# God's Handmaiden

## Other books by Gilbert Morris

*Jacob's Way*
*Edge of Honor*
*Jordan's Star*
*The Spider Catcher*

# God's Handmaiden

GILBERT MORRIS

**ZONDERVAN**™

GRAND RAPIDS, MICHIGAN 49530 USA

ZONDERVAN™

*God's Handmaiden*
Copyright © 2004 by Gilbert Morris

Requests for information should be addressed to:
Zondervan, *Grand Rapids, Michigan 49530*

**Library of Congress Cataloging-in-Publication Data**

Morris, Gilbert.
    God's handmaiden / Gilbert Morris.—1st ed.
        p. cm.
    ISBN 0-310-24699-7
    1. Working class women—Fiction. 2. Nightingale, Florence, 1820–1910—
Fiction. 3. Crimean War, 1853–1856—Fiction. 4. England—Fiction.
5. Nurses—Fiction. I. Title.
PS3563.O8742 G63    2004
813'.54—dc22

                                                            2003022152

Published in association with the literary agency of Alive Communications, Inc., 7680 Goddard Street, Suite 200, Colorado Springs, CO 80920.

*Interior design by Michelle Espinoza*

*Printed in the United States of America*

04 05 06 07 08 09 10 /❖ DC/ 10 9 8 7 6 5 4 3 2 1

# God's
# Handmaiden

# Kimberly

*May 1851–November 1852*

# Chapter One

Asoft but persistent touch on her lips brought Gervase Howard out of sleep instantly. Opening her eyes, she saw Mr. Bob staring at her. Smiling, she stroked the head of the huge cat.

"Good morning, Mr. Bob. How are you this morning?"

The cat at once began to purr, the rumbles deep in his chest humming as if generated by a miniature engine. He rose at once, arched his back, and yawned mightily. Placing his front paws on Gervase's chest, he began kneading her powerfully, eyes half shut with pleasure. The purring reached a crescendo, and although the claws of the cat were painful, Gervase did not object.

"You've been fighting again, Mr. Bob. Why do you have to do that?"

Mr. Bob was a dark-gray tabby with a large blunt head marked with a dark *M* and scarred from many battles. The only white spot on him was at the tip of his tail, and when he held it up straight, it always reminded Gervase of a candle.

For a time Gervase lay there, shutting out everything except the cat. She stroked Mr. Bob as he continued to knead her chest; then finally she pulled him down, rolling over so she could face him. He had big golden eyes, round as shillings, and he watched her carefully, still purring.

"You're all I have left, Mr. Bob."

The whispered words frightened Gervase, and her vivid imagination suddenly began to function despite her attempts to will the world away. Ever since the funeral, she had tried to blot out the details of her future, but now, graphically and powerfully, she could see her mother's face as it had looked in the wooden coffin — pale, worn, completely different from the way she had appeared in life. Gervase closed her eyes but the image seemed to magnify itself. She clutched Mr. Bob tightly and forced herself to think of her mother as she liked to remember her best. A series of images flashed in front of her — her mother smiling and laughing, her blue-green eyes dancing. Gervase remembered a time when she had come to her mother hurt and frightened — she could not even recall why now — and her mother had simply picked her up and spun around until Gervase was dizzy. Then she had pulled Gervase onto her lap and held her tightly, whispering comfort.

That poignant memory triggered others like it, for Gervase's mother had always known how to give comfort to her only daughter. Sometimes she had quoted Scripture, always with a fervency and a faith that Gervase had never seen in anyone else. At other times she had sung happy songs to Gervase, sometimes popular songs but more often hymns they sang together in the Methodist chapel they attended every Sunday. Often she would tell Gervase fantastic stories filled with wonder and hope. Somehow she had always been able to drive away Gervase's fears and anxieties.

The memories were jolted and driven away as Mr. Bob began to protest. He stiffened his legs and squirmed, saying, "Yow!" — which meant, as Gervase well knew, "It's time to turn me loose."

She released her grip and the big cat sat up and began washing his face. Then he gave himself a complete bath. Enviously Gervase thought, *I wish I had no more worries than you have, Mr. Bob.* But she did not dwell on this.

Throwing back the worn coverlet, she stepped out of the bed and stood for a moment, dreading the day. Then she dressed hurriedly, putting on her one good dress — the one she had worn to the funeral — and moved to the oak washstand. Slowly she washed her face and then, looking into the small mirror, brushed her hair. As always, for a moment she stared at herself, disliking what she saw, for she felt plain and homely. She had a thin face dominated by large blue-green eyes she had inherited from her mother. Her hair was light blond and came down well below her shoulders. There was a slight curl in it, and she quickly bound it up so it made a bun on the back of her head.

She looked down at herself, frowning, for at the age of fifteen she was very thin indeed. She knew other girls her age who had already blossomed into womanly contours. Another memory of her mother, whispering to her, *"You're going to be a beautiful young girl. Right now you are like one of the colts you see out in the pasture — all legs and awkward. But that will pass."*

Gervase quickly turned away and moved into the other room. Her only hope for beauty was that her mother had been a well-shaped woman with winsome features. *If I could only be as pretty as Mum!*

She halted abruptly and stared at the calendar her mother had made: a single sheet of paper with the weeks set out in pencil. Gervase touched it, sadness welling up as she remembered her mother urging her to draw birds at the top for decoration. She ran her fingers over the year, 1851, and the scrolled word *May.* She stopped at the number 5 and her throat grew thick — for she had circled the number when she came home from her mother's funeral.

Turning to avoid the calendar, she blinked back the tears and looked around the room. This was the only home she had ever known, and she was saddened further at the thought that this was the last day she would spend in it. There were only the two rooms, the bedroom and this one, the larger, which served for all other purposes. Two windows at one end of the room let in the feeble sunlight that illuminated it. She stared at the walls she had helped her mother paper. The wall covering had been salvaged from the dump — evidently, a wealthy patron had had too much. It featured small bluebirds and thrushes singing their hearts out. She had a painful memory of the day they had pasted the paper on, and she immediately moved toward the woodstove which served for both heat and cooking. The rest of the furniture included a pine table and four chairs — none of which matched — a settee, and beside it a lamp. A bookcase made of boxes was now empty, for Gervase had given away most of the books, keeping only a few. She had spent the week since the funeral getting rid of things, giving some of them away, selling some for what she could get, and now the room looked bare and alien — not at all like the warm, cheerful place in which she had grown up.

Deliberately pushing these thoughts from her mind, Gervase built a fire. She was very efficient at this and soon it was blazing. She had given away all the groceries to Mrs. Warden, who had a houseful of youngsters, retaining only enough for this final breakfast. She fried the last of the bacon and the one thin slice of ham, but when she sat and tried to eat, the food seemed to stick in her throat. When she picked up the last of the bread she had saved, the thought came to her, *This was the last loaf of bread Mum ever made.* The thought so distressed her that she quickly put the bread down and wiped her lips.

Mr. Bob came to press against her leg, and she broke the rest of the ham into small fragments and set it down. She watched as he wolfed the morsels down eagerly, then looked up and said, "Yow!" — which meant, "More, please!" Gervase snatched him and pressed her face against his fur, whispering,

"That's . . . that's all there is, Mr. Bob, but I'm sure we'll have plenty for you in our new place."

The thought of a new place disturbed Gervase and she got up at once. Picking up the bread, she went out the back door and began dividing the bread and tossing the crumbs on the ground. Quickly birds began to gather, mostly sparrows that were so tame now, they came almost close enough to take the bread out of her hand. It was a daily ritual for her, and had been so for so long that she could not remember when it first began. The birds chirped and made cheerful noises, scuffling in the dust and battling over the crumbs. "You don't have to fight. There's plenty today."

As she broke off bits of bread and tossed them on the ground, she lifted her head. This was the sight most familiar to her: a long line of identical houses jammed together so closely that one could scarcely squeeze between them. They ran in a curving circle down a hill, and all had clotheslines out back, most of them containing garments swaying in the breeze like lazy ghosts. Children were out now in a few of the yards, and she could hear their voices as they shouted and laughed.

It was a poor enough section of the small village. Almost all the inhabitants of the poorly painted houses worked in the garment mill. Smoke was rising in ragged gray streams from the chimneys of the dwellings, scoring the sky, which seemed clear of clouds for the first time this May.

There was nothing beautiful about the scene, yet Gervase Howard almost cried out as she realized that this would be the last day she would see it.

"Gervase? There you are, darlin'!"

Agnes Warden noted that Gervase was wiping furtively at her eyes, and felt a quick pang of pity. Gervase's mother had been Agnes's closest friend, and the heavyset woman was sad as she approached and stood before the young girl. Shifting her two-week-old baby girl to a more comfortable position, she said, "We're going to miss you so much, Gervase — especially Betsy here."

Gervase took the baby, cuddled her and touched her cheek, watching the bubbles that rose from the red lips. "I'll miss you, too, Miss Agnes, and . . . and the children." Misery was written across her face. "Oh, I wish I could stay here!"

Mrs. Warden made a comforting noise as she hugged her. "You'll be much better off with your uncle and aunt, luv. Everybody needs family, and it's a fine place where they live, ain't it?"

"I guess so. I don't know them, Miss Agnes."

The woman wanted to say something to comfort the young girl but nothing came. She had always loved Charlotte Howard and this daughter of hers, and the death had hit her hard indeed. Death was common enough in this place but it was never easy.

"I miss Mama, Miss Agnes!"

"Why, of course you do! You wouldn't be a good girl if you didn't — but the Lord took her to himself, dearie, and he's given you a home. You'll have your uncle and aunt to love you, and you'll make many friends."

Gervase handed the infant back. "The vicar is supposed to come and pick me up very soon, so I'll say goodbye now." She threw her arms around the woman, whispering, "Goodbye, Miss Agnes." Then she kissed the baby. "Goodbye, Betsy. Be a good girl." Agnes watched sadly as Gervase turned and walked blindly away.

For a long moment Agnes stared after the slight form of the young girl; then she turned and walked slowly back toward her own house. She was greeted by Bertha Willington, a tall, thin woman who lived in the house next to hers.

"How's she taking it, dearie?" Bertha asked.

"She's bleeding in her 'eart, she is, but there's nothing else for it."

"Wot about the aunt, the one she's a-going to? Is she a good 'un?"

"Oh, I never met her, and Gervase only met her once, years ago. But Charlotte said as 'ow she was a good woman."

"They wasn't too close, was they?"

"No. They lived too far apart, but she's quick, Gervase is. She'll make a place for 'erself."

"But I'll miss the both of them."

"So will I. She's a dear child!"

"Whoa, Geraldine, stop now! Do you hear me?"

The Reverend Gerald Howells tugged at the reins and brought the brown mare to a stop. She shook her head rebelliously and would have gone on, but Howells jerked the lines again, saying, "That's enough, now! You're too blasted ambitious!"

Reverend Howells sat very still in the small buggy, considering the task that lay before him. It had been a hard thing, the funeral of Charlotte Howard, as it always was when a child was left an orphan. Howells had developed a great affection for Mrs. Howard, for she was a faithful member of the church. She had little money to spare, but anytime there was work to be done or a case of need, she was always ready to give what help she could. The funeral had been better attended than he expected. He was surprised to discover how many friends Charlotte Howard had made in her brief lifetime. Her husband had died not long after they were married, and now there was only the child Gervase. It was to this problem that the minister now gave his thoughts.

Howells was not an impulsive man by any means. He liked his sermons well planned, as he liked everything else. It disturbed him when routines were broken, and often before a difficult interview he would go over what he planned to say. Now his lips moved as he reviewed the speech he had been working on. The mare's ears twitched, though she was accustomed to her master's soliloquies.

"Now, my dear Gervase, this has been very hard for you," Howells whispered. "You and your mother were so close — and with no father, even closer. I know your grief has been almost unbearable. But you must put that behind you, child, and I thank God that you have an uncle and an aunt who are willing to take you in. From all reports, they are respectable and good people indeed. Their invitation was most warm and you will have a good home. You will be lonely but that's only natural. Now you must look forward. Treasure your mother's dear memory, but she would want you to be happy in your new place."

For a moment Howells sat wondering how his speech would be received by the child, but he could do no better. Securing the reins, he stepped off the buggy and gave the mare a pat. "There, Geraldine, you behave yourself." Then he moved toward the house. He was a long, limber man and a busy one. This task of seeing Gervase safely embarked was the chore he had most on his mind this day.

When Howells knocked on the door, it opened almost at once, and he smiled and took off his hat. "Good morning, Gervase."

"Good morning, Vicar."

"I came a little early so I might help you take care of any chores remaining."

"Everything is ready. I'm all packed. Come in, please."

As the vicar stepped inside, he glanced around the room. It was a poor enough place, as were all the houses on the Row, but everything was clean and neat. He nodded. "The new tenants will appreciate moving into a home this tidy." He waited for the girl to respond, but he saw that her face was tense, and she seemed unable to speak. "Well now," he said as cheerfully as he could, "we may as well go a little early. Let me help you with your things."

"The box is in the bedroom, sir."

Howells went into the room and picked up the box, surprised at its weight. As he carried it out, he asked, "What do you have in here, Gervase?"

"All the things of my mother's that I could keep. Some of her books and a few pictures and some of my things that I had when I was a little girl."

"That's very good. You sold everything else, I suppose?"

"I gave a lot of it away."

"That's a good child." Howells went outside and loaded the heavy box into the buggy, then returned. Gervase was holding a rather large bag of some sort. "What is that, Gervase?"

"These are my clothes."

"And this?" Howells motioned to a wicker basket.

"That's Mr. Bob."

"Mr. Bob?"

"Yes sir, my cat."

Howells appeared disturbed. "You're taking your cat with you? I'm not sure that's wise."

Instantly Gervase drew up, her whole body taut. "Oh, sir, I have to take Mr. Bob with me! I've had him since he was a kitten."

"Yes, child, but — "

"I've got to have him, sir! I won't go without him!" Gervase blinked rapidly several times and her voice was unsteady. "I found him when he was just a little kitten, four years ago. He would've died if it hadn't been for me. I fed him with drops of milk and I can't leave him here, sir!"

Reverend Howells suddenly felt a great compassion for this girl. "Well, I'm sure your uncle and aunt will understand."

"I hope so," Gervase whispered, and then she looked the minister straight in the eye. "I won't stay if they won't let me keep Mr. Bob."

Howells was taken somewhat aback by this defiant statement. He knew that the child was afraid, as any youngster would be under the circumstances, but there was a purpose in her he had not seen before. He cleared his throat. "Well, I will write them a letter and ask them to let you keep Mr. Bob."

"Oh, thank you, Reverend!"

"There, there. Don't let that be a bother to you." Howells reached into his pocket and pulled out a small cloth purse. "This is a gift from some of the members of our congregation." He extended the purse and when Gervase took it, he nodded. "You might need a little extra."

"I wish I could thank them, sir. Will you thank them for me?"

"Of course I will." Howells hesitated, his rehearsed speech on the tip of his tongue, but somehow he felt it would not do. He cleared his throat and said briskly, "Well, are we ready to go?"

"Would you carry this, and I'll bring Mr. Bob?"

"Of course."

Gervase handed over the sack containing her clothes and picked up the wicker basket. From inside came a plaintive meow and Gervase said, "It's all right, Mr. Bob." She walked outside and the minister accompanied her. He put the bag in the back of the buggy and asked, "Do you want me to put your cat beside us?"

"Yes, please."

The minister took the wicker basket and his eyes widened. "He is a heavy cat!"

"He weighs over a stone."

"How did you figure that? You don't have scales, do you?"

"No, but we got flour in one-pound bags and I found stones that weighed the same. I put a board down and put him on one end and put the stones on the other until it balanced. He weighs sixteen pounds."

"A fine animal, and I'm sure he will be a comfort to you." The two got in the buggy and Howells picked up the reins. "All right, Geraldine, now you can go." He slapped the lines on the back of the mare, who started out at a lively pace.

As the buggy moved forward, Howells glanced at the girl, noting that her thin face was pale. She looked straight ahead for a time until they reached the top of the hill, and then she turned around. He had a full view of her face then. It was a good face, with a child's immature features. Her lips trembled but she said nothing. Finally she turned forward again, and he said cheerfully, "Now then. Have you ever ridden in a coach before?"

"No sir. I never have."

"Well, it will be an experience for you. I think you'll like it!"

As the wheels of the coach dropped into a pothole, all the passengers were jarred and thrown to the left. The coach had been practically empty when Gervase got on, but it had picked up passengers as they went along. It was the middle of May and hot and dusty so that perspiration ran down the faces of all the passengers. The coach seats had straight backs and no padding, making them uncomfortable. All morning long the coach had lurched over the rough road, picking up passengers and putting out a few, and eventually Gervase found herself sitting between a young man with a disagreeable countenance and a very large, rather silent man. She was holding Mr. Bob's basket in her lap, and from time to time he would meow and she would open the lid enough to slide her hand in and caress his head.

"Coaches is for people, not for mangy cats," the young man said harshly. He had a dirty face and his clothes were rough. He was evidently a working man, rather short and skinny. His teeth were bad and his breath was terrible. "I can't stand mangy cats!"

Gervase said nothing, for she was afraid. The other passengers seemed indifferent but the young man kept complaining.

Finally the big man sitting on the other side of Gervase turned. He was well dressed and wore a gold ring with a green stone on his right forefinger. "You have your cat there, do you, miss?"

Gervase quickly glanced at him and saw that he was smiling at her.

"Yes sir, I do."

"I've always liked cats myself. Look, now — you move over and take my seat by the window. Here, I'll hold your cat while you do that."

Gervase did not know what to do, but his smile encouraged her. She stood up and the big man moved to the center of the seat, holding the wicker basket high. "There you are," he said, giving it back to her after she sat again. "Now you can take him out of that box for a while and let him breathe some fresh air."

"This ain't no cat coach," the young man growled. "It's fer people."

The big man turned and leaned over, his weight crushing the smaller man. "You shut your mouth about this young lady's cat or I'll throw you through the window!"

The young man looked up, ready to argue, but something he saw in the big man's face caused him to reconsider. "None of my affair," he muttered sulkily and turned to stare out the window.

"Right enough," the big man said. He turned to Gervase. "Now, take your cat out and let him look around. He's been in that box all morning."

"Will it be all right?"

"I say it will be."

Gervase opened the lid and took Mr. Bob out. He stretched and sat in her lap and made no attempt to get away.

"Well, he's a right good one, ain't he now?" the big man said. He reached over and stroked the cat's head and asked, "What's his name?"

"His name is Mr. Bob."

"Well, Mr. Bob, let's me and you make friends. We got a way to go before we get to London...."

# Chapter Two

My word, Davis, you could be on time to breakfast, after all the trouble that our cook has gone to!"

Sir Edward Wingate held his fork as if it were a weapon and jabbed it toward his eldest son, adding, "I'll be bound you were fiddling around with that book of yours again."

"I'm afraid I must plead guilty, Father." Davis Wingate had come into the dining room expecting some such remark. His father had little patience with anything except riding and hunting and family. Anything outside these spheres failed to interest him. Crossing the room, Davis moved with the grace of a natural athlete. At the age of twenty-two, he was exactly six feet tall, was lean but muscular, and had the same good looks as his father — the same blond hair, wedge-shaped face, and cornflower blue eyes. His mouth was wide and when he grinned, there was a crooked quality to it, and a small dimple of which he was utterly ashamed appeared in his right cheek. He moved to the sideboard, where he picked up a razor-sharp carving knife, sliced off three pieces of ham, then dipped into the battered eggs and covered them with small mushrooms. He liberally filled his plate with fruits and came to sit next to his younger brother.

Ives, four years younger than Davis, was a smaller man — no more than five eight — and more finely built in every respect. He had a thin, rather delicate face and his hands were beautifully was brown and he had the same bright-blue eyes found in Davis, which they had both inherited from their father. "I think Father's right," Ives said. "You spend too much time reading those blasted books."

"All of you leave Davis alone," Lady Sarah Wingate said. She had a wealth of light-brown hair and rather dark blue eyes, and the traces of her youthful beauty still clung to her at the age of forty-nine. "You might be better off, Ives, if you too would spend some time broadening yourself."

"I don't need to be broadened with the stuff he reads. I tried that book you gave me, Davis, *Gulliver's Travels*. Nothing but nonsense! Imagine, Father," Ives said. "It's about a fellow who lands on a desert island inhabited by people no more than six inches tall."

Sir Edward shook his head. "Why do you want to read such trash, Davis? I can't understand it."

"I get tired of reading stock reports. I like to read something different."

"What were you reading this time?" Ives demanded.

"A book called *David Copperfield*."

"What's it about?"

"About a very young boy who has a cruel stepfather who beats him. He has a terribly hard time all through his life. Marries the wrong woman and has some people who despise him. It's written by Charles Dickens."

Ives shook his head in despair and gave his brother a look of disgust. He loved Davis but resented the privileges an older son always received. He delighted in besting Davis any way he could manage, and already at the age of eighteen attempted to win any young woman Davis showed any interest in. He had little patience with his brother's joy in literature and now said, "I can't understand you, Davis. Why in heaven's name would you want to read a book like that? As Father says, it's ridiculous. Isn't there enough misery in the world without reading books about people having hard times, like this fellow David Coppersmith?"

"Copperfield, Ives."

"Well, whatever. I'll never read it." Ives lifted a forkful of battered eggs to his mouth, chewed them thoroughly, then added, "Now, give me a good romance where good things happen to good people and bad things happen to bad people, and the lovers get married and live happily ever after."

Davis laughed. "That's more of a fantasy than *Gulliver's Travels* with its six-inch people. How often does that happen in the world?"

The argument went on for some time, with Davis feeling the criticism from his father and his brother more deeply than he revealed. He had had a great deal of practice at it, for although he had proved himself to be a good businessman and had pleased his father at the office, he took his pleasures in ways that neither his father nor his brother could understand.

Finally the breakfast was over, and Davis and his mother were left alone. He was leaning back in his chair sipping chocolate, which he loved, and telling his mother about *David Copperfield*. She did not read a great deal of fiction herself but at least she was sympathetic to his tastes. "You ought not to torment your father and brother as you do about your books. You know what they're like."

"Why, they're the ones who torment me! It would please Father if I read nothing but stock reports and bills of lading and reports from the House of Lords — all deadly boring, Mother."

"I suppose they are, but — " Lady Wingate did not finish, for the door opened. She turned to see Martha Miller, the cook, enter and come to a halt slightly behind her. "Yes, what is it, Martha?"

"Please, Lady Wingate, could I speak with you?"

"Why, of course, Martha. Go ahead."

Martha Miller had been the Wingate's cook for nearly fifteen years. She was a tall, strongly built woman with graying brown hair and gray eyes and had learned the tastes of the Wingate family so that the food was always pleasing. She was a cheerful enough woman, but now both Lady Wingate and Davis could see that she was disturbed.

"Well, it's like this, Lady Sarah. You remember that my niece is coming to live with George and me?" George Miller, Martha's husband, served as the gardener and in other capacities at Kimberly, the Wingate family home. Both were trusted, reliable servants for whom Lady Wingate felt considerable affection. "Why, I had forgotten, Martha. Is this the day she comes?"

"Yes ma'am, it is. But I just found out that Brodie is going to take Sir Edward to Brighton."

"I believe he is. Is that a problem?"

"The girl is coming by coach to London, and I had thought as how Brodie would pick her up. But now he can't do it. And Clyde's not available, either."

"Oh dear, that is a problem! Let me think — "

"Well, that's no problem," Davis said. "What time does the coach get in, Martha?"

"It's due in about three-thirty, sir."

"That will work out very well," Davis said with a smile. "I have to go into town this morning and do a few things at the office, but I'll be through in plenty of time. I'll be glad to go by and pick the girl up."

"Oh, would you, sir? That's kind, you are!"

"No problem at all. I've forgotten her name."

"Her name is Gervase Howard, Mr. Davis."

"Gervase? How do you spell it?"

"G–E–R–V–A–S–E. I don't know where my sister Charlotte got it."

"She must have been reading something by a poet, like Tennyson. What does the girl look like?"

"Oh, I have no idea, sir. I haven't seen her since she was four."

"Well, how old is she now?"

"Just fifteen, sir."

"I'll tell you what, Martha. If you will bake me one of those fine gingerbreads of yours, I'll guarantee to bring your niece home safely."

"Oh yes, Mr. Davis! I'll bake it for you first thing tomorrow."

"Good," Davis said, nodding firmly. "And you say you have no idea what the girl looks like?"

"Well, she was rather plain when she was a child."

"That's simple enough." Davis winked at his mother. "I'll bring all the plain fifteen-year-old girls there are on that coach, and you can sort the right one out."

"Don't be foolish, Davis," his mother scolded. "You be sure and take good care of the child."

"Why, of course! What'd you think I was going to do, eat one of her drumsticks?"

"You are awful!" Sarah Wingate said, laughing. This oldest son of hers had a streak of humor that sometimes offended people. She turned and said, "Don't worry. Davis is very reliable, Martha. He'll have your niece here safe and sound."

"Oh, thank you, ma'am! And thank you, sir. That makes me feel a great deal better." Martha started to turn and said, "And you remember, Lady Sarah, she's going to help me cook in the kitchen."

"I hope she will be a help to you, and we'll see about a wage after she proves herself."

"Thank you, ma'am. That will be very fine indeed."

After Martha left, Davis asked, "Can I bring you back anything from town, Mother?"

"Just bring the girl — and don't tease her. Her mother just died and she has no other relatives. She'll probably be very frightened."

"I'll be as gentle as you are yourself," Davis promised. He got up, kissed his mother, and left whistling a cheerful tune.

As the coach drew to a halt, Gervase clutched Mr. Bob's basket with both hands. She was extremely weary, for the trip had taken all day, with many stops. However, it had been made easier by the big man, whose name was Adams; he had spoken cheerfully to her and when the stage stopped at midday had helped her out and carried Mr. Bob. He had taken her into the inn, where he had bought her a meal of shepherd's pie. She had been too nervous to eat much of it, but he had encouraged her to drink the small beer that the inn offered.

"Now, young lady, we're in London. You say you're expectin' to be met?"

"Yes, Mr. Adams, by my uncle. His name is George Miller."

"Well, it's been a pleasure to make your acquaintance. Let me help you out." Mr. Adams clambered out of the coach, reached up for the basket containing Mr. Bob, and then gave his other hand to help Gervase down. "Here, you hold Mr. Bob and I'll see that your luggage all gets off. Coaches sometimes carry luggage away, as I know from sad experience."

Gervase stood while the burly man plucked her belongings from the top. "Is that all, now? The one box and the one sack?"

"Yes sir, that's all."

"Well, is your uncle here? Do you see him?"

"I've never met him, sir."

Mr. Adams looked somewhat disconcerted. "But how will he know you?"

"I expect my aunt will be with him. I remember her a little bit."

"Well, that's fine. I'll leave you then and God be with you."

"Thank you, sir. You've been very kind."

"You take care of Mr. Bob, now."

"Yes sir, I will."

A sense of loneliness descended upon Gervase as the big man grabbed a carpetbag and left with the others. The coach had stopped outside an inn which had a sign swinging from an iron rod: "The Red Eagle." The eagle looked more like a pigeon and was poorly done indeed.

For a time the place was very busy with people coming and picking up those who had arrived on the coach, but soon the crowd thinned. Gervase kept looking anxiously at every stranger who came, hoping it was her uncle. A clock from far away sounded three times. Finally there was no one left except the hostlers. They unhitched the horses and replaced them with a fresh team, and the stage pulled away. The street was rather wide and cobblestoned, and occasionally a wagon or buggy would come lumbering along. Gervase was growing apprehensive. The stage had been due to arrive at three-thirty but had come somewhat early, so she comforted herself by saying, "They didn't expect me here this early but they'll come soon."

Time dragged by slowly, and eventually a man with a red, beefy face, wearing a white apron much the worse for wear, came outside the inn. He stopped and looked toward Gervase, who was sitting on a bench in front of the inn. "Hello, missy," he said. "You waiting for someone?"

"Yes sir, I am."

"Come in on the stage, did yer?"

"Yes sir. I'm waiting for my uncle."

The burly man wiped his hand on the greasy apron and turned his head to one side. He had a shock of stiff black hair and deep-set black eyes. "Well, I reckon your folks is late."

"I'm afraid they are."

"I'll tell yer wot, missy. If they don't come pretty soon, you come on into my place, the Red Eagle. My name's Ben Horton. Ain't too good for a young lady to be out alone on the street."

"Thank you, sir. I will."

Horton went back inside and Gervase sat holding her hand on the basket. Mr. Bob was scratching and begging to be out, and she opened the basket and took him onto her lap. She stroked him and put him down so he could take care of his business, and then she picked him up again. She had kept part of the shepherd's pie, and she fished out some pieces of meat and fed them to him in small portions. Mr. Bob gobbled them down and mewed for more until all was gone.

The time passed even more slowly, and finally she heard the single chime that indicated the half-hour mark.

Gervase felt a touch of fear. London was a large city and she had never been more than five miles outside her little village. Her hands were unsteady as she stroked Mr. Bob's thick fur, and she prayed silently, *Oh, God, help me! Bring my uncle to me soon, please!* Her mother had taught Gervase to pray, as she had taught her so many things about God. Gervase remembered well the time of her conversion. She had only been nine years old, but the experience had been so real that she knew she would never forget it. She recalled even the smell of the small church where she had been sitting with her mother. The visiting minister had been a big bulky man with large expressive eyes that seemed to seek her out. He had cried, "Jesus stands at the door of your heart and knocks! Will you open your heart and let him come in?"

Mr. Bob nudged Gervase's face with his blunt head and she held him tightly, remembering how she had prayed that day a simple prayer: *Lord Jesus, please — come into my heart and make me good!* The tears had come then, but also a joy she had never forgotten.

Ten more minutes went by and Gervase held the cat and continued to pray. Then she heard loud voices. She looked up to see two young men who had come out of an inn farther down the street. They were laughing loudly and when they got closer, one of them said, "Well, look, Fred. 'Ere's a daisy!" The speaker was a tall, rather skinny man dressed in rough clothing, as was his fellow, who was short and muscular. The first whispered something that caused the other to laugh. The two came on, and Gervase made a belated decision to go inside the Red Eagle. She was still holding Mr. Bob, and she opened the basket and started to put him in, but the short man said, "Well, look at that, Hack. She's got a kitty cat. Ain't that sweet?"

"I always liked cats. Lemme hold him, girlie."

"No. He don't like to be held," Gervase said. She slipped the protesting Mr. Bob into the basket and latched the lid. She started to go inside but the tall man said, "Wot's your 'urry? Ain't we good enough company for you?"

Gervase was not totally unacquainted with drunks. She had seen enough of them in her small village, although she had kept away from them whenever possible. These two were deep into drink, she knew instinctively, and she could smell the raw alcohol on their breath. Neither of them had shaved recently and the tall one had yellow fangs for teeth. He leaned closer and put his hand on her shoulder. "Come on. Lemme see the kitty. I won't 'urt him."

"No, I want to go inside."

The short man said, "What's the matter? Don't you like us?"

"Sure she likes us, Fred. Don't you, sweetheart?"

"Please let me go." The tall man had grasped Gervase by the arm with a surprisingly hard grip, and Gervase struggled to get away.

"Here, you fellows let that girl alone."

The two men turned suddenly to see Horton, who had stuck his head out the door.

"You keep shut, Horton, or you know wot you'll get!" Fred said. He pulled a knife out of his pocket, opened it, and waved it. "Come on, if you wants to be a bloody hero. I'll cut your blinkin' ears off!"

"You hurt that girl and you'll have the law on you, Fred Simmons!"

A burst of raw raucous laughter and a curse was the only answer he got, and he ducked back inside the inn. Fred snorted with contempt and pocketed his knife.

"Wot you got in that little purse, sweetheart?" Hack inquired. He reached for it but Gervase snatched it away.

"That's mine!" she said.

"Well, you ought to buy a couple of old friends a pot of ale apiece, ain't that right, Fred?"

"Sure it's right. 'Ere now, missy. Tell you wot — we'll drink one with you."

"She's fresh out of the country, Fred," Hack said, grinning. "She don't know 'ow to behave."

"Then it's up to us to teach her."

"You let me alone!" Gervase said. She could not break the hold that Hack had on her, and her fear was turning to panic.

The two continued to pull at her, but their attention was caught by the sound of hooves on the cobblestones. Gervase looked between the men to see a light buggy pull up, the horse snorting. A tall man leaped out. She knew this could not be her uncle, for he was too young, but still he came straight up to them. He seemed to appraise the situation in an instant and he gave Gervase a reassuring look. "Well, this is Miss Howard, I take it?"

"Yes sir."

Fred and Hack turned to face the newcomer. Hack said, "Now, ain't he the fancy one, Fred! He's 'igh society, all right. Probably a duke. How you doin', Duke?"

Hack had released his grip on Gervase's arm, and she edged to one side, but Fred reached out and jerked her back. "You stay right where you are." He grinned at the newcomer. "Hey, Duke, I think you ought to buy us all a drink."

"That's right. Just give us a fiver and we'll go off and 'ave our own drinks."

The newcomer moved forward. He did not look at all perturbed. In fact, there was a slight smile on his face. "Your name is Hack?"

"That's right. Now wot does that get you?"

"And you want a fiver?"

Hack grinned. "Yeah, that ought to do me."

"All right. Here's your fiver." The tall man suddenly twisted his body and his fist shot out so fast that Gervase almost missed it. It struck Hack straight in the face, knocked him back against the wall, and he collapsed on the sidewalk. Blood was running down from his nose, staining his shirt, and he was moving his legs but could not seem to get up.

"And you. Would you like a fiver as well?"

Fred pulled his knife again but as he attempted to open it, he was struck an equally powerful blow that knocked him so hard against the building, the knife fell. Gervase was trembling as the tall man grabbed the weapon and heaved it down the street.

"Now, would you two want any more fivers, or will that be enough for you today?"

Hack was getting to his feet now, a look of pure hatred in his eyes. He glared at the tall man but said, "Come on, Fred. Let's get out of here."

Fred cursed the newcomer and the two staggered down the street.

The tall man turned to face Gervase and again he had a smile on his face. "My name is Davis Wingate. Your aunt asked me to pick you up."

Relief washed over Gervase. "Yes sir," she said a little breathlessly.

"I'm sorry I was late, but my horse threw a shoe and it took a while to find a blacksmith and get it replaced. Are you ready to go, Gervase?"

"Yes sir."

"These are your things? Good. Let me help you with them." He moved her box and sack into the buggy, then reached for the basket.

"I'll carry that, sir."

"What have you got in there?"

"Mr. Bob, my cat."

"Oh, I see. Well, come along."

As the buggy rumbled down the street, Davis glanced at his passenger. He could see that the girl was shaken. Her face was pale and her hands were not steady on the basket that held the cat. "What's your cat's name?" he asked.

"Mr. Bob."

"That's a nice name. Could I see him?"

The girl nodded and unlatched the basket. She took Mr. Bob out and put him between them on the seat.

"Well, he *is* a handsome fellow! Have you had him long?" Davis managed to engage the girl in conversation, and finally he said, "That was a pretty bad thing back there. Were you afraid when I was late?"

"Yes sir, a little."

"Don't blame you. I would have been scared stiff in a strange city."

"I was very glad you came, Mr. Wingate." She hesitated, then added, "I prayed and I knew God would take care of me."

"Very proper thing, and I'm glad I came along." Davis paused. "I was very sorry to hear about your mother," he said gently.

"Thank you, sir," Gervase whispered.

"I know you'll like it at Kimberly, though. Your uncle and aunt are very nice people. They've been there forever."

"Are you the master, sir, at Kimberly?"

"Me? No, not at all. That's my father, Sir Edward Wingate."

He continued to talk, trying to put the girl at ease, telling her what to expect, as the buggy cleared the inner city. The houses began to appear in larger plots, and eventually he said, "Our place is only six miles down this road. By the time we get there, we may miss supper, but I'm sure your aunt will fix us something." He almost put his hand on the girl's shoulder to reassure her but thought, *She's afraid right now and I'm a stranger. I'd better let her uncle and aunt take care of that.*

Gervase sat up straighter as Davis pointed with his buggy whip. "There's the house, Gervase. That will be your home from now on."

Gervase had been looking ahead for some time as the buggy climbed a gentle incline between deep woods on both sides of the road. Now she saw a large handsome stone building backed by a ridge of high woody hills. A stream that ran in front of it had been dammed to make a beautiful pond. She kept her eyes on the house while they crossed the bridge and drove to the front door, and then Davis drew up the horse as a young man came running out to take the reins.

"Take care of the horse, Bates."

"Yes sir. I will."

"Come along, Gervase," Davis said, smiling. "Your uncle and aunt will be anxious about you. I'm not sure they trusted me to bring you."

"Why not, sir?"

"Oh, they say I tease people too much."

Gervase smiled then, and for the first time Davis saw a trace of what might be beauty to come in the young woman. She was so thin and spindly, and the dress she wore was so ugly, that it had been hard to judge her. She had shown little signs of beauty. Now he saw that she had beautifully shaped eyes, and he knew that as she filled out, she would become a fairly attractive young woman. "Come along. I'll have Bates bring your things to your room later."

"Yes sir." Gervase got out of the buggy but hung on to the basket. They climbed the steps and Davis opened the door for her.

As they entered the house, Gervase could hardly speak. They had not come through the front door, so she could only imagine how glorious that must be. Instead they had entered what was apparently the kitchen. It was a huge room with high ceilings, two large stoves, a big fireplace at one end, and tables for food preparation lining the walls. She had no time to look further, for a woman who appeared vaguely familiar had come through the other door. "Gervase? Is this you?"

"Yes, Aunt."

Martha came forward and said, "I've been worried about you. Was your trip hard?"

"No ma'am. Not very."

"Well, thank you so much, Mr. Davis, for fetching her."

"You're very welcome." Davis put out his hand then, and Gervase, confused, did not know what he wanted. Then she saw his smile and she put out her own. His big hand swallowed hers and he bowed slightly. "Welcome to Kimberly, Gervase. You let me know if anyone doesn't treat you right."

"Thank you, sir — for all that you've done."

As soon as Davis left, Martha said, "You must be hungry, child. Have you had anything to eat since you left the village?"

"Just a little shepherd's pie."

"Well, I've kept some food hot for you. Come and sit down. You can eat and tell me about your journey."

"Thank you, Aunt Martha."

"What's that in your basket?"

"That's Mr. Bob. He's my cat."

Martha stared at the basket and then said doubtfully, "I'm not sure — "

"Oh, please, Aunt! He . . . he's my only friend. I have to keep him — please!"

Martha hesitated. The child had been through so much, and after all, how much trouble could a cat be?

"Very well. I think it will be all right. I'll have to talk to the housekeeper but she's a very nice lady."

"Thank you, Aunt."

"You sit down right here and I suppose you can feed the kitty. What does he eat?"

"Anything at all." Gervase sat at the table in the center of the kitchen and let Mr. Bob out. He stretched and then began to explore, as cats always do. He came to Martha when she brought him some chopped liver, and settled down to fill his stomach.

"Here. I've kept some mutton and there's still some warm soup left."

Gervase ate hungrily and her aunt sat watching her. "Was it very hard on you, the funeral?" Martha asked.

"Oh, yes ma'am, it was dreadful hard!"

"Well, naturally it would be. Oh, dear Charlotte! We were very close as children. I was four years older and when she was small, she was like my own baby. I played with her as if she were a doll."

Gervase suddenly could not eat, for her throat seemed tight. She felt the tears coming to her eyes, but she had no time for this, as a lady had just entered the room and now stood over them.

"Oh, Lady Wingate, this is my niece. Her name is Gervase Howard."

"How do you do, Gervase? I'm so happy you've come to stay with your aunt."

"Thank you, mum."

"Say Lady Wingate, Gervase."

"Yes, Lady Wingate."

"You're very welcome here, and your aunt says she's going to make a cook out of you."

"Yes ma'am — I mean, yes, Lady Wingate."

"Well, if you can become half as good a cook as your aunt, you'll never want for a place." The woman smiled and said, "Now I'll leave you two alone. We'll have time to talk later."

"Thank you, ma'am." Lady Wingate left the room, closing the door quietly behind her. "She seems nice," Gervase murmured.

"That she is!" Martha nodded firmly. "She and her husband both. Sir Edward — well, he *is* a bit grumpy at times, but he don't mean nothin' by it."

When Gervase had finished eating, Martha said, "Come along. I'll take you to your room."

"Mr. Davis said somebody named Bates would bring my things up."

"Oh yes. I'll have him bring them up, but you must be tired now. You can lie down. Is it too early for you to go to bed?"

"No ma'am."

"It would be good if you could go to sleep early. Come along."

Gervase followed her aunt out of the kitchen and down a hall. The house seemed enormous to her. She followed her aunt up a flight of stairs and then up another.

"Your room is on the third floor. The fourth, actually, but it's very nice."

Gervase had put Mr. Bob back in the basket and was carrying him as they ascended.

The last set of stairs led to a single door. "This is the only room up here. You'll be all by yourself. Will you be afraid?"

"No ma'am. I won't be afraid."

"This used to be the nursery for the boys when they were young."

Gervase stepped in and Martha put the lamp she was carrying on a table beside a large window. Gervase looked around; it was a very large room indeed. "The boys played all kinds of things in here when they were younger," Aunt Martha said. "It was a schoolroom then but the children all loved it. Look out the window. You can see the front of the grounds with what little light's left."

Gervase went to the window and saw the rolling green yard. It was getting dark now, however, and she could not see clearly.

The room had a sloping ceiling that was just a little higher than her head on one end but very high on the other. As for furniture, she noted the small bed with a brightly colored comforter and several pillows on top, a rocking chair, a chest, a dressing table. The carpet on the floor seemed very soft to her, for she had never had carpet, and she saw that the walls were papered.

"Oh, Aunt, this is too nice for me!"

"Not a bit of it! This will be yours from now on. Now I'll have Bates bring your things in." She came over and suddenly leaned down and took Gervase in her arms. "Will you be lonely in this room?" she asked, holding her close.

"No ma'am," Gervase said, returning the embrace. "Will you be far away?"

"No. I'm on the floor right below you. Just go down the stairs, the second door on the left. You'll meet your uncle tomorrow, and you can help me make breakfast in the morning if you're not too tired."

"Oh, yes ma'am, I will."

Gervase released her aunt then and Martha said, "Good night."

"Good night, Aunt."

As soon as she left, Gervase let Mr. Bob out of his carrier. He began prowling around, uttering soft, fluttering noises in his throat, as he did with strange things. Gervase was exploring the room when a knock came. She went at once to the door and found the young man she had seen outside. He looked about seventeen, not much older than she, and had a shock of raw red hair and a button nose. He was holding her box and her bag of clothes.

"Where will I put these things, miss?"

"In the middle of the floor will be fine." She waited until the young man plunked them down and then she whispered, "Thank you."

"You're welcome. Good to have you at Kimberly. My name's Bates."

"I'm Gervase."

"That's a funny name."

"I know. Everybody says that."

"Well, let me know if you needs anything." The young man left and at once Gervase began putting her things up. She found places for everything in the box. When it was empty, she decided to keep it. It had been specially made for her by Mr. Thomas, the blacksmith, for this journey, and it was one more tie to her old home.

Gervase found she was exhausted. She had slept little since the funeral and now her eyes began to grow heavy. She undressed, put on her shift, and got into bed, but remembered she had to turn out the lamp. Gervase got up, hesitated for a moment, then walked to the chest. She opened the bottom drawer and pulled out a small box. Sitting at the table, she adjusted the lamp and opened the box. She took out a bottle of ink, a turkey quill, and a notebook she was using as a journal. Opening the notebook, she dipped the quill and put the date at the top of the page.

*May 12, 1851*

She wrote very carefully by the yellow light of the lamp.

*I come to my ants today. She is verry nice, but my uncle was gone. When I got to London no one was there waiting for me, and two men bothered me. But Mr. Davis, he run them off. He talked to me all the way to this place and made me feel verry good. I will try verry hard to learn how to cook.*

Gervase reread the words she had written, blew on them as they dried, and then finally she added one more sentence.

*I miss Mum so much!*

She waited until the ink had dried, put everything back into the box, and then replaced the box in the lower drawer.

She knelt beside the bed, remembering how her mother would always kneel beside her. A sense of loneliness came to her but she prayed in a whisper, "Lord, thank you for this place, for my uncle and for my aunt. Help me to be a good girl here. And thank you for Mr. Davis." She got into bed expecting to lie awake, but fatigue overcame her and she drifted at once into a deep sleep.

# Chapter Three

A soft persistent touch on her eye woke Gervase. She did not move for a moment, but Mr. Bob continued to touch her in his usual fashion. His touch was so insistent that finally Gervase hugged him, saying, "Why do you always want to do that, Mr. Bob?"

The only response was a low rumble deep in the furry cat's body. Gervase continued to stroke the long silky fur but eventually he pulled away, crawled up on her chest, and stared down at her. He seemed to take great pleasure in looking deep into Gervase's eyes with his enormous golden ones. For a time she lay wondering what in the world a cat could be thinking, but finally she noticed that the pale morning light was beginning to filter through the window at the end of the room. Quickly she pushed Mr. Bob aside, rolled out of bed, and went to stare out the window. Her room faced east, so she saw the first milky light as it was gathering into an opalescent glow. Mr. Bob nudged her leg and then began mewing impatiently.

"Be still, Mr. Bob," she whispered, watching as a pale crimson glow finally divided the earth from the sky. She loved to watch the sunrise, the long waves of light rolling out of the east, and it was a fancy of hers to think of where the light had been before it touched her particular part of England.

Vaguely she was aware of faint sounds coming from somewhere in the house. She heard people walking, their faint voices sounding far away. Avoiding Mr. Bob, she lit the oil lamp, then moved to the washstand. Mr. Bob leaped up onto it and pushed his broad head against her. She rubbed him for a moment and said, "Now, you get down, Mr. Bob. I've got to wash." She took a sponge bath, then stood, hesitating, before the peg where she had hung her three dresses. Her best dress was dirty from the trip and she would have to wash it. The other two were not fit for such a great house, but there was nothing she could do about that, so she put on the brown one. She pulled on her black stockings, slipped her feet into her shoes, and then sat at the small dressing table, brushing her hair. She had very fine hair and as she brushed it, Mr. Bob insisted on sitting on her lap.

Finally she put the brush down, went to the chest, and picked up her mother's Bible, which was lying on top. Sitting in the rocking chair, she hesitated, then turned to the Psalms. Her lips moved as she read aloud in a faint whisper, "'Fret not thyself because of evildoers, neither be thou envious against the workers of iniquity. For they shall soon be cut down like the grass, and wither as the green herb. Trust in the Lord and do good; so shalt thou dwell in the land and verily thou shalt be fed.'"

She read the rest of the psalm, then bowed her head and whispered, "Oh, Lord, thank you for providing for me. Help me to be a good servant and please those who are over me. Be with Mr. Bob and keep him healthy. In Jesus' name. Amen."

She continued to read, and her pliant features changed as her eyes ran over the page. Gervase loved the Scriptures because her mother had always read them aloud to her. She had the eerie feeling that her mother was still reading. And she knew that as long as she lived, when she read the Psalms she would always be reminded of her mother's voice.

Finally she heard someone coming up the stairs to her room. Hastily she stood and replaced the Bible just as a knock sounded. She opened the door and found an elderly woman standing there. "Good morning, Gervase. I am Violet Peeples, the housekeeper."

"Good morning, Mrs. Peeples."

"I'm glad you're up so early. Some of the servants sleep like logs." Mrs. Peeples showed a displeasure by pulling her lips tightly together and shaking her head. "I'm glad to see you're an early riser."

"Yes ma'am. I always get up early."

"Well, come along. Your aunt will be expecting you to help her in the kitchen."

As the two started down the stairs, Mr. Bob padded along beside Gervase. Mrs. Peeples looked down and her eyebrows lifted. "I hope that cat won't be a problem."

"Oh no, ma'am! He's a very good cat."

They descended the stairs rather slowly, Mrs. Peeples hanging on to the banister. She turned to find Gervase watching her and shook her head. "My rheumatism is bad this week. The stairs especially hurt me a great deal."

"I'm sorry. Anything you want fetched from the upper stories, you just tell me, Mrs. Peeples."

The woman smiled. "There's the kind you are, girl." They arrived at the door that led to the kitchen, and Mrs. Peeples said, "You go ahead. Your aunt has already started the day's cooking."

"Yes, Mrs. Peeples."

Opening the door, Gervase found her aunt making dough in a huge bowl. "Good morning, Gervase."

"Good morning, Aunt Martha. I'm ready to help."

"Have you cooked much, Gervase?"

"Yes, some. But I have a lot to learn."

"Well, the first thing you learn is how to make bread. We bake every day here, bread and cakes, cookies, tarts. We need to get the bread into the oven first, and then all the servants will come in for an early breakfast. Here, I'll show you how to mix up the dough."

Gervase was very quick, and she willingly obeyed her aunt's instructions. As she worked, she looked around. The kitchen was almost as large as the cottage where she was born. The walls were whitewashed, and two of them were covered by pine shelves filled to capacity with pots, pans, cups, saucers, and many things that Gervase could not identify. The cooking utensils were made of iron, tin, and pottery. A bewildering array of bowls, measures, sugar tins, biscuit tins, and three large kegs were placed on the shelves between the high windows. "You'll learn all these things. Right in that box on that shelf you'll find the pepper box, the salt box, the sugar nippers, and sugar box. You'll learn them all quickly, Gervase."

"Yes ma'am."

"The fireplace we don't use for cooking, except on rare occasions. It was a blessing when somebody invented these stoves." Martha indicated the stoves, which had enormous ovens. "We can do the cooking for a week if we want to, in just these two."

"Will I be carrying the wood in?"

"No. Bates will take care of that."

When the bread was in the oven, Martha said, "Now we'll fix breakfast for the servants, then later on for the master and the rest of the house."

Breakfast for the servants was fairly simple, consisting of huge bowls of oatmeal, toast, and sliced ham served cold.

"Come along. Bring those platters in. I hear them already." The hallway door opened even as Martha spoke, and people began filing in. "You'd better put the milk on the table. They eat like starved wolves."

Gervase picked up the large pitcher and moved toward the kitchen table, where a small group stood gathered. She dared not look up for fear she would spill the milk. Someone said, "Who's this?" She glanced up to see a red-faced man with blue eyes staring at her.

"This is my niece, Clyde," Martha said. "This is Clyde Denny. He's the coachman and takes care of the horses. Clyde, introduce my niece to the rest of the household."

"I'm proud to do it, Martha." Denny was a cheerful-looking individual dressed in a white shirt and a brown vest with large buttons. "This is Daisy Pennington and Phoebe Rogers. They're maids, you see, and good 'uns, too! This is Robert Bates, the gardener's helper ..."

Gervase got as many of the names as she could but was too shy to look up much. She nodded at all of them. Just then another man came in. He glanced at her and grinned. "Well, you must be Gervase. I'm your uncle George. It's a pleasure to finally make your acquaintance," he said, holding out his hand.

Gervase shook his hand, saying quietly, "It's nice to meet you, too, Uncle."

"I gather you've met this motley crew?"

"Yes sir, I have."

"Don't trust any of them."

Clyde Denny hooted at that. "He's the one you want to watch out for, Gervase."

"What an odd name — Gervase." The speaker was Daisy Pennington, a very pretty young woman with blond hair and bright blue eyes. "Where'd you get a name like that?"

"My mother saw it in a book," Gervase said.

Phoebe Rogers, the other maid, had a wealth of brown hair and warm brown eyes. Both maids were wearing black dresses with white, delicate-looking aprons. "I wish *my* name was Gervase. I hate my own name."

"Why don't you change it?" Robert Bates asked. He winked at Gervase. "After breakfast I'll show you around the place."

"Stay away from him. He's a naughty boy," Martha commanded and looked askance at Robert. "You mind your manners, Robert. None of your tricks."

"Who, me?" Robert seemed hurt by her accusation. "I never tease anyone."

Laughter went up and then they all sat, and for a time Gervase was kept busy bringing food and drink. The meal was well under way when the hallway door opened again and a thin man with rather haughty features stepped inside. He was wearing a black suit with a narrow tie. He stopped suddenly and stared at Gervase. "Who is this?" he demanded.

"This is my niece, Gervase Howard. I told you about her, Mr. Wilkins." Martha turned and said, "Gervase, this is Mr. Silas Wilkins, the steward."

Gervase had no idea what a steward did, but she saw how the others looked at the thin man with some apprehension. She did not speak but instead curtsied.

"She'll be working with you in the kitchen, is that right, Martha?"

"Yes sir."

"See that she stays out of trouble, and I want to tell you —" Suddenly Wilkins twisted his head around and stared at Mr. Bob, who had leaped up on a windowsill and was licking his forepaw. "What is that?"

"Please, Mr. Wilkins, that's my cat."

Wilkins turned and put his frosty eyes on Gervase. "We will not have cats in this place."

A silence fell over the room and for a moment Gervase could not even speak. Then she began to plead. "Please, sir, he'll be no trouble. I'll take care of him."

"We will *not* have cats. They are filthy creatures."

"Now, Mr. Wilkins, they're not so bad," George Miller said.

"There will be no argument about this, George. You will get rid of that cat at once. I will not have him in the house." He stared sternly at Gervase, then turned and left the room.

Everyone seemed to be looking at Gervase and she could not think clearly. Martha came over and put her arm around her. "Now then. I'm sorry about this, Gervase."

"I have to do what he says?"

"He's the steward. We all have to do what he says," her uncle said, his face puckered in a bitter expression. "There's no call for him to take such an attitude. A cat will do no harm."

"He's always felt that way about cats," Clyde Denny muttered.

"Maybe we could keep him outside," Martha said tentatively. She saw Gervase's stricken expression but was helpless.

"You can't keep a cat out of a place," Daisy said. "I hate that man!"

Gervase was frightened for Mr. Bob. It was clear that there were no admirers of Silas Wilkins, but she sensed also that everyone was afraid to cross him.

"We'll see what can be done," Martha whispered. "Now, come along and have your breakfast."

But Gervase could hardly eat. There was a lump in her throat, and when Mr. Bob came and raised his front paws onto her legs, her hand was unsteady as she stroked his fur. She looked into his big golden eyes and right then and there made a resolution, but she did not speak of it.

When the servants' meal was over, Martha said, "We'll have to start breakfast for the master and the family now. Come along, Gervase."

Gervase did not remember much about the rest of that day. She stayed in the kitchen and did what her aunt told her, but her mind was working fast. She knew well she would not let Mr. Bob be harmed, and by the time noon came around, the plan was fully formed. She was given a little hope when her aunt told her she would beg Mr. Wilkins to reconsider, but later in the afternoon the answer was exactly what Gervase had expected. "Why is he so mean, Aunt Martha?"

"He's a sour, bitter old man. He should have been put out a long time ago. Nobody likes him."

"Why do they keep him here?"

"Oh, with Sir Edward and the rest of the family he puts on a better face than you just saw. He can be very pleasant with them but he makes life miserable for most of us."

The afternoon passed and woodenly Gervase went through the motions. She helped prepare the evening meal and afterward went out with her uncle George to see the garden, but her mind was on Mr. Bob.

Finally she went to her room, telling her aunt she was tired, and sat on the bed, holding Mr. Bob on her lap. "We'll run away from this place, Mr. Bob, first thing in the morning. I'll get a job somewhere in London. There must be someone who wants a girl who can wash or scrub for them. Don't you worry, now."

Mr. Bob reached out tentatively and shoved at her chest with his paw — which meant, "Rub my head." She complied and he began rumbling and purring deep inside. Gervase sat for a long time and then got up and began to sort her things. She knew she would have to carry Mr. Bob, for he could not be trusted outside his basket. She put inside the box everything she could not take and wrote a note.

*Deer Ant. I kant stay heer for I kant give up Mistir Bob. Thank you verry much for inviting me. I will be bak for my box sumday so pleeze keep it for me.*

She put the note on the table and weighed it down with one of the cups from the washstand. Then she got into bed and Mr. Bob hopped up with her.

She prayed fearfully but she knew she had no choice. "I'll never leave you, Mr. Bob. Don't you worry!"

As Davis reached the foot of the stairs, he caught a movement and turned his head to see Martha Miller come running down the hall.

"What's wrong, Martha?" Davis asked. He was very fond of Martha and always had a kind word for her.

Martha's face was pale. "Please, sir, it's Gervase!"

"Gervase? What's wrong? Is she sick?"

"No, but read this, please." She handed him a slip of paper, then began wringing her hands.

Davis read the note. "What's this all about, Martha? Why has she run away?"

"It's her cat. The steward told her she had to get rid of it. I was going to try to find it a home. I had no idea the poor child would do a thing like this."

"How long has she been gone?"

"I don't think it could be too long, sir. Violet said she saw her just about daylight."

"Only an hour ago? I wonder if Violet saw which way she went."

"Toward town, I suppose."

"Well, don't worry. She couldn't have gone far. I'll go get her."

"But the cat. Mr. Wilkins says — "

"Don't worry about that. I'll take care of Mr. Wilkins."

Davis went at once to the second floor, where he found the housekeeper and learned that she had seen Gervase moving eastward down the road. "I thought she was just out for a walk, exploring the place."

"Thank you, Violet."

Davis ran back down the stairs and dashed out to the carriage house. Clyde Denny was surprised to see him. "Good morning, sir."

"Hook up that light tilbury for me with Princess."

The tilbury was a small two-wheeled carriage with no top. The coachman did exactly as Davis commanded. In less than ten minutes Davis was in the tilbury, headed down the road. Princess, a lively bay mare, set off at a run. Davis had to brace his feet against the floor to keep his balance. He had gone only a mile when he saw a man walking toward him. He didn't recognize the man but he pulled up and said, "Hello there."

"Good morning, sir." The man was elderly with silver hair. He pulled off his hat and said, "What be you stirrin' for so early, sir?"

"I'm looking for a young girl. I think she's headed down this road."

"Why, indeed she is, sir! She's about three miles down the road or maybe a little farther. She was carrying a basket and a sack."

"Thank you very much," Davis said, nodding, then spoke to the mare.

He kept his eyes on the road ahead, and presently he saw a small figure trudging along. *Poor child! Not a very good welcome for her, I'm afraid. Those two toughs when I picked her up, and now this.* He saw Gervase turn around and look, and when he got even with her, he pulled the mare up and said cheerfully, "Well, good morning, Gervase."

Gervase's face was pale. She looked weary. He was surprised that she had gotten this far, carrying so much weight. "Good morning, Mr. Davis."

"Get in," Davis said.

"No sir, I can't do that."

Davis saw the way the young girl's mouth was set, and admired her determination. "Your aunt told me what happened, but it's going to be all right."

"I can't do without Mr. Bob, sir."

"Why, of course you can't, and I'm going to see that you don't."

He saw the light come to the girl's eyes. He also saw that her lips, which had been held tightly together, trembled slightly. Her hair, tied back simply, was almost the color of clear honey and made a rich yellow gleaming in the early-morning sunlight. "Whoa now, Princess," he said. Fastening the reins, he got out of the carriage and stood towering over Gervase. "Now then. I know you're upset, but if you'll trust me, I promise you'll never be separated from Mr. Bob. Not as long as you're at Kimberly."

"Really, sir? The steward, he said—"

"Will you trust me, Gervase, if I promise you?"

Gervase could hardly keep the tears back. She was weary and had become very frightened as she plodded along the road, with Mr. Bob meowing in protest every step. She thought of going to a strange town of which she had heard so much, and not much of it good. She knew nobody and had no friends, and now as she looked up into Davis's face and saw the kindness in it, she suddenly felt the lump in her throat. "Yes sir," she said, and she had to drop her eyes, for she felt them filling up.

"Fine! Let me help you. Come along, Mr. Bob." Davis put the basket on the seat and then stashed Gervase's bundle behind the seat. "Come along, now. Let me help you in. It's rather high."

Gervase took his hand, stepped up, and seated herself. She quickly wiped her eyes while he went around behind the carriage. *He's going to help me. I won't have to go away . . .*

Davis leaped into the tilbury, picked up the lines, and said, "Come on, Princess. Back home again." He turned the mare around, and as soon as they were headed up the road, he said, "Now, I have a proposition that I think will answer." He turned and saw that she was looking at him, her face still stiff. "Why don't you sell Mr. Bob to me?"

"No, I'd never sell Mr. Bob!" Gervase half rose, as if she would grab the cat in the basket and jump out.

"Now, don't be so quick. How about this: You'll keep Mr. Bob, just as you always have. He'll sleep in your room and you'll take care of him, but I'll own him. The difference is, you see, to everyone else he'll be *my* cat. And I'd like to see Mr. Silas Wilkins lay a hand on any of *my* possessions!"

Gervase could not answer for a moment. She was very bright and saw instantly what he was trying to do. "Thank you, sir," she whispered. "I ... I don't know what I'd do without Mr. Bob."

"Now, about the price." He reached into his pocket and pulled out a coin. "There. There's a guinea. We won't make out a bill of sale, but you and I understand it. I paid for him and he's mine."

"But you don't actually have to give me the money."

"Well, if you ever want to buy him back from me, you'll have to give me the coin back." Davis smiled. "I think it will work fine, Gervase." He put his hand on her shoulder, squeezing it slightly. "Anytime you want him back, I'll sell him to you."

Gervase once again felt relief wash through her. The weight of his hand on her shoulder was reassuring, and she said, "Thank you, sir. I know you're doing it for me."

"Nonsense! I've always wanted to own a fine cat like Mr. Bob. Now, suppose you let him out so he can enjoy this sunshine and fresh morning air."

Gervase quickly opened the basket and Mr. Bob hopped out at once. She put the basket in the back and saw that Davis was petting the cat. "Well, old boy," he said, "I hope you and I will get along."

Mr. Bob purred and Gervase stroked his head the way he liked. She could not speak, her heart was so full.

"We'll be back about in time for breakfast and we'll make our big announcement," Davis said, grinning.

"Yes sir." Gervase could say no more. She settled back and watched as the mare cantered along the road.

Martha was just serving breakfast to the servants when Davis and Gervase came in. Davis had Mr. Bob in his arms and Gervase was carrying the basket. Everyone looked up and a murmur went around the table. Mr. Wilkins was sitting at the head of the table. His mouth went tight as a purse, Gervase noticed, when he saw the cat. He rose and said, "Sir, the cat will not be here long."

"You're wrong about that, Silas. Miss Gervase," he said, and he turned to face the steward squarely, holding his eyes, "has sold this fine animal to me. I'm very happy with my new addition." He stroked the cat's fur but kept his eyes on Silas. "I'm going to have to ask all of you to be very careful with Mr. Bob. If anyone were to harm him in any way, I'm afraid I'd have to thrash him and send him packing without a reference."

A total and complete silence had fallen across the room, and Gervase was watching Silas Wilkins' face, which seemed to be frozen. His eyes were blinking rapidly, and his mouth was open, as if he were trying to swallow air.

"Now, Gervase," Davis went on, "will be in charge of grooming him, feeding him, and seeing that he's properly cared for." He stopped for one moment and said, "I would be very hard indeed on anyone who displeased me in this matter. Do you all understand?"

Immediately everyone at the table, except Silas Wilkins, murmured their assent. He stood there, apparently unable to move. Finally he saw that everyone's eyes were upon him, especially Davis Wingate's.

He nodded and muttered, "Very well." Tossing his napkin down on the table, he said, "I must be about my work."

As soon as Silas left the room, Clyde Denny laughed. "I always liked a man who loves cats. I can see Mr. Wilkins is a great cat lover."

Everyone laughed then, for it was a pleasure for all of them to see the sour steward get his comeuppance.

Davis handed Mr. Bob to Gervase. "Now then. Take good care of my cat, Gervase."

"Oh, yes sir. I surely will!"

Gervase was helping Annie Cousins, the scullery maid, wash the breakfast dishes. It was not part of her job but she liked Annie, who was only seventeen and rather plain but a great deal of fun. Annie turned to her, handed her a wet dish, saying, "Well, you've been here a month, Gervase. How do you reckon you like it?"

"I like it fine here."

"Did the steward ever say anything more to you about your cat?"

Carefully Gervase dried the dish and then put it on the stack. Shaking her head, she said, "He never mentioned it again, but he hates me. He'll hardly even speak to me unless he has to."

"I wish he hated *me* like that! He complains to me all the time."

The two continued to wash and when they were finished, Annie seemed to find something amusing, for she was grinning broadly.

"What are you smiling about, Annie?"

"Oh, nothing," Annie said. But she kept looking toward the hallway door.

Puzzled, Gervase glanced in that direction. As the two girls left the scullery and went into the main kitchen, suddenly the door opened and Gervase saw her uncle come in, bearing a cake. Martha was behind him, and the other servants filed in.

"Let's have the happy birthday song," Robert Bates said. He came over and got right into Gervase's face. "It's your birthday party! Happy birthday, Gervase!"

The servants then began singing "Happy Birthday," and Gervase, who had never dreamed of such a thing, did not even know how they knew it was her birthday!

"It's a big day when a girl gets to the age of sixteen," Clyde Denny said, nodding wisely. "It means she's getting to be a young woman. First thing we know, Gervase, you'll be gettin' married and having a whole houseful of babies."

"Oh, I won't either," Gervase said, blushing. She was sitting at the kitchen table, with the little gifts, all inexpensive, before her — a handkerchief, a shawl, some tinted ink. When she looked up, everyone saw that she could not contain the tears. "I never had a birthday party before," she whispered.

"Well, it's a custom where I come from to give everybody who has a birthday a kiss," Robert Bates said. He grabbed Gervase and kissed her roundly on the cheek before she could move.

"You're the world's worst liar, Bates!" Martha said, laughing. But she gave Gervase a kiss, too. "You look so much like your mother, it makes me want to cry."

Gervase hugged her aunt, and when they finally dispersed to their work, she gathered her presents and started to take them to her room. She had left the kitchen and reached the stairs when she heard her name called. She turned and saw Davis, who was holding a book in his hand. "How's Mr. Bob, my good cat?"

"He's fine, sir."

"What's all that you have there?"

"They're birthday presents. I couldn't believe it, sir! They had a little party for me with a cake and gave me presents."

"Indeed! And how old are you today?"

"Sixteen, sir."

"Well, happy sixteenth birthday," Davis said, smiling. "I'd like to give you a present, too. What would you like?"

Gervase stared at the book he was holding. "I never had a book, Mr. Davis."

"Here. Come along to the library and I'll sign it and put the date in it. It's one of my favorite books." Gervase followed him into the library. He sat at the desk, took out writing materials, and wrote for a few moments. "There. How's that?"

Gervase saw that he had written,

> *Here's to Miss Gervase Howard, my very dear friend — and joint owner of Mr. Bob. Happy birthday, and may you grow up to be as beautiful and happy as any young woman in England.*

Gervase took the book and examined it. "Jane Eyre," she said. "Is that who wrote the book?"

"No. That's the name of the young woman the book is about. As a matter of fact, you remind me a little bit of her."

"Really, sir?"

"In some ways. I'll tell you what. After you read it, we'll talk about it. Now I must run, but may I wish you again a very happy birthday, Gervase." He put out his hand and she took it. He squeezed her hand, nodded, and left. She made her way up the stairs and at once went to her journal. She wrote steadily for a few minutes.

> *My first birthday party. I wanted to cry, but it was because I was so hapy. And then Mr. Davis give me a book all of my verry own.*

She hesitated and then added,

> *He's so handsum — and so gud!*

# Chapter Four

Afaint but insistent scratching at the door attracted Gervase's attention as she sat at the dressing table in her shift, fixing her hair. She went to the door. Opening it, she looked down and suddenly made a face. "Mr. Bob, I've told you a thousand times not to do this!"

Mr. Bob looked up, holding a dead mouse in his mouth. His large eyes seemed to glow, as they always did when he brought Gervase a "present." Sometimes it was a dead bird or even an insect such as a grasshopper, but mice were his most common gift.

Gervase took the mouse by the tail and shook her head. "I do *wish* you wouldn't do this, Mr. Bob." But she knew such recriminations were useless, for he insisted on bringing gifts to her periodically.

Opening the window, she threw the dead mouse out, then moved to the washstand, poured fresh water in, and washed her hands thoroughly. She picked up her brown dress and struggled to pull it over her head. When she finally had it on, she looked down at herself. "I can't go around like this!" The year she had spent at Kimberly had marked a transition in her life. She had come as a scrawny, gawky, frightened girl, but the good food and the passage from her sixteenth year to her seventeenth had brought changes in her body, so now the fullness of her youthful figure was clearly outlined beneath the dress.

She stood there for a moment irresolutely, then shook her head. "I'll have to wear the other dress." She'd had to get rid of the clothes she'd brought with her, including her best dress, and now this one was much too tight for modesty.

She wrestled her way out of the dress and tossed it down, then suddenly hesitated. Picking up a pen, she went to the door, stood with her back to it, put her hand on her head, and carefully marked the spot. Twisting around, she peered at the mark she had put there a year ago when she first arrived. She was shocked to realize that she had grown almost two inches. She dated the new mark May 24, 1852. She was staring at the two marks when a knock came at the door, and she quickly said, "Just a minute." She slipped into a worn robe Mrs. Peeples had given her and opened the door.

"Good morning, Gervase."

"Why, Mrs. Peeples, you climbed the stairs! You must have hurt your knees terribly."

"They're very bad but I have some distressing news."

Gervase stared at the housekeeper. She had grown very fond of Mrs. Peeples, who was always kind to her. The woman stood as a barrier between Gervase and Silas Wilkins. "What's wrong, Mrs. Peeples?"

"Molly had to go home." Molly was the second-floor maid and had never been very satisfactory. She was very free with young men, and Mrs. Peeples constantly had to correct her. "I'm afraid you're going to have to take her place."

"But . . . I don't know how to do her work!"

"Well, you've become the best cook I've seen, except for your aunt perhaps, so it won't be hard for you to pick up Molly's duties. And it's a step up, you know. One of these days you could become a lady's maid, perhaps for the mistress."

The hierarchy in an English household such as this was very strict, Gervase had learned. The servants in a great house could amount to a small army. A fancy dinner with a ten-course meal and eighteen guests might generate as many as five hundred items to be washed. The women's clothes came in multiple layers of petticoats and skirts that were often changed several times a day, and all had to be washed by hand. The house was cluttered with intricately carved furniture and bric-a-brac, all of which had to be kept clean. The male staff was presided over by a butler or steward, and the female staff by a housekeeper. Each was addressed by the title of "Mr." or "Mrs." — the housekeeper always being a "Mrs.," whether married or not. Status was very important, Gervase had discovered quickly. The "upper" servants, which included the steward, the butler, and the housekeeper as well as the ladies' maids, had their own rooms. Others were the "lower" servants, the very bottom being a scullery maid.

"But I don't have anything to wear — a maid's dress, I mean."

"Molly left hers and you two are about the same size. My, you have grown, Gervase! Come down to Molly's room and try on her dress. I'll go with you."

Ten minutes later Gervase was standing in the middle of the room which Molly had shared with another maid. She was wearing Molly's black dress with a white apron and a pair of shiny leather shoes. She also wore a small white cap on her head.

"You look just fine," Mrs. Peeples said. "The dress is just a little too large for you."

"My other one was too small."

"Well, we'll get you fitted out. The family has company coming."

"Company, ma'am?"

"Yes. Miss Roberta Grenville and her parents, Lord and Lady Grenville."

"Are they very important people?"

"Well, they're of the nobility," Mrs. Peeples said, smiling. "Their family had a lot of money and a lot of property at one time but not as much now, I understand. But I can't be gossiping." She hesitated, then said, "Mr. Ives has been seeing Miss Roberta for some time. Talk is that they might marry."

"But he's in university. He doesn't have a profession, does he?"

"No, but he'll be a lawyer one day and then he can afford it. I'm going to ask you to be her maid — Miss Roberta, that is."

"But I don't know anything about being a lady's maid!"

"You just be polite and do what she tells you. You can carry water for her and see that her clothes are clean. Things like that. I'll tell her you're new. She'll be kind, I'm sure."

"How long will they be staying?"

"They'll be here a week, I understand."

Lord Grenville leaned forward and looked out the window of the barouche as the four-wheeled carriage traveled along the road, pulled by two teams of horses. "I say, the Wingate estate is quite impressive, isn't it, Alice?"

"Yes, it is." Alice Grenville was a rather pretty woman of forty-five. She had married late in life and had come from a family of considerable fortune. She had thought that Sir Winston Grenville had money, too, but she'd been somewhat shocked to discover that the Grenville fortune had diminished and now little was left except a fine estate and the title.

"I expect there would be good shooting here," Sir Winston said. "Look, there's a pheasant out there right now. By George, I'd like to get a shot at it."

"I am sure that you and Sir Edward will get your shooting in this week," Roberta Grenville said. She was a tall young woman, well formed, with black hair and brown eyes, and was dressed at the height of fashion. She suddenly leaned forward. "There's the house. It *is* rather impressive, isn't it?"

"By George, it is!" her father murmured.

"If I were to marry Ives, I suppose I would come and live here."

Lady Alice stared at her daughter. "You've not spoken of that before."

"Well, I must marry somebody, and Ives is an amusing young man." Roberta was amused at the attempts her parents made to marry her off. She paid little heed to them as a rule, for she had decided long ago that the man she married would be *her* choice — not her parents'.

"Well, he's only a cadet, a younger son," Sir Winston said. He stared out the window and added thoughtfully, "Sometimes I think our system is a bit unfair. Often the firstborn son isn't the brightest boy, but he always gets the best of everything. Doesn't seem quite right that the eldest inherits everything."

"You may be right, Father, but that's the way things are," Roberta said.

"Are you serious about him?"

"Oh yes. As I say, he's very amusing."

"What about the older son? What's his name?" Sir Winston asked hesitantly.

"His name is Davis. He's quite serious, Ives tells me," Roberta said coolly.

"You haven't met him, then?"

"No, I haven't. Ives speaks of him, of course, but not often. As I say, he's a more serious type. He works at the family business in London, and Ives tells me he likes to write. He's a great reader."

"Write what?" Sir Winston asked.

"Novels, I understand."

"What foolishness!" Sir Winston mumbled.

None of them spoke further until the carriage pulled up in front of the house. The doorman was there immediately to open the door and hand the ladies down. They were met by Ives Wingate, who came at once to make his bow and greet the family. The whole family was rather fond of Ives, and indeed his attention was centered at once on Roberta. "I'm so glad to see you, Roberta — and you too, of course," he said, turning to the parents.

"You have a beautiful home here, sir," Sir Winston said.

"You'll get to see a lot of it. My father's already talking about the entertainment he has planned for you."

"Shooting birds, I trust."

"Yes indeed! Come along. My father isn't here but my mother is."

Ives led them up the steps and when they were inside, his mother came, accompanied by two maids. She knew the Grenvilles, although in a very casual way, and spoke warmly.

"I know you must be tired after your journey."

She turned to one of the maids and said, "This is Daisy. She will take care of your needs. Daisy, show Lord and Lady Grenville to their room, please."

"Yes ma'am."

"And this is Gervase, Miss Grenville." Lady Wingate smiled sweetly and added, "She's new at her job. One of our maids left, so I'm sure you'll be understanding."

Roberta glanced casually at the maid and noted that she was very young — and rather nervous. "Of course. We'll get along, won't we, Gervase?"

"Yes ma'am." Gervase bobbed, and when Lady Wingate said, "Why don't you take Miss Grenville up to her room," she nodded and turned at once. "This way, ma'am."

Roberta followed the young woman up to the second floor, and when they were in the room, she looked around and said, "This is a very pleasant room indeed."

"Yes ma'am. All the rooms are pleasant."

Roberta suddenly laughed. "I'm sure they are." She studied the young woman carefully. Her dress did not fit, being somewhat too large for her, but Roberta didn't comment. "So you're new in this position. What did you do before?"

"My aunt is the cook. I helped her, Miss Grenville."

"Well, do you think you'll like it?" She did not really pay heed as Gervase answered, but after looking the room over, she said, "I think I'll take a bath and lie down. It's so dusty."

"Yes ma'am. I'll have fresh water brought up at once."

Roberta noted that Gervase did her best to please. *The poor thing seems frightened — but she's willing enough.* After her bath, the youthful maid helped Roberta into a robe.

"Brush my hair, will you, Gervase?"

"Yes ma'am." Gervase took up the brush and began to brush the young woman's hair.

"You're very fortunate to be in such an amiable household."

"Oh, they're all so wonderful to me, Miss Grenville! The master and his lady are as kind as can be. And Mr. Davis — oh, ma'am, I can't tell you how kind he is!"

Roberta concealed a smile at the girl's obvious feelings for Davis Wingate. "What about Mr. Ives?"

"Oh, he's fine, too, except he's gone at university most of the time."

"I'm anxious to meet Mr. Davis Wingate. I see you like him very much."

"Oh, Miss Roberta, I didn't say — "

"I could see the light in your eyes when you spoke of him. Is he handsome?"

"Why, I . . . I suppose so. He's very tall."

Roberta was aware that the young woman was disturbed by such conversation, and smiled. "Well, I'll be able to judge for myself. I think I'll lie down until dinner."

"Yes ma'am. Shall I come back and wake you up and help you dress?"

"Yes, Gervase. That would be very nice."

"So, the fair Roberta is with us," Davis said, smiling indulgently. "The angel whose praises you've been singing for how many months now?"

"Only four months," Ives said. The two were standing in the dining room, waiting for the others to come down.

"Have you started writing odes to dear Roberta's fingernails?" Davis asked with a grin.

"I'll leave the writing up to you, but she has very nice fingernails."

"I'm sure she does. I can't keep up with your love affairs, Ives."

"Don't be foolish! I haven't had any love affairs."

"Well, your infatuations, then. You always were easily infatuated."

Ives flushed. "I may have liked the young ladies a little bit."

"A little bit!" Davis laughed. "I thought for a while you were going through every suitable young woman in England, alphabetically."

"Now, that's not kind, Davis!"

"I'm sorry, Ives. I'm sure she's an admirable young lady."

"She is beautiful," Ives said, nodding. "I hope Father and Mother like her."

The two men talked until finally their parents walked in, accompanied by their guests. Ives moved forward at once, saying,

"I don't think any of you have met my brother, Davis. Davis, this is Sir Winston Grenville, his wife, Lady Alice, and their daughter, Miss Roberta Grenville."

"I am so glad to meet you all," Davis said, bowing. "Ives has of course spoken of you so often."

"What did he say, Mr. Wingate?" Roberta asked.

Davis was taken off guard by this sudden question. "I don't believe I could tell you all the rapturous words he gave concerning you, Miss Grenville. It would make you too proud, I fear."

"He hardly ever mentions you," Roberta said, smiling.

"I'm a very dull fellow, I'm afraid. Ives is the lively one."

"Come now. Let's go to the table. I'm starved," Sir Edward said.

They went into the dining room, which was very impressive indeed, even to Sir Winston and his family. It was a large room, twenty by twenty-two feet in size, with wall-to-wall green carpet and a long heavy linen rug under the table. The wallpaper was a bold green with a diamond-shaped gold mica pattern. A pair of silver George III two-light candelabras on spreading circular bases were giving out light, as was a glittering chandelier that threw shadows over the table. The table, which was made of mahogany and had turned baluster legs, was covered with the best French damask. Against the wall, the sideboard was enormous, with a serpentine mahogany front and a glossy marble top.

The silverware was gleaming, as was the snow-white tablecloth. As the company sat to eat, Roberta found herself between Ives and Davis. Sir Edward and Sir Winston began talking at once about hunting, while the two older women spoke about London society. Davis said little at first, for Roberta was bringing Ives up to date on the activities of their friends. Finally she turned to Davis and said, "I understand that you plan to be a writer."

Davis blushed slightly, for it was a touchy subject. "I write a little now and then."

"You want to be a novelist, I understand. Well, Mr. Charles Dickens is doing well, so I suppose the nobility can write as well as anyone."

"Have you read many novels?"

Roberta was a rather fetching young woman, all fair and smooth. Her dress fell away from her throat, revealing ivory skin, and her hair was as black as anything in nature. Davis could not help noticing the contours of her body in her dress and was somewhat shocked at his response. He was not much of a man for ladies, but he said to himself, *Well, Ives has picked himself a beauty!* Aloud he asked, "Who do you like? Sir Walter Scott?"

"I think he's a dreadful bore."

Davis laughed abruptly. "Most people are not quite so sharp."

"Well, I was thinking of *Ivanhoe.*"

"You don't like the book?"

"Ivanhoe is rather thick in the head. He has an opportunity to take a fine, lively young woman named Rebecca, and instead he turns away from her and marries the rather boring Lady Rowena."

Davis was amused. "That's not the common opinion."

"Oh no. Rebecca was a Jewess, so we stuffy English rule her out at once, but she's the much more attractive of the two."

Davis shook his head. "I've always thought so myself but never dared to say so."

"You should be more daring, Mr. Wingate. Life is so much more fun."

Ives sat listening as the two talked animatedly about novels. He was not a reader, so he did not take part.

The dinner went very well and afterward, when Davis had a chance to say a few words alone to Roberta, he said, "I monopolized your time. I should apologize to Ives and to you. Our arguments were almost a little too sprightly."

Roberta smiled, and she had a lovely smile indeed. "Men and women should argue, don't you think?"

Davis was intrigued by this fresh idea. "I haven't heard that advocated, I don't believe."

"Men don't listen to women but they should."

"I think you're right. Your ideas on fiction are quite interesting. We'll have to talk more about them."

"Well, we have an entire week. I would love it."

The week passed quickly for Davis. He found Roberta Grenville a fascinating woman. She spent most of her time with Ives, of course, but whenever Davis was able to engage her in conversation, he was always delighted with her sharp, penetrating ideas. And of course she was beautiful. He did not understand women enough to know that she had the art, picked up early in life by most beautiful women, of making men feel important — that is, whenever they chose to do so.

On the last morning of the Grenvilles' stay, Ives went shooting with his father and Sir Winston, leaving Davis to entertain Roberta. The two walked in the garden and stopped in the shade of some towering shrubs. They sat and for thirty minutes talked vigorously about the virtues of the English novelists compared with those of the French.

"I've never talked so much in my life, Roberta."

"I don't suppose you have anyone to talk to, about fiction at least. The family doesn't seem to be interested."

"Actually, they think I'm rather foolish."

"Well, I don't think you're foolish. I hope you keep up with your writing. Who knows?" She leaned forward suddenly and put her hand on his. "Someday I might be telling everyone that I was once very close to the famous novelist Sir Davis Wingate." Her voice had taken on a low timbre.

Davis laughed with some embarrassment. He was very much aware of her hand, and he covered it with his free hand. "I doubt that will ever happen, but it has been so good to have you here. I'll miss our conversations."

"Well, there's no reason why you should miss them."

Davis stared at Roberta. "What do you mean?"

"I'll be staying with my cousin Abigail in London. Her family has a townhouse there. Perhaps you'd like to call on them — and me, of course."

"I would like it very much."

"Here. I'll give you their address."

"When may I come?"

"Call and leave your card anytime. I'll tell the family you're coming. I believe they know your family slightly."

Davis took a deep breath. "Why, I will certainly do so."

The two continued to speak of writing, but eventually Roberta said, "You seem rather lonely."

"Most people don't see that in me."

"I see it because I have some loneliness of my own."

They were sitting so close, Davis could smell her faint perfume, and as she faced him, the fragrance of her clothes came powerfully to him and somehow slid through the armor of his self-sufficiency. She had a way of laughing that was very charming, but now she was quite serious.

"I'm sorry to hear that," he said. "You're so young and attractive and from a good family. Why, the young men must swarm around you!"

"I get bored with most of them. I do get lonely, I confess. I suppose everyone has their moments of loneliness."

"I suppose so."

"Perhaps we could help each other in that respect. We're not lonely now, are we?"

Suddenly Davis saw what he thought was a challenge in Roberta's eyes. He leaned forward and waited to see if she would move away from him, but she did not. Leaning even closer, he said quietly, "I suppose every man sees his own kind of beauty." He ceased to smile then and drew back. "You know, it's rather hard on me, but I see beauty in you."

"Why should that be hard?"

Davis hesitated. "Well, Ives is in love with you."

"Oh, Ives is in love with half the young women he meets."

Davis laughed. "You know him very well. He's very impressionable. But I wouldn't do anything to hurt him."

"I don't believe you would. But Ives will be off after another young woman soon enough."

Davis stared at her, not certain how to answer. Finally he said, "You don't think he's serious about you?"

"Oh, Ives is always serious about his romances," Roberta said, laughing. "He was serious about Cecily Holiman — and before that he was serious about my best friend, Laura Channing. He's a dear boy but rather flighty."

"And you, Miss Grenville — are you serious about him?"

"Why, of course not!" Roberta responded. "He's so young — in years of course but, well, in other ways. I really think he'll grow up someday and make some young woman a fine husband."

The two sat there talking, and then she looked at him and turned her head to one side. "You were about to kiss me a moment ago, weren't you?"

Davis felt himself redden. "Was I that obvious?"

"I usually know when a man wants to kiss me. Why didn't you?"

"Because of Ives."

Roberta did not speak and she did not move. Her eyes seemed to grow wider then, and Davis Wingate leaned forward and kissed her on the lips. She did not resist and when he drew back, he was confused. He started to speak but at that moment a voice said, "Mr. Wingate —"

Davis jumped up at once, and Roberta rose also to face Gervase. She seemed hesitant, and Davis realized she had seen him kiss Roberta. "What is it, Gervase?" he said almost harshly.

"Your mother asked me to tell you and Miss Grenville that she'd like to see you."

"Tell her we'll be right there."

"Yes sir," Gervase replied and hurried off.

Suddenly Roberta laughed. "I wish you could see your face." Sheer pleasure was dancing in her dark eyes. "Here we are at our first meeting — caught kissing by the maid! Now everybody in the house will know that you're courting your brother's sweetheart."

Davis stared at her, embarrassed, but then he forced a laugh. "I do feel like a callous schoolboy."

Roberta smiled. "This is like something from a book, isn't it? Young woman is brought to see youngest son, meets older son, who falls in love with her. How would you end a story like that?"

"It does sound like a piece of fiction, doesn't it?"

"Well, when you come to see me in London, we'll see if we can make it into a novel, you and I."

Gervase was lying in her bed with Mr. Bob sitting on her chest, treading on her with his front paws. Phoebe Rogers was sitting in the rocking chair, watching. The two had been giggling and laughing, for they had become fast friends. Phoebe had formed the habit of stopping by late at night. The two would smuggle sweets into the room and talk until bedtime.

"Why is Mr. Bob doing that? He looks like he's stomping on you."

"I don't know. He flexes his claws. Cats like to do that. This one does, anyhow."

"It looks like it would hurt."

"He's very careful." Gervase reached up and held Mr. Bob's head tightly, then pulled him forward and kissed him.

"You ought not to kiss cats right on the mouth!"

"Why not?"

"He's probably been eating mice."

"No, he's been drinking milk. He has a sweet breath."

Phoebe popped a sweetmeat into her mouth, sucked on it, and then crunched it with pleasure. She said, "Mrs. Peeples is really in a great deal of pain."

"I know. I feel so sorry for her."

"Well, you've got to where you do most of her work, Gervase. Everybody's talking about how well you know the house."

"I just help her when I can. Her knees hurt so badly, and her fingers are starting to hurt, too."

"I don't think she can stay long. She's just not able to do the work."

"I think she'll stay as long as she wants to. The master and mistress are very fond of her. She's been with the family for-ever, hasn't she?"

"Yes, she has."

Phoebe leaned forward, her eyes bright. "Did you know that Ives and Davis had a dreadful argument?"

"No. Who told you?"

"Nobody told me. I heard them myself. I was cleaning the room next to Mr. Davis's, and they left the door open."

"What were they fighting about?"

Phoebe's eyes opened wide and her eyebrows made arches of surprise. "What do you think? About Roberta Grenville, of course."

"You shouldn't be talking about what the family does."

"You don't want to hear it?"

Gervase pulled at Mr. Bob's ears and said stiffly, "Well, if you want to tell me, I suppose I can't stop you."

"Well, Mr. Ives was very angry. He said that Miss Roberta is his sweetheart, and he found out that Mr. Davis has been seeing her."

"What did Mr. Davis say?"

"Well, he didn't deny it, of course. But he said he's only seen her a few times. I thought they were going to come to blows. Mr. Davis seemed to feel pretty guilty about it. He is guilty, too. Back when her family was here, he spent all the time he could with her. Didn't you notice?"

"Yes, I noticed."

Gervase listened as Phoebe went on about the quarrel. Finally Gervase said, "You'd better get to bed, Phoebe. We have to be up early in the morning."

"I guess so. I'll just take the rest of these with me. If you eat them, you might get fat."

"Go ahead and take them."

Phoebe left and Gervase prepared for bed. When she was dressed, she took out her journal. She sat at the dressing table, looking back over what she had written for the past few months. She went to the entry in May when she had written,

> *I caught Mr. Davis kissing Miss Roberta today. I thought it was awful.*

She stared at that entry, then turned to the page where she had left off, and began writing.

*Phoebe just told me that Ives and Davis have had a quarel over Roberta Grenville. I saw this coming three months ago when I found them together out in the garden, but I didn't think Davis would do a thing like this to his own brother.*

Gervase paused and found herself staring at the wall, unable to write more. She did not move for a long time. Finally a frown came to her and she shook her head almost angrily. She began writing again, pressing hard against the paper, the strokes fast and furious.

*I said I'd be honest in this journal, that I would never say anything I didn't really feel. I can't help my feelings for Davis. I know it's wrong, but you can't help loving someone, can you?*

Gervase stiffened and then stared at what she had written. She went to the window and gazed out into the night. The soft breeze was making a sibilant, crying noise, and from far off came the sound of a lone dog barking. Finally she walked back to the desk. She sat, took a deep breath, and began to write.

*What a foolish, foolish girl I am! God has taken care of me, and I must get these foolish notions out of my head. I like Davis Wingate a great deal. That's natural, for he's kind and gentle to me always, but that's all it is!*

She shut the journal, put it in the drawer, and then got into bed. Mr. Bob came at once, as he did every night, and began shoving up against her.

"You can't have *all* the bed, Mr. Bob."

The big cat growled in his throat and settled down. An owl passed by the window, gave its ghostly cry, and the sound seemed to fill the room.

# Chapter Five

The dryness of August had loosened the earth so that as the afternoon breeze moved, it carried with it small flurries of dust. The sun dipped westward, and as Gervase looked in that direction, she saw the orange ball touch the horizon. The day's heat was out of the earth, and autumn's chill was beginning to make itself felt. She glanced at the young man who strolled beside her, and a smile touched her lips. She turned away quickly, listening as he spoke about the fair they had just attended.

Roger Osburn was only twenty-seven years old, but Gervase had always felt he was at least fifty in other ways, particularly in his habits. Six months earlier, when he had come to shoe the horses at Kimberly, Gervase had watched, fascinated, and the young blacksmith had evidently found her fascinating as well.

As the two of them walked slowly toward the house, Gervase looked up again at the sky. The late sun had ignited pools of pink fire in the clouds. "Isn't that a beautiful sunset, Roger?" she murmured.

Osburn broke off in the middle of a sentence and looked upward. "Why, it's right pretty," he responded and then immediately began speaking again of the horses he had seen at the fair. Though a young man, he had less imagination than anyone Gervase had ever seen. She had tried to talk to him once about books, and it was as if she had spoken a foreign language.

He never read unless it was something that had to do with farming or blacksmithing. Gervase made no further attempt to speak of the beauties of the evening falling upon them.

He had taken her out several times, including visits to church, which he liked. He had a fine singing voice, which was pleasing to her, but his interest in religion was more physical than spiritual. He had, for example, been very interested in the architecture of the chapel they had attended, and had insisted on taking her around and pointing out the intricacy of the work in the beams. Gervase, who was only mildly interested in church buildings, had cautiously tried to see what sort of spiritual life Osburn had. It was like stepping into an empty room, for the furniture in his head was purely worldly — horseshoes, barns, fields, crops.

As they reached the house, Gervase turned to Osburn and said, "Thank you for taking me to the fair, Roger. I enjoyed it so much."

"It was interesting," Osburn admitted. He had worn his best suit, the same one he wore to examine church architecture, a dark-brown wool suit that he wore winter and summer, and a bowler derby which he now removed and held behind him. He stood before her, his mild brown eyes fixed on her, and when Gervase said good night, he did not move. It was as if she had not spoken. "I've been thinking," he remarked in a prosaic tone of voice, "that you and me might get married."

Gervase had wondered when this proposal would come, but the offhanded manner of it caught her slightly off guard. Roger Osburn had never even attempted to kiss her or hold her hand. It was as if she were his sister or his maiden aunt! Gervase had some notions of romance — mostly from books, of course, and from observation of young people — and she had expected at least something more than this. "Why, Roger, I'm surprised."

"I don't see why. It would be a good thing, Gervase. My dad's gone on but my mum's still living. The house is all paid for. You could move right in."

*How like him to speak of marriage as a place to live rather than a man and a woman together.* Gervase of course had no experience in rejecting proposals. She did not know exactly what to say, except she knew she had to say no. Carefully she said, "I'm really not thinking of getting married. I'm very young."

"You're seventeen and I'm twenty-seven. That's about right." Osburn suddenly shifted his feet and he turned his head to one side. "I reckon you know I'm taken with you, Gervase." He leaned forward then and kissed her on the lips. It was the barest kind of a caress, not the sort of thing a man in love would give to a woman who stood before him.

Gervase almost smiled but caught herself in time. "I'm not going to get married for at least another five years or so."

Osburn weighed her words, and his mouth moved as he seemed to speak under his breath. Finally he nodded and said, "Well, I'll wait."

Gervase almost laughed aloud. It was as if she had asked him to wait for ten minutes while she got her hat! "I don't think you should count on that, Roger. There are so many young women who would make you a better wife than me."

Roger Osburn put his hat on and seemed not to have heard her words. "I'll be by to take you to church Sunday, Gervase. Good night."

"Good night, Roger."

Gervase stood watching Roger as he walked down the road. He was a sturdy young man with the broad shoulders of a blacksmith, and she well understood that marriage with him would be very . . . safe. He would never mistreat a woman. He would always be thoughtful about the material things of life, and she would never want for anything. But she could not help being amused, and she giggled slightly as she darted into the house. She went at once to Mrs. Peeples' room and found her sitting in her rocking chair as usual.

"You're home early, my dear."

"Yes, but I think we saw everything. Here, let me straighten up your room a bit."

Mrs. Peeples sat quietly, listening as Gervase spoke lightly of the things she had seen at the fair. She had suffered more from arthritis in the past year, and it had been Gervase who had taken the load from her. When she could not manage the stairs, it had been Gervase who had flown up and down and either carried out her instructions or passed them along to the other female members of the staff. She had become so necessary to the ailing old woman that now Gervase had been given a set of keys to the house so she would not have to come to the housekeeper for everything. Finally Gervase asked, "Could I fix you some tea?"

Without waiting for an answer, she went to the fireplace, put a kettle on, and soon it whistled cheerfully. By that time Gervase had set out the tea service, and she poured the tea and then the two sat sipping it. Mrs. Peeples said, "You've seen a lot of that young man Roger lately."

"Yes, I suppose I have."

Mrs. Peeples' hands were pained by the arthritis, but she covered her expression and looked over the cup. "He might make a good husband for you, Gervase."

Gervase suddenly laughed. "I suppose he would in some ways, but he's so . . . so dull."

Mrs. Peeples stared at her with astonishment. "Dull! What do you want in a husband? One of your heroes from the novels you read?"

"I wouldn't mind if the Count of Monte Cristo came asking for my hand, or Mr. Darcy from *Pride and Prejudice*."

Mrs. Peeples was a good housekeeper but lacked a sense of humor for the most part. "I don't understand you, Gervase," she said with a sigh. "Not that I would like for you to get married. I couldn't do without you around here, my dear."

"Well, there's no danger. I'm not going to marry him, and he's not liable to come dashing in and kidnap me. That would be exciting but it's not in Roger."

"What do you talk about?"

"About shoeing horses, of course. That's what he's mostly interested in."

This remark did amuse Mrs. Peeples, and she sat smiling as she considered how much the young girl had changed since she first appeared at Kimberly. She had been transformed from a skinny young woman into a very attractive one. She was wearing a green dress that made her eyes display their own hue of green. Her light-blond hair framed her face, and her eyes were dancing brightly, her face clearly expressive, as it usually was. "You're going to make some man a good wife, my dear," she said.

Gervase shook her head. "Not for a long time, I think." She got up and said, "Shall I help you get into bed, Mrs. Peeples?"

"No, I feel better tonight. You go along." As Gervase reached the door, she added, "Oh, Lady Sarah asked me to tell you to stop by before you retire tonight."

Gervase went at once to the back parlor. It was a smaller room than the main parlor, but Sarah Wingate liked it better. As Gervase entered, she spoke to Lady Sarah, who was sitting in one of the walnut Queen Anne side chairs, working on some sewing.

"Oh, good evening, Gervase. Did you have a good time at the fair?"

"Oh yes. It was very nice."

"I wanted to talk to you about the ball I've been planning."

"Mrs. Peeples said you would be having one. When will it be?"

"Next month, I think. Perhaps the middle of September. Sit down, my dear. I want to go over several things with you."

Gervase sat and listened intently as Lady Sarah outlined the ball.

"We will have possibly thirty guests, some of them overnight. I've made out a list, and those whose names I've marked we'll need to provide for. The others live close enough to get home after the ball."

Gervase took the list and ran her eyes down it quickly.

"You and Mrs. Peeples can go over the list, and of course I'll trust you to see that the refreshments are suitable. I know they will be, for you've become very good at that, Gervase."

"Thank you, Lady Sarah." Something troubled Gervase about the list, and she looked up and asked quietly, "Mr. Ives won't be at the ball?" She saw something flicker in Lady Sarah's eyes and instantly knew what the trouble was.

"No. He won't be coming."

Gervase didn't comment but instead asked questions and made notes. Finally she said, "I'll work on this right away."

"I'm glad you're here, Gervase. If it hadn't been for you, we would have had to replace Mrs. Peeples. She's almost like one of the family, she's been here so long. But you've taken the load off her."

"She's been very good to me, Lady Sarah."

"Yes, of course, but you've been good to her also." Lady Sarah smiled. "Why, you could be the housekeeper yourself, as young as you are."

Gervase nodded, then said, "I'll work on this and write everything down for your approval."

"Good night, Gervase."

As she left the parlor and headed for her bedroom, Gervase thought about the omission of Ives from the list. No one could live in a house as a servant without learning a great deal about the people who occupied the world of nobility. She had learned quickly that studying the lives of the Wingates and talking about them and laughing at their foibles was one of the chief forms of recreation for the servants at Kimberly. She herself did not participate but she listened.

*Ives and Davis are fighting over Roberta Grenville,* she thought. Something about this displeased her, as it always did, and she remembered how months ago she had written in her journal,

> *Mr. Davis should let Mr. Ives have Roberta. After all, he found her first and is interested in her.*

She had read that entry over many times but now somehow it seemed shallow to her.

As she entered her room, she was greeted by Mr. Bob, who had been asleep on her bed. She rubbed his broad head and held her fist out; he liked to shove his head against it. She stood for a moment thinking of the many things that would have to be done in preparation for the ball, the labor that would be involved during the event, the time that would be spent entertaining thirty people who would never give a thought to any of the work behind the scenes. Then she sighed and prepared for bed.

The house was like a whirlwind, packed with guests and extra servants, with new guests constantly arriving. Laughter filled the halls and the rooms.

The staff had risen early for several days in preparation for this day. Mrs. Peeples was having an especially difficult time, and all the work fell upon Gervase. She flew back and forth, up and down the stairs to Mrs. Peeples' room, always careful to ask permission to enter and just as careful to execute whatever order the housekeeper gave.

Some of the servants resented Gervase being so young and taking so much authority, but Gervase tried as best she could to explain that someone had to help Mrs. Peeples, and most of them were sympathetic.

She dashed into the kitchen and found Aunt Martha working at full speed to provide meals for over thirty people. Martha had tied her hair up, and the kitchen was filled with the smell of baking bread and roasting meat.

"How's Mrs. Peeples, Gervase?"

"Not very well. She's in such pain. I had hoped she'd have a good day for this ball."

"Poor woman suffers dreadfully."

"Let me help you, Aunt Martha."

"No. That young girl you hired does very well, the one with the awful name. I can never think of it — oh yes, it's Jemima."

"I don't think that's so awful. It's from the Bible."

"I don't care, it's awful! Here, let's go over the meals one more time...."

The two stood amid the bustle of the kitchen and discussed the menus. Finally Gervase put her arm around her aunt and said, "You've done fine, Aunt Martha. You're the best cook in all of England."

"I don't know about that." The remark obviously pleased Martha. She was very proud of her niece. Then she said, "Mr. Ives won't be here. I saw the list."

"No, he's not coming."

"He and Mr. Davis are like a pair of dogs fighting over a female."

"Aunt Martha, what an awful thing to say!"

Martha was a rather blunt, plain woman in her speech. Her brow wrinkled up. "Why, it's only the truth! I'll declare, with all the young women in England, it seems like two brothers could find one apiece instead of fighting over the same girl!"

Gervase did not answer and her silence somehow pleased Martha. "You never gossip about the family, and that's good. I'm ashamed of myself sometimes, but I do think Davis has behaved badly in this."

"I think I'd better go, Aunt Martha. I'll come back later to see how things are going."

As Gervase went to check on the third-floor maid, she thought back to the time when Roberta Grenville had first come. She had written the details of it in her journal, as she did with practically everything else, but the memory was clear. She had seen that Davis was attracted to the dark-haired woman even before he himself knew it, and as the months passed, she had been quick to observe the progress, as had all the members of the staff. Davis had gone to visit Roberta in London, and from that point on there had been a tension between the two brothers.

Phoebe Rogers ran up to her, saying, "Oh, Gervase, the Grenvilles are here and their rooms aren't ready!"

"I'll speak to them. You get Daisy and Helen, and all of you work on the rooms while I hold them here."

Roberta looked carefully at herself in the mirror and nodded with satisfaction. "This dress cost a king's ransom but it is nice, isn't it, Mother?"

"It was expensive," Lady Alice Grenville said, "but you do look wonderful in it."

The dress was a pale blue with a décolletage trimmed with lace. She was wearing an underskirt decorated with small flounces and flowers and an overskirt of a deeper blue gathered at the waist and very full, reaching just to her knees. Her hair was ornamented with flowers, and she had on elbow-length, snow-white gloves. Lady Alice admired the gown but a thought caused her to frown. "It's too bad about Ives."

Roberta shot a quick glance at her mother. They had already settled this matter and she disliked speaking about it further. "He's not happy, of course."

"Well, he was in love with you, Roberta."

Roberta touched her hair. "He'll just have to make adjustments — as we all do." She turned to face her mother, adding, "I never deceived Ives, not ever. I told him from the first that I'd never marry him."

"You never told me that."

"Didn't I? Well, we both know that I've got to marry well. Ives knew it, for I told him. I thought he understood but I suppose he didn't take me seriously."

"He must hate Davis."

"He's not happy with him but he'll find somebody else." A light knock at the door punctuated this remark and Roberta said, "Come in."

Gervase entered and stopped in front of her. "Is there anything I can do for you, Miss Grenville?"

"Oh, I think not. We're ready."

"Your dress is beautiful."

"Why, thank you, Gervase." Roberta studied the young woman dressed in a simple black dress with the usual white apron that upper servants wore. "You've grown up so much since the first time we met. Do you remember that?"

"Oh yes indeed, I do remember."

"Well, Davis speaks of you. He tells me how well you're doing — by which he means how many books you've read."

At this remark Roberta noticed how a faint flush came to the young woman's cheeks.

"He's been very kind to furnish books to me. I'm most grateful. If there's anything, just ask, please."

"Thank you, Gervase."

As the door closed, Roberta laughed. "Poor thing. She's always been infatuated with Davis."

"That's rather sad, isn't it? Many young men take advantage of servants. Do you suppose — "

"Davis? No, not in a million years! As a matter of fact, he's very protective of her. And she *is* capable. You know, Mother, I wouldn't mind having Gervase as my personal maid after — well, one day."

Lady Alice's eyes brightened and she said, "That will be something to think about, won't it?"

The ball was a success, as far as Davis Wingate was concerned. He danced every dance he could with Roberta, dancing with other young women only when his mother insisted. He was intensely proud of her, and the only thing that marred the happiness of the evening was the absence of Ives. This troubled Davis a great deal. He felt guilty about it but Roberta had assured him, "Ives doesn't really care for me. He's just infatuated, as he's been with many other young women. You know that, Davis. His pride is hurt but he'll get over it."

Finally Davis claimed Roberta for a dance, but instead of moving to the floor, he said, "It's getting warm in here. Let's go outside."

"Yes, it is a bit close."

The two went outside and overhead the stars were scattered across the ebony sky like brilliant diamonds. The music, filtered by the French doors, came to them softly as they moved along the walk between the shrubbery. Eventually Davis exclaimed, "I wish Ives could see things differently, Roberta."

"He will, Davis." Roberta took his arm and turned, and when he faced her, she looked up at him. She placed her hand on his chest and said, "He's very young. He'll find a woman he loves."

Davis had prepared himself for that moment. He knew exactly what he wanted to do, and he stepped forward and took her in his arms. She came to him willingly enough, and bending down, he kissed her on the lips. She fully met his caress, her arms going around his neck. She lay soft in his arms, her warmth a part of him, and her nearness stirred the hungers that had become very familiar. He held her tightly, aware of the softness and firmness of her body, and said, "I want to marry you. I love you, Roberta. I want you to be my wife."

Something came into Roberta's expression that Davis did not recognize, and he thought, *She's going to say no. She's thinking up some way to say it nicely.*

But Roberta put her hand on his cheek and left it there. "I love you, too," she said quietly.

"Do you? I was afraid you didn't."

"How could you think that, Davis?" Roberta pulled his head down again and kissed him.

He found himself almost unable to speak for the happiness. "Let's go inside and shout it out to everyone that we're going to be married."

Roberta laughed and shook her head. "No, don't be a fool! We'll have to tell our parents first."

"We'll go tell your parents first. I'll ask for your hand. What if they say no?"

"You know they won't. They're very fond of you. What if your parents say no to me? After all, we are rather penniless."

"That doesn't matter," Davis said quickly. "Come along. I want to announce it tonight."

Roberta smiled as he took her arm and practically hauled her back into the house. A strange expression crossed her face, and the thought that was uppermost in her mind was, *Well, Mother should be happy now. I've caught him.*

Gervase was helping the butler carry fresh drinks into the ballroom when suddenly she heard Davis's voice rise above the hubbub of conversation. She stopped dead still and saw that he was standing beside Roberta, her hand in his, and she knew instantly what was going to happen.

"Friends, I want you all to be the first to know that on this very evening Roberta has agreed to make me the happiest man in the world."

At once the two were surrounded by well-wishers. Gervase did not move but was unable to speak. She had not known until this very moment what a difference this might make to her. Long ago she had steeled herself against feeling anything for Davis Wingate, but now as she looked on his face — happy, smiling, beaming — she knew she had only deceived herself. Turning blindly, she made her way out of the room.

For the rest of the ball Gervase took care to stay away from Davis. She remained mostly in the kitchen, helping Aunt Martha. Finally, when the guests had all gone to bed and she had given the scullery maids their directions, she glanced up and saw Davis, who had started up the stairs. He called her name and came back down. Walking toward her, he smiled. "I suppose you heard the announcement?"

"Congratulations. I'm sure you'll be very happy, sir."

"Well, I think I will, but I have some good news for you." He took her hands and said, "Roberta wants you to become her personal maid after we're married. Isn't that wonderful?"

Gervase knew at that moment she would never live in the household of these two. She was able to conceal the feelings stirring within her and said, "That's very kind of Miss Roberta. I'll think on it."

"Think on it! What's to think on?" Davis squeezed her hands. "It will be a perfect arrangement. You can take care of Roberta and I'll take care of you two."

"I will give it some thought, sir."

"You always were a conservative young woman, just like Jane Eyre — very slow to move. But you'll have to do it. I will insist on it. Well, good night, Gervase."

"Good night, sir." Gervase watched him go up the stairs, taking them two at a time and whistling an off-key tune. When he disappeared, she turned and moved outside. The air was cold now, and as she walked, she was aware of the moon, a thin sliver veiled by diaphanous clouds. The stars seemed dull somehow.

# Chapter Six

November had come to England roughly, bringing bitterly cold weather and a foot of snow. The wedding of Davis Wingate and Roberta Grenville was now only two weeks away, and the servants, as usual, had covered the subject fairly thoroughly. Mrs. Peeples, troubled, had come into the kitchen to speak to Martha. Without preamble she said, "Martha, I'm worried about Gervase."

"Worried? Hasn't she been doing her work?"

"Oh, it's not that. She always does her work well, but she's lost that happy spirit she's always had. Haven't you noticed?"

"She's been rather quiet," Martha said. She was kneading dough and now brushed the flour dust away and looked up to face the housekeeper. "I'd been hoping that she would marry Roger Osburn, but she turned him down."

"Yes, I know. Has she said anything at all to you that might indicate why she's been so despondent?"

"No. As I said, she's been very quiet, Mrs. Peeples."

"She went to London and stayed gone for three days. She wouldn't say a word to me about why she was going."

"She didn't say much to me either. Just that she wanted to get away for a while and that she had never seen London. She was even quieter when she came back."

"Well, she's not a happy girl. She still visits with me, but she doesn't have anything much to say about what's on her heart."

The two women stood there talking quietly, and finally Martha said, "She goes on long walks these days. She's out there this afternoon, as cold as it is. She's going to catch her death!"

"I think you should talk to her, Martha."

Martha Miller shook her head. "It wouldn't do any good, Mrs. Peeples. I've tried." She glanced out the window and saw that tiny flakes of snow were beginning to fall again. "She's going to freeze to death out in that weather but she won't listen to me."

Gervase had dressed as warmly as she could. With the extra money Lady Sarah had insisted on paying her for helping Mrs. Peeples, she had bought warm boots, and they came in very handy for the long walks she was taking. In London she had found some inexpensive winter clothing, and now she hugged the blue wool redingote closely about her. The hood was over her head, but from time to time she looked up and let the fine bits of snow touch her face. They burned like fire for a moment and some landed in her eyes, making her blink.

The snow had made everything beautiful. The trees were rounded with clumps of white, soft and glittering in the afternoon sun. She turned back and passed the cottage of one of the farmers, and even the homely, weather-beaten house had obtained a certain dignity and beauty, with its rounded top and its windows almost up to their eyes in snow. The glass panes glowed from the fire inside. For some reason, as always, Gervase felt strange passing a house like that. She wondered what the people inside were like and what their problems and their joys were. She only knew that the woman's name was Leah and that she brought vegetables to Kimberly to sell, grown in her own garden.

The snowdrifts came up nearly to the top of her knee-high boots, and her coat dragged along the upper surface of the snow. Her boots made a crunching sound as they punched through the outer crust to the ground below. She walked out into a field of smooth, untouched snow. Looking back, she saw her footprints, the only impression on the perfect surface, and she found some pleasure in leaving her mark behind. Then she continued across the field.

Gervase had been unhappy for weeks now. Ever since Davis announced his engagement, she had known that life was going to be different for her. She felt foolish and ridiculous, for she was a servant in the house of a wealthy man with a title who knew her only as a young girl he would speak to and smile at from time to time. She had lived over and over again those encounters she'd had with him from the time she arrived, and it was easy enough to understand how a young girl could form a warm attachment to a very kind man. But as the months passed, she had moved from adolescence into womanhood and knew that what she felt for Davis was more than an attachment, more than an infatuation.

A movement caught her eye and she turned to find a fox that had suddenly appeared at the edge of a patch of gorse. He was an old animal with a silver coat, looking tired and woebegone. He stared at her. She expected him to flee, for foxes were secretive creatures. Something in his gaze brought pity to her heart, something she often felt for sick animals. "I wish you'd come to the house. I'd feed you. But you wouldn't, would you?"

The fox stared at her with dull eyes, and then almost painfully, it seemed, made his way back into the undergrowth. Gervase watched him go. The encounter saddened her. She sought the road again, where the footing was more secure. She had not gone more than a hundred yards back toward the house when she heard sounds behind her. Turning, she found it was a horseman, and her heart gave a little lurch as she recognized Davis.

The sound of the horse's hooves on the road were muffled. When he grew close, he lifted his hand. "Gervase!" He pulled up beside her and slipped off his mount, holding on to the reins. The horse was puffing, his breath turning to steam in the air, and Davis patted him on the cheek, saying, "Be still, Thunder." Turning to Gervase, he asked, "What in the world are you doing out walking in this weather?"

"I like it. It's so beautiful. Look, there are no sharp edges. Everything is smooth and rounded."

"But the sharp edges are under there, and when the snow melts off, they'll come back," he teased her.

"I know, but it's beautiful right now, isn't it?"

"Yes, it is. Would you like me to give you a ride back to the house?"

"No, I think I'll walk awhile longer."

"I'll join you, then."

"Yes, of course."

The two walked along and Davis was full of talk about the coming wedding. His eyes were bright and his face would not unsmile itself. Finally, as the house came into sight, he stopped and took her arm and held it, causing her to halt. "I haven't had a chance to talk to you, but I hope you've reconsidered Roberta's offer. She's very anxious to have you come live with us as her maid—and so am I, of course."

Gervase had been waiting for some time for this. She knew it had to come, and now she had her answer ready. She turned to face him and he seemed very tall. His features were clear and the cold air had reddened his cheeks. He had never looked so full of life and handsome to her as he did at that moment.

"I'm sorry, sir, but I can't accept Miss Grenville's offer."

"But Gervase, why not? If it's money—"

"It's not that, sir, not at all. Your offer was more than generous."

"Well, what is it, then? You know how much it would mean to me to have you in our home. We're going to get a place in London and you would get to see a lot of the town."

Gervase pressed her lips together and shook her head. "I'm very sorry to have to refuse, but you'll have to find someone else, Mr. Wingate."

"But I don't understand why."

"I'm going to be leaving Kimberly."

Davis stared at Gervase as if she had announced she was going to the moon. "Leaving Kimberly! Why, what in the world for? Everyone loves you here. You've made a place for yourself."

Gervase had anticipated this. "I've had an offer to work for a family in London, sir. Their name is Nightingale." She spoke very rapidly then, for she saw he was only waiting until she finished to argue with her. "I'll be a companion and a maid for their daughter."

"But why leave Kimberly? Do you know this family?"

"No sir, not really. But they've made me a very attractive offer and I've wanted a change."

Davis was obviously disappointed. Gervase saw it in his eyes and in the way he moved his feet impatiently. She knew him so well! His body language was as easy to read as his spoken word. Now, she knew, he would try to somehow change her mind, and for the next five minutes he did everything he could to do exactly that. But finally she said quietly, "I'm sorry, Mr. Wingate, but I feel I must do this."

"Roberta will be disappointed." Davis's lips drew together and he took his hat off and ran his hand through his hair. "And, blast it, so will I! I had looked forward to having you with us, Gervase."

"I must go in, sir."

"But wait. When will you be leaving?"

"Very soon, I think."

"Have you told my parents?"

"Yes. The Nightingales have already contacted them for a reference. I asked them not to tell anyone until I decided what to do."

"Well, Mrs. Peeples — you've practically done her work for her. Have you thought about her?"

"She's going to live with her sister in Plymouth. She hasn't announced it yet, but her sister has been urging her to come for some time. Her sister can take care of her better, and Mrs. Peeples is tired."

Davis stared at her and then shook his head. "This is a blow, Gervase. I hope you change your mind."

"I won't do that, sir. I must go now."

Moving up the road, she heard Davis mount his horse and then watched as he galloped past. The hooves of the horse threw tiny explosions of snow into the air. She watched him ride to the stables and then went directly into the house. She found Lady Sarah in the drawing room and informed her of her decision, which led to another uncomfortable ten minutes. Lady Sarah was grieved and made all sorts of promises, but when she saw that Gervase was fully persuaded to go, she said, "You'll be a loss, my dear, and if you change your mind later, there will always be a place for you here."

"Thank you, Lady Sarah. You've been so kind to me."

Gervase went at once to the kitchen and broke the news to Martha, knowing that her aunt would be disturbed. Martha could not accept it for a time. "You'll be among total strangers there. London's no place for a young girl to be alone."

"I checked out my new employers quite carefully. They're very respectable people, Aunt."

For some time she tried to reassure her aunt, but finally Gervase put her arms around her and said, "You've been so kind to me and we'll see each other. London's not so far."

"It won't be like having you here. I wish you wouldn't go. Why are you doing it?"

Gervase did not answer for a moment, and then she said, "I don't know. I just feel I need a change."

She took her leave then and went to her room. Her hands were not steady, for the scene with Davis had upset her and it had been difficult speaking to Lady Sarah and her aunt. She walked back and forth, Mr. Bob sitting and watching her with his huge golden eyes. Finally she sat and took out her writing materials. She thought for a moment about the Nightingales. She had seen in the paper their ad for a maid and a companion for their daughter, had gone to London and answered it, and had had an interview with them. She was impressed by Mr. and Mrs. Nightingale. They did not hire her but told her they planned to interview several young women and check their references. They would notify her by mail. She had gotten the letter just the day before and had slept little since. Now she began to write.

> *My Dear Mr. and Mrs. Nightingale,*
>
> *I was very happy to hear that you have decided to offer me the position we spoke of. I would be honored to accept your offer. I will have to give two weeks' notice here, but I will be in London by November the twentieth. If this is satisfactory, you need not write. If there are any questions, I will be here for the next two weeks. Thank you very much for the trust you have placed in me for this position.*

She put sand on the letter, shifted it around as it dried the ink, folded it, and then sealed it. Putting the letter aside, she took out her journal. She had filled, in the year and a half she had been at Kimberly, four large notebooks. It amused her now to look back and see the bad spelling and the atrocious grammar, but she could trace her growth, and she knew that a great deal of that was due to Davis Wingate, who had encouraged her to study and furnished her books and even paid for her to have a tutor for a time. She opened the notebook, put at the top,

*November 5, 1852*

> *I will be leaving Kimberly in two weeks. I never thought that I would. It was in my mind that I would —*

She broke off then and tried to think of a way to end the sentence, but finally simply crossed that line out.

> *I can't stay here. It would be too hard on me, and although it was kind of Miss Grenville to ask me to be her maid and Davis was so anxious, it is impossible.*

She sat looking at what she had written. Finally she wrote,

> *I've promised myself to only write honest things. I have loved Davis almost from the time I first saw him. It's foolish and ridiculous and I'm ashamed of it. But as I put it down on paper, I say what is in my heart. I could not be in the home where he was married to another woman.*

She dried the entry, closed her journal, and then put it away in the lower drawer. She prepared for bed, putting on her heavy flannel nightgown and her nightcap, and when she got into bed, at once Mr. Bob pushed his way in beside her. He radiated heat like a small stove, and in the coldness of the room she clung to him.

"We've got to go, Mr. Bob, and it frightens me. But you'll go with me. Don't worry. I'll never leave you."

Mr. Bob pushed his head against her and began to rumble deep down in his chest. Then he made himself into a ball beside her as she lay still in the bed.

# *London*

*November 1852–November 1854*

# Chapter Seven

Gervase carefully placed the dark-brown dress inside the carpetbag and closed it firmly. A fleeting memory came to her as she recalled coming into this room for the first time with a worn sackful of her pitiful clothes that she had brought from home. Quickly pushing the memory out of her mind, she looked around the room for a moment. Her eyes fell on the calendar she had made, and going to it, she drew a circle around November twenty, then pulled the pin that held it to the wall. Opening the carpetbag, she folded the calendar and placed it inside.

Her eyes touched on the bed where she had slept for so long, and then on the furniture that had become so familiar to her. All the drawers were empty now and the pegs stood out starkly, no longer bearing her clothes. The basket that was to convey Mr. Bob was on the bed, open. She had made a quilt pad for the bottom and now Mr. Bob was sniffing at it.

"I'm going to miss this place."

Gervase spoke the words aloud and then instantly rebuked herself. Shaking her head, she muttered, "I can't be feeling that way. It's time to go."

Everything was done. She had bidden farewell to her aunt and all the rest of the servants. Her packing was complete, and now she had nothing to do but get in the carriage with Clyde Denny, who was to take her to meet the London coach. Restlessly she looked out the window at the familiar scene. The snow had melted away, and the dead grass underneath reflected the moisture as the sun touched it with a powerful opalescence. Gervase had always liked the winter. She thought of all the times she had explored the woods to the north. It was there she had found a small pond where she had often gone to watch the fish as they came to the surface, sending concentric circles to the edge of the pond. She glanced toward the road that led to London, and a sadness came to her that she was forced to put down with an act of will.

"Miss Gervase, are you ready?"

At the sound of the voice outside her door, Gervase walked quickly across the room. Opening the door, she found her uncle George there with Robert Bates. "Yes, I'm ready," she said, smiling.

"We've come to give you a hand with your luggage. Bates, you take that chest. I'll take the suitcase and the cat."

"Oh, I can carry Mr. Bob, Uncle George." Gervase had not seen her uncle when she said goodbye to her aunt, and now she went to him and stood there for a moment, thinking of the many kindnesses he had shown her. "I can't tell you how grateful I am for all you've done for me, Uncle George."

"Well now, lass, it's been my pleasure and Martha's. Sad we are to see you go." He suddenly gave her a hug and a quick peck on the cheek. He had never done this before and it touched Gervase.

"I'll write to you as soon as I get settled."

"And you'll have to come back and visit," George said, nodding.

"I'll do that." Gervase smiled at Robert Bates, who had grown from a callow youth to a well-set-up young man during her stay at Kimberly. "Robert, I want you to be good. I'll be thinking of you."

"Why, I'm always good, Miss Gervase. You know that." He was holding her trunk easily on one shoulder. "Well, you'd better get downstairs. You may get a surprise." He winked at her uncle.

"Stop your foolishness," George said instantly.

Bates winked again and Gervase wondered what the young man meant. He was up to playing tricks on her and she would be on her guard.

The three of them went downstairs, Gervase waiting until last and carrying the wicker basket with a protesting Mr. Bob. "Be quiet, Mr. Bob," she said. "You're not hurt." When she reached the bottom of the stairs, she found Sir Edward and Lady Sarah waiting for her. This surprised her but not overly so, for both of them, she knew, had grown to like her, as she had become very fond of them.

"Well, I think you're making a mistake," Sir Edward said. "Here you have two good offers, one to be housekeeper here and one to be a lady's maid for Roberta when Davis marries her."

"It's so kind of you to ask me, Sir Edward, but I really feel I must go."

"Well, well, then. You've been a good girl. Here, tuck this in your reticule. A little parting gift."

Gervase took the envelope he held out and said in a flustered manner, "Why, Sir Edward, you didn't have to do this!"

"He wanted to and I insisted on it," Lady Sarah said. "Just a little bonus to help you get started in your new life." She came forward and kissed Gervase on the cheek. "There now. Let me hear from you when you get settled."

"I'll surely do that. Goodbye and thank you for your many kindnesses."

Gervase waited until the two men had gone out, carrying the luggage, then followed them, with Mr. Bob caterwauling all the way. As soon as she went outside, the morning sun struck her eyes, and she was stepping off the last step when suddenly she realized that it was Davis standing beside the carriage. Quickly she covered the expression that would have given her away, and forced herself to smile. "Good morning, sir."

"Good morning to you, Gervase. We have a good day for our trip."

Gervase looked around for Clyde Denny and saw him standing in front of the horses, holding them and grinning slyly at her. "I've lost my job this morning, Miss Gervase. Mr. Davis, he says he'll take care of carting you to London."

"That's right," Davis said. "I'm taking you to the Nightingale place."

"Why, you don't have to do that."

"It's something I want to do. Come now, let me help you in."

Gervase took his hand and he held hers firmly as she stepped up into the carriage. He closed the footstep, then the door, and walking around, he climbed in beside her.

"You treat them horses well, Mr. Davis," Clyde called as Davis spoke to the team and they moved out. "They're a little bit flighty."

"I'll do it, Clyde."

Gervase said nothing, for she was stricken with confusion. She had said all her goodbyes and had cut the ties that bound her so securely to Kimberly. She had not seen Davis and had been relieved, for she had not felt capable of saying her farewell to him so easily. This was one side of her thoughts. On the other side, she had been disappointed that he had not come to bid her goodbye. She knew now that he had planned it this way, and it was exactly the sort of thing that he often did.

The wheels spun over the frozen road, and from time to time would jolt into a rut that bounced both Davis and Gervase on the seat. She held carefully to Mr. Bob, not letting him out, until finally, when they had gone more than two miles without speaking, Davis turned and said, "Why don't you let Mr. Bob out? He'll get tired of that basket."

"All right." Gervase undid the latch and lifted the cover. Mr. Bob leaped out at once, and as she moved the basket, he sat there looking around in a self-satisfied way.

"You don't like that basket much, do you, Mr. Bob?" Davis said, smiling. He rubbed Mr. Bob's ears and the large cat leaned against him. Davis looked up and said, "You remember when I picked you up for the first time to bring you to Kimberly?"

"Of course I do!"

"Mr. Bob was tired of this basket then."

"I've never forgotten it."

Gervase sat there not knowing what else to say to Davis. It seemed they had talked everything out, and she was very much afraid he was going to pressure her to stay. She knew that was impossible.

After some time Davis said, "I was a little concerned about the Nightingales."

"Concerned! Why? Do you know something about them?"

"No, not a thing, but I made it my business to find out. William Nightingale is an interesting chap. Very rich, of course, and a rather handsome man, from what I hear."

"How do you know this?"

"Oh, a friend of mine is close to the family. I picked his brain a little. Mr. Nightingale's wife's name is Fanny. They have two girls. Did you meet them all?"

"I met Mr. and Mrs. Nightingale but neither of the girls."

"You'll have a time pronouncing the name of the older daughter."

"Why? What is it?"

"Parthenope."

"What's that?"

Davis laughed and shook his head. "Awful, isn't it? It's the Greek word for Naples."

"Surely they don't call her that."

"No. My friend said they call her Parthe."

"That's almost as bad."

"It is, isn't it?"

"What about the other daughter?"

"She was named after her birthplace, too — Florence in Europe. My friend was quite taken with her. She's a beauty."

"What else did you find out, Mr. Davis?"

"Well, their father's quite a fellow. He decided to teach the girls himself, and they learned Greek, Latin, German, French, Italian, history, and philosophy from him."

"My goodness! That's quite a list. I'm very intimidated."

"Well, I'm not sure exactly how much they learned. But anyway, those girls have been hauled all over Europe. I asked especially about the younger girl, since you'll be her maid. From what I've found out, she's very emotional, prone to exaggeration, and abnormally sensitive."

Gervase's heart sank. "She'll probably be very hard to work for."

"I think she's moody, all right, but my friend said she's really a lively young lady."

Davis continued to tell her all the affairs of the family. He shocked her a little when he said, "Miss Florence believes she's had a call from God."

"Really! To do what?"

"I'm not exactly sure about that. My friend wasn't, either — as a matter of fact, he said she didn't know herself. She's also given to excessive dreaming. Goes off into long spells of imagination. Nobody quite understands them."

"Well, I'm glad you told me all this, Mr. Davis."

"Look. Can't you call me Davis — without the 'Mister'? I should have told you to do it long ago."

"That wouldn't have been proper, for a servant to call her master by his first name."

"I suppose not but I'd like it all the same."

Gervase was quiet for a while, and then finally she asked, "It was nice of you to go to all this trouble to find out about the Nightingales."

"If they hadn't been respectable people, I would never have let you go live with them."

Gervase suddenly smiled. "You sound more like a father."

"Well, an elder brother, let's say." Davis shook his head with a short motion. "I'm still sorry that you're not coming to live with Roberta and me after we're married. I had it all planned out." Gervase had no answer for that, so she sat there silently. Davis did not pressure her, but he muttered, "I would have liked for you to have come to the wedding."

Gervase could not truthfully offer the normal response, "I would have liked to." Instead she said, "I'm sure it will be a beautiful wedding."

The two rode together for a time without speaking. Finally Davis said, "Did you ask the Nightingales about bringing Mr. Bob?"

"Yes indeed!" Gervase said quickly. "I wouldn't have taken the position if they hadn't let me bring him."

Davis took his eyes off the road to look at her. He seemed to study her deeply, but all he said was, "You're a loyal young woman, Gervase. I might have known as much."

She reached into her reticule and brought out a small item. Taking the paper off, she handed him the coin. "Here's the sovereign you paid me for Mr. Bob. I'm buying him back."

"By George, I'd forgotten that!" Davis laughed but shook his head. "Keep it, Gervase. Buy yourself and Mr. Bob a nice meal — lobsters or cod at a fine restaurant."

"They'd never let him in."

"For money they'd let an alley cat in!"

She sat quietly, holding the coin, and finally said softly, "I remember when you caught up with me when I was running away because the steward wouldn't let me keep Mr. Bob."

"He was a grouchy fellow. I was glad when he retired and we were able to get a more amiable man in his place."

Gervase did not answer, for she had been relieved also.

"I was worried about you," Davis said, smiling. "When I saw you all alone on the road with your little sack and your cat, by George I admired you!"

"Admired me?"

"Why, certainly! Not one child in a thousand would have had the courage to do what you did." He looked at her suddenly, then shook his head with wonder in his eyes. "You've grown up, Gervase. You were so skinny and gangly and now you're a beautiful young woman."

Gervase could not answer. She kept her face turned away, and finally he said, "I didn't hurt your feelings, did I? I meant well."

"No sir, you didn't hurt my feelings." She turned and gave him a brilliant smile. "You made me feel very good indeed!"

The house Davis pulled up to was a good-sized plain square structure of the late Georgian period. It was not as ornate or large as Kimberly, but there was a neatness about it and the grounds were well laid out.

"Whoa, boys!" Davis said, stopping the horses. He held the lines and looked at the house with a critical eye. "A very nice place," he said. "I understand they've added quite a bit to it since they bought it."

"It's not as beautiful as Kimberly — but few places are."

Davis seemed reluctant to get out. He watched as a man came around the house and approached them, obviously a servant. Giving a sigh, Davis got out of the carriage and came around. He reached out his hand and when Gervase took it, he handed her down. She would have withdrawn her hand but his grip tightened. He stood holding it without speaking. Gervase was embarrassed. His hand was warm and large, and he held her so firmly that she could not pull back.

"Please, you're holding my hand, Mr. Davis!" she whispered.

Davis ignored her plea. "By heaven!" he exclaimed. "I hate to let you go, Gervase! I've become accustomed to you. Why, you're just like a younger sister to me."

Gervase could not free her hand. She knew that the servant was standing there staring at them, and she felt this was the wrong way. "Please let me go, sir!"

"I suppose I'll have to," Davis said but retained her hand. Then suddenly he lifted it, kissed it, and said, "Promise to write me."

This had not entered Gervase's mind, but he reached out and took her shoulders. "I'm not letting you go until you promise."

Gervase looked up into his face and knew that at times like this he could be very stubborn. "I will write you and tell you about getting settled."

"And I'll answer you back." He hesitated, then kissed her on the cheek. "Goodbye, and think of me." He got into the carriage, gave her one look, and shook his head and spoke to the horses. They moved off and Gervase stood watching him go, knowing that this closed the door on a part of her life, and she could never open that door again.

# Chapter Eight

O h, you brought your cat! Do let me see him, my dear."
The speaker was a tall, attractive woman looking to be in
her late fifties. Mrs. Fanny Nightingale was handsome and had
proved to be very agreeable as she welcomed Gervase into her
home. "I like cats very much. Mine died about six months ago.
I had him for twelve years."

"Oh, I'm so sorry."

Mrs. Nightingale turned her head to one side and smiled
sadly. "You do become attached. Well, let me see this fellow."

Gervase set the basket on the floor and unlatched the lid,
and Mr. Bob hopped out. He turned his golden eyes on Fanny
Nightingale, and when she leaned over and put out her hand,
he pushed his head against it. "Well, you *are* a handsome thing!
How old is he, Gervase?"

"He's six. I raised him from a small kitten."

"Well, I hope he's a good mouser. We're having trouble with
that these days."

"Yes. He always brings them to me as a gift," Gervase said
dryly.

"They do that, don't they? One doesn't know what to do
with such a present."

"I'm very anxious to begin work, Mrs. Nightingale."

"Well, your mistress won't be back until tonight, but it will
give you time to get settled in, you and — what is your cat's name?"

"Mr. Bob."

"You and Mr. Bob, then, can get settled in. Here, I'll have one of the servants take you up to your room. You're probably tired after your trip. Why don't you lie down and take a nap. You can meet Florence as soon as she comes in." Mrs. Nightingale guided Gervase through the double doors that led out of the foyer. "Maggie," she said, "come here, please."

"Yes mum?" The speaker was a very large woman — not fat, just large. Gervase had to look up at her and guessed that she was close to six feet tall. She had a florid complexion, green eyes, and red hair. There was a plainness about her but real strength in her features.

"Maggie is one of our maids. This is Gervase Howard, Maggie. She's to be Flo's new maid. Take her up to the room that we decided on."

"Yes, Mrs. Nightingale."

"I'll have Simms bring your luggage up," Mrs. Nightingale called out as the two ascended the stairs.

"Thank you, Mrs. Nightingale."

The woman called Maggie did not speak until they had reached the third floor. "Your room's right down here," she said. She led the way to a door on the end and opened it. "It's a nice room. You'll like it, I think."

She had a broad Scottish accent, and Gervase smiled at her as she stepped through the door. Gervase took one look around and said, "Oh, this is a lovely room!"

The room she stood in was no more than twelve by fourteen feet, but it seemed roomier because of the height of the ceiling and an oversized window that admitted bright beams of yellow sunlight. The floor was covered with dark-red carpet, and a hearth rug was in front of the small fireplace.

"You have your own fireplace, you see," Maggie said. "Simms will keep you supplied with coal."

"That will be nice. I've never had a room with a fireplace."
Putting Mr. Bob down, Gervase ran the palm of her hand over
the wallpaper. It was very delicate, with elaborate scenes of
Indians, trees, and animals. "What lovely paper," she said.

"Miss Flo picked it out. She has quite an imagination. You
know her, do you?"

"No. I've never met her. Only the master and the mistress."
Gervase examined the room's furnishings. There was a tall
poster bed made of cherry, with a bedspread of a red printed
cotton. The dressing table was a walnut Queen Anne on cabri-
ole legs, and a carved clothespress with two open doors above
and two drawers below was backed against one wall. A maple
rocker with green cushions was placed beside the window, and
in one corner stood a small washstand with a beautifully
designed ceramic pitcher and basin.

"This is very nice indeed, Maggie! I didn't hear your last
name."

"It's MacKay. I'm from Scotland."

"Yes, I suspected that."

Maggie laughed and spread her arms out in a wide gesture.
"I can't hide the way I talk or the way I look, but it's proud I
am of old Scotland."

"Have you been here long, Maggie?"

"Only a year."

Just then a servant arrived with Gervase's belongings.
When he left, Maggie asked, "Shall I help you unpack?"

"That won't be necessary. Perhaps you could tell me a little
about the establishment here."

As Gervase quickly discovered, Maggie was quite a talker.
Her request opened the floodgates. For a while the two simply
stood in the room, but eventually Maggie took her downstairs
to the kitchen, where she fixed tea, and they sat at the large
kitchen table as they talked.

Gervase also found out that Maggie was intensely curious. She interrogated Gervase about her past, and Gervase was willing enough to tell some of this. She found herself liking Maggie very much, for the big woman was outspoken, cheerful, and offered to be of help.

"What about Miss Florence?" Gervase asked finally.

"Ah, well, you'll have to find out for yourself aboot that." Maggie took a large swallow of tea and then filled her cup again. "She's got an imagination, that one has, and a mind of her own." She laughed and shook her head. "Mr. and Mrs. Nightingale have a time with her, for she's as stubborn as a mule." Then, as if she had said too much, she added quickly, "But she's a very sweet lady. Easy to get on with once you get used to her ways."

"How old is she, Maggie?"

"Thirty-two her last birthday but she seems much younger. And her sister is just one year older."

"Neither of them have ever married?"

"No, not a bit of it! And a shame, I call it." Maggie leaned forward and whispered, "Miss Flo, she could have married half a dozen times — but she's peculiar."

"Peculiar how, Maggie?"

"She's said for years that God's put a call on her."

"A call to do what?"

"Ah, that's what nobody knows — not even she herself. But she's never married because of that feeling. And as for Miss Parthie, why, she's not as bright as Miss Flo and she has spells."

"What kind of spells? You don't mean fits?"

"No, no!" Maggie threw her hands up. "Nothing like that! She just goes into long months of being sad. I suppose she could have married, but somehow she never did."

"Is Miss Flo very fussy about her clothes?"

"No more than most fine ladies. She loves clothes and she likes to dress up and look nice. That's why you've been brought here, I suppose."

"What about her last maid?"

"I don't think she ever really had one she liked very much. She can't bear stupid people."

"Oh dear, she won't like me, then!"

"No, you're vury quick. I can tell that. Don't be afraid to speak up to her. Not impudently, mind you, but she likes to try her wits on people. She gave up on me a long time ago, though she likes the way I iron her clothes." Maggie said finally, "Why don't you go up and take a nap? I'll come for you as soon as Miss Florence comes home."

"Thank you, Maggie. I am a little tired." Gervase went back to her room and found Mr. Bob already curled up on the bed, apparently waiting for her. She took off her dress, lay down, pulled the coverlet over herself, and fell asleep instantly.

Gervase was awakened by Maggie with the word that Miss Florence was home. She quickly dressed and arranged her hair and went down. She found her new mistress in the library, and one glance revealed that Miss Florence Nightingale was more attractive than Gervase had imagined. She looked far younger than her thirty-two years and had a most lively expression. Florence had thick chestnut hair, her color was delicate, and her gray eyes were sharp and bright. She had perfect teeth, smiled easily, and was somewhat taller than Gervase, with a willowy figure. She was wearing a day dress of light green with bell-shaped sleeves. Over her shoulders and arms she wore a large bright-red shawl with a fringe border. Her first words were, "So, you have brought your cat with you. What is his name, Gervase?"

"His name is Mr. Bob, ma'am."

"We all like cats around here. He'll be a happy addition. Now, let's sit down and I want to hear all about you. And then you may hear some things about me." Her eyes danced and she said, "I wouldn't want to tell you everything or you might turn tail and run away from this place."

Gervase smiled as she took her seat. "I'm sure I wouldn't do that, ma'am. And about myself, well, there isn't really much to tell."

Florence Nightingale turned her head to one side and studied Gervase. "And what is it you want to do with your life?"

Gervase went completely blank. "With my life, ma'am?"

"Yes. Everyone has to decide what to do with his or her life. Do you intend to be a lady's maid until you die?"

"Why, I don't think so, Miss Nightingale. I suppose I would, someday, like to get married and have a family, as most women do."

"But what do you want to do until then? Do you have a mission?"

Gervase laughed. "My mission, Miss Nightingale, is to please you and do a good job in my work as long as I'm here."

"Well, that's a refreshing answer! I might as well tell you right now, I'm a rather difficult woman to work for. As a matter of fact, I find myself difficult at times."

"Oh, really, ma'am, I doubt that."

"You won't doubt it after you've been here a time! Now, tell me all about yourself."

For the next thirty minutes Gervase answered questions, and by the time the half hour had fled, she was exhausted. Miss Nightingale seemed to be satisfied and she said, "Well, suppose we go upstairs and I'll show you all my things. I'll expect you to keep them in place, of course. I will need someone to help me dress, get ready for bed — oh, all the things ladies expect of their maids." She hesitated, then said, "I may as well tell you that I have a mission from God."

Gervase almost said, "I know," but she caught herself just in time. "That must be very fine indeed."

"No, it's *miserable!*" Florence Nightingale shook her head and her lips grew tight together. "I get upset with God sometimes because he won't tell me what the mission is."

Gervase did not know what to make of this, so she simply said, "I'm sure he'll tell you when he's ready for you to know."

Suddenly Florence began to laugh. She had a good laugh that started deep inside somewhere and bubbled over. Her eyes squeezed together, and finally she said, "That is a very good answer, Gervase. Come along and I'll show you your duties."

"Well, how are you getting along with Miss Flo?"

Maggie MacKay had proved to be a stout friend to Gervase. The big woman was always ready to help and always ready to listen, which was a godsend. Gervase smiled almost wearily at her. "She's a very difficult woman to please at times."

"She is that but you've done well, Gervase. I can tell she likes you very much."

The two women were in Maggie's room, to which they had retired after the evening meal. They sometimes went there and talked together. Maggie was a reader of novels herself, and the two found a great deal in common. She was the kind of friend Gervase needed, for Miss Flo was a hard taskmaster. She was never unpleasant, but she liked things done exactly as she laid them out, and could grow sharp when anyone failed.

Maggie picked up a newspaper from the table beside her chair and began to comment on the stories. Gervase was listening quietly but sat up sharply when Maggie said, "Mr. Davis Wingate." Maggie looked up and said, "Wingate? Isn't that the family you worked for?"

"Yes, it is. Davis Wingate is the oldest son. What does it say?"

"It says here that he was married to a woman named Roberta Grenville." She ran her eyes over the article. "It must have been a very fancy affair." She suddenly gave Gervase a very direct stare. "Aristocratic sons sometimes get after pretty young maidservants. Did he ever try to make love to you?"

"Maggie!"

"Well, I don't know the man. I only know that it's common enough." Maggie noted that Gervase's cheeks had grown flushed and that her hands were moving nervously. Her eyes narrowed and she said, "I take it he did, from the way you're acting."

"He certainly did *not!*"

"Well, you don't have to bite my head off," Maggie protested. "I just asked."

"Mr. Davis was as kind to me as anybody has ever been." Gervase recounted the time when Davis had met her and saved her from harm when she arrived in London. She spoke glowingly of how he had provided her with books and had not forgotten her seventeenth birthday. She ended by saying, "He's the finest young man I've ever known, and I won't hear anything against him."

Maggie leaned back and crossed her arms and stared at her. "Maybe," she said softly, "you liked him *too* much."

Gervase jumped up. She rarely got angry but now her face was red. "You're a suspicious woman, Maggie MacKay!" She stormed out of the room, slamming the door behind her.

Maggie sat staring after her. After a time she tapped her lower lip with her forefinger. "Well, you know, I've always said that when you throw a rock at a pack of dogs, the only one that'll yell is the one that gets hit. I reckon as how Miss Gervase Howard is a little too fond of that man and doesn't want anybody to know it." She shook her head sorrowfully, for she liked Gervase a great deal. "Too bad. She'll just have to swallow her medicine and forget about it."

# Chapter Nine

Maggie's green eyes glowed with curiosity as she walked into the library. She stopped before Gervase, who was reading a book, and extended an envelope. "A letter came for you, Gervase. I brought it right in."

Gervase placed a marker in the book, put it to one side, and took the envelope. She glanced at it and then looked up. "Thank you, Maggie."

"Ain't you going to read it?"

"Later, I think."

"It comes from that man you're so struck on — Davis Wingate."

"I am not struck on Davis Wingate, Maggie!" Despite herself, Gervase felt her cheeks grow warm. "I wish you would not insist on saying things like that."

"Well, why does he keep writing to you? He's a married man, ain't he?"

"Yes, he's married. We're simply friends. That's all. He wants to know how I'm doing."

Maggie shook her head firmly. "I bet that fancy wife he married don't know about all this, does she?"

"I have no idea, and there's nothing in our letters that she couldn't read."

"Well, you know what the Bible says about that. People who play around with burning coals are going to get burnt."

Exasperation showed itself in Gervase's tone. "The Bible doesn't say anything like that and you know it!"

"Well, it should!"

"I don't want to talk about it, Maggie. Now, go on about your business."

"Well, la-di-da! Ain't we the fancy one now." Maggie sniffed and turned away. She moved rather lightly for such a large woman, and only when she was out of the library and her footsteps grew faint did Gervase open the letter. She had written to Davis a brief note a week after she settled in at the Nightingales', and he had promptly written her back a very short note. He had, however, requested that she answer him, for, as he said,

> *I'm interested in your well-being and you will need a friend. I'd like to be that friend.*

She had been with the Nightingales for eight months now, and she had received nine letters from Davis, all very brief. Mostly he told her about the family and the servants and the things at Kimberly he knew would interest her. Her letters were similar — newsy, cheerful, and witty — and he often said how much he enjoyed getting them.

Breaking the seal, Gervase eagerly read the letter.

*August 2, 1853*

*Dear Gervase,*

*I enjoyed your last letter immensely, and I was especially amused — or should I say grieved? — at the "gift" that Mr. Bob brought to you. I know you must have been horrified to find the baby rabbit deposited on your chest when you woke up. I know Mr. Bob meant well, and I am glad to hear that you were able to nurse the little fellow back to health and set him free. Please don't chastise Mr. Bob for things like this, for he has a generous heart.*

*Your uncle and aunt are doing very well, and the new housekeeper, Mrs. Smith, is very amiable and pleases my parents and the other servants very much. I was glad to hear that you had heard from Mrs. Peeples and that she is improving down on the coast. Maybe the weather there will cure her rheumatism.*

*I have had no one to talk to about the novel — or should I say the fragment of an unending novel? For that is what it seems to be. When you were here, we talked so much about it and I made great progress, but no one is interested in such things now at home. I have been thinking about trying to make contact with a publisher. I even thought of going to see Mr. Dickens, but I know he is a busy man and must have dozens of would-be writers banging on his door. So I suppose I shall forge ahead alone. Perhaps before the millennium begins I will be able to finish it. If I do, I will certainly dedicate it to you, for you have been my only encouragement.*

*I will close this with a hope and a wish that your life there will be full and that you will be happy.*

*Yours sincerely,*
*Davis*

Gervase read the letter through twice and was struck by one important omission: not once did Davis mention his wife, Roberta. This seemed strange to her and she could in no way account for it. She wondered about that as she folded the letter and put it in her book.

*August 8, 1853*

*My Dear Mr. Wingate,*

*Indeed, my life here in London is full and I am happy. I feel very blessed.*

*Speaking of blessing, there has been a great deal of talk here lately about a new minister in London. His name is Charles Haddon Spurgeon, and he has turned London upside down with his preaching. He is pastor of the new Park Street Baptist Church, a man of unusual power.*

*I went to hear Reverend Spurgeon last Sunday. I have a new friend here, one of the maids, whose name is Maggie MacKay. She is a zealous Christian — somewhat too zealous, I sometimes think. She is what has often been called an "enthusiast" and tells me that she has been known to cry aloud in services. When I discovered this, I was halfway inclined not to invite her, but she is a good soul.*

*We arrived at the church, which seats fifteen hundred people, but there could not have been fewer than three thousand in it. The service commenced with a hymn which was sung by the congregation — and never have I heard such singing! There was no need of an organ in that congregation, for the voices of the people were loud indeed, and Maggie was not the quietest.*

*Mr. Spurgeon got up and led a prayer which was one of the most remarkable I ever heard. He prayed first for confirmed believers, then for declining ones, and then for the unconverted. I wish you could have heard him preach. He is really only a boy, no more than nineteen, I believe, and I have never heard anyone like him, Mr. Wingate! You are aware that most ministers read their sermons. Some, I understand, even have a prompter with a manuscript in hand if the preacher stumbles over a word. Most sermons come out as quite literary, perhaps, but not particularly dynamic.*

*Reverend Spurgeon had no manuscript, and I must say he flew like a captive eagle set free. His heart seemed to be burning and he had a desire to communicate with all the fervency in him.*

*His appearance is against him. He is quite short, no more than five feet six, and somewhat thickset. He has a very large head and his teeth protrude and his eyes are slightly crossed. No one would ever call him handsome, I'm afraid.*

*As he began his sermon, he pulled out a bright-blue polka-dot handkerchief from his coat pocket and flourished it about while he made a point. He looked quite comical, really — but how he did preach! As I say, I have never heard such preaching. It was so simple and it went directly to my heart.*

*I say that advisably, for many sermons have gone to my head, but this one went straight down deep inside me. Perhaps because I was feeling somewhat depressed. He spoke of blind Bartimaeus, the beggar who called out to Jesus, you remember, in the tenth chapter of Mark. Every-one told him to be quiet, and Mr. Spurgeon so well showed how this man would not be quiet but cried out even louder. And then he described how Jesus stopped dead still and said, "Bring him to me."*

*That was the essence of his sermon — that Jesus wants us to come to him. That no matter how much others may ridicule us or discourage us, still Jesus the Savior calls to us.*

*Isn't that a wonderful thought? And I am very excited about going back to hear Reverend Spurgeon again. If you have an opportunity, I hope you will go hear him.*

Gervase looked down at what she had written and laughed ruefully. "I've written him a book! That won't do." She again began to write, saying briefly,

*I have run on far too long. As I mentioned before, I am very happy here, serving Miss Florence. She is a wonderful lady. Some-times a little sharp but I don't mind that. Give my best regards to all there who would be interested.*

*Sincerely yours,*
*Gervase Howard*

She put the letter aside, intending to post it the next day — and also determined that Maggie would not know that she had written it.

Leaving the library, she started down the hall, but she heard Florence call to her from upstairs. "Gervase, come up here a moment, please."

"Yes ma'am."

Gervase mounted the stairs quickly and turned into Florence's bedroom. She had left it immaculate, but now the bed was covered with books and papers, and Florence was sitting right in the middle of them. Her face was excited and she said, "I have wonderful news!"

"What is it, Miss Flo?"

"I've been asked to take over the nursing situation at an institution here in London."

Gervase knew that Florence Nightingale was greatly interested in nursing as a way to serve God. She also was aware that Florence's parents and her sister were violently opposed, arguing that it wasn't ladylike. Gervase understood that Florence was sharing her news with her maid because she had no one else who would be sympathetic. She went to the bed at once and stood smiling down. "That is marvelous, Miss Florence! I know you'll do a wonderful job. What is the name of the institution?"

"It has a rather awful name: The Institution for the Care of Sick Gentlewomen in Distressed Circumstances. Isn't that frightful?"

"It is a little unhandy, ma'am."

"I simply call it the Institution." Florence bounded out of bed and paced the floor, her face alight.

"I'm convinced that this is what God wants me to do. It all began back in 1837, Gervase. I knew God was calling me to something special, but all this time I've been waiting for him. Did I ever tell you about Dr. Elizabeth Blackwell?"

"No ma'am, you never did."

"She was one of the first women doctors in England. I met her in 1851 and later I went to a place called Kaiserwerth. There's where I got my first taste of real nursing. It was very spiritual" — Florence made a face — "but very poor nursing."

"Will you have to move, Miss Florence?"

"Yes. I will have to move to the Institution. So I'll be leaving you."

"Leaving me!" Gervase exclaimed in dismay. "But ma'am, I want to go with you."

"Why, Gervase, you don't know how rough the living will be there! I will be in charge, but I've been there and it's terrible. Very dirty, and caring for patients can be a rather nasty business."

"I don't care, Miss Florence! I'm your maid. You take care of the patients, but you'll need somebody to take care of you."

"What a sweet thing to say! Are you certain you want to do this? I can recommend you to some of my friends. I'm sure I could find you a place."

"No ma'am. I want to go to the Institution with you."

Florence came over, her eyes dancing. She kissed Gervase on the cheek, the first time she had done such a thing. "That would be so helpful. You're right — I do need someone to take care of me. All my attention will be on the new program. Oh, it's going to be wonderful, Gervase!"

*"I'm going to turn the world upside down!"*

In the months that followed, these words of Florence Nightingale echoed in Gervase's mind.

Gervase knew nothing about nursing, but she quickly discovered that those who were serving as nurses at the Institution knew no more than she. They really were little more than cleaning women, many of them incapable of tending sick people.

Florence Nightingale swept into the Institution and at once began a revolution. She invented a scheme for having hot water piped up to every floor. She had a windlass installed, which was a lift to bring up a patient's food. When some members of the committee that oversaw the Institution complained, she told them firmly, "A nurse should never be obliged to quit her floor except for her own dinner and supper. Without some system, a nurse is converted into a pair of legs." The committee was too stunned to argue, and Florence Nightingale forged straight ahead, giving the committee the sensation that they had unknowingly released a genie from a bottle.

"They are nothing but children in administration, Gervase," she stated. "And they're not capable of administering anything."

⟨≈⟩

During this period, Gervase learned that she had an undreamed-of gift for nursing. She was strong, patient, quick, and most of all, she was not afraid of getting her hands dirty — or any other part of her person.

Miss Nightingale was delighted at this. Early in their stay, she found Gervase cleaning, without a tremor, a patient who had soiled herself. Later Miss Nightingale said, "That is the sort of thing that eliminates many women from our profession. They are unable to bring themselves to do it."

Gervase had smiled. "I'm glad I'm of help to you, Miss Nightingale."

"You would make an excellent nurse if God calls you in that direction."

These words stayed with Gervase, and as the months rode on, she became more and more efficient. She learned very quickly and became Florence Nightingale's right hand. Gervase was very young and had a mild manner, but at times she could flare up with a bright anger. When she caught some of the so-called nurses feeding their patients with dirty silverware, she had leaped at them with a fury, so that many began to complain to Miss Nightingale, "That nurse of yours is too hard!"

Florence Nightingale had laughed. "She's no harder than I am — and I am never wrong!"

Gervase grew close enough to Florence Nightingale that she was not surprised when late one night at the Institution, as they were both drinking tea after a hard day, Florence confided to her the essence of her ambition.

"I'm going to have to produce a new type of nurse, Gervase. These women know nothing and want to know nothing. I am going to find women who are called to a higher life of service."

Gervase listened and finally said, "I'd like to be one of those, Miss Nightingale."

"You already are. What would I do without you, my dear?"

Gervase went away carrying that in her heart, and somehow a resolve came to her. She knew somehow that she was going to be the kind of woman, the kind of nurse, that Florence Nightingale spoke of.

The next day she got a letter from her aunt — poorly written, poorly spelled, but warm with encouragement. However, it began with unwelcome news.

*March 23, 1854*

*Deerest Gervase,*

*Mr. Davis ain't happy in his mariage. Miss Roberta never has enuff money and don't mind complaining befour the servants. She throws it away as iff it was watter, and she shouts at Mr. Davis when he dont give her everything she asks for.*

All day long this disturbed Gervase and she had no one to share it with. She tried to push it out of her mind, for she did not like to think of Davis being unhappy. She knew she would never be more to him than she was — a friend — but the thought that he was miserable bothered her greatly.

This was still on her mind later that day when Florence grabbed her as she left one of the wards.

"Gervase, it's happened!"

"What's happened, Miss Flo?"

"England and France have declared war on Russia!"

Indeed, the troubles in the Crimea had been in the newspapers for some time. England did not want Russia to advance into territories that she considered her own. Along with France,

England had threatened the Russians with war if they did not pull back — and now it had happened.

"What does it mean, Miss Flo?" Gervase asked.

"It means our army will be sent to the Crimea, and as in all wars, it means there will be many wounded." Florence's face grew serious and rather sad. "And it means many will die for lack of proper nursing."

"But it's always been that way, hasn't it? I mean, women have never gone to the battlefields."

"They never have, and if they had, many men would be walking around alive today who are buried in some foreign field."

Gervase watched the older woman's face. "Well, there's nothing you can do about it."

"Isn't there?"

"Why, no. I wouldn't think so."

Any comment such as that got Florence Nightingale's back up. "I have a friend who is in government, Mr. Sidney Herbert. I think he'll be of some help."

"To go to war?"

"That's where the nurse is needed, Gervase, and one way or another I'm going to do all I can to serve God in that way!"

# Chapter Ten

Gervase sat reading the October 2, 1854, issue of the *London Times* as she waited for Miss Flo to come downstairs. She was concerned mostly with the progress of the war raging in the Crimea, and the story gave her little encouragement.

> The British army, which landed a force at Varna, has been decimated by a cholera epidemic. More men have died from that disease than from the bullets of the enemy. The army, which left in September, had won the Battle of Alma, but the wounded are dying by the hundreds.

The news was gloomy, as it had been since Florence and Gervase left the Institution and returned to the Nightingale home. Florence had been reluctant to leave, but since she had fulfilled her contract with the Institution, there was nothing to do but return home. Leaving had been difficult for Florence — indeed, she had felt something like despair, for the work had been her life.

Gervase heard the sound of footsteps, and looking up, she saw Miss Florence descending the stairs. She rose at once and said quickly, "Miss Florence, could I speak with you a moment?"

"Why, of course, Gervase. What is it?"

"I have just received word that my aunt is ill, and I need to go help care for her, Miss Flo."

"Well, of course you must. I hope it's not serious."

"I hope so, also. She's a strong woman and I'm hopeful that it's minor, but my uncle is worried."

"Then you must go at once. Do you need anything? Medicines? Money, perhaps?"

"Oh no, I think she needs me there more than she needs any medicine."

"You go ahead and make the arrangements, then, and write to me by post as soon as you have news." Florence looked down at the newspaper and shook her head. "This war is getting worse. William Howard Russell has written of the horrors of the medical situation in the *Times*."

"Yes, I've been reading it."

"England is stirred up over losing our men to disease through carelessness." A deadly anger underlay the voice of Florence Nightingale and she looked up. "Go ahead. I'm praying that I'll be able to help, but you must see to your aunt now."

"Thank you, ma'am. I'll say goodbye before I go."

Gervase went at once to find Maggie. She found her dusting the furniture on the second floor and said at once, "Maggie, my aunt is ill. I must go to her."

"Oh, that's too bad, Gervase. I hope it's not bad."

"I have a favor to ask."

"Why, certainly. What is it?"

"Could you take care of Mr. Bob while I'm gone?"

"Why, I'll treat that darling better than he's ever been treated."

"That will take a load off my mind."

"When will you be leaving?"

"Immediately. I shouldn't be more than a week."

"My prayers will be with you, darlin'."

"Thank you, Maggie. I knew I could count on you."

Lady Sarah's face revealed little but Gervase could tell that she was troubled.

Gervase had gone to her aunt as soon as she arrived at Kimberly, and had been relieved, for Aunt Martha's illness was not serious. Later that afternoon Gervase had gone walking outside despite the cold weather. October had brought sharp breezes, and rain had dampened the land, making the cold worse. Then Lady Sarah had called her in, and Gervase had stood in the parlor beside the fire, thawing out, and related to her former employer what she had been doing.

"Nursing? Well, that sounds very interesting. Isn't it hard?"

"Yes, it is, but I like it very much."

"And this woman, Miss Nightingale. Is she a gentle-woman?"

"Oh, certainly! She's very well educated and at one time she moved in high society."

"I don't think I've met her."

"The family travels, mostly in Europe."

Lady Sarah questioned Gervase further. When the older woman did not mention Davis or Ives, Gervase asked, "I trust Mr. Davis and his wife are fine?"

"Oh, they're in good health."

"And Mr. Ives?"

The question seemed to unsettle Lady Sarah. She twisted the ring on her hand nervously and seemed to be searching for an answer. "He's in good health, too," she said shortly.

Instantly Gervase knew that the situation was not good. Lady Sarah was not a woman easily disturbed, yet the question had brought furrows to her brow and she had quickly changed the subject.

After Gervase left Lady Sarah, she stepped outside to continue her walk and met Clyde Denny, who was exercising one of the horses. He slipped out of the saddle and came to greet her, the ruddiness in his face evidently reinforced by something stronger than tea.

"So good to see you, Gervase. You're looking fine. Like a real lady." He winked and said, "Why, I don't mean that. You always looked like a lady."

Gervase laughed. "It's all right, Clyde. How have you been?"

That question was enough to send Clyde off, for he was a very wordy individual. He was also somewhat of a gossip, and he screwed his face to one side, smacked his lips, and winked at her again. "Too bad about Mr. Davis."

"Why? I heard he was very well."

"Oh, he ain't sick or nothin', but he ain't a happy man, Gervase. Not a bit of it."

"What's wrong, Clyde?" Gervase knew she shouldn't ask this question, but it popped out before she could think.

"Well, you know I never gossip — "

"Oh, I know that well, Clyde."

"Him and his missus don't team together too well. You know that Mr. Davis was always a working, serious kind of chap. Not at all like Mr. Ives, you remember. Well, his wife, she likes excitement, and that excitement is pretty expensive at times."

Gervase did not answer, but her silence did not slow down Clyde, who continued for some time listing the things he had noticed. Particularly the arguments between Davis and his wife.

"Of course," he said, shrugging, "Mr. Davis, he's a quiet sort and never would raise his voice to a woman, but Miss Roberta — my word! She don't mind peelin' anybody's potato! I'm not surprised she would lay me bare, but her tongue's awful sharp for Mr. Davis."

"I'm sorry to hear it."

She ended the conversation as soon as she conveniently could, and determined to listen to no more gossip about the family. As she walked along the hedges, she looked up to see dark birds scoring the sky. They made harsh, raucous cries and then disappeared into the west.

The time passed quickly and soon Gervase found herself back in the old routine. On the third day of her visit, she was helping Annie Defoe, who was filling in as cook until Aunt Martha was able to take up her duties again. This was familiar territory for Gervase. She was laughing at Annie, who was a rather comical woman given to imitating various people. She was impersonating the local bishop when Roberta walked in, her face twisted in anger. "Annie," she said, "if you can't do more than imitate your betters, I think you'll need to find another place."

Fright crossed the cook's face. "I'm sorry. Indeed I am, Mrs. Wingate."

"Come with me, Gervase."

Gervase got a warning look from Annie as she followed Roberta out of the kitchen. Roberta turned and said, "I'm going to have to ask you not to encourage Annie in her ridiculous imitations."

"I think she meant no harm, Mrs. Wingate."

"I'm not debating this with you, Gervase. You will do as I say. Is that understood?"

At that instant Gervase understood something very clearly. This was a woman who had changed a great deal. Roberta had always behaved in a kindly fashion but that was gone now. *It's because of Davis and the letters we write each other,* Gervase thought. She was not wrong, for Roberta stared at her a long moment in silence and then said, "It's not fitting for a servant to be exchanging letters with a married nobleman. I won't mention this matter again."

Gervase did not have a chance to answer, for Roberta turned and walked away. Gervase was somewhat stunned at the change in the woman, and pity for Davis came to her.

*You never know what a person is like until you marry them.* The thought troubled her, and she knew she would be writing no more letters to Davis.

⟡

Martha was a strong woman and was well again within a week. Gervase was pleased at her aunt's quick recovery and planned her trip back to London. Clyde was going to take her as far as the post, where she could ride with the post carriage back to the Nightingale estate. Leaving the stable, Gervase circled the garden, not wanting to pass close to the house. Darkness had fallen and she suddenly saw two forms. One of them she recognized instantly as Roberta Wingate. She could not see the man clearly but she knew it must be Davis. They had not been around Kimberly all week during her visit, and Gervase had been glad of this, for she did not want a confrontation with Roberta over her relationship with Davis. She moved on quickly and entered the house, and that night she slept poorly.

She rose early the next morning, for she had arranged with Clyde to leave at nine. Her bag was packed and she took it down with her. She went into the kitchen, where Annie fixed her a good breakfast. Gervase tarried, drinking tea until it was almost time to go. Then she stood and said, "Goodbye, Annie. You've done a fine job filling in for my aunt."

"No one cooks like Martha," Annie said.

"That's right, I think, but it's good of you to say so."

Picking up her bag, Gervase left the kitchen. She was somewhat startled when Davis intercepted her in the hallway. He came toward her very quickly and gladly, and behind him Roberta stood watching them, a strange expression on her face.

"Why, Gervase, you're leaving and I haven't had a chance to see you." He put out his hand and she took it automatically. She had a glimpse of Roberta's face, saw the anger there, and could not think of how to answer him.

"I'm sorry I missed you," she said finally.

"Well, you don't have to go right away. Look, I have to return to London tomorrow morning. Stay overnight and we can make the trip together."

"I think Gervase needs to be back at her position, Davis," Roberta said. "Come with me. I have something to say to you."

"In a moment, Roberta." Davis glanced over his shoulder and something passed between him and his wife. Gervase saw the woman's face harden, and Roberta walked away, turning into the parlor.

"I don't think I can do that, Mr. Wingate."

"We're back to 'Mr. Wingate,'" Davis said quietly.

"Yes sir. I think it must be so. And I must tell you that — " Gervase hesitated, then said, "I don't think it would be proper for me to write anymore."

Davis glanced back involuntarily to where Roberta had stood. "I see," he said grimly. He had lost his gaiety. He bowed his head and seemed to be in deep thought.

"I'm sorry, sir, for I've enjoyed your letters," Gervase said.

Davis did not answer. He was staring at his feet. Finally he looked up, and his face had an expression Gervase had never seen on it before. He looked tortured and his mouth was twisted in a cruel way. He stared at her for a moment, then said, "A man pays for his mistakes. Goodbye, Gervase." He turned and walked rapidly away, and Gervase noticed that he did not go into the parlor but went out the side door.

Throughout her journey back to London, she was troubled by the exchange.

# Chapter Eleven

When Gervase arrived at the Nightingale house, she found that Miss Flo had gone to a friend's home for a brief visit, taking Maggie with her. Gervase was relieved by the thought of some time alone, for she was in low spirits. She kept to her room for the most part, but on the third day after her return she encountered Mr. Nightingale in the library, where she had gone to return a book.

"Why, Gervase, here you are!" Mr. Nightingale, a tall, good-looking man, was standing in front of the fireplace. He came forward at once, shook her hand, and welcomed her home. "Sit down and tell me what you've been doing."

Gervase sat and gave a brief account of her visit. Not wishing to dwell on her circumstances, she adroitly changed the subject by asking, "Mr. Nightingale, I really don't understand the war in the Crimea. It's so confusing. Could you possibly explain it to me in a simple fashion?"

Talking was what William Nightingale did best! He beamed at her, saying, "Why, my dear child, the Crimean War is a simple affair and can be easily summed up in a few words. On March twenty-seventh of this year, Britain declared war on Russia over territorial matters. Basically, Russia was moving into Turkey, and Britain objected to this. The British joined with France and Turkey and landed an army in the Crimea to stop the Russians. After the French and British had fought and won the Battle of Alma, they marched down to Sevastopol, where the Russians had built a large fortress. When they reached Sevastopol, they sat down for a long winter siege. That's what the whole thing has been."

"But our men are dying, the papers say, and most politicians can't understand why our army hasn't won and come home."

"They're fools, Gervase! It's not difficult at all to understand." Nightingale paced the floor, waving his arms wildly as he spoke. "This war, up to now, is undoubtedly the most poorly managed war of the century, perhaps of all time. The public considered Britain to be invincible. But since our great defeat of Napoleon at the Battle of Waterloo, under Wellington, the army as we knew it ceased to exist."

"But . . . how can that be, sir? What happened to it?"

"Why, the army, for all practical purposes, was dismantled. Capable officers were sent into retirement. Training camps were stripped down to a bare minimum, and the processes by which the British army was to receive food and clothing and care for the wounded were almost completely demolished!"

"What a shame!"

"You may well say so! This past spring, as the war began, confidence was high. The Royal Guard was a magnificent body of fighting men as it marched through London to embark for the Crimea—you probably remember it, don't you? But what the crowd cheering them did not know was that behind these splendid troops, the flower of the British army, there were absolutely no reserves. These troops were doomed to perish and when they did, the ranks were filled with raw recruits with no military experience and no backing from those in England who should have supported them."

Gervase stared at the man, saying, "But that's not right, sir!"

"Of course it's not right—but that's what has happened. The troops marched out to do battle, some thirty thousand men, but when they embarked for the Crimea, there were not enough transports to take both the army and its equipment across the Black Sea. Thirty thousand men were crammed in rightly enough, but pack animals, tents, cooking equipment, hospital supplies, medicine chests, bedding, and stores — all had to be left behind. In fact, only twenty-one wagons were brought for thirty thousand men going into action. Dr. Alexander, the division's staff surgeon, claimed, 'They have landed this army without any kind of hospital transport, litters, or carts.'"

Gervase listened as Mr. Nightingale spoke fervently and with more than a trace of anger. Finally he said, "I have a letter from a friend who went through the whole thing — here, let me read to you what he says."

Nightingale went to his desk, rummaged through the drawer, then pulled out a sheaf of papers. "Now, listen to this," he said.

"'We won the hard-fought Battle of Alma, but what to do with the wounded? There were no bandages, no splints, no chloroform, no morphia. The wounded were handled without feeling, like cordwood. They lay on the ground or straw mixed with manure in a farmyard. Arms and legs were chopped off without anesthetics. The victims lay on old doors or sat in tubs. Surgeons worked by moonlight because there were no lamps or even candles, and a cholera epidemic broke out which brought death by the hundreds. Dr. Menzies, the senior medical officer, was informed that many hundreds of battle casualties from the Battle of Alma, and another one thousand cholera cases, were on their way to Scutari, which was simply an enormous barrack, the headquarters of the Turkish artillery.

"'When the men arrived at the Barrack Hospital in Scutari, there was nothing. Dying men lay on the floor, wrapped in blankets saturated with blood and ordure in which they had been lying since they had fallen on the battlefield. There was no food. There were no kitchens. There was no one to attend to them. There were only a handful of doctors. Many of the wounded lay without a drink of water all the night and the next day. There were no cups or buckets to bring water in. There were no chairs or tables, certainly no operating room. And the men, half-naked, lay in long lines on the bare filthy floors of the huge dilapidated rooms.'"

"But that's . . . that's terrible, sir! The poor soldiers!" Gervase said with indignation.

"Yes, and you can imagine what Flo said when she read this letter! It was all I could do to keep her from packing up and getting on a ship!" Nightingale snorted. "Fortunately, the public has been alerted. William Howard Russell, war correspondent for the *Times,* has documented the sufferings of the sick and wounded. Not only are there few surgeons, not only are there no dressers and nurses, there is not even linen to make bandages. These men must die through the neglect of the medical staff of the British army, who forgot that old rags are necessary for the dressing of wounds.

"Russell's stories have created a sensation. The country is seething with rage. I still can't believe it!"

Gervase listened intently as Mr. Nightingale spoke of the dying men in the Crimea, but she only half heard him. She was thinking, *Miss Flo will never let this continue! She'll do something.*

<hr>

Sidney Herbert was an admirer of Florence Nightingale, but more importantly, he was the secretary of war, the man responsible for the sick and wounded. Herbert had followed Florence's career with avid interest. In the midst of the public's outcry for action from the government, Herbert wrote a letter to her. The letter said in part,

*I know of but one person in England who would be capable of organizing and superintending a group of nurses to care for our soldiers. The selection of the nurses will be very difficult. The challenge of finding women equal to the task — full of horrors and requiring knowledge, goodwill, substantial energy, and great courage — will be immense.*

*My question simply is, would you listen to the request to go and superintend the whole thing? I must not conceal from you that I think the ultimate success or failure of the plan will depend upon your decision. Your own personal qualities, your knowledge and your power of administration, and among greater things your rank and position in society gives you, in such a work, advantage which no other person possesses. I know you will come to a wise decision. God grant that it may be in accordance with my hopes.*

As Secretary Herbert sent this letter, he informed his staff, "If Miss Nightingale will not do this work, gentlemen, I fear it will never be done!"

⤳

Upon her return, Florence was delighted to see Gervase. But the next day she received Sidney Herbert's letter.

She accepted the assignment, and the nation was stirred by her appointment — which was made by the full cabinet. No woman had ever been so distinguished before.

At once Florence threw herself into the task of recruiting and training a group of nurses to serve in the Crimea. As there was at that time no organization training nurses, the work was a pioneer task. She at once enlisted Gervase and Maggie, and the days were filled with activity.

Gervase was excited but as she spoke to Maggie, it was with some apprehension. "I don't see how she can do it, Maggie. It's such a big thing!"

"She'll do it, don't you fear."

The two women were sitting outside the large room where a number of volunteers had come to make themselves part of the new nursing service. The voices rose in a gabbling sound and Gervase shook her head. "Some of those women wouldn't be fit to nurse a dead rat!"

"I know. Miss Nightingale's worried about it." Maggie glanced over to where Florence was writing, and kept her voice low. "It's worn her down."

"Yes. She knows that if this mission fails, there will probably never be good nursing in England. Not ever."

The two women talked quietly, and finally Florence rose and walked over to them. Her face was calm but pale. "Well, it's time to begin selecting the women who will serve. I suppose you've looked over the candidates in there."

"Yes ma'am, we have," Gervase said, nodding. She wanted to say more but feared discouraging Miss Nightingale.

"Everyone is asking," Florence said, "if women can nurse men under such conditions. The eyes of the nation are fixed on the hospital in Scutari. If our nurses do well, the profession will never again be despised, and a prejudice will have been broken."

Maggie listened as Florence spoke, and then said, "Some of the women out there are very poor quality."

"I know they are, Maggie. We are authorized to take forty, but if we do not have that many qualified volunteers, we will go with what we have." She glanced at the room where the volunteers were waiting. "Many of them are here only for the money. We must find out those women and be certain they do not go. Come along, then. It's time to begin." She hesitated, then said, "I will have the final authority, of course, but I trust your judgment. If you see anything that would disqualify any of these women, please make it known to me. Come now. We must begin. Time is short!"

Selecting the nurses did not take long. The quality of the volunteers was low, and indeed some had come for money. The wages were to be twelve to fourteen shillings a week with board, lodging, and uniforms. No young women were accepted, the majority of the chosen being stout older women. A uniform dress was provided which was extremely ugly. It consisted of a gray tweed dress, a gray worsted jacket, a plain white cap, and a short woolen cloak. The women also would wear a Holland scarf over their shoulders. There was no time to fit individual wearers, and some women got sizes either too large or too small. The uniform had obviously not been designed to make the wearer attractive!

The rules were very strict. No nurse was to go out alone; she had to be with either a housekeeper or three other nurses. In no circumstance was any nurse to go out without leave. The party was also to be nonsectarian. Fourteen professional nurses, who had experience at serving in hospitals, were engaged, and the remaining twenty-four were all members of religious institutions: Roman Catholic nuns, Dissenting deaconesses, Protestant nurses, or Anglican sisters. These nurses from religious institutions were required to accept Miss Nightingale's authority.

Gervase and Maggie became an integral part of the selection process. Some volunteers were out of the question. Each woman was interviewed at least three times, and the interviews often revealed a troublesome background. Many nurses had been drunken or promiscuous, and these were of course eliminated at once. Those volunteers from religious orders were neither drunken nor promiscuous, but many of them were more concerned about the souls of their patients than about their bodies and had no medical training whatsoever. Miss Nightingale said once with exasperation, "These self-devoted women, fit more for heaven than a hospital, flit about like angels without hands among the patients. They soothe their souls and leave their bodies dirty and neglected!"

Time was also pressing, and one evening after a hard day of working under Miss Nightingale's direction, Maggie and Gervase finally sat and had a few moments to speak before going to bed. Maggie, being larger and stronger, had borne the physical stress better than Gervase, but even her face was lined with strain. Sipping from a large cup of the tea they had brewed, she shook her head. "I don't see how nursing wounded men could be worse than this getting ready to go," she murmured.

"I think it probably will be," Gervase answered. She was so tired she could hardly speak, but she had risen to meet the challenge. "I think it's going to be terrible."

"Some of these women are worthless. They shouldn't be permitted to go."

"I think you're probably right, but we don't have time to weed them out anymore. I know Miss Nightingale is worried about it."

The two women sat there letting the fatigue soak out of their bones, and finally Gervase gave Maggie a curious look. "What is it you really want, Maggie? Do you want to be a nurse all your life?"

"I don't know, Gervase."

"Wouldn't you like to get married and have a husband and a home?"

"I'm too big and ugly for that."

Gervase stared at Maggie. "You are large," she said, "but you're certainly not ugly, and you'd make a good wife."

"I'm plain and that's the truth of it." Maggie shrugged. "I came to that a long time ago. I saw other women, small and pretty, and the men were drawn to them, but they weren't drawn to me. So I gave it up."

Gervase shook her head. "I think that's a mistake. You have all kinds of good qualities."

Maggie laughed. "The men watch women go along the street. They don't look for good qualities. They look for a pretty face and a shapely figure."

"Maybe some men, but there are others who value the things you have — honesty, goodness, loyalty. You have all those."

Maggie suddenly dropped her head, and Gervase saw that a strange expression had crossed her face. The big woman did not speak but Gervase knew she had touched a nerve. Pity for Maggie came to her then, and she wanted to comfort her, but the words would not come. After a long silence Gervase stood up. She put an arm around Maggie and squeezed her. "I am going to pray for you to find a husband."

"That'll be a difficult thing."

"Nothing is too difficult for God. Come now. Let's go to bed. We'll be leaving in two days."

"What are you going to do with Mr. Bob?"

Gervase hesitated. "I don't know," she said. "I thought about sending him back to Kimberly and letting my aunt and uncle take care of him."

"That probably is the best plan."

"He's never been separated from me. I think he'd be unhappy — and I know I would."

"Well, you can't take him with you, so you'd better send him to your aunt."

"I'm thinking about it," Gervase said. "Let's go to bed."

On Saturday morning, October 21, 1854, the party of nurses under the direction of Miss Florence Nightingale left London

Bridge. They were to travel by way of Boulogne to Paris. As the nurses lined up to board the ship, Maggie looked for Gervase. Once Florence stopped her and said, "Have you seen Gervase?"

"No ma'am, I haven't. She should be here. It would be very difficult if she didn't make this journey, but she'll be here, Miss Nightingale. She's very strict about keeping her obligations."

Florence was called away to see to the loading of medical supplies, and Maggie was kept busy herding the band of nurses up the gangplank. They were all aboard except for the last three when Maggie saw Gervase coming toward her. She was carrying a wicker basket in her hand, and when she drew near, Maggie said, "That's not Mr. Bob, I hope."

Gervase said, "Mind your own business, Maggie." She pushed past Maggie and went up the gangplank. Maggie stared after her and then suddenly smiled. "She's a stubborn young woman. I wonder how Miss Nightingale will take this. She won't like it, but if we're at sea, she can't make Gervase take that animal back — which is probably what Gervase intended."

Indeed, that had been Gervase's plan. She had tried to force herself to send Mr. Bob back to Kimberly, but she had grown so fond of the big cat, and he of her, that she could not. She knew she was risking the loss of Miss Nightingale's confidence, but in the end she had simply put Mr. Bob in the basket and brought him on board.

The interview that had followed was not pleasant. She had gone to Florence after the ship sailed for Boulogne, and confessed what she had done.

"I know it was wrong of me but I just couldn't help it. You see, he's been my only friend, almost, and I was afraid he wouldn't be cared for."

"You shouldn't have done this, Miss Howard."

"I know, ma'am, but I promise you I'll take care of him. He won't be a burden on anyone."

"Your whole time and thought and energy should be devoted to the sick men."

"Yes ma'am, I know. I was very wrong."

Miss Nightingale stared at the young woman and hot words rose to her lips. Florence was a woman of great strength who did not like to be crossed, but something about Gervase Howard's face stopped her. Florence knew a little of her background and had become convinced that there was great potential in this young woman. Finally she shook her head and even managed a smile. "If that cat is one bit of trouble, both you and he will go back to England on the next ship."

"Yes ma'am."

"All right, then. You keep Mr. Bob out of my way."

"Oh yes, Miss Nightingale. I will."

By the time the party reached Marseilles and was ready to embark for the Crimea, two of the nurses had already eliminated themselves by getting drunk. They were sent back immediately, and Miss Nightingale made it clear that if she had to go alone to the Crimea, then so be it.

On October 27 the party boarded the *Vectis* to sail for the Crimea. As they hurried on board, Gervase and Maggie discovered that she was a horrible ship, built for carrying fast mails, not for carrying passengers. The vessel was infected with huge cockroaches and was so notorious for her discomfort that the government had difficulty manning her.

Gervase found out that she was a good sailor, and after the first day so was Maggie. On the second day out, the *Vectis* ran into a gale and Miss Nightingale was prostrated by seasickness. The two women cared for her very carefully, since she was unable to even sit up.

The trip gave Gervase and Maggie time to think about what they were doing, and Gervase became more serious as they approached their destination. "I have a feeling that this is going to be worse than we expected, Maggie."

"It's going to be bad," Maggie agreed, sitting on her bunk in the small room she shared with Gervase. "I've just heard that there was a Battle at Balaclava and there were hundreds — maybe thousands — of men wounded. They'll all be shipped to the Barrack Hospital."

"Well, that's what we're here for, isn't it?"

"But from the talk I hear, that hospital isn't much. Terrible, as a matter of fact."

"Well, God will simply have to take care of us."

By the time the ship reached Constantinople, Miss Nightingale was on her feet. She had come up on deck and joined Gervase and the rest of the nurses. She looked across the water toward Scutari, where the hospital was. It had been raining heavily but now the rain had stopped, and a few fitful gleams lit up the shore. It was not a pretty sight, and as the ship nosed into the harbor, Gervase noted the bloated carcasses bobbing on the tide. On the shore she saw a pack of starving dogs fighting among themselves, and the shore itself was filthy. A cold wind blew out of the north, and as they disembarked and passed through the enormous gateway of the Barrack Hospital, she was reminded of the words from Dante, "Abandon hope all ye who enter here."

Scutari was a cold, muddy, filthy place that gave off a terrible fecal odor, and as they were met by Dr. Menzies, the head of the physicians, and Major Sillery, Gervase whispered to Maggie, "This is an ugly place, Maggie, and I don't think we've seen the worst of it yet!"

# Chapter Twelve

Whatever romantic notions the nurses might have had concerning the Barrack Hospital had vanished as soon as they set foot inside the building.

Its form was a hollow square with towers at each corner. One corner had been burned and could not be used. There were four miles of beds and everything was filthy and dilapidated. Sanitary defects made the hospital a pesthouse, and men died like flies due to diseases brought on by filth, overcrowding, and insufficient food.

As Gervase picked her way along, following Miss Nightingale and her two male escorts, the stench hit her almost like a blow. She had not known that an odor could be so overwhelming, and she whispered to Maggie, "It's almost like walking into a wall of stink, it's so awful."

Maggie was moving through the sea of mud and refuse that made up the ground, and as tough as she was, her face was pale. "How could it be this bad?" she asked.

Gervase gritted her teeth and fought off an impulse to throw up. She was holding Mr. Bob's basket in her right hand and a small carpetbag in her left. "Miss Nightingale said it would be bad like this. You remember?"

Indeed, just the previous night Florence Nightingale had gone over the situation for the two women. They had sat in their cramped quarters while she explained that there were three departments responsible for maintaining the health of the British army, and none of them had any connection with each other. One department might order supplies, but unless another paid for them and still a third delivered them, there would be no supplies. Officials were trained not to spend money, never to risk responsibility, and for the most part were helpless within the system.

Gervase heard Major Sillery say, "Miss Nightingale, I'm sorry to say that we don't have any fit quarters for your ladies."

"What do you have, Major?"

Major Sillery was a tall, thin man with a pale complexion and a bushy mustache covering his mouth. He glanced at Miss Nightingale and said, "We'll do the best we can for you, but we're not prepared to take care of a group of women."

Miss Nightingale did not answer, but Gervase understood at once that this was going to be the standard reply to their requests.

When she saw their quarters, Gervase could not believe her eyes. Miss Nightingale stood staring at the officer. "You mean, only six rooms for forty women?"

"I'm dreadfully sorry but that will have to do."

The rooms were damp, filthy, and unfurnished except for a few chairs. Miss Nightingale stared at the major, who fidgeted for a moment and then, muttering something about his duties, walked away. Dr. Menzies apologized again for the poor accommodations and took his leave.

"We'll do the best we can, ladies," Miss Nightingale said. "Come. We'll divide up into these rooms and make ourselves as comfortable as possible."

One of the rooms was occupied by the dead body of a Russian general, and Miss Nightingale ordered the two men assigned to help her to remove the corpse. The room was not clean and there was nothing to clean it with.

"What are we supposed to sleep on?" a nurse complained.

"There are your beds, along the wall," Florence said.

The nurse stared at the raised wooden platform along the perimeter of the room. There was no bedding and the wood was rotten. The nurse, whose name was Irene Moore, a heavyset middle-aged woman with brown hair and brown eyes, opened her mouth to protest. But when she saw Miss Nightingale's expression, she quickly closed it.

"It won't be so bad, Irene," Maggie said, grinning. "You've got enough padding on you to make yourself comfortable. Think about what the skinny ones will have to put up with."

Gervase and Maggie found what evidently had been a small kitchen, a room no more than eight by ten feet, but at least there was room to lie down. Once again there was no furniture, but Maggie by some means cajoled a soldier into finding them two pads and a table and a couple of rickety chairs. They settled in, then sat at the table, eating the food they had brought from the ship in a small knapsack. Maggie remarked, "Mr. Bob won't have any troubles. This place is full of rats."

Mr. Bob had been freed from his basket and now was prowling around, growling softly in his throat. "He'd better be careful. Someone might eat him," Maggie said. She saw the expression on Gervase's face and laughed. "Of course that won't happen."

"I'll be glad when we can do some work to make all this rough living worthwhile," Gervase said. She picked up Mr. Bob and lay with him on her mat as weariness set in. "Tomorrow, maybe, we will be able to help these poor fellows. . . ."

⟨≈⟩

"But they're just *ignoring* us!" Gervase protested. She had found Miss Nightingale and asked her when they would begin work. She had received no answer. "Why won't they use us?"

Florence said, "They think their authority is being challenged, Gervase."

"But we just want to help."

"I know that, but that's the way a hierarchy is. Men are afraid of their positions. They are territorial and refuse to give up any authority."

"The poor men — "

"We'll just have to wait. We can't accomplish anything without the confidence of the doctors."

"So we're going to do nothing?"

"We're going to wait until the doctors ask for help. I must demonstrate that I do not wish to interfere nor attract attention. And it's going to take self-control. Until we're officially instructed, we'll just have to watch men suffer. The medical team is understaffed and overworked."

The day passed slowly and a few stores arrived. Gervase and Maggie helped sort out old linens and count the packages of provisions. The hardship did not end with that. They had to stand in a corridor to get a pint of water a day; they had to eat out of tin bowls, wipe them with paper, wash their faces and hands in them, wipe them again, and drink tea from them.

"I could put up with all this if I knew we were doing some good," Gervase complained bitterly to Maggie. "I'd like to drown these doctors! They say they're called to serve the sick, but let them die without help!"

For several days the two had to listen to the men and watch them as they cried out for the simplest of care and did not get it. The nurses, almost as a body, blamed Miss Nightingale, but she was steadfast in her command that they would have to wait until the doctors asked them for help. "None of you is to enter a ward except at the invitation of a doctor," she said. "No matter how badly you want to or how great the need."

The first breakthrough came when Miss Nightingale began to cook "extras," as she called them. She had brought food supplies with her and began at once providing meals for her own nurses. She also, with the doctors' permission, provided pails of hot arrowroot and port wine for the Balaclava survivors. Within a week she was in charge of the kitchen and for five months supplied the poor soldiers as they came in from the battlefield.

On November 9, 1854, an enormous influx of wounded and sick poured into the Barrack Hospital, and its very magnitude caused the entire situation to change. These men came in suffering from dysentery, scurvy, starvation, and exposure, and there were many more on the way. The troops were riddled with cholera, and the men had abandoned their packs, so they arrived with nothing.

The Russians had attacked at Inkerman and the British were barely victorious. But winter was coming and it was obvious that Sevastopol would not fall until spring.

The weather changed and icy winds began to lash the land. The troops on the battlefield had no fuel. They burned everything that could be burned and then froze. The authorities were overwhelmed, and as the sick and wounded began to flow into the Barrack Hospital, Miss Nightingale's hour finally arrived. In desperation the doctors turned to her, and Florence called her nurses together. Her face was alight. "This is our time," she said. "We must prove ourselves invaluable, to set an example for those who will come after us."

The situation was indeed desperate. The sick poured in until the enormous building was packed. Every bed was filled and men were laid on the bare floor.

The doctors varied widely in skill and commitment. Miss Nightingale wrote of them, "Two of them are brutes and four are angels — for this is a work which makes angels or devils of men."

Gervase was tried in a crucible, for she had never seen such filth nor knew it could exist. It was indescribable: men lying with gaping wounds covered with vermin. There were no pillows, no blankets, and the soldiers' uniforms, which had been their sole covering for a week, were stiff with blood and filth.

But now the nurses had what they had come for — those with noble motives. Those who had come only for money began at once to clamor to go home.

Gervase worked from the time the sun came up until long after dark. She had become acquainted with many of the patients, and one of them, a soldier named Tommy Deakins, had touched her heart especially. He was a young man, no more than eighteen, and had been shot in the stomach. The doctors had turned him aside, saying it was hopeless, and Gervase had done what she could. She had cleaned him up, tried to get him to drink a little wine and eat a little, but his stomach wound prevented it.

He lived for two days, and on the evening of the second he lay with his pale face covered with sweat, gasping in pain. Gervase bathed his face with a damp cloth and could do no more than listen as he poured out his fears.

"Me mum tried to get me not to join," he whispered. "I should've listened to 'er!"

Gervase wanted to encourage him by saying he would get better, but she could not bring herself to a lie of this magnitude. She finally said, "Tommy, are you a Christian?"

"Yes mum, I am. I was saved when I was twelve years old."

"Then you will go to be with the Lord Jesus."

Tommy Deakins turned to her and reached out his hand, and she held it. He looked so young, more like a six-year-old than a young man. "That's right, Miss Gervase. But . . . I'll never marry, never have a kid of my own . . ."

Gervase sat there listening as he spoke his regrets. Two hours later he seemed to have slipped away, but he opened his eyes one more time, and when she leaned over, he said, "It makes it easier, havin' you 'ere while I'm crossing over, miss. It surely do! Thank you for coming to help."

Those were the last words Tommy Deakins spoke, and Gervase broke down and wept. She was still weeping when Maggie came, lifted her, and forced her to go to bed.

"He's so *young*, Maggie."

"They're all young. Whoever's responsible for this, I hope they burn for it!"

❧

The conditions did not get any better as the days wore on. Gervase worked with the others. She lost weight on a pitiful diet, and even Irene Moore began to lose the fat she had brought with her.

Mr. Bob flourished. Not on rats, although there were plenty of those. He made the rounds with Gervase, and to her surprise she discovered that he was as good as medicine to many of the wounded and sick men. Most of them loved to pet him, and Mr. Bob was always open to that.

One soldier, a middle-aged man named Alfred Williamson, was particularly fond of Mr. Bob.

"I do love cats, Miss Gervase," he said. He was sitting against the wall, holding the bowl of soup Gervase had brought him and stroking Mr. Bob. "We've got four cats at our house."

"What are their names, Sergeant?"

"Rex, he's the oldest. A fine strong tabby. Twelve years old. He rules the roost. And there's Contessa, midnight black and a pest of a cat if there ever was one." Sergeant Williamson smiled. "But we keep her all the same. And then there's Chester. He must weigh fifteen pounds. Big as a panther almost and black as night. And there's Percy—a fat butterball!"

"You have how many children, Sergeant?"

"Two children, Bobby and Heather, and I'll be seein' 'em again now that I'm going to be sent home."

"I'm glad you'll get to be with your family." Gervase had knelt down to be on his level. She watched the hope glow in the soldier's eyes as he spoke of his home and his family.

Finally he said, "I think you're an angel, Miss Gervase. Indeed I do! I don't know what us poor chaps would have done if you and the others hadn't come to take care of us."

"I'm no angel, Sergeant."

"To us poor blokes you are! If you hadn't got to me when you did, my wife would be a widow. And little Bobby and Heather would be orphans if it weren't for you—and think what would have happened to all our cats!"

At that instant Gervase looked up to see Florence Nightingale walking along the long line of wounded and sick men. She was carrying a lantern, and the light shed its yellow corona over her face. Gervase said, "There's the one you want to thank, Alfred. None of us would be here if it weren't for her."

The two watched Miss Nightingale as she stopped, spoke to the maimed and broken men, and moved along, speaking more encouragement.

Sergeant Alfred Williamson kept his eyes on her. He was still stroking Mr. Bob, and when his hand paused, Mr. Bob pawed at him as if to say, "Don't stop that now."

"She's a saint," Williamson whispered. "That's what she is."

Gervase Howard put her hand on his, saying, "I think you're right, Alfred. If she's not a saint, I don't know who is." She studied the woman and said, "There's a verse in the Bible that reminds me of Miss Nightingale. Psalm 132, verse 17. It says, 'I have ordained a lamp for mine anointed.'"

Alfred stared at the tall woman walking among the suffering. "Why, it do sound like her, don't it now?"

At that moment Florence became aware of the two. She gave Gervase a quick smile, nodded to the sergeant, and then held the lantern high as she moved down the dark corridor.

"'A lamp for mine anointed,'" Gervase whispered. "And that's what she is — a woman anointed by God!"

# The Crimea

*November 1854–July 1856*

# Chapter Thirteen

From where he sat, by moving his chair to one side, Davis had been able to watch a pair of industrious sparrows as they built a nest in a crevice of the building across the way. He did not know enough ornithology to identify the species, but he had begun to admire them. Even now as he watched, the one he assumed to be the male arrived back at the construction site, carrying a long twig in his beak, grasped firmly by the middle. He alighted on the granite ledge and considered the width of the crevice and then hopped toward it. His engineering sense was in error, for the twig was longer than the width of the gap, and when the ends struck the jagged edges of the broken stones, he bounced backward. Dropping the twig, he stood staring at it with an angry eye — or so Davis fancied — then picked it up again and made another assault, with the same result.

At this instant the female, who had been only barely visible inside the crevice, came bounding out. Her beak was moving and she was hopping up and down.

"Giving the old boy a peeling," Davis said with a grin. "Just like a female!"

Leaning forward a little, Davis watched as the female picked up the twig by one end and easily carried it inside. The male stood staring, then hopped to the edge and launched himself into the air. The female did not appear for a time, and Davis watched until she came out and looked up into the sky. He could see her bright eye and the silken down of her brown breast. He could almost, indeed, see the tiny heart beating rapidly. He admired the beauty of the small bird until finally she too flew away in search of material for her new home.

Reluctantly Davis turned from the window. "You're getting to be quite a sluggard, old boy," he murmured to himself, shaking his head ruefully. "Watching birds build nests doesn't serve the purpose of keeping this business afloat." He bent over and began studying the first of a stack of papers on his desk, only vaguely aware of the humming sound of voices that came from the outer office. The door was closed, but still he could hear the voice of Jamie Madden, their youngest clerk, relating his conquest of a young woman named Alice. It was a familiar thing, for Madden seemed to know an unending list of young women, and all of them fell to his charms — at least to hear Jamie Madden tell it.

Davis put the heels of his hands against his eyes and rested his elbows on the desk. He sat listening to Madden, whose tale finally ended. Abruptly the door opened.

"Hello, Davis. Sorry to be late."

"It's all right, Ives. Come on in and sit down. Will you have some tea? There are a few sandwiches left over from noon."

"No thanks," Ives said, shrugging. "I ate lunch on the way in." Ives was wearing a tight-waisted short redingote, a frock coat that had set the style in the United States and had found its way to England. It had tight sleeves, flaring skirts, large white revers, and a velvet collar. His light-blue trousers were tight-fitting and fastened underneath his black patent leather shoes. He pulled off his hat, which had a rather high crown, and tossed it on Davis's desk, then ran his hand over his hair. "It's getting blooming cold out there. I expect it's going to snow."

He sat and leaned back, a well-knit, handsome young man of twenty-two. Davis got up and walked to the door. "Renton, bring us some tea, will you?"

"Yes sir."

Closing the door, Davis returned to his desk. He did not sit but stood beside the window and looked out. The male bird had come back, and even as Davis watched, the female arrived. They disappeared inside the crevice, the male bearing a bit of paper, the female a long piece of straw. "Those birds are quite a lesson."

"What birds?"

"There's a pair of birds building a nest over there, in a hole in the marble. I've been watching them. You'd think that by this time of year they would have a nest already built, wouldn't you?"

"Maybe they're like the grasshopper."

"What grasshopper?" Davis asked, turning around.

"You know. The grasshopper and the ant. That old story." Ives flashed a grin at his tall brother. "I've always thought it was like us."

"What are you talking about, Ives?"

"Well, as bookish as you are, you should have made the application. The ant worked all summer gathering food, and the grasshopper played his fiddle or something. Chased after women, maybe — lady grasshoppers." Ives laughed and said, "Then when winter came, the ant was all snug and had everything ready, while the poor grasshopper came to his door freezing. He turned him away."

"I think that's from Aesop's Fables," Davis said. "I didn't know you read that."

"I didn't. The minister spoke about it three weeks ago at church. When he was talking about the grasshopper, I think he was looking at me. A lazy idler."

"I doubt he had you in mind." Davis smiled but his smile was troubled. He sat and the two men talked until a clerk brought in the tea. As soon as he left, Davis took a sip and remarked, "Have you heard about Creighton?"

"Creighton St. John? Your bosom friend at Oxford?"

"Yes."

"What about him? He's still in the army, isn't he?"

"Yes. He's a major now and he's getting his regiment ready to go fight in the Crimean War."

Ives shook his head and then sipped his tea. Looking over the cup, he said, "You always said St. John was one of the smartest fellows you ever knew. I never understood why he went into the army. That's for chaps who can't do much else, isn't it?"

"No, I don't think so. Some men in the military are duds, of course, but so are some in the stock market. I could reach out and put my hand on a few of them on this very floor."

"That war won't amount to anything. We'll have the Russians on the run before you know it."

"What makes you say that?"

"Well, we have the best army in the world, haven't we? They beat Napoleon."

"That was very nearly before you and I were born. According to Creighton, the army's just a shell of what it used to be."

"Well, I think it's really none of our business. That's what Creighton and his fellows are paid for, isn't it, to fight the wars? Not for a gentleman."

"Somebody has to fight the wars besides the regular army."

Suddenly Ives laughed. He had a good laugh which began deep in his chest, and his eyes danced as he said, "I know what's going on in your head. You'd like to be going over there with him, wouldn't you?"

"What are you talking about?"

"I haven't read many of those novels you keep giving to me, but I've read enough to know that in them war is seen as a great adventure. You're too romantic, Davis. War's not a great adventure. It's a nasty mess, from all I've read in the history books. It's not for gentlemen. Leave it to the professionals."

"If all Englishmen had done that, we'd be speaking French by now, or Spanish!"

"You don't think the Russians are going to invade us, do you? That's ridiculous!"

"No, and I'm not sure about the virtues of this war. All I know is that England has forces all over the globe, from the Sudan to the Crimea. It's the British Empire we're talking about here, Ives. Doesn't that mean anything to you?"

"Of course it does," Ives said, "but I'm not going to run out and take the king's shilling. There are plenty of young fellows who don't have any work to do. I'll leave the great adventure to them — or to romantics like yourself."

"Speaking of people who don't have much to do," Davis said, "I have a letter here from Professor Jennings."

Immediately Ives became defensive. He put the cup down, clasped his hands together, and sat up straight. "I can guess what it says." His voice was brittle and the fun was gone from his eyes. Jennings was Davis's old professor, now an administrator at Oxford.

"I would rather guess you can't. He simply says that — "

"He says that I'm a no-good loafer and that I don't attend classes or take my studies seriously."

"Actually, he says a little more than that, Ives. He says you're in danger of having to leave if you don't start working harder. What's wrong? Why are you having so much trouble? You're not stupid."

Ives got up and stood stiffly before Davis. "Why did he write to you? Why not to Father?"

"Because we're old friends, and he knows that Father doesn't know much about what goes on at Oxford."

"You're not my father, Davis. And you don't understand. You loved it at the university and I hate it."

"What's wrong with it, Ives? It's not a hard life."

"It's the same old thing every day, and the professors, some of them, are a thousand years behind the times. They're as dull as dishwater."

Davis sat there listening while Ives poured out his discontent. Finally, when the younger man fell silent, Davis said, "I get sick of coming to this office, Ives, but I come because it's my duty. It's what must be done."

Something passed across Ives' features then and his shoulders seemed to slump. "The oldest son never understands the younger one, Davis. He gets everything, and the younger one goes around picking up the crumbs."

"That's not true," Davis said, but he knew it was very close to the truth. He felt a sudden burst of affection and thought, *Perhaps I haven't done enough for Ives.* Rising, he moved around the desk and put an arm around his brother's shoulders. "Look, Ives, you find out what you want to do — what you really want to do — and I'll help you do it."

"Even if it means leaving the university?"

"Even if it means that. I want you to be happy, Brother."

"That's decent of you, Davis. I'll give it some thought." He suddenly struck Davis on the shoulder. "You're a thousand years old, all duty, and I know you don't like this work. You'd rather be living in an attic somewhere, writing the great English novel, wouldn't you?"

Davis did not have an opportunity to reply, for the door opened and Roberta came through. As usual, she was wearing the latest in fashions, in this case an outdoor dress with a bodice cut close to her figure. Her dome-shaped skirt was long and full and gathered into the waist, emphasizing her figure. A bonnet framed her face, and above her bodice a ruby set in gold lay against her skin. It twinkled with a candescent glitter, catching the light from the window. "Are you ready, Davis? Oh, hello, Ives. I didn't know you were here."

"Hello, Roberta. You look beautiful today, as always."

"Thank you, dear." Roberta's eyes were bright and she turned to Davis. "Are you ready?"

"Ready?"

Roberta suddenly lost her smile. "Yes. It's opening day at Ascot. You promised to take me today."

Ives saw Davis's expression change and thought, *He's forgotten all about it. That'll be trouble.* Like his parents, Ives was very much aware that Roberta was a hard woman to please. Her lips grew tight and both men saw that she was angry.

"I'm sorry, Roberta. I don't know what's gotten into me," Davis murmured.

"You can leave the office for one afternoon."

"Ordinarily I could, but there's a meeting two hours from now. It's been set up for weeks. I have to go."

Roberta stared at Davis, the planes of her cheeks growing hard. She was not a woman who cared to conceal her emotions, and now she said in a brittle voice, "You're not married to me! You're married to this office, Davis!"

"Oh, that's not right, Roberta. I simply forgot."

Ives stood back, looking for an opportunity to leave. He had been present at these arguments before and they were always unpleasant.

Suddenly Davis said, "Ives, be a good chap. Take Roberta to Ascot, will you?"

"You can't assign me as you do your clerks, Davis," Roberta snapped, her eyes icy.

Ives stepped forward at once and took Roberta's arm. It was full and strong under his touch. He said quickly, "Don't be angry, Roberta. Davis is just like the rest of us men. He's a little forgetful. Come along. I planned to go to the races anyway."

His words soothed Roberta's brow at once. She smiled and said, "Were you really, Ives?"

"Of course I was. Come along. Davis will make it up to you, won't you, Davis?"

"Yes, I will. I promise."

Roberta sighed and shook her head. "All right. Let's go, then. We're going to be late. My carriage is downstairs."

As the two walked to the door, Ives turned and grinned. "We'll talk later about this business of what to do with my life, Davis."

"Of course. Let's have lunch tomorrow or whenever you can."

Roberta asked, "What business is that?"

"Davis called me in to bawl me out for neglecting my work at university."

"Have you been?"

"Certainly."

Roberta laughed. They headed for the stairway. "You are a rascal, Ives Wingate."

"But you don't mind rascals, do you?"

"No, I don't. Come along. I don't want to be late."

Opening day at Ascot was always an exciting affair for the cream of London society. The men wore what amounted to a uniform — long cream-colored coats, striped trousers, and tall hats — and the women outdid themselves, vying for the most spectacular dresses they could find. The opening day crowd was certainly more concerned with fashion than with horses.

Roberta, however, had placed a large bet on a horse called Queenie, and she cheered him home as she and Ives stood beside the rail. When Queenie came in first, she turned and in her excitement threw her arms around Ives, crying out, "I won! I won!"

Holding her rather tightly, Ives said, "Yes, you did." She stepped back and he asked, "What are you going to do with all your winnings?"

"I'm going to spend it on something utterly frivolous."

"That would be a sin," Ives teased her. "I'm afraid I would have to report you."

"To Davis?"

"Oh no. To your guardian angel. We have long talks about you from time to time." Ives shook his head and said, "I'm afraid this is going to be a very evil report, Roberta Wingate."

"Here. Go cash this ticket in; then we're going to the Walker House and we'll order the most expensive thing on the menu."

"I will have a lot to tell your guardian angel. Her name is Cleo, by the way."

"A female guardian angel? I rather like that. She'll understand how it is with us women. Go now and get the money."

Roberta was waiting for Ives when he returned. Taking the bills he handed her, she stuffed them into her reticule. "Come along now. I'm starved."

When they arrived at the carriage, Ives said, "We're going to the Walker House. Do you know where it is, Dixon?"

"Yes sir. I think as how I do."

"Well, take us there and in a hurry."

Getting inside the carriage, Ives found that Roberta had taken her gloves off and was counting the bills. "You know, Ives, I love money," she said, crinkling the crisp bills and even pressing them to her cheek.

"That's something else to tell Cleo. It's a sin to love money."

"Why, of course it isn't. Where did you get an idea like that?"

"I think from some old book I read once."

"What old book?"

"It's called the Bible, I believe, or something like that."

"You are a fool, Ives!"

Ives laughed and said, "Here. Let me help you count it. As a matter of fact, you'd better let me hold it for you."

With a laugh Roberta handed him the bills and said, "Yes, but let's spend it all today."

"That might take a little doing. This is quite a wad you have here."

"We'll find a way, you and I." She suddenly turned to face him. "Do you remember the first time you took me out? You didn't have enough money to pay the bill at the restaurant. I had to help you."

"I'd forgotten that. But we had a good time that night, didn't we?"

"Yes. We always have a good time."

Her words seemed to hang between them, and finally he pushed the bills into his inner pocket and asked, "Have you heard about Creighton St. John?"

"You mean Davis's idol?"

"His idol? He's a good friend."

"He's his idol," Roberta said flatly. "Davis is always talking about Creighton. He admires him so much, I think he'd like to have an image of him carved out of stone."

"Oh come, Roberta. They were just good friends in school."

"He thinks Creighton is having a wonderful time — and he's having a terrible time."

Ives stared at Roberta. "It's not that bad." Even as he rode beside her, he was aware of her fragrance, and he felt, as he always had, the sway of her body and the vibrance of her personality. She was a well-shaped woman with features quick to express her thoughts, and she had a love for excitement and the good things of life, a sentiment echoed in his own spirit. "I think he gets bored with life at that office. I would, wouldn't you?"

Roberta shook her head. "Let's not talk about Davis," she said shortly.

Ives did not argue but changed the subject. They arrived at the Walker House, went inside, and were seated at one of the better tables. They ordered, as Roberta had said, "the most expensive thing on the menu." In this case, oysters with Saratoga potatoes and Catawba white wine. This was just the beginning, and by the time they had sat there for an hour, they had sampled several of the more exotic dishes.

The Walker House was a combination of a restaurant and what would be called, in later years, a nightclub. The tables were arranged around an open space, and an orchestra played while couples danced.

"Come on, Ives. Let's dance."

"I'm too full," he protested but he got to his feet. They were playing a waltz and she came to his arms at once. As they moved around the floor, she said, "Tell me about your love life, Ives." Her eyes gleamed and her face was only inches from his.

"Haven't got one."

"I don't believe that for a minute. You always drew women."

Ives did not answer and for one moment she saw he was serious. "You know, Roberta, we've heard the songs about broken hearts that never get put together again. I thought they were romantic nonsense, but I don't believe they are."

Roberta blinked with surprise. He had never spoken like this. "We were very close, weren't we, Ives?"

"Yes. I thought so, but that's over."

Roberta did not answer for a time. She felt his hand on her back, and as always his touch excited her. Finally she said, "I'm sorry, Ives."

"Couldn't be helped. You chose Davis and I've got to swallow my medicine."

They made a complete turn of the floor in silence. Then Roberta said in a tight voice, "I had to marry Davis — to save my family."

"Don't ever tell Davis that," Ives said quickly. "It would break his heart."

"He knows it."

"No, I don't think he does. Davis is so smart about some things but he's not very smart about women."

"You're right about that."

The two finished the dance and when they arrived at their table, she said, "Let's go to the theater. The Russian ballet is in town."

"We'd get out too late."

"It doesn't matter. Come along."

"I don't know anything about ballet. I never understood it. I always just wonder why they didn't get taller girls instead of dancing on their toes."

Roberta laughed and pressed herself against him. "Come on. I'll explain it to you. It'll be fun."

"It'll be awfully late when it's over."

"I'm a grown woman and can choose my own time for coming in. I'm not on a leash, Ives."

Ives stared at her and saw the rebellious spirit there. "No, you're not," he said. "Well, let's go see the ballet."

When Davis arrived at Kimberly, he found his mother downstairs. "What are you doing up this late, Mother?"

"I was waiting for you. I thought you'd be in earlier."

Davis hung his coat on the hall tree and put his arm around her. "You shouldn't have stayed up."

"I don't mind."

"Did Roberta get back earlier?"

Sarah Wingate did not answer for a moment. Finally she said quickly, "She hasn't gotten in yet."

"Well, she went to the races with Ives. They probably went out to have a late dinner."

The two walked slowly down the hall, Davis keeping his arm around his mother. "I was supposed to take her to Ascot but I forgot."

"She gets lonely, Davis."

"I know. It was my fault."

"She's a woman who likes activity. You'll have to take her to more places."

Davis shook his head. "She loves parties and I hate them."

Sarah did not answer but she knew Davis had summed up his marriage.

She and Edward had seen it very shortly after the wedding. Roberta was a woman who liked high society. She loved parties and activities, while Davis had always been fond of solitary pursuits. There was nothing Sarah could do about it, and she looked up at him and said, "I'm sorry you two aren't getting along."

"My fault, I suppose. I'm an old stick-in-the-mud."

"You certainly are not," Sarah said.

"Well, I have one supporter, anyway."

Ignoring his words, Sarah said, "What is it you want to do? I know you don't like going to the office. Couldn't we hire someone to take your place?"

Davis thought about his mother's words. They had paused at the stairway that led to the bedrooms on the second floor. He looked at a statue of Venus, thinking, not for the first time, how cold she looked, with no warmth of expression. "We quarrel a lot about children. I want them and she doesn't."

"I know. She's told me. She made that very plain."

"We didn't even talk about it before we married. That was my fault."

"Your father and I are worried about you. Would you like another career? We're proud of what you've done with the business, but we want you to be happy."

"I don't know, Mother. I've always thought, ever since I was a boy, that I might do something meaningful. Oh, it's not that what I do at the office is meaningless. It has to be done, but I would like to leave something behind other than an account in a bank somewhere."

"Have you thought about what you would like to do?"

"No. I haven't let myself think about it."

Sarah touched Davis's face. "You think about it, Son. Life is very short. Nothing is sadder than someone who reaches the end of it and looks back and decides he hasn't done what he's wanted to."

Davis kissed his mother. "All right. I'll think about it. Now off to bed with you."

"Good night, Son."

As his mother went up the stairs, Davis walked to the kitchen. There he was surprised to see Martha. "Why, hello, Martha. What are you doing this late? Not working, I hope."

"No. I got hungry. Thought I'd fix myself a bite to eat."

"Could you fix me a bite, also?"

"How does battered eggs and some fresh mutton sound? Very good meat it is."

"It sounds just right."

"I've made tea. Sit down until I get the eggs ready."

Ten minutes later the two were sitting at the table eating the hot eggs and the mutton, which was very good indeed. "Your cooking is the best, Martha."

"You always say nice things."

Martha was somewhat pale after her recent illness, and Davis said, "You're recovering very well but I think you came back to work too soon."

"Not a bit of it. What good does it do a body to stay in bed all day?" She drew an envelope out of her pocket. "I got a letter from Gervase yesterday."

Instantly Davis said, "Really! How is she doing?"

"You won't believe it, Mr. Davis. Did you ever hear of Florence Nightingale?"

"Of course I have. There's some sort of fuss in Parliament about whether to send nurses to the Crimea. I've been following it."

"Well, they settled it. They asked Miss Nightingale to take forty nurses and go help take care of the wounded soldiers, and Gervase is going with her as one of the nurses."

"You don't tell me!" Davis leaned forward, his eyes fixed on Martha. "What else does she say?"

He listened as Martha read portions of the letter, and then she said tentatively, "You two used to write, Mr. Davis. She misses your letters. She told me that."

Davis could not answer. He remembered vividly how Roberta had made it clear that she thought it improper for him to exchange letters with a former servant.

"What about Mr. Bob?"

"Oh, he's still with her. You know her and that cat."

"Yes, I do." Davis suddenly felt depressed. He got up and found a smile. "That was a fine midnight snack. Thank you, Martha. And when you write to Gervase, give her my best."

"I doubt if that'll be possible, sir."

"Why not?"

"Because I doubt if the mail gets to the Crimea. She'll be gone, I think, by the time a letter reaches London."

Davis looked at the woman, his expression unreadable. "Well, good night."

Martha watched him walk out of the room. She folded the letter slowly, put it in her pocket, and looked around the kitchen where she had spent so many years. She was thinking of Gervase and what a strange world she would be in. She murmured, "Take care of her, Lord." Then she turned the lamp down and left the kitchen.

# Chapter Fourteen

Christmas was two months away, but already snow was blowing lightly across the drill field, the tiny flakes sweeping the frozen ground and forming small patches of white where they came to rest. To Davis the snow looked like crumpled newspaper by the fence row, and he pulled his coat tighter about his throat. "It's freezing out here today, Creighton."

"It is a bit nippy." Major Creighton St. John was a tall thin man with brown hair and a pair of direct gray eyes. His uniform made a bright splash of crimson against the monochromatic terrain, and he pulled his hat down more firmly over his forehead, saying, "A bit hard on the men but they've got to be toughened up."

Davis had come out to visit his old friend and had found himself in the midst of maneuvers. He watched as the artillery rolled their cannons into position and fired them, using blank shells that made thunderous explosions. The soldiers, clad in red coats and with bayonets fixed, made charges and counter-charges and shouted as if they were playing rugby. Major St. John turned to the short, muscular captain and said, "Captain Taylor, exercise the men for another two hours."

"They're pretty tired, sir."

"They've got to be in better condition."

"Yes sir."

"Come along, Davis, to my office. No sense in your freezing to death out here."

The two went into the tent that had been set up on the training ground. Both men kept their coats on. "Sit down. How about something to drink?"

"It sounds good, Creighton — or should I say Major?"

"Oh, you only have to call me that if you wear the uniform." St. John had a thin face, his nose was sharply prominent, and his wide mouth twisted sideways when he grinned or laughed. He rummaged around, found the bottle, poured two glasses, and said, "Here. This will warm you up."

Davis took a swallow and then coughed violently. "What is this?"

"I don't tell secrets. It's my drink that's going to make me rich."

"If it doesn't kill me first." Davis smiled.

Major St. John threw himself into a chair and pulled his coat closer around him. "I hate cold weather," he said. "I wish we were going to the Sudan or somewhere blistering hot."

"What's the weather like in the Crimea?"

"Rotten. Wet and nasty. We'll be bound to lose men to sickness."

"How do your troops look?"

Creighton took another swallow of the potent drink, gritted his teeth and shut his eyes. When the jolt had passed, he said rather morbidly, "They're not ready for combat, Davis."

"Couldn't you hold them back longer for training?"

"There's no time. We're all the reserves that are available." He stared at Davis and said, "I'm not sure about this war. England's let the army go to pot — the navy too, for that matter. As soon as war comes, everybody gets patriotic, but when it's over, the first cry is, 'Cut back on the army. Send the sailors home.' Then when another war comes along, there we are."

"Like the poem by Kipling?"

"What poem is that?"

Davis closed his eyes and quoted with feeling,

*"I went into a public 'ouse to get a pint o' beer,*
*The publican 'e up an' sez, 'We serve no red-coats 'ere.'*
*The girls behind the bar they laughed and giggled fit to die,*
*I outs into the street again an to myself sez I:*
*'O it's Tommy this, an' Tommy that, an' "Tommy go away"*
*But it's "Thank you mister Atkins," when the band begins to play!*
*Then it's Tommy this, an' Tommy that,*
*An' "Tommy's 'ow's yer soul?"*
*But it's "Thin red line of 'eroes" when the drums begin to roll!'"*

"I'd forgotten that — but it's the rotten way things are," Creighton muttered. "Nobody loves a soldier in peacetime, but when the guns start booming, everybody wants to call them heroes."

Davis sat quietly sipping his drink, listening as Creighton spoke of the plight of the regiment. Davis had been impressed with the enthusiasm of the men, but when he mentioned this, Creighton shook his head.

"Enthusiasm won't last long when you come under fire. You see the fellow right next to you get his head nipped off by an artillery shell, it sort of dims enthusiastic spirits. It takes a long time to make a trained soldier, Davis. You don't turn them out in thirty days, and that's what most of these troops have had — thirty days' training." He took another drink and shook his head, almost in despair.

"What about your officers?"

"Well, a couple of them are all right. Most of them are too old. Still fighting the last war. I did have a good aide. Lieutenant Summerton. Some fool used live ammunition and shot his foot off in a mock battle."

"So he won't be able to go with you?"

"I mean he won't be a soldier at all. His foot is ruined."

"What did you do to the one who shot him?"

"Impossible to tell which one it was. They're all green and you can't watch every one of them all the time. I'm going to miss James. He was my strong right arm." Suddenly Creighton looked up and stared at Davis. His eyes sparkled and he said, "I'll tell you what. Why don't you join up as my aide? Lieutenant Davis Wingate. How does that sound?"

Davis laughed. "Don't be a fool, Creighton."

"I'm not. Look, I know you, Davis. You're sick to death of that office. This'll be an adventure for you."

"An adventure that might get my head taken off."

"All adventures are a risk."

Davis stared at his friend. They had come to Oxford on the same day and left the same day. Those years had forged a strong bond, but now he was uncertain. "You're joshing, aren't you?"

Creighton straightened. "Well, I was joking, but it doesn't have to be a joke."

"Of course it does. I'm no soldier."

"Neither are those poor fellows you saw out there. Neither is most of the staff. I'm telling you, Davis, we're scraping the bottom of the barrel."

"But you said yourself you can't make a trained soldier quickly. Especially out of a stockbroker."

Creighton suddenly had become excited. He said, "Here. Have another drink."

Davis held his glass out and shook his head. "You're not going to get me drunk enough to make me think I can join the army and leave for the Crimea next week and be any good."

"Look. What do you think an aide does?"

"Well, he helps his commanding officer."

"That's right. He writes letters that the commanding officer doesn't want to write. He keeps up with the quartermaster and makes sure the supplies are where they should be. He runs errands. That's what he is — an errand boy. You'd make a great errand boy, with that mind of yours. You never forgot anything in school."

Davis took a drink and stared at St. John. "It's impossible," he said.

"Why? Because of your work at the office?"

"Yes. That, for one thing."

Creighton laughed. "What if you had a heart attack and died before you got back there? Would they close the office?"

The liquor was getting to Davis. He never got drunk, but still his thoughts were running more loosely now, if not as coherently as before. "I think I have been drinking this punch too long."

Creighton grew utterly serious. "I wish you would come along, Davis. I know you're a married man, but really it won't be that dangerous. You might be carrying some messages under fire, but basically I think it will be a siege operation — one of the most boring kinds of warfare. I need somebody I can trust implicitly. You could pick up what you need on the way there."

Davis was staring at Creighton incredulously. "I can't believe you're serious."

"Think about it, Davis. This war won't last long. It's going to be short and sharp, and I need somebody desperately. I might put it that your country needs you, but I think I have another argument that would be even more telling with you."

"What argument is that?"

"It would get you out of that office you hate!"

Davis had pulled fresh socks on and slipped into the bed. The sheets were cold and he waited until Roberta came in beside him. He pulled her around and she came to him expectantly.

"Roberta, I want something."

"I can guess that." The room was semidark, with only one small lamp burning, but he could see the outlines of her face, and her eyes were laughing at him.

"I want us to have a baby."

Instantly Roberta stiffened. "We've talked about this, Davis. Don't start again."

There was an urgency in his voice. "I know you like to go out and do things, and you're afraid a baby would tie you down. But we can hire people to take care of the child. You'll have plenty of freedom."

"I'm not going to argue about this, Davis. It's something I'm not ready for."

Davis Wingate was basically a calm, easygoing man, but suddenly anger rose up in him and he spoke almost before he thought. "You're no wife, Roberta!" She began to pull away but he pulled her back. "There's more to life than shopping for clothes and going to parties. A man wants a woman who will bear him children. That's what marriage is, growing together and—"

"I don't want to hear this!"

"Well, you're going to hear it, and another thing—I've let you do anything you wanted to, given you anything you wanted, but that's going to stop!"

The quarrel grew more virulent and finally Davis could stand it no longer. He got out of bed, pulled on a robe, and left the room. Hot words lingered on his lips but he bit them off. He was half hoping she would call out to him, but only silence came. He found a spare room and lay down and tried to think calmly. He had been unhappy in his marriage for some time, but now this scene with Roberta had brought to the surface all the resentment he had harbored. "She'll have to listen to reason," he muttered. "She'll just have to...."

Davis left before Roberta rose the next morning, and did not see her for the next three days. He went to visit Creighton again. He stayed at the office late. He took long walks in the cold streets, thinking, trying to discover what sort of man he was — and what sort of woman he had married.

On the third night he was standing beside the Thames, where he had come to watch the river flow silently by. It was growing late and he knew that the neighborhood was not safe, but he didn't care. For a long time he stood as silent as the river. He heard the far-off cries of boatmen, and once he heard the shrill whistle of a boat as it came downstream, but he did not move.

Afterward he could never tell at what exact moment he made his decision, but he always thought it was at this instant when he stood beside the Thames and saw his life as clearly as he had ever seen it. He did not speak and no one spoke to him. But when he left the Thames and took a carriage to his home, he knew that something had changed in him. He had reached a fork in the road and had made his choice.

The dinner was good, as always, but Davis had said scarcely a word. He had picked at his food, and Roberta, as well as his parents, knew that something was bothering him. Roberta did not speak to him directly at all, but finally his mother asked, "Aren't you feeling well, Davis? You've hardly eaten a bite."

"I have something to tell you." Davis looked up and saw alarm in his mother's eyes, and his father suddenly straightened. Roberta had fixed her eyes on him, her lips drawn together in a thin line.

"There's no easy way to say this, but I've enlisted in Creighton's regiment as his aide."

A total silence fell across the table. For a moment everyone seemed paralyzed, and then Sir Edward exclaimed, "But that's impossible! You're not a soldier."

"I've talked it all out with Creighton. He needs someone he can trust. I know I'm not a soldier, but I can be of some help to him."

"You can't do this!" Roberta blurted. "It's impossible! It's those stupid romantic novels you're always reading! You'll get yourself killed."

Davis did not answer her. He was looking at his mother and saw the pain in her eyes. "I'm sorry if you're upset. I knew you would be, but I'm leaving early in the morning to join the regiment." He got to his feet suddenly and looked at the three of them. "I know you'll want to talk about this, but nothing is going to change my mind, so please don't try." He turned and walked out of the room.

Roberta waited until he was gone before saying, "It's only a romantic notion. I'll talk him out of it."

"I don't think you can, Roberta," Sarah said slowly. "You haven't ever seen Davis in the mood he's in now. He's always been easygoing, but when he makes his mind up, it's impossible to change it."

Sir Edward said, "Please try." His face was twisted in distress and he shook his head. "It's the worst decision he could make!"

"You're just doing this to punish me, Davis."

Davis turned to face Roberta. He had not known whether she would argue with his decision, but she had followed him out of the dining room and stepped into the bedroom, where he had begun putting a few things together.

"I don't want to talk about it, Roberta. I'm going and that's all there is to it."

Roberta hesitated. Indeed Sarah was right: she had never seen him like this. She watched as he methodically went through his clothes, picking out some and putting them on the bed. Finally she went over and touched his arm. When he turned to her, she looked up at him. "Davis, you think you can get your way by making this gesture, but it won't work. I'm not going to have a baby."

"I see that now. I'm not doing it for that reason."

His words were calm but Roberta saw the steely resolve in his face. For a moment remorse came to her and she said quietly, "Look, Davis, we both know by this time that we weren't 'made for each other,' as the poets and the novelists say, but we can have a good life." She put her hands on his chest and said urgently, "You have romantic notions about life. I don't. In our world marriage is for life. Divorce isn't an option. We're different, you and I. We want different things and we have to learn to live with those differences. One of those things has to do with children. You want them and I don't—for now. Let's just live together and say no more about it. You'll break your parents' hearts and you know it."

Davis looked down into her face. Her beauty had always moved him, but it did not do so now. "That's not a marriage, Roberta," he said quietly.

"It's all we can have, Davis. Make the best of it. It's what most men and women have. You got your ideas of marriage from romances, but that's not the way life is."

Davis knew that his arguments would be useless. He said, "I'm sorry it has to be this way. We did make a mistake, Roberta, but I'm going and that's all there is to it."

Roberta was shocked. She prepared for bed and when she lay under the covers, she thought about what she could say to change his mind. *He'd be a fool to go. He could get himself killed.*

Finally Davis slipped into bed, and Roberta moved over against him. She touched him and whispered, "Please don't go."

His only answer was to turn over and say in a voice that sounded almost dead, "Goodbye, Roberta."

# Chapter Fifteen

The year 1855 came to the Crimea with deadly force. The air in the ward was frigid, so cold that Gervase's fingers were numb as she tried to remove the bandage very gently from the face of the young soldier. He flinched and she cried quickly, "Oh, I'm so sorry, Thad."

"It's . . . it's all right, ma'am. Go ahead."

Gervase cupped her hands, blew on her fists, and flexed her fingers. "I'll get you another blanket as soon as I change your bandage," she said. The bandage covered half of the young man's face, and she knew that the unsteadiness in her hands was not only due to the almost-Arctic cold. January had come bringing even colder blasts of frigid air than those of the months preceding, and blankets were scarce. Each man had only one, and even now Thad Thomas's thin body was shaking almost violently. He was lying on one of the hard, raised platforms, with only a thin pad stuffed with dry grass for a mattress. He wore his uniform, which was the warmest thing available. His hands were outside the cover, and Gervase saw that they were clenched into tight fists. "I'm sorry to be so rough. I know it's painful."

"You go right ahead, Miss Gervase."

The bandages were made of linen that had come from England in bales. The nurses had worked hard to wash them, for some were unclean, and then to cut them into strips.

Gervase carefully removed the bandage as gently as she could. The wound before her was frightful. A shell had gone off very close to Thomas's head and had chewed the right side of his face. It had destroyed the right eye and torn the flesh out in chunks, leaving the side of his face a mass of bleeding nerves. Gervase had heard one of the doctors whisper to another, out of the wounded soldier's range of hearing, "He's going to make it, but he'll be an ugly mess for the rest of his life, I'm afraid. No way to give him back a face."

"Where's your home, Thad?" Gervase asked, hoping to take the young man's mind off the pain. There was very little morphine, she knew, and that was saved for the very worst of cases. She knew that the pain must be terrible.

"I come from Dover, ma'am."

"What a beautiful place."

"Yes ma'am. I've always thought so."

"What about your family?" Gervase worked as quickly as she could, listening as the soldier shared a few basic facts about his family. She laid bare the bleeding wound, letting nothing show in her face. She knew the young man's eye was on her, and she smiled at him and said, "Go on. Tell me some more." As he spoke haltingly, she cleaned what was left of his face. The eye had been torn out of the socket, and she could see the cheekbones and even part of the jawbone where flesh had been ripped away. Gently she cleaned the remaining tissue and began to apply another bandage.

"Well, you'll be going home soon, Thad," she said cheerfully.

"I guess so, but I don't care."

"You don't want to go home?"

"I've nothing to go home to, Miss Gervase."

"Are you married, Thad?"

A long silence followed and the young soldier closed his remaining eye. "I was going to be when I got back."

"Why, that's wonderful! Tell me about your fiancée."

"Don't reckon I'll have one."

Instantly Gervase knew what was on the young man's mind. She began to summon up all the encouragement she could think of. "Why, she'll be happy to have you back. What's her name?"

"Her name is Gwen, ma'am — but I don't think I'll be seeing her. I don't want her to see me like this."

"I think that's very wrong," Gervase said as she worked on the bandage. "Gwen would be very hurt. I'm sure she loves you."

"She loved what I used to be, but no woman could love a face like this. They won't even let me have a mirror, it's so bad. It is bad, ain't it, Miss Gervase?"

"It's a serious wound, but look at the good side of it, Thad. You've seen what goes on here. Men go out with no legs. Think how much harder that would be. One poor fellow had both hands blown off." She recounted other crippling wounds.

Finally Thad said, "But I'll be a horror to look at. How could a woman love a fellow with only half a face?"

"Let me ask you one question, Thad, and mind you tell me the truth."

Surprise caused Thomas to twist his head so he could face her. "Why, what is it, ma'am?"

"If Gwen had an accident and was harmed in some way — like this, for instance — would you still love her?"

"Yes, I would, ma'am. That wouldn't make no difference to me."

"Of course it wouldn't. It wasn't just part of your face that Gwen loved. It was *you*. You'll go home and you'll have, maybe, some adjusting to do. But you're going to get well. I think your face will fill in, the flesh will grow, and it'll be a badge of honor for you. Gwen will love you for what you've done for your country. I think you ought to write to her right now, today. You haven't told her about your wound, have you?"

"No, I ain't. I was afraid to."

"You write to her right now, and if you'd like, I'll add a note to go with it."

The young man struggled to sit up on his bunk. He touched the bandage and said, "I guess I'll do that, Miss Gervase, if you'll give me a piece of paper and something to write with."

"I'll do it right now. I'll get you a blanket too."

Gervase went at once to get the wounded soldier paper and a blanket, already composing in her mind what she would say to Gwen.

She moved down the line and when she got to the third bunk, she said cheerfully, "Well now, Marvin. Could you eat a little warm soup, do you think?" The man on the bunk did not answer, and when Gervase leaned over, she saw that his eyes were open, staring straight up, and his jaw had dropped. Suddenly Gervase felt nauseated and dizzy. She quickly sat on a camp stool and could not move for a time. Death had come to be such a common thing, and yet at times like this she would be stricken dumb. She began to tremble and struggled to control herself.

A hand touched her shoulder and she started. Twisting, she saw Florence Nightingale standing there. "Is he gone, dear?"

"Yes. He was talking just yesterday about going home, Miss Nightingale. I . . . I had such hopes for him."

"So did I." Florence's face was pale, but she stood as straight as a soldier and for a moment she did not speak. "It never gets any easier, does it, Gervase?"

"No ma'am, it doesn't." Gervase stood then and said, "It's harder on you than it is on the rest of us. You have not only men like Marvin and Thad to worry about but also all the other things that trouble you so. Nobody could do it but you, ma'am!"

Indeed, Florence Nightingale did bear a heavy burden. She was a slight woman who had never been robust and had been accustomed to luxury and now was living in almost unendurable hardship. To add to this, she had been victimized by petty jealousies, treacheries, and misrepresentations, both at the hospital and in England. The work that Miss Nightingale did was hard enough to have crushed most women, yet her administrative work was a fright. All day long, callers thronged her: captains of ships for transporting patients; officers of royal engineers; nurses; merchants; doctors; chaplains. She handled these one after another. At night she slept in a storeroom, in a bed behind a screen. During this time she wore a black woolen dress; white linen collar, cuffs, and apron; and a white cap under a black silk handkerchief. She spared herself nothing, but day after day, and week after week, carried on the work that would have broken strong men.

Dr. John Hall, chief of medical staff of the British Expeditionary Army, was a powerful man — and the enemy of Florence Nightingale. He was a martinet and despised those who worked under him. He was furious at the adulation that was poured on Florence Nightingale and did his best to discourage her work and make it even harder.

But even then the influence of Miss Nightingale was extraordinary. She could make men stop drinking, write home to their wives. One of the soldiers, named Kinglake, said, "The magic of her power over men was felt in the bloodstained room where operations took place. There, perhaps, the maimed soldier, if not yet resigned to his fate, might be craving death rather than meet the knife of the surgeon, but when they saw the honored lady in chief standing beside them with lips closely set and hands folded, decreeing herself to go through the pain of witnessing pain, the men would be strengthened and go on to do what they did."

The troops worshiped her. One soldier wrote, "What a comfort it was to see her pass even. She would speak to one and nod and smile to as many more. We lay there by the hundreds and blessed her shadow when it fell across us." The troops even gave up bad language. As one soldier said, "Before she came there was cussin' and swearin', but after that it was holy as a church."

Standing near Marvin's bunk, Gervase felt unsteady. She found that her hands were trembling. Florence Nightingale looked carefully at her pale features.

"I'm sorry to be so weak, ma'am," Gervase said.

"You're not weak. Go take a break. Have a cup of tea. I'll have the body removed. The bed is needed."

"They always are."

Miss Nightingale shook her head and passed her hand across her forehead. "I just had word that there was another battle and many men were wounded. They're on their way, should be here any moment. We'll have to make room for them somehow. You and Maggie do what you can."

"Yes ma'am."

"But now go. Take a few minutes off. It might help if you would pray."

"I will, and for you too, Miss Nightingale."

Gervase made her way to the kitchen and discovered that there was tea already made. One of the nurses who handled the cooking smiled at her sympathetically. "You look plum pale, Miss Gervase."

"I'm sure we all do."

The nurse, whose name was Emily, shook her head. "It don't ever end, does it now?" She was an older woman who should have been at home amid the comforts of her own house, but here she was in the Crimea in the midst of blood and disease and filth.

Gervase sipped the tea and listened as Emily spoke cheerfully about the meal she was working on. But Gervase couldn't stop thinking about Miss Nightingale. "Why does she do it?" she asked. "Why do any of us do it?" She found no answer and fatigue had made her groggy.

When she finished her tea, Gervase went to her room. She sat wearily on her cot but was afraid to lie down. Sleep was an overwhelming desire, and to combat it, she pulled the small wooden box from under her bed and removed her journal, pen, and ink. Balancing the notebook on her knees, she began to write.

*January 4, 1855*

> *It seems it will never end. Every day they remove men's bodies from the hospital, and as soon as they're gone, the beds are filled again with new patients. Most of them are terribly wounded, and we can tell almost by looking that some of them will not make it. But Miss Nightingale never gives up, and the rest of us will not allow ourselves to do so.*
>
> *I think so often of home now, of Kimberly. I think of it in the springtime. The cold here makes it seem like heaven almost.*

Suddenly Mr. Bob came bounding in with something in his mouth.

"Oh no, not another gift, Mr. Bob."

Mr. Bob had captured a mouse that was still alive. Quickly Gervase removed the tiny creature and held it in her hands. He seemed uninjured, and she knew cats often kept mice simply to play with.

"Shame on you, Mr. Bob. This poor fellow deserves better."

The mouse nestled in her hand and Mr. Bob sat down in her lap. Gervase stroked his long silky fur. The cold weather always made his coat beautiful. As always, he began purring like a miniature engine, his eyes half closed with pleasure as she rubbed his ears and stroked the base of his tail.

For a time Gervase sat there, holding the mouse in one hand, stroking Mr. Bob with the other. Eventually she said, "That's enough, Mr. Bob." She got up and for a moment stood irresolutely, not knowing what to do with the mouse. If she put him down, Mr. Bob would catch him again. So she walked quickly away while the big cat curled up on her cot for a sleep. She went outside and to her right saw clumps of dead grass. She put the mouse down nearby. For a moment he seemed confused. Then he turned and stood on his hind legs, facing her. He folded his tiny hands together and for a moment looked as though he were praying. His bright eyes watched her and his nose twitched violently. Finally he turned and scurried away, hiding himself in the tall grass.

<hr>

"Well, they're unloading the wounded out in the courtyard," Maggie said. She and Gervase had worked hard to get as many beds ready as possible. "I don't know where we're going to put them."

"We'll find a way. How many empty beds do we have?"

"Nearly thirty, but that won't be enough," Maggie said pessimistically.

"We'll do something."

Maggie suddenly laughed. Her face was red and chapped with the bitter cold, and she wore gloves with the fingers cut out. She blew on her hands and shook her head. "You're a caution, Gervase! Always looking on the bright side of things.

Why don't you ever just give up and gripe and complain, like the rest of us?"

"I never hear much complaining from you, Maggie," Gervase said, smiling. She pushed a lock of hair from the big woman's face. She had to reach up to do it, of course, and a wave of affection for the woman came to her. She patted Maggie's cheek. "Come along, now. It's going to be fine."

The two left the ward and moved outside. The cold hit them like a fist, and the pale sun now settled westward. It touched the tops of the faraway mountains, seeming to break like the yolk of an egg. Yellow color spilled out, making the barren country almost beautiful. The air was pearl-colored, and the smoke from the cooking fires rose in tall spirals which were tossed about as they found the higher currents. Two doctors were moving the wounded as they were unloaded from the three wagons that had drawn up. There were cries from the injured men as they were placed on the earth, and those cries seemed to tear at Gervase's heart.

A tall officer was helping to unload the men. His back was to her but she recognized the uniform of a lieutenant. He bent to put a middle-aged man, whose face was contorted with pain, on the ground. Gervase approached him and said, "Lieutenant, can you help us move the wounded inside?"

The officer straightened and turned to her. The bill of his cap shaded his eyes, and he had not shaved recently, so a scraggly beard covered his face. "Gervase," he said quietly and stepped toward her.

For a moment Gervase could not think — and then recognition came to her. "Davis," she whispered, "it's you!"

"Yes." He removed his cap and she saw that his face was much leaner than she remembered it. His eyes were sunk back into his head and weariness scored his features. He held his hand out.

She took it with both of hers and for a moment simply held it. "I didn't know you were here. When did you join the army?"

"I enlisted a couple of months ago." He smiled then and some of his weariness seemed to wash away. "I'm glad to see you," he said quietly. "I knew you were here, but I haven't had a chance to come."

"Why did you join the army?"

Davis hesitated. "We'd better get these poor fellows in out of the cold. We can talk later."

"Yes, of course," Gervase said. "Come. We have beds all ready. We're a little short of blankets but we'll find more."

Gervase was glad then that there was work to do, for she could not think clearly. She threw herself into the labors of getting the wounded men settled, and of course as soon as they were inside, there was the work of cleaning them up, changing bandages. She was much aware of Davis, who stayed with the men as the nurses performed their duties. He moved from bed to bed, speaking to each man. While she worked, Gervase had time to sort out her thoughts, and finally she went to him to say, "Davis, you look tired. Are you hungry?"

"Famished. We've had nothing but turnips for the last week."

"Oh, how awful! Come now. We'll get you something from the kitchen. The men will be fed very soon but I'll fix you something."

Neither of them spoke until they got to the kitchen. The cook was busy fixing broth for the wounded and supper for the rest of the men. It was a bustling place indeed, and Gervase simply moved among the others there, as she often did when she prepared special meals for her favorite patients, those who needed it particularly. She fixed two plates, found two cups, and put them on a wooden tray. Leaving the kitchen, she said, "Come along. We'll eat in my room."

Davis fell into step beside her and she led him to the small room. "You sit on that cot and I'll sit on this one. Move that box for me to put the tray on."

He pulled the box out from under Maggie's bunk and Gervase set the tray down. He sat heavily and stared at the food. "I never knew I was such a glutton, Gervase. I've done nothing but think and dream of food for the past week."

"A steady diet of turnips will do that. Eat now, Davis."

He smiled.

"What are you smiling about?"

"I'm just glad to see you," he said. Actually, he was glad that she had left off the "Mister." The use of his first name sounded so natural and good to him.

The meal was very simple, as were all meals at the Barrack Hospital, but there was some ham, two boiled potatoes, and dried peas that had been cooked until they were tender. The bread was hard but Davis ate everything, washing it down with the steaming hot tea.

When they finished, he leaned back against the wall and rested his face on his palm.

"You look so tired, Davis," Gervase said.

"I am tired."

"Are you too tired to talk? We could do that tomorrow."

"No, of course not." He leaned forward then and looked at her. He began to speak, telling her about his friend in the army, Major St. John.

Gervase listened and when he finished, she said, "Your family must have been shocked."

"*Shock* is not the word for it." Davis grinned ruefully. "I really couldn't reason with them, because there's not much reason in things like this."

"I think there is. I honor you for doing such a fine thing."

"You're the one who deserves that — you and Miss Nightingale. All England is talking about her, Gervase. Stories about her in all the papers. I believe she could be elected prime minister," he said with a grin, "if she were to run."

"She has such a hard time here. I wish people knew."

"I've heard a little about it, but tell me more."

Gervase told him about the envy and petty spites Dr. Hall had created. She told him also about another band of nurses who were sent for Florence Nightingale to be responsible for but who were not under her orders. "It's just been terrible, Davis. They were totally untrained, they came without any money or any supplies, and we had no place to put them."

"Why were they sent?"

"Dr. Hall did it, I think."

"Why does he hate her so much? I can't believe it."

"He's an evil man. He wants publicity and power and he resents the attention Miss Nightingale is getting."

Finally Gervase saw that Davis could hardly sit up. His eyes were heavy and she said, "You need to sleep."

"Sleep," he groaned. "I've forgotten what that is."

At that moment Maggie walked in. Davis stood at once, as did Gervase. "Maggie," she said, "this is Lieutenant Davis Wingate."

Maggie recognized the name instantly and, after acknowledging the introduction, said, "Gervase talks about you a lot, Lieutenant."

"Does she, now? What does she say?"

Maggie shook her head. "I'll not repeat it."

"Probably best," Davis said. He pulled himself together and said, "I'll go visit the men one more time, the poor chaps."

"Then we'll find you a place to sleep."

"It doesn't matter. I could sleep on the bare ground."

"We can do better than that," Gervase said.

"It's nice to meet you, Miss MacKay."

"And I'm glad to meet the famous Davis Wingate," Maggie said, smiling.

He looked at her, startled, and then shrugged and left the room.

"So that's the man I've heard so much about. My, he is a handsome fellow!"

"He's a fine man. I'm proud of him. He didn't have to come over here."

Maggie stared at Gervase and a thought came to her. She opened her mouth, suddenly closed it, and then said, "Well then. I'd better go find the poor man a place to sleep."

"Oh, I'll do that, Maggie. I know you're tired."

Maggie stopped, half turned, and said, "You want to take care of him, don't you?"

Gervase flushed. "Of course."

Maggie shook her head but said no more. From the door of their small room, she watched, troubled, as Gervase made her way down the hall.

The next two days went very quickly. Davis grew angry when he saw how badly the wounded were treated. Gervase said, "You're seeing the best of it, Davis. Before Miss Florence came, the wounded were on the floor in the filth, dying like flies."

The two were sitting outside the wall of the main building. Mr. Bob had accompanied them, and now he pushed his face against Davis's boot. Davis picked him up. "Well, you're looking very fat."

"It's the mice and the rats. He stuffs himself all the time."

"They didn't object to you bringing him?" Davis asked.

"I didn't ask. I simply brought him."

The two talked for some time and then Maggie appeared. She came over at once and said, "Well, Lieutenant, you're getting royal treatment."

Davis was stroking Mr. Bob. "How's that, Nurse MacKay?"

"I noticed you've made the best nurse among us your own."

"I demand the best of treatment," Davis said, smiling.

"Well, you're spoiled, as all men are."

"But I deserve it." Davis found that he liked Maggie a great deal. He talked with the big woman awhile, then handed Mr. Bob to Gervase, stood, and said, "I'll leave you two to talk about me."

As soon as he walked away, Maggie turned to face Gervase. She did not speak for a moment, and Gervase suddenly found herself troubled by the expression on the big woman's face. "What's wrong, Maggie?"

"Be careful, Gervase."

Gervase stared at her. "What are you talking about?"

Maggie did not answer right away, and then she said, "I'm not a romantic woman myself. I would be if I had the chance, I suppose. But a fine-looking chap like that can be a danger."

"Don't be foolish!"

Maggie simply said, "He's a married man, Gervase. Don't play with fire." She turned abruptly and walked away, leaving Gervase to stare after her. She almost called out but then she closed her lips. She watched Maggie disappear inside the building, and then put Mr. Bob on the ground. "Go catch a mouse," she said absently and rose to go back inside.

"I have to get back to my post," Davis said. He had come to find Gervase, who was working on Miss Nightingale's correspondence, something she often did.

"I'm sorry you have to go."

Davis shrugged. "It's what I came for." He hesitated, then said, "I thought I'd go into the village and buy a few things to take back to some of the fellows. Would you go with me? You probably know the shops."

"I'll go but there aren't many shops. This was just a small village, no more than five hundred people, and suddenly there are hundreds or even thousands here."

"Then come along. You can guide me."

The two left the hospital and walked down the worn path. The troops had left their mark, for everything seemed dirty and shabby. A few hungry dogs lying on the ground stared at them and barked halfheartedly. They apparently lacked the strength to get up.

Gervase took Davis to the few shops and he made his purchases, and then they started back. When they were within a few hundred yards of the hospital, he said, "Let's go look at the sea."

"All right. If you like."

They walked down to the coast. Davis put his purchases down, and the two stood beside a large rock overlooking the sea.

"It's so restless. The sea, I mean," Davis said.

They stood there silently, listening to the waves as they lapped the shore. They could hear vaguely the noise of the hospital, but here on the shore most of that was covered by the sibilance of the waves.

Finally Davis said, "I've been so confused lately, Gervase."

Startled, Gervase turned to him. "Confused about what?"

"About what to do with myself."

Gervase did not know how to answer. He had always seemed so assured and now she saw that he was troubled. "What's wrong, Davis?"

He suddenly turned to her, and his eyes fixed on her face as if he were memorizing her features. "You know what a keystone is, Gervase?"

"Yes. It's the top part of an arch in stonework, isn't it? Part of a door."

"Yes. You know that if a keystone trembles, the arch will carry the warning along its entire curve. And if that keystone falls, the arch will fall, and there'll be nothing but confusion — no design at all. That's the way I've felt lately, that I haven't understood what the keystone in my life is."

"The Bible says that Jesus should be the keystone," Gervase said simply. She realized then that she had been waiting a long time to say this to this tall man. He was faithful enough in his religious duties — she had seen that when she was at Kimberly — but he seemed to have no concept that Jesus Christ was a living force.

Davis stared at her. "You really believe that, don't you? That Jesus is the very center of the life of a Christian."

"That's the way it should be. Sometimes we put our own keystone up there. For some people it's money, for others it's fame. For some it could be something as simple as ... as, oh, maybe a house or a horse. It doesn't matter what it is, Davis. If Jesus isn't there, the arch won't stand."

Davis was very still. "We've never really talked about things like this, have we?"

"No, we haven't — but I've wanted to."

"Why didn't you?"

"I suppose I'm just a coward. Christians are supposed to be witnesses but I've not been faithful. But to me Jesus has to be the biggest thing in life."

Davis stood quietly for a time, studying her. Her long, composed lips held back, he thought, some hidden knowledge. Those lips were curved in an attractive line, for she had a pleasantly expressive mouth. The light ran over her and shaped her, revealing the soft lines of her body, the womanliness of shoulder and stance. She made a little gesture with her shoulders, and he thought of how everything she did spoke of goodness and faithfulness. He knew there was, in this quiet woman, a fire that some man would call forth someday. And suddenly, despite himself, he wanted to be that man.

"You'll never know," he said finally, "how much I admire you." He put out his hand suddenly and touched her cheek, marveling at its smoothness.

There was a silence between them and he quickly removed his hand. He saw that she was unsettled by what he had done, and he said quickly, "What will you do when the war is over?"

"Keep nursing," she said rather briefly.

"Will you marry?"

His question seemed to trouble her. "I don't know, Davis. I don't think so."

Instantly he said, "You should. You'd be a wonderful wife."

He watched her eyes then and saw that he had touched something deep in her heart. At that moment she seemed to draw away the curtain of reserve, and something like a challenge came to her. He felt deeply the turbulence of her spirit. Suddenly he knew that pain which comes to a man when he sees beauty in a woman — and knows it can never be his.

"We'd better get back," he said quickly. His words seemed to hurt her and he did not know why. He felt somehow that she had been expecting him to say more, but he could not think of what. He spoke then to cover his confusion. "I'll probably be coming back with more wounded."

"Be careful, Davis. Take care of yourself."

The moment was awkward. Davis knew it had been important, but he was bound by ties he could neither ignore nor forget. The thought of Roberta came to him so sharply that he almost blinked. He was a man of profound honor and now he said almost brusquely, "I'll say goodbye, then."

"Goodbye."

The words seemed bare and without warmth, and as the two walked back, Davis found in himself an emptiness he had not known existed.

# Chapter Sixteen

Lieutenant, take these orders up to Captain Fogerty. Be quick about it. They're urgent."

Lieutenant Davis Wingate took the envelope Major St. John extended toward him. He did not fail to mark the look of fatigue etched on his commanding officer's face. Davis had noticed that men, after so many weeks under fire, developed a stare that was instantly identifiable. He knew he himself had such an expression. Saluting, he said, "Yes sir."

"Oh, Davis?"

"Yes sir?"

"Look out for yourself. It's rather hot in that area." The officer suddenly moved forward. He hit Davis on the shoulder and grinned. "I can't spare you, you know."

For that moment Davis relaxed. "I'll watch it, Creighton. I can't spare me, either."

The two of them laughed, and then Creighton straightened and put on his official face. "Get back as soon as you can."

"Yes sir."

❧

The broken field through which Davis ran, crouching low, had been under attack for over three weeks. The Russian cannons had found a company of French there and had sent their large projectiles over, blasting deep craters. It looked more like the landscape of the moon, Davis thought, than anything on earth. He skirted the wounds in the earth, slipping once and nearly falling but catching himself. Straight ahead lay safety, but the sounds of battle still surrounded him. He could hear the rifle fire, a thin popping, to his left and behind him, and to his right the artillery — either Russian or English, he could not tell — were making their mighty booming coughs. He had delivered the orders and run all the way back, dodging through trees and over the torn ground, but now directly before him lay a line of scrub trees that offered some cover. His breath was coming in short spurts and he heard himself gasping deep in his chest.

When he was no more than thirty yards from the trees, suddenly he felt someone tap him on the left arm. Since he was running as fast as he could, he couldn't imagine it. He looked down at his arm and saw that his coat was bloody, and then the pain struck him and he realized he had been shot. He took another step, then whirled to see, to his left, a rifleman reloading. He was a small man, dressed in a uniform of disreputable rags, and he was intent on getting a shell into the chamber to kill Davis.

With his right hand Davis reached down and tried frantically to unsheath his pistol. The world seemed to be whirling but finally he felt the leather holster give way. He grasped the revolver, and as he turned sideways and raised it, he saw that the rifleman had succeeded in loading his weapon and was bringing it up to firing position. Davis could not move any faster. It seemed as though he were underwater, so slow was his arm to level the pistol. He looked over the sights and saw the eyes of the Russian, a bright brown, staring at him.

Davis pulled the trigger, felt the pistol kick, and almost instantaneously heard the crack of the rifle. He felt something tug at his hat, but then he saw the enemy soldier fall backward.

A roaring seemed to fill Davis's head. Quickly he made a tourniquet out of his belt and tied the arm to stop the bleeding. Then he walked over to the soldier. The man was lying on his back but he was not dead. He had been shot high in the chest. Fright was in his face and he held up his hand in a pleading gesture. Davis knelt beside him. The blood was crimson in the snow and spreading over the wound like a red flower.

For a moment Davis hesitated, and then he seemed to come back to himself. Awkwardly he pulled a handkerchief out of his inner pocket with his right hand and tugged at the man's shirt. He put the handkerchief inside, over the wound, and it was instantly reddened. Pulling out his hand, he took the Russian's hand and placed it over the handkerchief and pressed, saying, "Hold it — hold it!"

The man said something in Russian and held the handkerchief in place.

Davis could not leave the soldier here to bleed to death, so he said, "Come," and tugged at him. The Russian got to his feet but staggered. With his good arm Davis pulled the man's free hand over his shoulder. He staggered forward and the Russian stumbled along with him. It seemed as though the tree line ahead were now miles away. Their boots scrabbled across the dust, and Davis noticed that the sole of the Russian's boot was flapping so that he saw his exposed foot.

*Don't think I can make it* ... The thought flew through Davis's mind but finally they were there. He saw movement ahead and cried out the password, and then just as he was falling down, he saw that the tourniquet had slipped and his entire side was soaked with blood. The world began whirling but it was English soldiers who came rushing toward them. He tried to give an order but his tongue failed to function. The world had grown silent, and he felt the cold snow as it pressed against his face.

Creighton St. John's face was stern. "Sergeant, I want you to get Lieutenant Wingate to the hospital as quickly as possible."

Sergeant Clyde Patton nodded. "Yes sir. I'll take care of it. We can't afford to lose the lieutenant. He's the best we've got."

"You're right about that."

"What about the Russian? He's in bad shape."

"Take him along. Maybe headquarters there will be able to get something out of him about the enemy's position. But hurry, Sergeant Patton."

"Yes sir!"

The darkness had been a thing of permanence, as solid as granite, and he had been embedded in it like a fly in amber. When from time to time his mind would come back, all he was conscious of was the pain in his arm and a buzzing sound, like the noise of bees. He could not think of what the sound would be, and the pain was so great that he did not care to try. Finally, after a long time, he discovered what the sound was — voices. He could not make out what they were saying, but there seemed to be a great many of them.

Occasionally he was conscious of hands touching him. Sometimes there was a feeling that they were light and almost like gauze, and other times there was a roughness to them that caused him to cry out.

After a while he knew a little more. He opened his eyes and saw forms and faces, but by that time fever had gripped him. He would feel himself burning. His tongue was hot in his mouth, as hot as a burning coal, and his skin felt as though it were flayed.

From time to time he would drop back into the coolness of the stonelike darkness, and this was a relief. He had no concept of time. He could have been there for an hour or while the pyramids were built.

The light came to him then, and he realized there was a coolness on his face which felt exquisite. He knew he was lying flat on his back and that his flesh was not burning as it had been.

Then the voices came to him, and he understood that two of them were speaking of someone. He tried hard to listen and finally they came sharp and clear.

". . . the fever has broken and he'll be better, I think, from now on."

"Yes, I was so afraid of the infection, but it's gone now and the wound looks clean."

"It's healing well. I'll leave you with him but I believe you've won your battle. You need to lie down. You've worn yourself out with this one."

"I'll find time later, Miss Nightingale."

The voices ceased but Davis suddenly felt a clearness in his mind. He realized that something was lying over his eyes, and as he reached up, he felt a touch on his face and the damp cloth was removed. He opened his eyes and a face came before him. He could not focus for a moment, and then the woman's features swam into place.

"Gervase," he said, and his voice sounded like a frog croaking. His throat was dry and his lips seemed to be baked, they were so stiff.

"Davis, you're awake!"

He reached out and she took his hand. He felt light and the room seemed to be whirling, but he waited until it stopped. "Where . . . where is this place?"

"It's the hospital. You were wounded. Don't you remember?"

"Wounded. Oh . . . yes. I was shot in the arm."

"Yes. You lost so much blood on the way here, we thought you were going to die."

He saw that her lips were soft and her eyes were large and luminous. "You've been here all the time?"

"Don't talk. I want you to try to drink some water."

Words had never sounded sweeter to Davis Wingate. When she brought a small cup, he guzzled thirstily. She let him have three swallows and then said, "No more for right now. You must take it in small doses."

"That's the best drink I ever had."

Davis turned his head and saw he was in an enormous room with cots lining the walls and many more in the middle of the floor. "I'm in the hospital," he whispered.

"Yes." Her hand was on his forehead and she kept it there. It was deliciously cool, and he did not speak until finally she moved it. "I must have been in pretty bad shape."

"You were. Your sergeant wouldn't let us alone. He was afraid you wouldn't get good attention. He's been waiting for you to wake up. I must go tell him. He wants to get word back to your commanding officer. He's worried, too."

She disappeared and Davis lay there. He tried to move his left arm and found that it was bound tightly. Then Sergeant Patton's face was above him. "Well, you're back in the land of the living, are you, sir?"

"Yes, Sergeant. Lucky to be here."

"Glad you are. You were in worse shape than that bloody Russian."

"Did he live?"

"Yes. They're holding him with some other prisoners."

"Thank you for bringing me, Sergeant."

"There's a boat going back right away, but I ain't leavin' until you're well and able to go, sir."

"Thank you, Sergeant."

When Gervase came back, she gave him more water. He drank it and then set the cup down. He lay there quietly, studying her face, and she became restless. "Why are you staring at me, Davis?"

He did not answer but put out his hand, and when she took it, he said, "I've missed you."

The simple words caused Gervase to look away. She said nothing but sat there holding his hand in both of hers until he dropped off to sleep again.

⤳

"I tell you, you're going to have a relapse if you insist on doing so much," Gervase said. She had found Davis walking around speaking to the wounded men in his ward, and now she turned to Sergeant Patton, saying, "Sergeant, isn't there some way you can control this man?"

Patton gave her an astonished look. "Why, ma'am, he's an officer! I'm only a sergeant."

Davis laughed and came to stand before the two. "All right. Sergeant, I order you to make me do whatever Nurse Howard commands."

The sergeant grinned broadly. "What will it be, ma'am?"

"Take him outside where he can sit in the sunlight."

"Right you are. Come along, Lieutenant. You heard the orders."

Gervase smiled as she watched them go. She changed more bandages for half an hour and then went outside to check on the two of them. Davis was sitting on a camp stool and the sergeant was kneeling beside him. As she approached them, she heard Davis making strange noises that sounded like, "Dit da, da dit dit dit." She saw he was holding a piece of paper. "What's that, some kind of foreign language?"

"No, it's a code. Sergeant Patton here worked for Samuel Morse, the famous American inventor. Have you heard of him?"

"I don't believe so."

"Oh, it's quite the thing, ma'am," Sergeant Patton said, his eyes bright. "He invented the telegraph."

"The telegraph? What's that?"

"It's a machine that sends electrical impulses over a wire. I mean, you could string a wire from London all the way to Scotland, and you sit down with a little machine and touch it. It makes something we call a dit, and way up in Scotland that same impulse is picked up. Here's the code." He fumbled in his pocket and handed her a small piece of cardboard with letters written next to strange combinations of dots and dashes. "A dit is the same as a dot. You see, this is an *A* — a dot and a dash."

"How do you make a dash?"

"A dash, or da, is made up of two dits. An *A* on a telegraph would be dit and then just a split-second pause and then dit dit. So you have all the alphabet there, and you get very proficient. You can send quite a few words per minute."

"It would certainly be quicker than sending a message by mail," Gervase said, smiling.

Davis said, "It's fun too. Sergeant, give the nurse one of those codes."

"You can keep that one, miss. I have copies."

Gervase asked, "What are you going to do with the code, Lieutenant?"

"We're going to learn it while I'm here and then we'll go to work for Mr. Morse as operators. He'll need competent operators in England, won't he, Sergeant?"

"That he will. It's the comin' thing, I tell you." Sergeant Patton stood and said, "I think I'll wander around a bit. You keep your eye on him, miss."

"Of course I will."

As soon as the sergeant left, Gervase looked at the card and said, "So if you wanted to say 'to,' it would be da for *T*, and *O* is da da da?"

"Yes. They even have a signal now for distress."

"How do you mean, Davis?"

"Well, say a ship's in distress. A crewman could flash a bright light to spell out S.O.S. — 'Save our ship.' And maybe sooner or later they'll invent a wireless telegraph." Davis grinned. "Come now, it'll be fun. Let's see which of us can learn the code first."

"I don't have much time for games but I'll look at it." Gervase thought a moment, then asked, "How would you like to visit the Russian whose life you saved?"

"How is he doing? I'd forgotten about him."

"He's doing very well. The bullet took him high in the chest. If it had gone any lower, it would have pierced a lung and he probably would have died. I've been tending to him."

"Does he speak English?"

"No, but he has a friend among the other prisoners who does, so he translates for me."

"I'd like to see him."

"I don't know if you should walk that far."

"We'll take it easy. Come along. You can introduce me."

"Ivor, this is Lieutenant Wingate, the man you shot — and who shot you."

The translator, a swarthy man, grinned and translated the words. At once Ivor, who was sitting on a chair, started to get up, but Gervase pushed him back. "You be still," she said.

Ivor caught her meaning and he reached his hand out toward Davis. When Davis took it, the Russian, instead of shaking

Davis's hand as he expected, raised it to his lips and kissed it. A torrent of words flowed out of his lips. Davis was embarrassed and he looked to the interpreter. "What'd he say?"

"He says you are an angel sent from God, that he knows you are a Christian man because you have saved his life. And he thanks you from the bottom of his heart."

"Well, nobody ever called me an angel," Davis said, grinning. He retrieved his hand and nodded. "Tell him he's very welcome."

As the translator spoke, Ivor pulled something out and held it up. Davis leaned forward. "That's your wife and babies?"

The translator listened and then said, "Yes. And he thanks you for not making his wife a widow and his children orphans."

Davis was surprised at how small the man was and what a humble fellow he seemed. The enemy had sometimes seemed to him cruel and vindictive, but as he began to ask about Ivor's life, he discovered that the man had been conscripted and forced to go to war.

"We were all conscripted and made to fight. If they left it to us" — the translator grinned sourly — "we would all go home."

Ivor was saying something else and he was pointing at Gervase. The translator listened and nodded. "He says you are an angel, also. You have taken care of him and saved his life. He would bow down and kiss your feet, only he cannot."

Gervase flushed. "There's no point in that," she said, smiling. "That's what we came for."

Davis and Gervase talked with Ivor for some time, and Gervase promised to come back and bring the prisoners something good to eat. Ivor bowed over and over again, and thanks tumbled from his lips.

Pulling themselves away, they walked back toward the hospital. Gervase said, "That was wonderful, wasn't it?"

"Yes, it was. You don't think about them as being such gentle men, but they're just like us, I suppose."

"I thought it was nice that he thinks of you as a Christian."

"You're more of one than I am, Gervase, and I think he saw that."

"Aren't you a Christian, Davis?"

"I don't know, really. I was sprinkled when I was a baby. I've attended church and taken Communion, but that's not it, is it?"

"No, it's not."

He looked at her carefully. "It's different with you. I can tell."

"I don't know how different I am. I don't think of myself as a good Christian at all."

The two walked slowly back and Gervase spoke of her faith. When she made him go to bed and rest, she waited until he lay back and said, "You need Christ in your life, Davis. You see how dangerous it is out here."

"You're right about that. We'll talk about this before I leave."

"You won't be leaving anytime soon."

"I must get back as soon as I'm able. Probably two or three days."

She shook her head but saw that he was determined. "We'll talk more later."

Davis had prepared to leave but told Sergeant Patton, "Sergeant, you go out and hold the wagon. I need to say goodbye to Gervase."

"I said goodbye to her already. She's a good 'un, ain't she, sir?"

"Yes, she is. I won't be long."

Davis went searching for Gervase and found her in the kitchen, helping with the cooking. The kitchen was filled with noisy talk and he said, "Can we go someplace where we can say goodbye properly?"

"Of course, Davis. I think it'll have to be my room, though. Everywhere else is so busy."

"That'll be fine. I can't stay long."

The two made their way out of the crowded kitchen and five minutes later they were at Gervase's door. He left it open as he followed her into the room and stood before her. "I've got to go back, but I just wanted to tell you that there's no way I could ever thank you, Gervase, for your care."

"That's why I'm here."

"I know, but — " Davis grinned faintly. "I think I got a double portion of your care."

"Perhaps you did — for old time's sake."

"I've thought about those old times so much," he murmured. "It's hard to believe you're the same spindly little girl I picked up at the coach station."

"That seems like another world, doesn't it?"

"Yes, and it was a good world."

"I know," Gervase whispered. "I think about it a lot."

Davis was watching her and something came to him. He wanted to speak, to tell her how much she meant to him, but he could not. Then, without meaning to, he leaned forward and with his good hand pulled her close. "You've been so wonderful," he said. He lifted her hand and kissed it, then released it. Gervase did not speak for a moment, and then she said quietly, "I think it's best that we not be together, Davis. It's too dangerous."

Davis Wingate knew exactly what she meant. When he kissed her hand, he had felt something that had been lying dormant in him, and now he knew that what he felt for this woman was not the same kind of love he had felt for the child she had been when he first met her. He bowed his head for a time and chewed his lower lip. Then he straightened and said, "I doubt if I'll see you again, unless I come to bring more wounded."

"The war will be over soon and you'll be going home."

Davis stared at her, then said in a toneless voice, "Yes, home. Goodbye, Gervase." He turned and walked away without another word, and as he left, Gervase watched him until he disappeared. She stood there silently, not moving, and then took a deep breath and went back to her duties.

# Chapter Seventeen

Sevastopol, the objective of the British forces, fell on September 8, 1855, and from that time on it was merely a matter of waiting.

Gervase kept busy, for although the rate of the wounded slowed and finally stopped completely, there were plenty of patients to take up her time.

As the months passed slowly by, Gervase had no word of Davis. She had known when he left that he would not come back unless he was bringing wounded or was injured again himself, and it became habitual for her to deliberately put him out of her mind.

Finally the summer came, and in June late one afternoon she was sitting outside with Maggie. Their duties were much lighter now, many of the wounded having been shipped back to England.

Maggie said, "I'll be glad to get back home."

"What will you do, Maggie?"

"I'll stay with Miss Nightingale. She's talking about starting a school for nurses. Maybe I could help."

"That sounds like such a good thing to do."

"Maybe you could do that, too. We could get us a place together."

Gervase smiled at her. "I'm still praying for God to send you a husband."

Maggie laughed. She had learned to accept her single state and shook her head. "It'll be you that the young men will come flocking around, not a giant like me."

The two sat there for a long time. Finally Gervase said, "Look. There's a ship coming in."

Maggie stood and put her hand over her eyes. The summer sun was hot and strong, and though it was going down, it was still very bright. "I think they've come here to catch the ship for England. They're not wounded at all."

The two women watched as the troops disembarked. Gervase said, "You must be right. They're not making any attempt to get to the hospital."

"They'll be getting on those two big ships that pulled in last week. I wish we were going on them."

"We'll be going soon enough."

Davis appeared without warning. Gervase was cleaning up the dispensary when suddenly she heard his voice. Her heart skipped a beat, it seemed, and she turned and gasped, "Davis!"

"Hello, Gervase. The bad penny turns up again."

"Were you on the ship that came in?"

"Yes. We're leaving in two hours, but I couldn't leave without seeing you."

"Here. Come along. There's no one in the kitchen now, I think. Maybe we can find something."

They went to the kitchen and only a couple of women were working there. Gervase got two cups, filled them with tea and put cream and sugar in them, and then said, "Come now. We can talk down here."

They made their way to the end of the long tables and sat next to the wall. "You're looking so good, Davis. How's your arm?"

Davis lifted his arm and flexed it. "Perfect. I have a little scar there but that's no matter." He leaned forward, saying, "You look tired."

"I think that's chronic in this profession."

"When will you be going home?"

"Miss Nightingale hasn't said yet, but the hospital is emptying out fast. I don't expect it'll be long. Maybe next month."

They sat drinking their tea and both felt the strain. Gervase was remembering their parting and was sure that was in his mind, too. "Does your family know you're coming?"

"I've written them. They should get the letter before I arrive."

She asked about Sergeant Patton and discovered that he was already on the ship. Davis smiled and said, "Have you practiced your Morse code?"

"Not very much. I don't see how I would ever use it. I don't intend to be one of Mr. Morse's operators."

Davis hesitated, then said, "I must get back. I just wanted to let you know I've healed completely."

"I'm so glad, Davis. You came very close to death."

"Yes, I did. And since we talked to Ivor, I've been thinking about this matter of becoming a Christian. I've decided that I never have been one, really."

Gervase smiled and said, "You'll find Jesus. He's seeking you, and if you start seeking him, the two of you will find each other."

Davis got up and put his cup down. He came around the table and stood looking down at her. "Will you write me, Gervase?"

Gervase dropped her eyes. She did not speak for a long time, and then she said, "I don't think so. It wouldn't be proper. You must see that, Davis."

He did not speak and she saw the distress, the regret, in his face. He started to say something but broke off suddenly and could not finish his sentence.

"Goodbye. May God bless you, Davis."

He did not even offer to shake hands but turned and left rapidly. Once again, as she had years before, she shut the door on Davis Wingate and locked it and threw away the key.

On July 16 the last patients left the Barrack Hospital. Florence Nightingale and her nurses left on July 28, 1856.

The trip home was uneventful and when they stepped ashore, Gervase suddenly felt weary and tired beyond bearing. Maggie was standing beside her. The big woman put her arm around her and said, "Come on. We'll go find us a place to live, and Miss Nightingale will find a place for us to serve."

Gervase smiled up at her friend. "All right. That's what we'll do, then."

The two women made their way down the gangplank and joined the milling crowd, then found their way off the dock and soon were lost on the busy streets of London.

# A New Calling

*August 1856–October 1857*

# Chapter Eighteen

A s Gervase looked at the date on the front page of the *London Times*, a tiny shock ran along her nerves. Sitting in a room at the hospital, she stared at the date for a moment, then closed her eyes and leaned back in the chair. *One year — it was one year ago today that Maggie and I set foot on England again after the war. A whole year — and where has it gone?*

Indeed, the year had passed quickly for Gervase since she returned from the Crimea. At first she had felt at loose ends, not knowing what to do, and for several weeks she had sought vainly for work as a nurse. There had been no openings, and just when she had begun contemplating seeking work as a maid or a cook, Florence Nightingale contacted her.

"I'm beginning a new work to train nurses. I'll be working under the auspices of Gray's Hospital, Gervase. I would like for you and Maggie to be with me."

A warm feeling touched Gervase as she thought about this woman who had become famous all over England as a result of her Crimean experience. Florence's labors in the Crimea had produced two figures, both heroic — the soldier and the nurse. Never again was the British soldier to be ranked as a drunken brute, the scum of the earth. He was now a symbol of courage, loyalty, and endurance. And never again would the nurse be considered only a tipsy, hard-drinking sluggard. Miss Nightingale had stamped the profession of nurse with her own image.

After the war, however, Florence Nightingale never made a public appearance, never attended a public function, never issued a public statement. Instead she threw herself into the work of creating a training program for nurses. To do this, she had to struggle with the powers that existed, exactly as she had done during the war itself. But she threw herself into the task with all the resolution that marked her character.

Both Gervase and Maggie had given themselves to the work, and it was good that they were there, for Florence Nightingale suffered from ill health much of the time. She needed all the support of these two women, and throughout the year they had labored long and hard for the cause that Florence Nightingale had set before them.

The work at the hospital had been hard but Gervase had learned much. During the long days, and sometimes long nights, she had soaked up all the expertise she could from doctors and from Florence Nightingale herself. The pay had been meager but she had cared little for that. It had been enough to sustain her, and she and Maggie had found a comfortable apartment which they had worked hard to make into a home.

"What are you doing? We've got to leave, Gervase."

Maggie MacKay came surging into the room, a bundle of energy as always — a large bundle of energy! Maggie had not grown fat but she was still oversized, and her green eyes danced now as she stood looking down at Gervase. "Have you forgotten? We're going to see Tom Thumb."

"Oh, Maggie, I'm so tired!" Gervase protested. "I don't think I can do it."

"None of that!" Maggie reached down, pulled Gervase to her feet, and held her by both arms. "You're going to that performance if I have to drag you! Come along and change your clothes."

With a short laugh Gervase surrendered. Maggie usually had her way, and besides she had been looking forward to seeing

Tom Thumb. P. T. Barnum had brought part of his circus to England, and everyone was talking about what a wonderful show it was. Maggie had managed to obtain tickets and bullied Gervase so that she had finally agreed to go.

Quickly the two women changed out of their uniforms, left the hospital, and made their way to the theater where P. T. Barnum had put up an enormous sign: "Tom Thumb — The World's Smallest Human Being!"

The crowd was pressing in, but Maggie had obtained reserved seats, so they made their way down to the front of the large venue. After they had taken their seats, they were rewarded by several circus acts that Barnum had brought with him — a group of rather amazing tumblers, contortionists who could tie themselves into knots, and a troupe of clowns who performed acrobatically and kept the audience roaring with their remarks and jokes.

Finally P. T. Barnum himself came out into the spotlight and took a bow as the audience called his name and applauded him. He was a rotund man with a pair of sharp eyes. He was dressed in a cream-colored suit with a black tie and a pair of shiny black boots. His voice was loud and clear as he said, "And now, ladies and gentlemen, my dear British cousins, you are ready to meet the man whom I find one of the most amazing human beings it has ever been my good fortune to encounter. May I present General Tom Thumb!"

The orchestra gave a roll of the drums and a diminutive figure came sailing out from the wings. He was wearing the uniform of an American general and waved a ten-inch sword in his hand.

"He's so tiny!" Gervase whispered. "He can't be over two feet tall."

"But he's perfect in every detail," Maggie said.

Indeed, Charles Stratton *was* tiny. Barnum had found the child, who was twenty-five inches tall and weighed fifteen pounds and had a three-inch-long foot, in Bridgeport. The astute showman had at once signed up the little youngster. Stratton was only five years old at the time and weighed no more than the family's pet dog.

Barnum had created a sensation, for the young fellow had learned very quickly to perform a variety of roles. As the act progressed, he performed as a soldier, waving his tiny sword and singing "Yankee Doodle Dandy" in a tiny but perfectly clear voice. He changed uniforms and performed a military drill. As Gervase and Maggie applauded and cried out their approval with the rest of the audience, he came out as Cupid, wearing flesh-colored tights and holding a bow and carrying a quiver of arrows. As little David from the Bible, he staged a mock battle with two Goliaths, the giants of Barnum's American Museum — Colonel Goshen and Monsieur Bihin. He even offered, as a finale, a pocket-sized portrayal of Napoleon.

The two women laughed and applauded until their hands hurt, and finally when the performance was over, they made their way out of the theater. During their trip home on the horse-drawn trolley, they spoke of what it would be like to be as small as General Tom Thumb. "I wonder what he'll do for a wife when he grows up?" Gervase said. "But then, he may grow to be normal size."

Finally Gervase grew quiet, and Maggie caught a glimpse of her face. She saw there the traces of fatigue, for Gervase's physical stamina did not equal her own, which was tremendous. There was something more there that Maggie had long tried to understand. She had developed a great affection for Gervase Howard, and she knew there was, somehow, a sadness in her that she had never been able to explain. Finally she asked, "What about Leslie Maddox?"

"What about him, Maggie?"

"Well, he used to call on you but he stopped."

"I wasn't interested."

"But he was such a fine man. Good-looking too."

Gervase shook her head and didn't answer. Maggie thought over the past year and brought before her mind, besides Leslie Maddox, two other men, both eligible, who had shown an interest in Gervase. She had gone out with them a time or two but nothing had come of it. Now a thought came to Maggie and she asked in an offhanded fashion, "Do you think you'll go visit your aunt Martha and your uncle soon?"

"No, I don't think so, Maggie."

"You might see Mr. Wingate."

Gervase suddenly bowed her head and stared at her feet. "I will not be going back to Kimberly anytime soon."

"Mr. Wingate used to write to you before the war. Have you heard from him since he got home?"

"No. It wouldn't be proper. He's nothing to me, Maggie. Please don't speak of him again."

Maggie was surprised at the sharpness of Gervase's voice. She said no more but filed it away in her memory. *She hasn't forgotten him. I saw how the two of them were together at the hospital — the way they looked at each other. Too bad, but she's got to get him out of her mind.*

The two arrived at their destination, stepped off the trolley, and went at once to their small apartment, which consisted of a sitting room and two bedrooms. Gervase said, "Good night. It was fun going to see Mr. Tom Thumb."

"Good night, Gervase."

Gervase entered her room, where she picked up a letter lying on her dressing table. It had come just as she left for work, and she had put it aside for later. She knew her aunt's handwriting and was glad to hear from her. Sitting at the table, she opened the envelope and by the light of the lamp read her aunt's letter.

Her aunt Martha was a terrible speller, so bad that Gervase often had to use her imagination to make out what was being said. She struggled through the first page, which simply gave a list of the day-by-day activities of her aunt Martha and a quick summary of how the servants were doing. Turning over the page, Gervase stopped suddenly, for she read the words

> *I feel so sorry for Mr. Davis. He has to putt up with his wife and it's verry bad. I don't know why itt is, but they never seam hapy. It hurts me to sea Mr. Davis so sad.*

Gervase finished the letter, folded it carefully, and put it in the drawer of her dressing table. She undressed quickly, put on a shift, and got into bed. Mr. Bob, who had been waiting for this moment, leaped up and pushed against her. It was August, the weather was hot, and Mr. Bob was like a furry furnace. Still, he persisted, and Gervase stroked his silky fur.

Despite herself and all the resolutions of the past, she could not keep her mind away from Davis Wingate. Her aunt's brief words had caused her to imagine what life must be like for him. Finally she rolled over and as Mr. Bob shoved himself against the small of her back, she began to pray. It was a desperate prayer, almost an agonizing one. *Oh, God — take him out of my mind! I can't stop thinking of him, so I ask you, just blot him out of my memory!*

❧

"Oh, this letter just came for you, Miss Howard."

"Thank you, Mrs. Travers."

Gervase had just come home from a shopping tour. It was one of her rare days off, and she took the letter and glanced at it. She did not recognize the writing for a moment, but then it came to her. *It's from Davis's mother, Lady Sarah.*

She had never received a letter from Lady Sarah Wingate. She went into her room and sat, then stared at the letter for a moment before opening it. It had been a month since she prayed so hard for God to remove Davis from her mind. The prayer had been partially answered. She had filled up her life with work and activities so that she had little time to think of other things. It had been a struggle but it had been successful.

Now, however, the letter disturbed her. She could not think of why Lady Sarah would be writing her. With a decisive motion she broke the seal, opened the letter, and began to read.

*My Dear Gervase,*

*This letter will bring sad news to you, for I know how fond you have been of our family. I do not know how to say this, but Davis has had a terrible accident. He took a fall from the cliff that borders the beach. You know the place. There are rocks below, and it was a wonder that he was not killed instantly. He suffered severe head injuries, and I am grieved to tell you that he has not recovered consciousness since.*

*We rushed him to the hospital, and Dr. Thompson was there and cared for him, but he could do nothing. He called in specialists, but none of them have been able to help my poor son.*

*Davis is alive, but he is totally unable to speak or even to move. He is in a coma, and the doctors are mystified. They are not optimistic at all, and I fear they are not telling us the worst.*

*After Davis spent a week in the hospital with no improvement, Dr. Thompson agreed to let us bring him home. Roberta hired two attendants to take care of him in his pitiful condition. We have fixed a room up on the first floor, the green room you remember — the largest of the bedrooms — but our hearts are so grieved, I can hardly write this letter.*

*I am writing you because I feel that the Lord has put you on my heart in a special way. I believe I was thinking of how you cared for him in the Crimea when he was wounded. I have never been a great believer in those people who are always saying, "God told me to do such*

*and such." I love the Lord, but he has never spoken to me directly —
until now.*

*I have been praying for a long time, unable to eat, and your face
came before me as I prayed. I asked the Lord why that was, and the
answer that came to my spirit was, "Gervase must care for Davis."*

*You may think I'm a foolish woman, but I do believe God was in
it, Gervase. We have heard such wonderful things of your nursing
experience, and I am so worried about poor Davis. Would it at all be
possible for you to come and take over his care? The two assistants
who have been hired are not trained at all, and I am unhappy with
some of the things that go on.*

*I realize this is a lot to ask, but I do ask it. If you cannot come,
I will understand. Please, if you could decide to do this quickly, it
would give me great consolation. If you cannot, I will try to find somebody else. But I am continuing to pray that you will be the one to care
for Davis.*

> *Yours affectionately,*
> *Lady Sarah Wingate*

Gervase was thrown into a strange emotional state so
strong that she could barely hold the letter. Her hands were
trembling. The thought of Davis being close to death struck
her like a blow.

Getting up, she paced the floor. Thoughts swarmed through
her mind, the first being, *I can't do it! I can't bear to be around him.
God, I've asked you to take him out of my mind — and now I'm asked to
be with him!*

After a time she grew somewhat calmer. She sat and read
the letter again, and then she rose, went over to the bed. She
knelt, put the letter before her, and began to pray.

※

"I'm very confused, Miss Nightingale. I just don't know
what to do."

Florence had listened quietly as Gervase spoke. She had said nothing until now, but she had studied the face of the troubled young woman who sat before her. She noted the trembling in the hands and the twitches of the mouth, and finally she asked, "Why are you so troubled, Gervase?"

"Because I love this family very much, Miss Nightingale. I grew very fond of them when I was a servant in their house."

The answer did not appear to satisfy Florence. She continued to study the face of Gervase Howard. Florence herself was a believer that God spoke to people. God had spoken to her three times in her own life, giving her directions as to which way to take. She did not find it at all strange that Lady Sarah Wingate would receive a word from God. She said as much then to Gervase. "It seems to me that you have your answer in your hand."

"What is that, Miss Nightingale?"

"Lady Wingate says that God has put you on her heart."

"But he hasn't spoken to me."

"That's not necessary. God doesn't have to go around and speak to half a dozen people. You know your Bible. You know that God often would give a word to one and to one only. When Paul was struck down on the road to Damascus, he was helpless and blind. But God spoke to a man called Ananias. He told Ananias what to do, and Ananias went and gave the word of God and ministered to the apostle Paul. I think the same situation exists here."

Gervase bowed her head for a moment, and when she looked up, her eyes were intense as she studied Miss Nightingale's face. "You counsel me to go?"

"I do. If you discover you have made a mistake and you shouldn't be there, you can always come back. But I believe we should always listen when God speaks."

Gervase suddenly grew calm. She sat quietly for a few moments and then nodded. "Thank you, Miss Nightingale. I will need to go at once if you can spare me."

"I would never stand in the way of anyone who is hearing the call of God," Florence said, smiling. "Go, and my blessing be with you."

~

Maggie was helping Gervase pack. She had received the news of Davis Wingate's injury and had peppered Gervase with questions. Gervase was putting her clothes into a small trunk and finally said, "You know as much as I do, Maggie. You've read the letter."

"It doesn't tell us much about the problem. I've never heard of such a thing."

"Neither have I but I've got to go."

Maggie continued to help Gervase, and when the trunk was filled, she suddenly put her arms around Gervase and held her. "My prayers will go with you. You know that. If you need me, call and I'll be there the next minute, before you know it."

Gervase felt a sense of safety in the circle of the big woman's arms. She held her fiercely and then said, "I'll write you, Maggie, as soon as I find out anything. And now I must go. The coach leaves in less than an hour...."

# Chapter Nineteen

As Gervase descended from the carriage, she straightened her back and stared at Kimberly for a moment. She held Mr. Bob's basket firmly as memories came flooding back, and despite herself, a feeling of dread came over her. The past had a power to touch, and she well understood this. Sometimes in the night, memories of childhood would come back, mixing in with her dreams so that reality and that world were intermingled. Now just the sight of the stately house somehow frightened her. She did not believe in omens, yet the happy days she had known in this place seemed far away, set back in a place blurred by the passage of time.

Quickly she turned to the driver who had brought her from the station, paid him, and said, "Thank you very much. You may leave the luggage here."

"Thank you, miss. And good day to you."

Gervase heard her name called then, and she turned to see Lady Sarah, who had come outside. She was surprised to see her come down the steps and hold her arms out, but Gervase quickly set Mr. Bob down and took the embrace — and felt the better for it.

"Bates, take Miss Gervase's luggage to her room, the one next to Mr. Davis's."

"Yes mum. Good day to you, ma'am." Robert Bates still had the same pug-nosed, alert appearance. His red hair was redder than ever and his eyes bluer, and he grinned impishly. "Good to see you again. Indeed it is, ma'am."

"Thank you, Robert. You're looking well."

"Is that Mr. Bob you've got there?"

"Yes, it is. I couldn't do without him."

"Come along, Gervase. You must be exhausted after your long journey."

"It wasn't that bad, Lady Sarah."

"Well, I have tea and a small snack prepared. We'll be having dinner soon, so I don't want to spoil that. Your aunt's been cooking all day. They're all so anxious to see you."

The two women ascended the stairs and entered the house. Gervase smiled and spoke to Daisy Pennington, saying, "You're looking fine, Daisy. Prettier than ever."

"Thank you, Miss Gervase. It's so good to have you back."

"Would you please take Mr. Bob to my room?"

"That I will, miss."

Gervase followed Lady Sarah into the drawing room, and as soon as they were inside, the woman turned and said, "Sir Edward has gone to London on business. We're finding out how much of a burden Davis bore, keeping it going. Here. Sit down. Let me give you tea."

Gervase sat while Lady Sarah poured the tea. "You use sugar and cream, I believe."

"Yes ma'am. I'm surprised you remember after all this time."

Lady Sarah hesitated, put the cream and sugar in, and then handed the cup to Gervase. "It seems like another life. So much has happened."

"I was so shocked to get your letter."

"I knew you would be. I should have written earlier, right after the accident, but everything was happening and I couldn't seem to pull myself together."

"Is there any change at all in his condition?"

"No. Not a bit." Lady Sarah sat, picked up her cup, and sipped it. Her hands were unsteady, and there was a slight twitching around her mouth as she tried to gain control of herself. "It's been like nothing I ever dreamed of, Gervase. If he had been killed at once, it would have been a terrible shock. But that happens often and I suppose we get accustomed to such things. But poor Davis! To have to look at him lying as still as death and totally helpless. It's . . . it's hard to bear."

Compassion welled up in Gervase and she put the cup down. Leaning forward, she said, "Tell me what Dr. Thompson said."

She listened as Lady Sarah repeated the doctor's words. There was nothing new in them and finally Lady Sarah fell silent.

"Can't he move at all?"

"No. Well . . . well, for some reason he's able to swallow. The doctors can't understand that. He can only take liquids, so we have to make fine broth, as fluid as possible. Dr. Thompson thinks it's a reflexive response."

"I suppose you get him into a sitting position and then spoon it in a little at a time?"

"You're so quick, Gervase! Yes, that's exactly what we do."

"And these two attendants. They've had no training?"

Lady Sarah shook her head and her lips drew together in a tight line. "We only have one now. We had to get rid of the other one. This just happened yesterday. He was drinking."

"But have they worked in hospitals?"

"Not that I can find out. Roberta hired them. She said a friend of hers recommended them."

For a time the two women sat there, with Gervase trying to get every bit of information she could from Davis's mother. Suddenly a voice sounded and she turned to see Roberta Wingate enter. Gervase rose at once and said, "Good afternoon, Mrs. Wingate."

"Hello, Gervase." Roberta's tone was neutral at best, but there was disapproval in her eyes, and at once Gervase understood that she was still thinking of her displeasure over the letters she had exchanged with Davis.

"I was so sorry to hear of Mr. Wingate's accident."

"I'm sure you were." Roberta was wearing a lime green cashmere tea gown with a tight-fitting bodice. Her hair was done up in the latest fashion and she looked beautiful. But the coldness in her eyes set that off, at least for Gervase.

"I might as well tell you, Gervase, that I was not in agreement with Lady Sarah about sending for you."

"I'm sorry to hear that. What is your objection?"

Roberta tossed her head and a look of distaste passed across her features. "It's not suitable for a woman to take care of a man. There are . . . certain things that would be entirely out of place."

"If you mean by that," Gervase said evenly, keeping a pleasant expression only by effort, "bathing patients and taking care of their elimination, then you have to understand that's what I did in the Crimea."

"I'm sure it was very noble and all that, but it's better for a man to take care of those things."

Lady Sarah spoke up at once. "We've already discussed this, Roberta. I'm afraid Sir Edward and I are going to have to insist. We feel that Gervase is better trained to take care of Davis than the men you found."

An angry light flared in Roberta's eyes but she said, "Have it your own way," then turned and left the room.

"I'm sorry about that, Gervase. Perhaps I should have told you."

"She feels as many other people do — that there are certain aspects of taking care of the sick which aren't suitable for women. But I haven't found it so."

Lady Sarah rose and said, "I'm glad you're here." She held out her hands and Gervase took them. Lady Sarah's features were worn and marked with fatigue. "I'm *very* glad you're here," she said warmly. "Come, I'll take you to Davis."

The two women left the drawing room and walked down the broad hall. "We've kept Davis on the first floor. We have a bedroom on this floor, as you remember, and we put Davis in it. We've converted the small study into a bedroom. It will be yours, right next to Davis's."

"That will be convenient."

Gervase accompanied Lady Sarah to the end of the hall. When Lady Sarah opened the door, Gervase stepped inside, and her eyes immediately went to Davis. She saw his tall figure lying under a sheet, and he seemed to be sleeping, so peaceful were his features.

But at the next instant she caught the odor so familiar to her from her work in the hospital. Her glance went at once to the large man who had risen from a chair next to one of the windows. He tossed the paper down and stood staring at her.

"This is Emmett Bailey," Lady Sarah said. "Bailey, this is Miss Gervase Howard. She will be in charge of my son's care."

"Yes mum." Bailey was a hulking fellow with pale blue eyes set too close together. He was obviously very strong, but he had started going to fat and bulged out of his clothes. His hands were overly large and looked rough, like a farmer's or a black-smith's.

Gervase said, "I trust we will work well together, Bailey."

Bailey did not answer, merely nodded, but there was a sullen expression on his blunt features. "I can't do it all," he muttered.

"You won't have to do it all," Gervase said with asperity. She walked over to the bed, lifted the sheet, and then turned and put her gaze on Bailey. "The patient has soiled himself. Why hasn't he been cleaned up?"

"I ain't had time." The answer was insolent, and a clash of wills took place at once between the big man and Gervase. She studied him for a moment and then turned to face Lady Sarah. "Would you please excuse yourself, Lady Sarah? My patient needs care and at once. I'll be asking for several things that I don't see here."

"Anything you ask for, Gervase. If you can't find it, let me know." Lady Sarah took one agonized glance at the still form of Davis, then turned and fled the room.

As the door shut, Gervase stood directly in front of Bailey. "This patient hasn't been cared for."

"I cleaned him up this morning. I had it all to do myself. I can't do everything."

"You will address me as Miss Howard. Or Nurse Howard. You understand that?"

For a moment Gervase thought Bailey would walk out of the room. Anger flared in his pale eyes. "All right, Miss Howard."

Gervase studied him for a moment and said, "You're on trial here, Bailey. I haven't seen anything to indicate you're able to do your job, so you have one chance."

She waited for him to answer but he obviously was not going to.

"We're going to put the patient in that chair right there. Then you're going to take that mattress out. It's totally ruined. Why didn't you put an oilcloth sheet over it?"

"I ain't had none."

"Well, we'll get one, then. Come help me get him into the chair."

Bailey, for all his sullenness, was tremendously strong. He lifted Davis and put him in the chair, and then she said, "I'll take care of him. You remove the mattress and take it outside."

"What'll I do with it?"

"Burn it—but before you do that, get a fresh mattress and put it on this bed. Then go to the kitchen and get oilcloth from the cook. Tell her I asked for it. Is there fresh linen here?"

"I reckon so."

"You will say, 'Yes, Miss Howard.' Do you understand that? If you can't, get out."

Bailey straightened, shocked by the intensity of Gervase's gaze. "Yes, Miss Howard." He went quickly to the bed, pulled the soiled mattress off, and dragged it out. "Where will I get another mattress?" he called out.

"Go to any bedroom you find and take one. If anyone asks what you're doing, tell them it's my order."

Gervase was angry to the bone. She could not bear to see patients mistreated, and obviously Davis Wingate had received very little care. She stood beside him, holding him in the chair, and waited until Bailey came back dragging a mattress. He put it on the bed and spread out the oilcloth he had gotten from her aunt.

"Come here and be sure he doesn't slip while I put the covers on," Gervase said. She quickly put a sheet over the bed and then nodded. "Now put the patient back in the bed."

Bailey lifted Davis, letting his head drop back.

"Hold his head, you clumsy oaf! Don't let it fall like that!"

Gervase supervised Bailey's efforts, then said, "Now go get hot water, fresh cloths, and towels if there aren't any here. We're going to bathe him completely. If I ever see him in this condition again, you'll be dismissed immediately. Now get out!"

For the next hour Gervase worked over the limp body of Davis Wingate. She bathed him thoroughly, then rubbed light oil all over his body. She spoke only once to Bailey, who stood sullenly by, doing her bidding. "Didn't anyone ever tell you about bedsores, Bailey?"

"No one said nothin' about that."

"Look. There's one beginning right here. When a patient isn't turned, he gets bedsores. So from now on the patient will be turned constantly. No more than four hours in one position. Back, then one side, and then the other side. Even on his stomach for a change. And it'll be done gently."

By the time she had Davis completely cleansed and placed on his left side with a pillow holding his head up, a knock sounded at the door. She opened it and Sir Edward was there with Lady Sarah. "My dear, I'm so glad to see you," he said with relief in his voice.

"It's good to see you, Sir Edward. I've missed you." She felt his hand press her own and sensed his sincerity. "Come in and see how we're doing with your son."

The two came and stood beside the bed with Gervase.

"Why, he looks so much more comfortable," Lady Sarah said, "and that pleasant smell! What is it?"

"It's a little oil, Lady Sarah. When anyone has to stay in bed for long periods of time, they need to be kept very clean and they can't lie in one position. I was shocked to find out that Davis had been left on his back all this time. He has the beginning of a bedsore."

Sir Edward shot a glance at Bailey and his mouth tightened. "I wasn't aware of such things."

"I'm so glad you're here to see to that," Lady Sarah said. "Now, what else can we do?"

Gervase had thought about this a great deal. "The biggest danger is that the muscles will lose their tone. He must be exercised every day as much as possible."

"Exercised! But he can't move."

"If the muscles move, whether he moves them or someone else does, it will keep them flexible. Look. Like this." Gervase took Davis's right arm, which was outside the sheet. She lifted it slowly and then lowered it, then lifted it again. "This should be done at least fifty times a day and then the elbow should be flexed like this. Every muscle possible has to be exercised."

"Where did you learn all this, Gervase?" Sir Edward asked, somewhat in awe.

"From Miss Florence Nightingale. She's talked with doctors all over the world, and she's found that this treatment, when used, is most effective. When Davis regains consciousness, he mustn't be withered, his muscles weakened."

"You . . . you believe he'll recover?" Sir Edward asked with hesitation.

"I'm going to believe that he is. I don't know when but I assure you, Sir Edward and Lady Sarah, from now on my life is devoted to one thing — seeing Mr. Davis up and walking around and smiling again. That's my calling."

Tears came to Lady Sarah's eyes. "Bless you, my child! It's so good to have you with us."

The two stayed for a time, and as soon as they left the room, Sir Edward straightened and took a deep breath. "By George," he said emphatically, "I'm so glad that young woman is here!"

"She gives me hope, Edward."

"It's hard to believe that anything good will come out of this, isn't it?"

"God isn't dead," Lady Sarah said as they walked slowly down the hall. She put her hand on his arm and turned him around. "God told me to send for Gervase, and I think he did so for a purpose. We've got to help her every way we can."

"I've never liked the looks of that fellow Bailey."

"Neither have I. Davis wasn't being cared for properly at all, and he looked so awful! Now he looks so . . . so peaceful."

"Where did that Bailey chap come from?"

"He was recommended by one of Roberta's friends."

"Well, he hasn't done much that I approve of, but Gervase will see to it. She'll be looking out for Davis."

"Yes."

Later that day when Sir Edward made another visit to the sickroom, he had a word with Gervase. She looked at him directly and said, "The attendant's a heavy drinker. Have you noticed the veins in his nose and how bloodshot his eyes are? I can even smell it."

"I've noticed that."

"He's not very responsible, I think."

"If he doesn't suit, discharge him."

Gervase hesitated. "That may make trouble with Mrs. Wingate. She hired him."

"You let me worry about that, my dear! You do what you must, Gervase. Oh, by the way, Dr. Thompson is coming late this afternoon. I know you're anxious to see him."

"Yes, I am. I don't know him."

"He's a fine doctor. Comes highly recommended."

Dr. Thompson was a middle-aged man with a full black beard and jet-black hair. He was short and thickset and had stubby fingers, but there was a manner about him that Gervase liked at once. She had been around so many physicians and something about Dr. Thompson gave her confidence. As he examined Davis, he asked questions and then answered her own as honestly as possible. Finally he said, "We are working in the dark here, Miss Howard. Nothing like it in my experience, but I have written to other doctors all over the kingdom, trying to find out something about this situation."

"I'm sure you'll learn something, Doctor."

"Tell me about your time in the Crimea. By George, I so admire that woman Florence Nightingale!"

"Well you might. She's a marvelous woman."

Dr. Thompson listened as Gervase spoke about her experiences at the Barrack Hospital. He interrupted her several times and obviously was interested in the quality of nursing.

"Did you ever run into a case like this one?"

"As a matter of fact, Dr. Thompson, there was one. One of the soldiers, a sergeant, got a wound in the head from a shell. The injury itself wasn't bad and the doctors weren't afraid of that. But he was unconscious, just as Mr. Wingate is. He stayed unconscious for three weeks. We had to feed him as best we could and he lost a great deal of weight."

"But did he recover?"

"Yes sir, he did. No one knows why. For three weeks he didn't say a word, his eyes were closed, he didn't move. And then one morning he suddenly opened his eyes and began speaking, his voice very feeble and faint. After that he recovered rapidly."

"I wish we knew more about cases like this."

"I believe in the kind of treatment that Miss Nightingale has found effective." Gervase explained that she was convinced that exercising the muscles was the best medicine.

"I have heard of such things but it's so time-consuming. Most patients can't afford it and most doctors don't even know about it." His black eyes were keen. "I don't think you can do this all by yourself. You have some help?"

"I have an assistant, sir."

"Make sure you follow this treatment. We pray God that it will work." Dr. Thompson smiled. "Well, I have no instructions for you, Miss Howard. You are far more qualified than I to take care of a patient in this condition. I'll come by often and you let me know if there's any change at all."

"Certainly, Doctor, and may I say I think Mr. Wingate's very fortunate to have you as his physician."

"Well, thank you, Miss Howard. It's kind of you to say so. And I think he is most fortunate to have you as his nurse."

# Chapter Twenty

Martha stirred the mix in the large bowl vigorously but kept her eyes fixed on Gervase. The two women were sitting in the kitchen, where Martha was preparing to bake and at the same time listening to Gervase speak of her experiences in the Crimea. From time to time Martha shook her head. Finally she exclaimed, "My, what a terrible time that must have been!" She put the bowl down and, pulling out large dollops of dough, began to form the loaves that would be placed into the oven. "We've missed you so much, Gervase. George and I talked so often about the possibility of your coming back."

"I didn't suppose I ever would," Gervase said. She was sitting at the table, peeling an apple, and paused to cut off a slice and nibble at it. "If it hadn't been for poor Mr. Wingate's accident, I probably wouldn't have come here."

"Oh, it's a terrible thing! A fine, strong man like him, helpless as a baby." Martha patted the dough, set it aside, and started forming another loaf before saying, "Do you think there's any chance, dear, that he'll ever come out of it?"

"There's always hope, Aunt Martha — always!" Gervase smiled and said, "This is a good apple." Rising, she said, "I've got to go take care of my patient now. The broth you've been making him is very good."

"The poor man. I wish I could do more."

Gervase left the kitchen, and as she made her way to the sickroom, she reviewed the past three days. She had settled into a routine and had schooled herself never to say or even think a discouraging thought. She was well aware that the Wingate family was stricken by Davis's plight, and she had made it a point to be cheerful at all times when around them. Only at night, when she was alone in her room, did doubt creep in on her. When that occurred, she would throw herself into a spiritual battle — reading promises in the Scriptures, singing hymns, and at times even speaking aloud her resistance to the Devil. She had never done this before but she found it to be very effective.

The sun was throwing bright bars on the carpet in Davis's room, through the French doors and the windows on either side. Motes moved in the sunbeams like tiny dancers, but Gervase had no time for this. She glanced at Bailey, who was slumped in the chair as usual, reading a newspaper, then began to examine Davis. Indignation rose in her and she turned to face the big man.

"Bailey, you haven't done a proper job of cleaning up the patient."

The attendant threw the newspaper down and got to his feet, a scowl on his face. "I done the best I could!"

"Well, your best isn't good enough! Now you'd better go, because you're coming on duty at three o'clock and you'll stay on until midnight. Do you understand that?"

"I ain't deaf!" Bailey said, his tone dripping resentment. He turned and walked out, closing the door with more force than necessary.

"Something's got to be done about that man." Gervase considered for a moment, then went to the washstand and filled a pan with the lukewarm water. She pulled out Davis's shaving things, tested the razor, stropped it a few times, then put the articles on a tray and brought them to his bed. Setting them down, she said cheerfully, "Well now, Mr. Davis Wingate. How would you like a nice shave?" She ran her hand over his cheek and shook her head. "You've got to be neater than this. I want your cheeks to be like a baby's skin."

Expertly she worked up a white lather on the brush and applied it to Davis's still face. During her time in the Crimea, she had become quite adept at shaving men. It had all begun with a young soldier who had lost both hands when a shell exploded. She had practiced on him and later others asked for this service.

She picked up the razor and, turning Davis's head, moved it smoothly down the cheek. She worked efficiently, moving his head from side to side and working very carefully under his nose.

"There," she said when she had finished. "How does that feel?" She cleaned his face off with a damp cloth, then applied some lotion and brushed his hair back. "You look very handsome today, Davis Wingate," she said. "Now you're going to get a first-class workout."

Pulling the sheet back, she began moving his right leg by bending his knee and pushing his leg until it would move no farther, then stretching it out. As she did, she sang to him bits of songs, interrupting herself to speak to him exactly as if he could hear her.

She exercised him for an hour, and by then she herself was tired and perspiring. The room was warm and she wiped her face, then washed her hands and sat beside him. "Now it's time for a reading. Today I'm going to read the eleventh chapter of John, one of my favorite chapters in the whole Bible. Do you remember it, Davis? I'm sure you do."

She began reading in a clear voice, carefully articulating the words. "'Now a certain man was sick, named Lazarus, of Bethany, the town of Mary and her sister Martha. . . .'" She read the entire chapter and then laid the Bible down and stood.

"Isn't that a wonderful story? I remember a sermon by Mr. Spurgeon at the Metropolitan Tabernacle. Oh, it was such a great message! He said that Mary and Martha must have been terribly disappointed — and Lazarus too, of course — when Jesus didn't come. But when the disciples asked him about it, Jesus said that the sickness was for the glory of God."

Taking Davis's hand, she stroked it as she spoke. "They had seen Jesus do miracles, Mr. Spurgeon said, and now he was letting one whom he loved die."

From outside, where gardeners were working in the beds, came the sound of voices. They sounded happy and carefree, and as a counterpoint came the song of a thrush which had perched just outside the window.

For a time she paused to listen to the bird. Then she said, "But Jesus did come and he raised Lazarus from the dead. I've always thought that was so wonderful but a little puzzling too. Where do you suppose Lazarus went during that time when he was dead? Mr. Spurgeon said he probably hated to come back. There he was in heaven, and now he had to come back and die all over again. I suppose he was the only man who ever died twice. Do you think so, Davis?"

She talked for a long time, then finally put his hand down and laid her own gently on his chest. "I'm going to pray for you now, and I'm going to ask that the same Jesus who raised Lazarus from the dead will bring you back from wherever you are. If you can hear me, Davis, you pray with me."

She prayed then and found herself caught up in a zealous prayer that was unusual for her. She was a calm young woman as a rule, but she was astonished to hear herself crying out with all the fervency within her.

Finally she stopped and gave a half laugh. "There, I've become a shouting Methodist, I suppose." She stood there for a moment looking at his face, thinking of the times when his eyes had flashed and how he had laughed so that his whole expression lit up. She leaned over and whispered, "I'm going to take care of you, Davis, and God is going to bring you out of this!" She hesitated for a moment, then kissed his forehead. Straightening, she said, "There! You see what a forward woman I am." She sat in the chair and began to read, listening from time to time to the thrush's song and letting her glance fall on the still figure that lay on the bed.

As Gervase sat quietly at the table, taking her meal with the family, she suddenly remembered the small house she grew up in. The whole thing could probably have fitted within the large dining room of the Wingate family home. She looked at the gilt-wood side serving table, at the two George III candelabras shedding their light, at the china cupboard which displayed the best crystal glasses. *This is such a beautiful room and Davis has had so many meals here.* Even as she thought this, she prayed silently. *God, bring him back to himself and to this place and to his family again.*

She glanced at Roberta, who sat to her right on the opposite side of the table. Ives sat beside her, and the two were talking of the popular drama they had both seen. Gervase let her eyes travel down to Sir Edward, who had barely touched his food. *He doesn't look well. He's not eating right, and I don't think he sleeps well, either.*

Her glance then ran to Lady Sarah, who was wearing a dark-blue satin dress that matched her eyes exactly. She was an attractive woman, and Gervase knew that she also was suffering over the illness of her son.

Mrs. Smith, the relatively new housekeeper, appeared from time to time, checking to be sure that the food and the wine were replenished. She was a small woman, dark-haired with warm brown eyes, and she had made a good place for herself here at Kimberly.

Sir Edward suddenly said, "I suppose the food situation was bad in the Crimea, Gervase."

"It was very bad, sir. Especially at first. Miss Nightingale had to spend her own money to buy food for the wounded."

"That's terrible!" Lady Sarah cried. "How in the world could such a thing happen?"

"England really wasn't ready for a war," Gervase said. "Someone said England's always trying to win the current war with the last war's tactics."

Ives gave her a curious glance. "Wasn't it a pretty nasty business over there?"

"It was very hard, sir."

"You must have suffered quite a bit," Ives remarked.

"Oh, I didn't mean on me. I meant on the poor soldiers." She hesitated and then said, "I wish you could have seen Davis. He worked so hard and did so much for the wounded, and his commanding officer told me that he was one of the best soldiers he'd ever had."

"Did he really say that?" Sir Edward asked, his eyes lighting up. "It's good to hear."

Ives was toying with his wineglass. "Gervase, how much hope is there for Davis?"

Gervase knew this was on all of their minds. She said quickly, "There's always hope. With God nothing is impossible." She spoke of how she had seen many terribly wounded men who seemed certain to die but survived.

"But this is worse," Roberta said quickly. "The doctors don't even know what to think."

"It is a difficult case but I believe that Mr. Wingate will recover."

"I spoke with a doctor in London about my husband," Roberta said, her eyes fixed on Gervase. "He said that all these things you are doing, these exercises, are a waste of time. He never heard of such a thing." She turned to face her in-laws, saying, "I think it's simply a waste of money."

Lady Sarah said in a voice that was soft but covered a steely ring, "I think we can spare the money, Roberta."

Gervase noted then that Roberta, who was outspoken to a fault, could not meet Lady Sarah's eyes. She dropped her head and shoved her fork savagely into the piece of beef on her plate.

"While we are on the subject," Gervase said, "I must tell you that I think Bailey is not suitable for his position."

Roberta looked up, her eyes flashing. "He's strong and he's able to handle Davis. I chose him myself."

"I know, Mrs. Wingate, but there's a lot more to taking care of a patient than just moving him physically."

"Well, I'm satisfied with him!" Roberta said, and there was challenge in her expression as she glared at Gervase.

"I think," Gervase said carefully, her voice well modulated, "that you were deceived in the man. He drinks and he doesn't carry out my orders." She glanced quickly around the room and saw the others staring at her. "I've been meaning to bring this up privately with you, Sir Edward, but I think it's very important that Mr. Wingate be kept absolutely clean, that he be turned every four hours without fail, and that he be exercised."

"It's foolishness!" Roberta snapped.

Ignoring his daughter-in-law, Sir Edward said, "What do you suggest?"

"I left orders for Bailey to exercise the patient exactly as I taught him, and I laid a trap for him."

"A trap? What are you talking about?" Roberta asked.

"I put a piece of very fine thread over his ankles. It would be impossible to exercise him without disturbing that thread. I'm going now to see if it's still there." She looked then at Roberta and said evenly, "If it is, I'm afraid he will have to be discharged."

Sir Edward got up at once. "I'll go with you, Gervase."

"And I'll go, too," Roberta said angrily. She wanted to say more but, seeing that Sir Edward was watching her with a hard expression in his eyes, she shut her lips.

Gervase had not intended to make a spectacle of this, but she saw that they were determined. She led the way as all of them left the dining room and turned down the hallway. She opened the door to Davis's room and went in, followed immediately by Lady Sarah and Roberta and then the men.

Bailey was sitting in the chair, as he usually was, but he sprang up at once. His face was flushed and he was overwhelmed by the presence of the family.

"Bailey," Gervase said evenly as she stood before him, "did you exercise the patient as I told you?"

"Why . . . sure I did."

Gervase watched him for a moment and then turned and moved to the bed. She picked up the sheet and lifted it to expose the lower part of Davis's legs. She did not speak but her eyes went to Sir Edward. He came over and saw the fine thread still in place. "It's exactly where I put it, sir."

Sir Edward turned and his face was florid as he stared at Bailey. "You are discharged! Be out of this house within an hour!"

It was clear that Bailey had been drinking. He started to bluster but Ives stepped forward. "You heard what my father said. Come with me. I'll see that you get your wages to date. Come now!"

Gervase watched as they left, and Roberta gave her a look that could have killed. She turned and walked out.

"Roberta's upset," Lady Sarah said, "but this was the right thing to do."

"It leaves you in a rather hard place, Gervase," Sir Edward said. "We'll have to find someone else."

"I have a suggestion to make, sir."

"A suggestion? What is it?"

"I've worked for several years with a woman named Maggie MacKay. She was with me in the Crimea. She's a large woman, very strong, and the best nurse I have ever seen."

"Do you think she would take a position here?" Lady Sarah asked at once.

"I think she would."

Sir Edward's jaw was tense, but his eyes went to his son lying on the bed, still as a human could be. "Get her here, Gervase. Write a letter now and I'll have Brodie take it personally. Tell her to name her wages. You must have help, and this woman sounds as if she'd be a godsend."

"I'll write the letter right now, sir. And thank you both." She hesitated, then added, "I'm sorry if I've disturbed Mrs. Wingate."

"She'll get over it," Sir Edward said. "You write your letter and I'll find Brodie."

Gervase straightened Davis's sheet and smiled down at him. "Now then, you're going to get some really fine care. Maggie's the finest woman I know."

The scene with Bailey had taken something out of Gervase. She knew she had made an enemy of Roberta Wingate, and that somehow the woman would get her revenge. But she could not think of that. He had to be dismissed.

As Gervase walked to the washstand, her cat strolled in. "Mr. Bob, what are you doing in here?"

She picked him up and sat in the chair with him in her lap. She stroked his fur and said, "Would you like a song, Mr. Bob? What would you care to hear?"

Mr. Bob yawned hugely and began to lick his paws.

"You're not much of a music critic." Gervase looked at Davis and asked, "What would you like, Mr. Wingate? Something sad or something happy?" She thought for a moment and then lifted her voice and began to sing,

*"Amazing grace, how sweet the sound*
*That saved a wretch like me*
*I once was lost but now am found*
*Was blind but now I see...."*

# Chapter Twenty-One

M aggie, you have a visitor."
Maggie MacKay had just administered a strong dose of laudanum to a patient in great pain. She laid the man down, whispering, "You'll feel better now. Just lie still." Straightening, she looked at Sister Marie and asked, "A visitor? Who is it?"

"I couldn't say but he asked for you. He's out in the office. A country type, I think."

Maggie turned and left the ward, moved to her left, and after making two turns stepped into the receiving room, where she found a large man waiting for her.

"Is this Mrs. MacKay?"

"I'm Maggie MacKay."

"I'm Brodie McLean, ma'am. I have a letter for you from Miss Howard."

As she took the letter, Maggie glanced at the man who stood before her. He was very large indeed! She guessed he would top six inches over six feet, and he was strongly built. He had a squarish face and his hair was neatly trimmed. His eyes watched her with some curiosity, and she noted that his hands were the largest she had ever seen.

Opening the letter, she read it quickly. It was very brief.

*Maggie,*

   *I need you desperately! Mr. Wingate is in poor condition, and I have just lost the assistant who was here when I came. Good riddance, but I need you, Maggie. If you can come, Sir Edward and Lady Sarah would be most grateful, as would I. If you can come with the bearer of this letter, please do! The need is great.*

*Love,*
*Gervase*

Maggie folded the letter and said, "You know what the letter says?"

"Yes, Mrs. MacKay. She'd like vurry well for you to come to her."

The burr of old Scotland was in the man's voice and Maggie looked at him more closely. "You're from Scotland, are you?"

"Yes ma'am, I am indeed!"

"Well, I've got to talk to my superior, and if she gives me permission, I'll need to go to my apartment and pack everything."

"Miss Gervase said for me to do whatever you say."

"Very well. Wait here and I'll go make the arrangements."

The arrangements were easy enough to make. Miss Nightingale listened as Maggie explained the situation, and then said, "Well, you must go to her at once, Maggie. Stay as long as you need to. Then when you want to come back, the door will be open."

Maggie left the hospital, and Brodie McLean waited as she packed. There was a great deal to do, for Maggie had decided to give up the apartment. The position at Kimberly sounded as if it would be long-term.

The last trunk, the largest of all, would not close, she had crammed so many things into it. She pushed at it futilely but then the big man stepped forward and said, "Let me help you, ma'am." He leaned over and closed the trunk easily, fastened the latch, then picked it up as if it were filled with feathers. "Is this the last, Mrs. MacKay?"

"Yes. I'm ready." He motioned for her to go first and she stepped out of the room. Having already settled with the landlord, she went out to the carriage. It was a large phaeton and was loaded heavily with all the baggage.

"Do you think the horses can pull such a load?"

"Oh yes. There's no problem." McLean put the big trunk on, tied it down, and then came around and held out his hand. Maggie stared at it for a moment, not knowing what he wanted, then flushed. She took it and he helped her inside the carriage. As he stepped in on the other side to sit beside her, she said, "I'm *Miss* MacKay, not Mrs."

"You're not married, ma'am?"

"No. I've never been married."

The big man was silent and Maggie turned to meet his gaze. There was a strength in the man, obviously in his body but also in his eyes. "There's a waste of a woman," he remarked.

Maggie stared at him and then flushed again. "Drive on. We need to get there as quickly as possible."

"Yes, Miss MacKay."

"You don't have to call me 'Miss' at all. My name is Maggie. They call me Sister Maggie at the hospital."

"Sister Maggie it is, then."

Maggie sat still, somewhat stunned over the rapidity of what had taken place. Finally she turned to face the driver and asked, "How long have you been in this country?"

"Seven years. My good mother died and there was nae other kin there."

Thinking he might have a wife, Maggie asked curiously, "Do you have a family here?"

"Me? Oh no. Just myself."

"What part of Scotland was your home?"

"I lived in a wee village called Tilly Fourie," he said. "That's just east of Aberdeen."

"Tilly Fourie! Why, I've been there many times."

Brodie McLean turned to her, his eyes wide. "You tell me that!"

"Yes. My home was in Banchory, not twenty miles from there."

"I've been there often. Through it, at least." He smiled broadly and shook his head with surprise. "We're fellow Scots, then. Always good to find a countryman — or countrywoman, I might say."

"It is strange," Maggie remarked.

"Did you ever go to the fair at Aberdeen?" he asked.

"Oh yes. Every year. We might have seen each other."

"No, I don't think so. I would have remembered you. Be sure of that."

Maggie was somewhat at a loss as to how to take the big man. He seemed a simple fellow, yet she sensed a wit in him. He began to speak easily of the old country and she found herself opening up to him.

Gervase flew out of the house and embraced Maggie, who leaped to the ground before Brodie could help her. "I'm so glad to see you, Maggie!"

"And I'm glad to see you, too."

"Miss Florence didn't object to your coming?"

"No. She thought you probably needed me more than she did."

"Where shall I put the baggage, Miss Gervase?" Brodie asked. He had dismounted and was standing at the rear of the carriage.

"In my old room upstairs. I think you'll have to make several trips."

"I brought everything," Maggie said. "It didn't sound like we'd be going back soon."

"No, I think you're right," Gervase said. "Well, come along."

Maggie reached down to pick up a heavy suitcase but felt her hand being pushed aside. "Now, Sister Maggie, you let me take care of this baggage. As the Scripture says, 'Bear ye one another's burdens.'"

"There you have it," Gervase said with a laugh. "I suppose you've been peppered with quotations. Brodie knows more of the Bible than anyone I ever saw and can find a Scripture for everything."

Maggie smiled. "Thank you, Brodie. Do you read the Bible a great deal?"

Brodie's face changed. "I canna' read," he said, "but I remember everything."

"That's true. He could quote a whole sermon, I think."

"I missed out on learnin' how to read, or maybe I'm just too stupid."

"Of course you're not. Don't say that!" Maggie said, speaking rather sharply.

"Maybe I'll be able to read when I cross the river to the other side."

"You don't have to wait until then," Maggie said. "I could teach you to read myself."

"I doubt it, Sister Maggie. My head's as thick as a block of wood."

Maggie MacKay shook her head. She loved a challenge and said, "If you're smart enough to remember that much Scripture, it wouldn't take much for you to learn your letters."

"I've told him that myself," Gervase said, smiling. "But he's a stubborn fellow. Now come along. We need to get you settled."

❧

The lamps were turned down and Maggie and Gervase were having a cup of tea. They had moved a table between the two chairs across from Davis's bed, and now as they drank the tea, Gervase felt the fatigue run out of her. "I'm so tired," she said. "If you hadn't come, Maggie, I don't know what I would have done."

"You're wore out, dearie. As soon as you finish that tea, you go right to bed."

The two had gone over the care of the patient carefully. Maggie was a powerful woman and could turn Davis quite easily. She agreed wholeheartedly with the treatment Gervase had prescribed.

Now as the two sat, she studied Gervase. Her thoughts ran along familiar lines. She suspected that Gervase had feelings for this man, feelings she kept tightly bottled up.

Gervase suddenly said, "Maggie, I haven't told you another part of the treatment."

"And what's that, Gervase?"

"Well, when I first came and saw Davis — Mr. Wingate — lying there so still and unable to move, I thought, *What if he can hear us?* Nobody was speaking to him, Maggie. So . . . well, when I'm alone with him, I talk to him. Just cheerful things. Sometimes I sing to him or read to him. If he can hear, it must be a comfort to him."

"Of course it is, and I'll do the same thing. Is that what you'd like?"

"Yes, Maggie." Gervase's eyes danced and she said, "You could always sing so well."

"I have just the thing for him," Maggie said. She got up and stood beside Davis. "What you need is a good dose of poetry, and there's only one poet whom I trust, and that's Bobby Burns, a fine Scotsman." She winked at Gervase and then began to quote as Gervase left the room,

*"Oh, my love is like a red, red rose,*
*That's newly sprung in June.*
*Or my love is like the melody,*
*That's sweetly played in tune.*
*As fair art thou, my bonnie lass,*
*So deep in love am I,*
*And I will love thee still, my dear,*
*Till all the seas go dry.*
*Till all the seas go dry, my dear,*
*And the rocks melt with the sun!*
*And I will love thee still, my dear,*
*While the sands of life shall run.*
*And fare thee well, my only love,*
*And fare thee well a while!*
*And I will come again, my love,*
*Though it were ten thousand miles!"*

Gervase stood at the door listening to the beautiful poem and looking at the gentleness on Maggie's face. *She has such love,* she thought, *and no man to give it to.*

She started down the hallway toward her own room, but Ives suddenly turned the corner, coming out of the library. Seeing her, he asked, "Is there any change?"

"Not really, but now that Miss MacKay is here, he'll get much better care."

Ives studied her face. "Why do things like this happen, Gervase? Doesn't God care?"

"Why . . . of course he cares, Mr. Ives."

Ives dropped his gaze, then without another word suddenly turned and walked rapidly toward the stairs. Gervase watched him, wondering, and said aloud, "He's hurting for his brother. He surely is."

⌇

The knock came and the door opened at once as Ives looked up from his book. Roberta entered and shut the door behind her. She was wearing a nightdress, for it was after midnight. Ives stood and she came to him and put her arms around him.

Ives did not return the embrace, and she asked, "What's the matter, Ives?"

"I . . . I feel terrible, Roberta!"

"About what?"

"About us — the way we've treated Davis."

At once Roberta became aggressive. She held him closely and whispered, "We couldn't help ourselves! We were in love long before I married Davis."

"You should have married me. I tried to get you to marry me."

"We'd have had nothing, not even a roof over our heads."

Ives sighed. "He's my only brother, Roberta. I've betrayed him. I can't bear to think of it!"

Roberta Wingate was not a brilliant woman but she was a clever one — especially where men were concerned. She had been over this before with Ives, and it always ended the same. She would whisper to him about how love can't be denied. She would caress him and sooner or later he would cease to resist.

And so it happened, as ever before. As he weakened, Roberta hid the smile and pressed herself against him. "We love each other, Ives — that's all that matters!"

# Chapter Twenty-Two

Maggie sat in the chair beside Davis as he lay as still as stone. On her lap lay the thick black Bible whose cover was worn and thin and whose pages were even more so. Her voice was the only sound in the room.

> *"And I turned to see the voice that spake with me. And being turned, I saw seven golden candlesticks;*
>
> *And in the midst of the seven candlesticks one like unto the Son of man, clothed with a garment down to the foot, and girt about the paps with a golden girdle.*
>
> *His head and his hairs were white like wool, as white as snow; and his eyes were as a flame of fire;*
>
> *And his feet like unto fine brass, as if they burned in a furnace; and his voice as the sound of many waters.*
>
> *And he had in his right hand seven stars: and out of his mouth went a sharp two-edged sword: and his countenance was as the sun shineth in his strength.*
>
> *And when I saw him, I fell at his feet as dead — "*

Maggie broke off suddenly and glanced toward the bracket clock that sat in the center of the mantel over the fireplace. Every day for her three weeks at Kimberly, she had studied the clock, loving the chiming sounds as it tolled the half hours and the hours. She kept her eyes fixed on it now as it chimed with its silver voice. It was a George III ormolu-mounted tortoise shell and enameled clock made for the Turkish market. There was something exotic about it that Maggie liked, the dome top and the flambeau finial and the pierced trellis sound frets.

Her lips moved as she counted the chimes, and then she turned back toward Davis and said cheerfully, "Well now. Eight o'clock. Almost time for your supper. I'd better be goin' to get it now." She closed the Bible and stood. "That's the Lord Jesus we were reading about, Mr. Davis. I like to think of him sometimes like this. Of course, I like to think of him being born in the manger, a human child just like the rest of us, but that was only half of it, wasn't it? He's now seated at the right hand of the Father, just as John saw him here in the book of Revelation."

She patted his arm. "I don't understand that book too well but I love to read it. My father read it all his life. As a matter of fact, he had a dog he named Revelation. When I asked him why, his eyes sparkled and he said, 'Because just like the book in the Bible, I don't understand a thing about him. He's totally mysterious.'" Maggie laughed and shook her head. "Well, I'll be goin' to get your meal."

But as she put the Bible on the shelf and turned to leave, the door opened, and to Maggie's surprise Roberta Wingate entered, bearing a tray with something under a silver cover and a glass of milk.

"Why, Mrs. Wingate, what's this?" Maggie asked. Her mind was working quickly, for Roberta had never offered to help with the care of her husband. Sometimes whole days went by when she did not come to the sickroom, and as for any of the more unpleasant aspects of caring for an immobile patient, she had never once volunteered.

"I thought I'd bring my husband's meal," Roberta said. She was wearing a light-blue dressing gown made of velveteen and lace, with an overdress of cashmere. Her hair was piled high on her head in one of the newer fashions. Setting the tray on the table beside Davis's bed, she said, "I put a little special seasoning in it, although I'm sure he won't know the difference."

"Well, that's very kind of you, Mrs. Wingate," Maggie said at once. She waited for Mrs. Wingate to leave but the woman made no move.

"I thought I'd have a try at feeding him myself."

"It's a little difficult, ma'am. It's very slow. A spoonful at a time."

Roberta glanced at Davis. "He has to be sitting?"

"Yes ma'am," Maggie said doubtfully. But there was determination in Roberta Wingate's eyes, so Maggie adroitly pulled Davis up to a sitting position. She was a very strong woman and needed to be, for it took strength and skill to lift Davis and put pillows behind his back for a bolster. They had to be arranged on each side so he would not slip down, but she was expert in this skill.

Roberta lifted the silver cover, revealing a bowl of soup. She filled the spoon as Maggie covered Davis's chest with a large cloth and tucked it around his neck.

"I don't know why it is, Mrs. Wingate, that he's still able to swallow."

"He was able to do that from the first." Roberta leaned forward and carefully touched the spoon to Davis's lips, but she found them tightly closed. "What's wrong? Why doesn't he take it?"

"I'm sure I don't know, ma'am. He usually does."

Roberta made another attempt but Davis's lips were sealed tight. She frowned. "I don't understand. Don't you just feed him like this?"

"Yes ma'am. Usually he takes it right away. I've never seen this before."

Roberta tried a few more times but had no success. Then she turned away with an impetuous motion. "Well, I tried," she said with asperity. "I'll leave it to you." She put down the spoon and left the room quickly, closing the door behind her.

"Well, what's wrong with you, Mr. Davis?" Maggie took the spoon and tried to feed Davis, but his lips were still tight. Surprised, Maggie shook her head. "I'll have to ask Miss Gervase about this."

She put the cover back over the broth and sat, keeping her eyes fixed on Davis's face. She wondered about the incident, for it was strange indeed. A thought came to her and she muttered, "Maybe there's something in that new seasoning that he doesn't like." It did not seem likely and yet she had some time before Gervase would come to relieve her. Making her decision, she left the room and went at once to the kitchen. She poured out the soup Roberta had brought and found the broth they had been feeding Davis in the evenings. She put it on the fire to heat, and then as she stood there pondering the strangeness of it all, she was startled when a voice said, "Good evening, Sister Maggie."

"Oh, hello, Brodie." Maggie turned to face the big man, who came to stand before her. "How have you been doing with your reading?"

"Not as fast as I'd like, but wud ye like to hear me?"

"Yes, I would."

Brodie took a book from the side pocket of his coat. It was a child's book which Maggie had found for him, very simple. Opening it, he began to read. He had actually done very well at learning his letters, and when he finished reading and looked up, there was a glow of pride in his eyes.

"That's very good, Brodie. You're doing so well."

"I can't wait until I can start to read the Bible. But there's sae many long words in it!"

"You'll be reading like a minister in a year. Wait and see."

Brodie looked down at Maggie, his face bright with pleasure. "I can't begin to tell you how much it means to me."

"I've enjoyed it, Brodie. I truly have."

Indeed, Maggie had enjoyed being with Brodie. They had spent many hours together when they found the spare time. They had talked about Scotland, and their love for Robert Burns tied them even closer together.

Finally Brodie slipped the book in his pocket. Something seemed to be on his mind, for he stood there rather awkwardly.

"Is there anything wrong, Brodie?"

"No, not wrong. I've just been wondering about something."

"Wondering about what?"

"I'm wondering — if you have a sweetheart."

Maggie felt her face growing warm. "No, I never have."

"That's vurry hard to understand."

"No, it isn't. Men want small, pretty women. What's hard about that?"

"Some men, I suppose, but those of us who are oversized, what wud we do with a small woman? Wear her as an ornament on our watch chain?"

The issue had always depressed Maggie. She usually steered conversation around such things and had put all thoughts of romance and marriage out of her mind.

"I'm just too big, Brodie."

"Too big? No!" Brodie moved very quickly. He reached out and lifted her toward the ceiling as if she were a child. "You're not too big for a fellow my size."

"Brodie, put me down!"

Maggie felt strange being held so lightly and so easily. All her life she had seen men help women smaller than herself, picking them up sometimes and placing them in carriages, simply showing off their strength, but no man had ever done this with her. She put her hands on his arms and felt her face glowing. "Please put me down."

Brodie obediently lowered her to the floor and said, "Now, you see? You're nae too big at all for the right man."

"You're very strong, Brodie, but that doesn't change me. I'm a plain woman."

Brodie suddenly grew serious, and he held her eyes with his own and whispered, "'Behold, thou art fair, my love; thou art fair. . . . Thy lips are like a thread of scarlet, and thy speech is comely: thy temples are like a piece of a pomegranate within thy locks. . . . Thou art all fair, my love; there is no spot in thee.'"

Maggie could not move for a moment. In all her life, no man had ever paid her a compliment, and now the beautiful words from Solomon's song had been applied to her. Speechless, she stood there looking into Brodie's face. She had heard many cruel remarks about her personal appearance, but there was nothing but warm respect and admiration on the face of Brodie McLean.

She stammered, "Th–thank you, Brodie. That's lovely."

"Only true, Sister Maggie. Now, I have been wurking up to ask you a question."

"Ask me what?"

Brodie cleared his throat and seemed to find difficulty speaking. "Maybe you wud allow me take you to chapel on Sunday."

"Oh no, I couldn't do that!" Maggie said at once, flustered by his request.

Maggie saw grief and embarrassment on Brodie's face. "I shouldn't have asked you, a rough fellow like me."

Maggie MacKay was a sensitive woman, for all her size. She hated to hurt anyone, and she suddenly understood that she had hurt this man — who was, she knew, sensitive for all his size. Something came to her then and she said, "I'm sorry, Brodie. I didn't mean to be so abrupt. If you'd like, I'll be glad to go to chapel with you."

Brodie's face immediately broke into a smile. He was not a handsome man, but there was a strong masculinity about him, and his eyes began to glow as he said, "Well, that's vurry good. You'll like the minister at the chapel where I go."

"I'm sure I will."

Brodie left the room and Maggie found that she was shaken. It had been only a brief encounter, but nothing like it had ever come to her before. Her hands were unsteady as she poured the warm broth into a bowl. Walking toward Davis's room, she found herself looking forward to going to church in the company of a strong man.

When she entered the room, she discovered that Gervase had already come to relieve her.

"I wondered where you were," Gervase said, smiling.

"Well, it's a strange thing. Mrs. Wingate brought some soup down for Mr. Davis, and you know what? When she tried to feed him, he closed his lips tightly and wouldn't take it."

Surprise washed across Gervase's face. "He's never done that before."

"I know. It was very strange. She gave up and left, and when I tried to feed him, it was the same. She said she put in some extra spices. I thought maybe he didn't like it."

"Well, let's see if he likes this."

Gervase took the tray, put it down, and when she put the spoon to Davis's lips, they opened and he swallowed obediently. "Well, he's taking his broth fine right now. I don't understand what happened."

"Maybe it was the spices."

Maggie watched as Gervase fed Davis, and when Gervase finished and removed the cloth from his neck, Maggie picked up the tray. She hesitated for so long, however, that Gervase asked, "What's wrong, Maggie?"

"Well, nothing."

"Come on. I can see something's troubling you."

"Gervase, Brodie asked me to go to chapel with him Sunday."

"He did? Well, that's fine. You two are getting along so well."

"But I've never done that before. I've never gone with a man anywhere. I was always too plain and outsized."

Gervase put her hand on Maggie's arm. She had to look up into the woman's face as she said, "When you stand beside Brodie, you don't seem large at all. And you look fine. I'll tell you what. Why don't we get you a new dress. You haven't had one since I've known you."

"That's vanity, Gervase."

"No, it's being a woman. We're going to make you look especially nice. Now, go along with you."

Midnight arrived and the ormolu clock chimed twelve silver notes, filling the sickroom with their melody. Gervase waited until the last note had sounded, then stood up, her book in hand. She had been reading *Jane Eyre* to Davis for over a week and now had come to the end. "Midnight, Davis, and we're at the end of the book. I hope you liked it. I think it's a wonderful story. You gave it to me for my birthday, remember?" Gervase opened the book and looked down at the page. "They had such trouble, Mr. Rochester and Jane Eyre. She reminds me a little of me. A plain woman coming to a big house, exactly as I have done, and then falling in love with — " She broke off then and shook her head. "Well, it's just a story, but it's so wonderful the way it ends. She says simply, 'Reader, I married him.' So that's the way books should end. A man and a woman getting married. And listen to this. She tells at the very last what it's like to be married to the man she loves:

"I have now been married ten years. I know what it is to live entirely for and with what I love best on earth. I hold myself supremely blessed — blessed beyond what language can express; because I am my husband's life as fully as he is mine. No woman was ever nearer to her mate than I am: ever more absolutely bone of his bone and flesh of his flesh. I know no weariness of my Edward's society: he knows none of mine, any more than we do of the pulsation of the heart that beats in our separate bosom."

Suddenly Gervase's voice broke and she was shocked to hear herself utter a little sob. Quickly she pulled her handkerchief out and covered her face. When she removed the handkerchief, it was damp with the tears that had come unbidden to her eyes. "Do you think I'm foolish, Davis? I suppose I am."

The silence was heavy in the room, and Gervase stood beside Davis, looking down into his face. He was, in her mind, the handsomest man who had ever lived. The sickness that had removed some flesh from his cheeks might make him look weaker but not less handsome. She stroked his blond hair.

"I'm an incurable romantic, just like Jane Eyre, Davis. I fell in love with you when I first came to this place. You didn't know that, did you? When you rescued me the first time we met, I loved you for it. And during the weeks that followed, when I was so lonely, you were always so kind. I couldn't help myself, Davis."

She suddenly dropped the book and put her hands on his cheeks as it struck the floor. "I couldn't help loving you, and I still can't. I've tried to put you out of my life, my love, but here I am, still in love with you." Her voice broke slightly as she said, "And it's just as hopeless now as when I was a child." The tears came to her eyes and she could not stop them. She pulled her handkerchief out again and tried to gain control of herself, turning away from the bed. Finally she overcame the tears and turned and said, "Well now, aren't you happy to have such a miserable — "

Gervase broke off suddenly. Davis's eyes were open. This was not unusual, for they often were. But something was happening. He was blinking in an erratic fashion. This had happened once or twice before, but something about it was different this time. She leaned over him and saw, with a shock, that his eyes were focused on her. Always before they had stared blankly at the ceiling or the wall.

"Davis, can you hear me?"

A frantic blinking, but there was some method to it. Some of the blinks were very quick, other times his eyes closed very slowly.

*He's trying to say something to me.* Gervase could hardly breathe, for an iron band seemed suddenly to be clamped around her chest. "Davis, if you can hear me, blink twice."

Instantly Davis blinked two times.

"Now blink once," Gervase whispered.

Davis's eyes were fixed on her. Then very slowly and deliberately they closed for just a moment and opened again.

"Oh, Davis, you're there! You can hear me! Can you speak at all?"

The eyes blinked very definitely twice, but then as she watched, she saw him blink three times very quickly, then three times very slowly, and then three times very quickly. Having done that, he stared at her, and there was a pleading in his eyes. His lips did not move, but there was intelligence and something like panic in the eyes that watched her.

Suddenly something triggered a memory that Gervase had long buried. It was of that time back in the Crimea when Davis had been outside the hospital with his sergeant. She remembered it clearly. Davis had said that the sergeant once worked for Mr. Morse, who had invented something called a telegraph. And then the memory came flashing back. "The code! S.O.S. would be a distress signal, you said." She looked at Davis. "Is that what you've done? S.O.S.? Is that what you're doing, Davis? Blink twice if it is."

*Yes.*

"I don't remember much of the code, but I still have it among my things." She leaned over and put her hand on his cheek. "It is the code, isn't it? And when I learn it, you can speak to me through it. Is that right?"

*Yes, yes, yes.* Davis kept blinking twice and she caressed his cheek. "Oh, my dear," she whispered in a broken tone, "you're there. It's you and you're alive and trying to speak to me. Thank God, Davis! Oh, thank God!"

Davis slipped off into sleep soon after revealing his consciousness, and as soon as Maggie came to relieve her, Gervase left. For reasons she didn't fully understand, Gervase said nothing to Maggie about the change in Davis.

In her room, she opened the trunk and at the bottom found the things she had brought back from the Crimea. The small piece of cardboard with the words *Morse code* written at the top was there. She pulled it out, sat on her bed, and stared at it. "A — dot dash," she said aloud. "B — dash dot dot dot." She studied for two hours, some of it coming back to her. She tried spelling out a few simple words, but finally she fell on her knees and began to pour out thanks and praise to God. "You're a miracle-working God," she cried, and the tears came. But they were tears of joy. "I know you're going to do a complete healing. Help me, that I might reach Davis down in that place wherever he is."

# Chapter Twenty-Three

When Gervase came into Davis's room, the first thing she did was ask Maggie quickly, "Did anything unusual happen today?"

"Why, no," Maggie replied. "What could happen? He's just the same."

"Oh, I don't know. I guess I've just lost too much sleep. You go ahead now. I'll take over."

As soon as Maggie left the room, Gervase went to Davis and saw that he had opened his eyes. "Davis, blink twice for yes and once for no. Can you hear me?"

Davis blinked his eyes firmly twice. *Yes.*

"Are you in pain?"

He blinked once. *No.*

"Can you feel anything at all?"

*No.*

Gervase hesitated. "Do you want me to tell your family?"

Davis blinked once emphatically.

"But Davis, it would make them very happy."

He blinked a series of noes very hard, and she saw that he was disturbed.

"Well, are you thirsty?"

*Yes.*

"Would you like something other than water?"

*Yes.*

"What is it, then?" She guessed wine and milk, and finally she said, "Spell it out. I've been working on the code."

Gervase watched carefully as he spelled out *tea*.

"You want hot tea?"

*Yes.*

"All right. I'll fix you some right now."

Gervase hurried to the kitchen, and as she went about the business of heating the water and making the tea, her heart was beating rather rapidly. She was very excited, and when she came back, she used all her strength to lift him and prop his back against the walnut headboard. "Now, do you think you could drink out of the cup instead of a spoon?"

*Yes.*

Holding the cup to his lips, she tipped it and saw that he swallowed eagerly. "Don't drink too fast. There's plenty of time."

He finished the cup and she put it down. "Have you been conscious a long time?" She saw his struggle and said, "A week? Two weeks?"

*Do not know.*

She hesitated and saw that he was blinking at her.

*Thanks.*

"For taking care of you?"

*Yes. I was going mad.*

This took some time to spell out. She missed some of the letters, but she discovered that she knew more than she had expected she would. "I'm so glad we're able to communicate, but now listen to me. When I do your therapy, you must try to help. Don't just lie there. When I lift your arm like this, you try to lift it with me. I know it seems impossible, but just visualize your arm and strain as if you were picking up something."

*Yes.*

She laid him down and for the next hour she worked hard, moving his arms and legs very slowly. She could not tell that there was any progress, for his limbs seemed dead. She spoke cheerfully to him all the time, and finally, when she was finished, she asked, "Do you want to sit up?"

*Yes.*

"What can I do for you? Do you want me to read something special to you?"

She saw that he was staring at her in a peculiar way.

"What is it?"

*You love me.*

The words brought a rich flush to Gervase's cheeks. She put her hand on her cheek, as if to hide it. "I . . . I didn't know you could hear me. Don't think of it, Davis. It could never come to anything. I just want to see you get well."

Quickly she picked up a book and began reading it. She was happy that he was showing progress, but disturbed that her heart had been laid open to him.

Three days passed before Dr. Thompson came, but now he was poking and poking at Davis. Gervase said nothing but stood watching as the physician examined him carefully, looking into his mouth, pulling his eyelids up to look at the eyes. Finally he turned and said, "There isn't any sign at all, Miss Howard?"

Gervase hated to lie to the good man. "I'm not discouraged, Doctor," she said.

"Well, that's good. I'm surprised at the tone of his muscles. I believe that therapy you thought of worked. Some of the doctors I wrote to have answered me, and they have given positive reports of things like this."

Gervase talked with Dr. Thompson about the care of the patient, and finally when he left, she looked down at Davis. "I feel as though I'm lying to Dr. Thompson. He ought to know what's happening."

*No, no, no.*

"I can't see why. You don't even want me to tell your family?"

*No.*

"But why not?"

*Not now.*

Gervase was puzzled and troubled by this. "It doesn't seem fair, Davis, but I'll do as you say."

*I hate this.*

"You'll be well one day."

*You disgusted.*

"Me disgusted? Why, of course not." She did not understand. "What do you mean?"

*Nasty job.*

"Oh, I was used to that. It was good training in the Crimea. You know how bad it was, but it got me ready to take care of you." She smiled then and put her hand on his chest. "Now I'm going to read to you. *Pickwick Papers*? Will that suit?"

*Yes.*

Gervase sat beside him and began to read. The only sound was her voice, that and the ticking of the ormolu clock on the shelf. She read for almost an hour, and then suddenly she heard a noise. She thought that perhaps Mr. Bob had gotten into the room, for it had sounded like a cat's cry.

There was no Mr. Bob, however, and she began reading again. She had not read half a page when another sound came, a soft hissing sound that mystified her. Getting up, she walked to the window, which was partly open, and thought, *It must have been something from outside.* She was going back to her chair when suddenly her glance fell on Davis's face. His eyes were blinking frantically.

"What is it, Davis?"

*Toe, toe.*

Gervase looked down and saw the big toe on his right foot twitch.

Hope rose in her and she asked excitedly, "Did you do that? Can you do it again?"

*Yes, yes!*

She watched and the toe twitched. "Do it three times in a row." The toe twitched three times and she cried out, "Davis, it's a miracle!"

*Yes.*

"Now," she said, "God is doing a work, but you're going to have to help. I want you to try very hard to move that toe. Concentrate all your strength on it."

The two of them focused on Davis's toe, both of them willing it to work.

Finally Gervase said, "I think that if your toe can come back, your foot can. And if your foot can, your leg can. Davis, I believe God's going to heal you. Do you believe that?"

There was a long pause.

*Yes.*

Maggie looked up at Brodie. They were sitting in the chapel together. It was crowded, so his arm was touching hers. He was holding a hymnbook, and she thought, *How strange it is to have to look up to a man.*

The congregation was singing one of her favorite hymns, and Brodie, she had discovered, had a glorious voice! It rose above all the singers about him, over all the congregation, and many were turning their heads to look. He sang the words on a clear pitch that seemed to fill the chapel.

> *"Fairest Lord Jesus*
> *Ruler of all nature,*
> *Oh, thou of God and man the son,*
> *Thee will I cherish,*
> *Thee will I honor,*
> *Thou my soul's glory, joy and crown.*
> *Fair are the meadows,*
> *Fairer still the woodlands,*
> *Robed in the blooming garb of spring:*
> *Jesus is fairer,*
> *Jesus is purer,*
> *Who makes the woeful heart to sing.*
> *Fair is the sunshine,*
> *Fairer still the moonlight,*
> *And all the twinkling starry hosts:*
> *Jesus shines brighter,*
> *Jesus shines purer,*
> *Than all the angels heaven can boast."*

When the song ended, she whispered, "You have such a beautiful voice, Brodie. I never heard a man who could sing like you can."

Brodie's face grew crimson and he did not answer.

Maggie sat beside the big man during the rest of the service and knew a strange contentment. She had felt odd buying a new dress, and Gervase had helped her pick it out. It was of a pale light-green color, and as she looked at herself in the mirror, she had seen a new Maggie. Gervase had insisted on working with her hair, too, and had pronounced, "You have beautiful hair and you look wonderful."

The service ended, and as Brodie and Maggie walked out into the morning sunshine, Maggie said, "That was a marvelous sermon."

"He's a bonnie preacher, he is."

The two left the walkway in front of the chapel and cut across the yard. The grass was bright green, and overhead the sky was a glorious blue. Fleecy white clouds floated along gently, and the sun cast its warm beams over them as they moved toward the area where the buggies were parked.

Suddenly Maggie stepped in a slight depression. She would have fallen but Brodie heard her cry and reached out to steady her. "What is it, Maggie?"

"It's my ankle. I twisted it."

"Well, here, lean on me. We'll get you home and you can doctor it. It's nae broken, is it?"

"No. Just painful." She tried two or three steps, wincing with each effort.

Suddenly Brodie swept her up in his arms. "You can't walk on that ankle. You'll make it worse."

He carried her the rest of the way. Maggie could not say a word. She was furiously embarrassed and was certain that everyone was watching.

Reaching the buggy, Brodie placed her gently in the seat. "There you are," he said with a smile, then walked around and stepped into the vehicle. As he sat beside her and picked up the reins, Maggie finally regained her composure somewhat.

"No man could do that but you, Brodie."

"Well, God gave me strength if he didn't give me brains."

"You've got brains enough!" she said sharply.

Brodie drove the horses until they were stepping smartly along the road back to Kimberly. He did not speak for a time and Maggie finally turned to face him. "When I was a girl and it was obvious I was going to be oversized, I used to pray that God would make me smaller."

"Well, that was foolish. God made you like you are." He winked at her. "Just the right size for a good-sized man. All these other women seem like toys to me." He took her hand and squeezed it. "You're just right."

Maggie felt the width of his hand swallow hers. He had huge hands but they did not seem outsized on his large frame.

"How is Mr. Davis getting along, Margaret?"

She did not answer at once but finally said, "Everyone has always called me Maggie except my father. He always called me Margaret and wouldn't let anybody call me anything else in his presence. I always liked the name but I've never liked Maggie."

"Well then. We'll make everyone call you Margaret."

Maggie suddenly laughed. "I don't see how we'd go about that."

As they wheeled along the road at a fast clip, Maggie said, "I can't see much change in Mr. Davis. But you know, Brodie, for the last few weeks or so Gervase has been different."

"Different how?"

"It's hard to say, but she somehow seems more content and happier. I don't know why."

The two spoke of Davis's plight and other things until they reached the house.

"I don't want you to carry me in. It would look so odd."

"I don't care what it looks like. You can't make it up the stairs on an ankle like that."

Brodie would take no argument, and he got out, picked her up, and headed straight for the house. They were met at the door by Phoebe Rogers, one of the maids, who exclaimed, "What happened, Maggie!"

"I just twisted my ankle. I'll be all right."

"Can I bring you anything?"

"No, I think with some compresses it will be all right, just a little tender. Thank you, Phoebe."

Maggie's room was on the fourth floor, and when they were halfway up, she asked, "Aren't you getting tired?"

"Not a bit," Brodie said, smiling cheerfully. He carried her to her room and put her down. "There," he said. "You want me to go get Miss Gervase to help?"

"You might go by and tell her. Maybe she knows a trick or two with sprained ankles."

He did not leave but stood smiling down at her. "So, you like it when I call you Margaret?"

"Very much."

"Then Margaret it is." He did not seem inclined to go, and finally he said with a peculiar light in his eye, "We've gotten to be good friends, haven't we, Margaret?"

"Yes. Very good."

"And how then am I to thank you for teaching me how to read?"

"You just say thank you, and I say you're welcome."

"It doesn't seem enough." He put his hand on her forearm. "Don't you think somethin' else might be appropriate?"

Maggie stared at him, unable to answer. He was smiling and he suddenly put his arms around her. She knew he was going to kiss her, and she had never been kissed by a man before. He was so strong that she was a little fearful, but his caress was gentle, and she found herself responding to it.

He drew his head back and said, "Well now. My love is like a red, red rose. I'll go for Miss Gervase, and I'll come to see how you are later."

Maggie watched him as he went down the stairs, singing under his breath. She could not move for a minute, for something had come to her as he kissed her.

"I love this big man," she whispered. "And I never thought anyone would love me."

For three days Gervase worked overtime. Maggie's ankle was sprained more than she had thought at first, and the stairs gave her problems. Gervase had demanded that she rest as much as she could. They had doctored it with cold compresses and liniment, and now for the first time since the accident she was doing better. But Gervase was worn out.

She entered Davis's room carrying a fresh stack of linens and put them in the mahogany clothespress. When she went to Davis, she saw he was excited. His eyes were rapidly blinking a message.

*Fingers!*

Quickly Gervase looked down, and sure enough his right forefinger was moving back and forth. The other three fingers also seemed to be moving slightly.

"Oh, Davis, that's wonderful! That whole side of your body is coming awake, and soon the other side will." She looked at his eyes, and then her eyes went to his lips. They were moving slightly and she knew he was trying to talk. "Can't you speak at all, Davis?"

He gave up finally and then blinked, *No.*

"What are you trying to tell me? Take your time. We have plenty of that. Are you in pain? Did something bad happen?"

*No. Wonderful.*

"What is it, Davis?"

The process was slow but he began by blinking, *You gave hope.*

"I'm so glad," Gervase whispered.

*Didn't know Jesus.*

"Oh, Davis, is that so?"

*Yes. Was lost. But now believe.*

Gervase saw that tears were running down Davis's face. Snatching her handkerchief, she wiped them away. "And did he come in, Davis?"

*Yes, yes, yes!*

"I'm so happy, Davis. You've been born again! I'm so glad."

Gervase suddenly took his hand and held it to her cheek. He was watching her with expressive eyes, and she whispered, "Thank God. Maybe it took all this to bring you to him, but now you are part of the family of God. Saved forever!"

# Chapter Twenty-Four

As Gervase wrote in her journal, the lamp beside her on the table threw its corona of light over the paper and then over the farthest part of the room. It twisted shadows into odd shapes, and shredded yellow gleams on the walls and floor. The only noise in the room was that of her pen scratching, a sound broken only when she stopped to dip the pen in the inkwell. She had been writing steadily and now she expelled a sharp gust of breath, put the pen down, and flexed her fingers as she read what she had written.

*Fall is here, and the trees are showing the reds and yellows and golds. I love this season! Winter will come, but for now everything is crisp and somehow holy.*

*Davis has kept improving since the moment he began blinking at me. First his toe and then later the fingers on his right hand. Now he is able to move both hands, the fingers at least, and he has some movement in the lower part of his legs. Every time I go to the room, he's excited and it's like an adventure.*

*Things change so quickly. I read in a book by some poet — I can't remember his name — that sometimes a person bends to pick up something that fell out of his hand, and when he gets up, the world has changed. That's the way it seems with Davis's recovery. For a long time there was nothing but now every day there's new improvement.*

*He is so hungry for God! He wants me to read the Bible to him. Indeed, it is a new birth. He's just like a child. He gets so excited, he*

*can't signal me fast enough with his eyes, and I have even laughed at*
*him — the first time I've done that in a long time.*

*He hasn't said anything more about what I said about loving*
*him. He's very grateful, but we both know that what I feel for him is*
*a very private thing. He's a married man and that's all there is to it.*

She slowly put the journal away and then went into his
room. She found him awake and ran her hand down his cheek.
"You're getting bristles," she said. "I think we'll shave."

*Wish I could.*

She read his eyes as they blinked rapidly, for she had
become an expert, practically, in the use of Morse code. "Someday you'll be able but now it will have to be me. Come, let me
help you sit up."

She struggled to move him, for she had not Maggie's
strength. As she did, she reminded herself that it was no longer
"Maggie." Her friend had informed her, and everyone else, that
she now wished to be called Margaret. Gervase was sure that
somehow Brodie was involved in the name change, but she had
said nothing.

When she finally got Davis upright, his head leaning
against the headboard, she gathered all the materials for shaving and soon had his face covered with lather. She took the
razor and began shaving him, her face intent on the task. Once
she shifted her eyes and saw that he was watching her closely.
She smiled and said, "There aren't many lady barbers."

*Glad there is one.*

"Well, let's get under your nose now. That's the most delicate part." Carefully she moved the blade across his upper lip
and then completed the shave. She wrung out a cloth in the
warm water, cleansed his face of the remaining lather, and put
on some lotion. His eyes moved.

*Good barber.*

Gervase suddenly laughed. "Don't try to get around me, Davis Wingate! When you're well, you'll shave yourself."

His eyes were fixed on her and he blinked out the word he often gave her.

*Thanks.*

His gratitude touched Gervase and she stood looking into his eyes. "I'm glad I was able to help."

She was startled when she suddenly heard a voice. "You're still talking to him."

Gervase whirled to find that Roberta Wingate had entered the room. Her eyes were as cold as polar ice as she advanced to stand directly before Gervase. Roberta glanced down at Davis and shook her head, then looked up. "You were always in love with him."

"No, you mustn't say that!"

"You think I didn't know? *Everybody* knew it. You were foolish over him when you were a girl. All the servants knew it. Even Sarah saw it."

"I always admired him. He was so kind."

Roberta laughed but there was a hard edge to the sound. "You poor little fool! You come here with all your nursing ways and your talking and singing and reading. He's just a vegetable. Can't you understand that?"

Gervase could not move as Roberta flayed her with her words.

"You may as well leave here, Gervase. Either he'll die or he'll get well." Roberta smiled cruelly then. "You'll lose him either way. Why don't you leave and make life easier for yourself? Find a man of your own."

Gervase could not answer. All her words seemed to be frozen as Roberta turned and left the room, slamming the door behind her. Gervase's back was to Davis, and she could not think of how to face him. Finally she did turn, trying to put an impersonal expression on her face.

He was watching her intently, and then his eyes moved.

*Don't mind her.*

Gervase could not face him squarely. She was embarrassed and humiliated that he had heard these things. Finally she cleared her throat. "It's true. I have always cared for you, Davis. At first, just as a child. You were always so kind. I don't know when that changed. But we mustn't speak of it or even think of it."

Quickly she turned from him and moved across the room. She busied herself with the small chores to be done in a sick-room, and then finally she picked up her Bible and went to face him. "I think I'll read from the book of Mark. It's always been a wonderful gospel to me. Everything moves so fast and Jesus is always reaching out and touching people."

*That will be fine,* he answered.

Gervase sat and began to read. She was drained and felt that Roberta had left her nothing but a quivering mass of nerves. It was bad enough that she loved a man she could never have, but for him to hear all these things made it worse.

For nearly an hour she read steadily, clearly. She knew the book so well that she could almost read it without thinking, but she forced herself to focus on the words.

She was reading from the fifth chapter when she heard a slight noise. She turned quickly and looked around the room. Seeing nothing, she continued where she had left off, at the twenty-eighth verse. "'If I may touch but his clothes, I shall be whole. And straightway the fountain of her blood was dried up; and she felt in her body that she was healed of that plague —'" Once again the sound came to her. Getting to her feet, she walked around the room, searching the floor to see if an animal had somehow gotten in. She went to the window and listened intently but did not see anything.

As she turned, her eyes fell on Davis's face, and she saw that his lips were moving! "Davis, are you trying to speak?" she cried. She moved to him, putting her face close to his. "Speak if you can."

The words, when they came, were very faint, a mere whisper. Yet she heard them clearly. "Don't ... feel ... bad."

"You spoke! You can talk!" Gervase said. In her excitement she took his face between her hands and held him there. She stared into his eyes, tears in her own. "It's God working in you!"

Then she saw he was trying to speak again, and when she put her ear close to his lips, he said, "Don't let ... Roberta ... hurt you."

"Oh, I won't, but let me go tell your family! They'll be so happy."

"No. ... Don't tell ... anyone."

"But Davis, why not?"

She saw something change in his eyes, and his lips grew very still. Finally she said, "Please, Davis, tell me why you don't want anyone to know of your improvement."

The words came then, in a whisper but clearly definable. "I'm afraid, Gervase."

"Afraid? But you're getting better all the time."

"Afraid of ... Roberta."

"You're afraid of your wife? Why?"

For a moment his lips twitched, and then she heard him speak more clearly. "I didn't fall, Gervase. ... I told Roberta ... I was leaving her. ... She said she'd ... kill me if I did."

Gervase suddenly knew what was coming, and her eyes were filled with horror.

"We walked ... along the cliff. ... She pushed me."

Gervase could not speak. She stared at his face and whispered, "She tried to kill you?"

"Yes . . . and she'll . . . try again."

Suddenly Gervase understood some of what must have been going on in Davis's mind, and compassion went through her. She put her arms around him, pressed his face against her chest. "I won't let her harm you, Davis. I swear I won't!"

# Trial by Fire

*October 1857–January 1858*

# Chapter Twenty-Five

Davis had slept a great deal for two days after regaining his speech. When he was awake, however, he made great progress, so that by the third day he could speak coherently, though without much force. Gervase had trouble sleeping and did not press him for details until he could speak more easily. A vague sense of unreality possessed Gervase as she tried to grasp the significance of what Davis had said.

But finally she determined to know the full truth. She waited until very late, when the household was asleep, before broaching the subject.

"Davis, I can't believe it. I knew you were unhappy, but —" She could not go on. His eyes were fixed on her face, and the torment in them she could read clearly.

The quiet was broken by the ormolu clock striking the half hour. The notes seemed to hover in the air and then faded away, and silence possessed the room again.

At last Gervase spoke. "I knew you were unhappy in your marriage. Aunt Martha told me that in a letter, but it's so . . . so terrible! I can't take it all in."

For a moment Davis's pale face remained absolutely still, his eyes filled with bitterness. Then he began to speak. The whisper became stronger, and his words easier to understand.

"Our marriage was always wrong, Gervase. I knew it only weeks after the wedding. Things began to fall apart. She didn't care for any of the things I cared about. All Roberta wanted was a world of parties, the theater, balls — while I liked solitude. She cared nothing for my writing. She made fun of it."

Davis paused and Gervase asked, "Are you tired of lying down? Would you like to sit up?"

"Yes, please."

Gervase managed to pull him up into a sitting position, then propped his pillows around him. She put his left hand on his lap but held tightly to the other. When he was comfortable, she said quietly, "I'm so sorry, Davis."

"Sometimes a man makes a fool of himself with women. I was not an expert. Never was."

"So you were unhappy even before you enlisted."

"Absolutely miserable. As a matter of fact, I think that was part of the reason for my enlisting. Simply to get away from Roberta and the constant quarrels."

"Do you think she changed after you married?"

"No, I think she was always a selfish woman. I saw traces of it in her but it got worse after we married." He closed his eyes for a moment. Gervase held his hand and waited. Finally he opened his eyes and said, "By the time I got back from the war, I knew everything between us was over." He hesitated, and then he whispered, "I found out she was seeing another man."

"Oh no!" Gervase exclaimed. "How awful."

"I don't know how many others there had been, but what broke my heart was that the man she was having an affair with was my brother, Ives."

Instantly Gervase remembered that she had seen a few signs which had troubled her concerning Ives and Roberta. One memory came very clearly to her. She had been returning to the house after running an errand and had seen Ives and Roberta almost hidden by the shrubbery. He was holding her hand and she was standing close, looking up into his face and smiling. At the time, Gervase had tried to believe it was innocent, but now as she thought on it, she remembered that certain of the household had hinted at an intimacy between the two.

She squeezed Davis's hand tightly and asked, "Did you confront her about it?"

"Yes. I had horrible thoughts, Gervase. I thought about —" Davis lowered his voice. "I thought about doing violence to them, but thank God I didn't."

"Did you confront Ives?"

"No, I never let him know I was aware of their affair. We were never very close but I always loved Ives. I think he was a victim."

"You accused Roberta, then?"

"Yes, it was quite a scene. She denied it at first but I knew I was right. Finally she admitted it. She said she never loved me. It was always Ives."

"What did you do, Davis?"

"I'm not a violent man, but I was so deeply hurt that I could hardly bear it. I told her our marriage was over. I told her I was going to divorce her."

"Would you have?"

"No, not really. Divorce just isn't done among our people. Some pretty bad marriages have stayed together in our family. No, I would have put up with it, I suppose. But I was angry, and I shouted at her and told her I'd throw her out and let all the world see what she was." Davis fell silent.

Gervase asked, "What happened then?"

"Roberta's a pretty good actress. She cried and told me she was sorry, but I didn't believe her. I said, 'You'll be out of here. I won't have you in this house.' Other terrible things."

Stroking his hand, Gervase waited. He seemed to be gathering strength and she said, "You're speaking much more clearly."

"I guess my voice is rusty, I haven't used it in so long." He hesitated and then said, "She put on a good act, Gervase. She begged for forgiveness but I wouldn't bend. Finally, three days after the quarrel, I told her I was going to tell my parents what had happened. She asked me to come for a walk while we talked it over, and I did. We had often done that, walking out on that cliff by the sea. You know the path along the edge?"

"Yes, it's rather frightening. A sheer drop of I don't know how far, with those awful rocks like teeth at the bottom."

"I always liked it. You can hear the sound of the surf. I always felt free there somehow. Anyway, we took a buggy out there and began walking. I'd always put her on the inside, away from the lip of the cliff, and I did this time. She begged me and pleaded with me not to tell and swore she would never again have anything to do with Ives or any other man, but I was half mad, Gervase. I turned away from her, I remember now, facing out over the cliff. I couldn't bear to look at her! I remember saying, 'You've made this trouble for yourself and now you'll have to wallow in it.'"

Gervase said quietly, "And she pushed you over?"

"Yes. I was right on the edge and when her hands caught me in the back, I think I cried out, but there was no help."

"I don't see how you kept from being killed."

"Well, the drop isn't as sheer as it appears. There are some outcroppings. Rough enough, but I hit a couple of them on the way down. When I struck bottom, it was on my back, and the tide had washed in some sand. I would have been killed instantly if the rocks had been more exposed. Of course, when I hit bottom, that was all I knew. But after I recovered consciousness, I overheard some of the help say that a fisherman found me."

"A fisherman?"

"He was walking along the beach. He ran for help and a party came and carried me in."

"So you didn't know anything until you woke up here in this bed?"

"That's right, and I couldn't move or speak. It was awful! Worse than anything I could ever imagine. I could hear people talking but I couldn't move. I heard what the doctor said, and I heard my parents begging him to do something. And all the time I was trying to cry out, 'Help me! Do something!' But of course I couldn't."

"It's a miracle that you're alive, Davis."

"Yes, I know that." He licked his lips then and asked, "Could I have some water?"

Instantly Gervase placed his hand on his lap, got up, and poured a glass half full of water. She held it carefully to his lips and he took small sips. Finally he'd had enough and she put the glass down. "You're going to get well, Davis," she said. "I know you are."

"Now you know why I didn't want you to tell my parents. She's very clever, Gervase. As long as I was helpless, I couldn't reveal what she had done. But she knew that if I recovered consciousness, she would have to find a way to prevent my telling. When I get stronger, that will be the time to tell my family."

"We'll just have to pray that God will perform a complete miracle." Gervase put her hand on his cheek. "Poor man. I'm so sorry that you had to suffer all this."

"Gervase, you'll never know what it meant when you came. Those two oafs couldn't take care of a sick dog! And then when you talked to me as if I could hear, I found hope. I loved the songs you sang and the way you would read to me. You were an angel from heaven! I loved you when you were a child, but never so much as when you came to me when nobody else would."

Gervase felt her face growing warm. She could not allow him to speak of love, for he was a married man. She said briefly, "Well, it's time for your exercises. You have some movement now and you can speak. We've got to make you strong enough to get you out of that bed." She began to raise and lower his arms. "Come now, help me. Lift. . . . Lift. . . ."

⤙⤚

Ives stood in the middle of his room the next morning, uncertainly staring at the door. He had come back from university and spent the night. Just past midnight, Roberta had come to him — but he had turned her away. She had tried to cajole him but this time he had somehow managed to deny her. Now as he thought of it, he whispered, "I never saw her so angry. She can't bear rejection."

From the half-open window, he could hear the voices of George Miller and Brodie McLean as the two discussed what new plantings should go into a bed just outside his window. He waited for a moment and then took out a handkerchief and wiped his face. It was cold in his room, for fall had come with its biting breezes, but it did not seem cold to him. He dreaded the affairs of the day. He could not face his parents without terrible guilt clawing at him, and it took all the strength he could muster to make himself go to the sickroom and put in an appearance.

Leaving his room, he walked down the stairs, then turned and made his way down the hall. As he did, he glanced up at the pictures of former Wingates, arranged in order. Their faces seemed to look down on him in dour disapproval, and they were a solemn enough lot, at least when they posed for their portraits. Ives clamped his teeth together, thinking, *You wouldn't be very proud of what the family has produced in me.*

When he reached the door of Davis's room, he hesitated. Then he straightened his shoulders and shook his head. "Got to do it," he muttered. He opened the door, stepped inside, and saw Gervase standing beside Davis. She was shaving him but looked up. "Come in, Mr. Ives."

"I didn't know you were a barber, Gervase."

"Yes, I had to be in the Crimea. One poor young soldier had lost both hands. He was so depressed and he looked so shaggy, I offered to shave him. I'm afraid I made a hash of it. I cut him twice, I think. He made a joke of it, saying, 'Well, those aren't the worst cuts I've had lately.'" She shook her head and grief showed in her eyes. "They were so brave. Most of them so young." Gervase leaned over then and drew the razor expertly down Davis's cheek, wiping the lather on a towel she held. "Would you like to try it?" she asked Ives.

"No, it's all I can do to shave myself." He stood on the other side of the bed and watched as she carefully shaved his brother. When she finished, she wiped off the rest of the lather with a hot wet cloth and then applied some shaving lotion. "There," she said to Davis, "now you smell better than I do."

"You've always talked to him, Gervase, haven't you?"

"Oh yes."

"Even though he can't hear you?"

Gervase paused, holding the shaving things. "It does me good, Mr. Ives, and I think, *What if he can hear?* How awful it would be never to be spoken to."

Ives dropped his head and stared at the floor. He could not think of a single thing to say, and finally, when she came back from putting away the shaving equipment, he said, "I wish there were something I could do for him."

"Well, you can pray."

A bitter twist moved on Ives' lips and he shook his head almost violently. "Not me," he muttered.

"Why not you?"

"Because I'm not a man who prays."

"Don't you know the Lord?"

The simple question disturbed Ives. "No," he said, "I don't."

"Well, I hope you will find the Lord Jesus."

The words struck Ives like a hot iron. Suddenly the guilt that had been building up in him seemed unendurable. He turned to face Gervase and saw her calm eyes watching him. "I've never been close to Davis," he said, his voice unsteady. "To tell the truth, I've always been resentful of him."

"Why would that be?"

"Oh, the usual. He's the oldest son. I'm just a cadet. Everything for him, nothing to me. I didn't notice it much when we were boys, because there was little difference, but when he came to his majority and I grew older, I realized he would always be first. It wasn't his fault of course but I did resent him."

Gervase said carefully, "That's probably a very common thing, but I hope you don't resent him anymore."

Suddenly Ives wrenched himself away. He walked to the window and stared outside. Brodie McLean was shoveling in the dirt, the shovel looking like a toy in his huge hands. Ives watched as the dirt flew, and then said in a wretched voice, "Of course I don't resent him now. I just wish he could hear me. I'd try to make it up to him for the way I've felt."

Gervase came over then and stood beside Ives. She touched his arm and he turned around quickly, surprised. "I think," she said, "you ought to say these things to him."

"He can't hear me."

"But you can hear yourself — and God can hear you. And one day Davis will hear you, too. I'll leave you two alone."

Ives watched as the young woman left the room, and for a moment stood there irresolutely. Then something came to him that he could not explain. He knew she had touched something deep in him, and he walked over and stood above Davis. He put his hand over Davis's and noticed that his own hand was trembling. The flesh beneath his touch was warm, and although Davis's eyes were closed and it seemed he could hear nothing, Ives began to speak. "Davis, I am sorry that I've been jealous of what you had. You've always been good to me, a good friend, a good brother — and I haven't been what I should have been!"

A struggle took place in Ives Wingate at that moment. He thought of his life, of his infidelity, of the sin against his brother, his own blood, and then he swallowed hard and said, "I haven't been faithful to you. I've had . . . an affair with Roberta, and I can't expect you to forgive me. You couldn't, even if you could hear me." Tears suddenly came to his eyes, and he struggled for words as they ran down his face. Finally he squeezed Davis's hand. "I'm sorry, Brother," he said brokenly, then whirled and, pulling a handkerchief out of his pocket, wiped his face. He left the sickroom resolved to end the affair that very night, and did not even see Gervase at the far end of the hall.

Gervase came at once to Davis. His eyes were open and he said, "That was a good thing, Gervase."

"What did he say?"

"He confessed his sin with Roberta and asked my forgiveness."

Gervase brushed back a lock of his fair hair. "And did you forgive him, Davis?"

"Yes, I did!"

The two of them were silent; the clock sent its silver chimes into the room. Mr. Bob came to push Gervase with his blunt head, and when she ignored him, he glared at her and stalked off, offended.

# Chapter Twenty-Six

As Gervase walked along the edge of the woods that bordered Kimberly, the odors of fall made a thick fragrance around her. The wind roughed up the fallen leaves in the thicket as she passed by. She savored the wild odors of the earth, even though they created a sense of dissatisfaction in her. A smoky haze made a blue ceiling over the land, and though the noonday sun was warm, winter was in the air.

A noise overhead in one of the towering oaks made her look up, and she saw a large red squirrel, his eyes bright as buttons, chattering at her angrily. He made such a comic figure as he frisked his tail around, rebuking her for breaking into his territory, that Gervase smiled. "Don't worry. I won't find your nest and steal your acorns." She watched as the squirrel scampered around the tree and then disappeared into the foliage.

Turning, she continued to walk, watching the clouds as they tumbled across the gray sky and thinking of the strangeness of her life. She was an introspective woman, and now she tried to arrange her thoughts into some kind of orderly pattern. She believed in her deepest heart that life, even at its worst, was good. A woman was made to laugh and to cry, to work and to love. If she failed to do this, her spirit would shrivel and she would lose the name of womanhood itself, leaving nothing behind when she departed from this life. Gervase was deeply convinced that God was in all things, but she knew just as certainly that a woman had to play her part. God would put choices before her but a woman had to make the right one.

As she came to the end of the walk and turned back toward the house, she paused for a moment and lifted her arms to the sky, stretching and feeling the blood beat in her temples. She held the position, reaching her fingers out as if trying to touch the sky, and in that moment she had what the theologians call an epiphany.

She had come across the word in her reading and had looked it up. It simply meant a revelation of sorts—when one suddenly, without any teachers, knew something that God wanted one to know. She let the moment sink in, and when she lowered her arms to walk quickly toward the house, she felt a new strength, a new excitement. "I know you're going to do great things, God," she whispered. "I just don't know how to go about helping you. But then again, maybe you don't need help." The thought amused her and she laughed aloud. "As if I could help you, God, who created all things!"

She entered the house and went at once to the kitchen, where she found her aunt Martha busy with the cooking. She had boiled the potatoes until their swollen interiors made fluffy beads through their cracked skins; a huge tub of corn was awash in its own milky juices; and next to it, in a smaller pan, bobbed small round peas drenched in butter. Gervase took a deep breath, enjoying the spicy fragrance of an apple pie, and then she said, "It all smells so good, Aunt Martha."

"It ought to, the way I worked on it." Martha smiled at her niece. "You've been out walking. That's good. You have color in your cheeks."

"I want to fix a plate to take to Davis's room," Gervase said, adding hurriedly, "I may not want to come back."

"Help yourself," Martha said. "There's plenty."

Quickly Gervase cut a large slice of the roast beef, added a baked potato, some peas, and then cut a slice out of the pie and put it on a smaller plate. She added a glass of milk and, putting it all on a tray, left the kitchen, feeling somewhat dishonest. She made her way to the room and said to her friend, "Margaret, you go get something to eat. I've brought a lunch in here."

"That looks good," Margaret said. She got up, took one look at Davis, and said, "You didn't bring his broth?"

"No, I'll get it later. You go on and get some rest."

As soon as Margaret left, Gervase put the tray on the small table. "Lunchtime," she said.

Davis opened his eyes and whispered, "I'm starved."

Gervase helped him into a sitting position and then began cutting the roast beef into bite-sized portions. For a week now Davis had been eating solid food, and the nourishment of it showed in the brightness of his eyes. He could speak almost as well as before the accident. She mashed the baked potato, put a dollop of butter on it, and put salt on the vegetables, and he said, "Can't tell you how good it is to eat something solid!"

"I'd think so. Here, this ought to be good."

Davis took the bite of roast beef and chewed it. When he had swallowed that, she followed it with some of the potato and then tried to balance the peas on a fork. They kept rolling off and she said, "Oh, let's just use the spoon."

Davis smiled. "Just use your fingers. I don't care. You don't know how wonderful it is to be eating something besides that broth."

Gervase fed him, and though it was only a mundane affair, something she had done for many sick people, she was aware that something warm lay between her and this tall man who had become almost like a child she was caring for. It was something strong and unsettling to her, and somehow she was sure Davis felt it. She studied his face as he watched her, and the

300

sunlight shone in his eyes and built up solid angles at the base of his ears and at the bridge of his nose. He had long, full lips and a wide chest. He was a strong man physically, and it grieved her that he was losing his muscular strength. Still, he was getting better. She helped him finish the vegetables and beef and gave him some of the pie, then asked, "Have you felt any more movement?"

"I have a surprise for you." He smiled then and to her amazement bent his right arm. "I can't pick it up yet but I can bend it. See?"

"That's wonderful, Davis! I'm so happy. What about the other one?"

"It's coming along — not as well, but it seems the right side always awakens first."

Gervase praised him for his efforts and then they had an hour of therapy. By the time they were through, he was able at least to lift his arm from the shoulder a couple of inches, and finally he exclaimed, "This is so tiring. It's worse than digging a long ditch."

"But you're coming back to life. Isn't it exciting, Davis! Just think. One day you'll be walking, running, and doing all the things you used to."

"If I do, I'll know who to thank for it."

"Yes, the Lord is good."

"But you are his handmaid, and you've been the instrument to bring me out of that dark place where I was ready to lose my mind."

"Say nothing of that."

"How can I keep from it? You know, during the long time when I had nobody to talk to me, I thought a lot about my earlier life. And I was amazed to discover how much of you I had tucked in my memory. I remember so well the time I took you fishing down by the pond. Do you remember that?"

"Oh yes. It was the first fish I ever caught."

"You caught three of them, and we had to clean them, and you ate them for supper. I've thought about that. It was so clear in my mind, like seeing a drama on a stage. You were such a scrawny, bony, and scared little girl, but not that day. I remember how you laughed when you caught that first fish."

"It was a wonderful day for me, Davis. It was only two weeks after I came to Kimberly, and I didn't know how to do anything. I was awkward, and when you took me out and spent part of your day with me, I could hardly believe it." She laughed and touched his cheek. "You were kind to a frightened, lonely girl."

"Well, the frightened, lonely little girl has been transformed into a beautiful and gifted woman. I'm so proud of you, Gervase."

Gervase dropped her eyes, for she felt them burning. She could not allow the moment to be prolonged and said, "Well, we can't dwell on all that, I suppose. Now it's time for a bath."

"I look forward to the time when I can take my own."

Gervase laughed. "So do I."

⁓

Brodie found Maggie standing on the back porch. He had a wheelbarrow full of tools but he put it down at once and went to her. "Good afternoon, Margaret. What are you doing?"

"Just out to enjoy this cool weather. Isn't it a beautiful fall?"

"It is indeed. If I were back in Scotland, now it wud be harvesttime. I miss that, you know. Someday I'd like to own a little place. Raise some vegetables of my own."

"I always worked with my mother in our garden at home."

The two stood there talking, watching the sky as it darkened. It seemed to grow dark very early, and finally he said, "Come for a walk with me."

"All right. Where shall we go?"

"It doesn't matter. I'd just like to spend a little time with you."

He led her down to where the path wound around the rose garden, and he commented, "The roses are all gone now. Beautiful they were."

"Yes, but they'll be back next spring."

"Yes indeed, they will." They reached the edge of the woods and for a time did not speak. "One of the things I like about you, Margaret MacKay, is that you know how to be silent."

Margaret laughed. "I don't think you remember all the times I talked your ear off."

"You know how to talk too, just not all the time. But that's only one of the things I like about you."

"What are the rest?" Margaret asked, smiling. "I need to hear them. No man ever told me these things before."

Suddenly Brodie turned, took her by the shoulders, and pulled until she stood looking straight up at him. "That's what you need to hear for the rest of your life — good things from a man."

Margaret looked up at him and, as always, admired his rugged strength. He was a thick-bodied man, well padded with muscle, and not an ounce of fat on him. He was the strongest man she had ever seen, easily picking up loads that two or three men would have struggled with. Standing so close to him, she felt very small, almost like a little girl. "What are you saying, Brodie?"

Brodie's broad face was serious but there was a light dancing in his eyes. "I'm saying I want to say good things about you as long as I live, and I can only do that if you'll marry me."

The world seemed to stand still for Margaret MacKay at that moment. Years before, she had given up all hope of such things as marriage, a man, a home — and now this man, whom she knew to be strong in both body and spirit, was asking her to become a wife, perhaps even a mother. She could not speak, so great was the emotion that seemed to rush through her very veins. She found her throat tightening and she blinked to keep the tears back.

"Do you really wish it, Brodie?"

"I must have you, Margaret." The words were simple, but then Brodie put his arms around her and drew her in. She lifted her face, took his kiss, which was so gentle and reverent that she felt it was almost like a blessing. Then she threw her arms around his neck, pulling him closer. There was a hunger in her, and he responded, his arms tightening about her, pressing her against his strong form.

When she drew back, she smiled and said, "Yes, Brodie, I'll be your wife."

"You make me very happy, Margaret."

"And you make me feel like . . . like a woman for the first time, Brodie."

"A woman you are — and a bonnie one! Let's walk some more and we'll talk about marriage." They had not gone three steps when he suddenly said, "Now, who do you think should wear the pants in the family?"

Margaret was startled. She looked and saw his eyes dancing with fun. "We'll talk about that, Brodie."

"Davis, what's wrong! Are you choking?"

Indeed, Davis seemed to be. He had taken only three spoonfuls of the soup Gervase had brought, but then when she tried to give him a fourth, he had pushed the spoon away with his tongue. His face was pale. "Something's . . . wrong." Suddenly he began to throw up, gagging and choking.

Alarmed, Gervase grabbed the washcloth and cleaned him up until the spell passed. "What is it?" she demanded.

"Something . . . wrong with that soup!"

Gervase looked at the soup. She had picked it up from the kitchen, where she had instructed her aunt Martha to leave it. Gervase had heated it and brought it straight to Davis's room. Now she took the spoon and tried it. It was a simple vegetable soup that her aunt made so well, but as she tasted it, an alarm began to sound in her head.

"It does taste peculiar."

Davis was breathing hard and his eyes were watering. He blinked to clear them and said, "It burns, Gervase. I think it's poison."

His words seemed to hang in the air, and then Gervase said, "It doesn't taste right."

"Did you fix it yourself?"

"No, Martha fixed it but she left it out for me."

The two were silent, and finally Davis said, "I thought at first it just contained different spices, but there's something else in it."

Gervase lifted the spoon to taste it again, but he said abruptly, "Don't put that in your mouth, Gervase."

She lowered the spoon to the plate. "Do you think it's Roberta?"

"I hate to think such a thing but she tried it once before. Remember? She wants me dead. I'm a threat to her as long as I live. She's afraid that if I remember things, I'll have her arrested for attempted murder."

"Before we make too many guesses, let me go see if anybody else has gotten sick over this. That might be best."

Gervase left the sickroom, carried the soup back to the kitchen. She casually asked her aunt if she had done anything different to the soup.

"Why no, we all had it for lunch. Here, let me taste it."

Martha took a spoonful of the soup and at once made a face. "This is awful! I don't know what's wrong with it."

"Well, maybe some bad spices got in it."

"Bad spices in my soup! That's never happened before."

"Don't worry about it, Aunt Martha."

When Gervase returned to Davis's room, she said at once, "Everyone ate the soup and nobody was harmed, but Aunt Martha knew that something was wrong with this."

"It was Roberta."

"I think you're right," Gervase said. She looked at the door, as if she expected the woman to enter. "From now on I'll get all your meals myself. We'll have to be very careful."

"You're always having to look out for me. I wish for one time I could look out for you, Gervase."

She smiled. "You always have. Now it's my turn."

"It's hard to keep Margaret from knowing I'm all right. I have to keep my eyes shut."

"Let's do some more exercises. See if you can double up your leg."

"All right," Davis said grimly. "I've got to get out of this bed!"

# Chapter Twenty-Seven

Davis had improved tremendously over the past six days, so much so that hope for a full recovery was now blossoming in Gervase. His strength was coming back so swiftly that he could now feed himself and could struggle into a sitting position on his own. She had asked him tentatively about telling his family but he had still been reluctant. "Just let me wait until I can walk, then we'll tell them," he had said, and she had agreed.

Gervase had been invited to join the family for dinner on Thursday evening. Lady Sarah had made the request herself. Although Gervase felt uncomfortable, knowing what she did about Roberta, she felt it necessary to go.

She left her room and went down to the dining room, where the others had already gathered. Sir Edward came to her at once, saying, "Well, you're late, Gervase. Probably the first time you've ever been late for anything in your life."

"Not really, Sir Edward." Gervase smiled up at him and thought, *If anyone wants to know what Davis will look like when he's an older man, all he has to do is look at his father.* "I'm sorry. I was delayed a little."

"No problem. We're all ready. Here, you're going to sit at my right hand. I want to hear more of those stories about your time in the Crimea."

Roberta was seated across the table, at Lady Sarah's right. Lady Sarah smiled. "Those were adventurous times, weren't they, Gervase?"

"Yes, I'm afraid they were. Mostly very uncomfortable." Gervase tried to keep anything from showing in her face. As she studied Roberta Wingate, she still found it hard to believe that the woman was as cold-blooded as a venomous serpent. Certainly it didn't show in her face! She was smiling and gracious, for this was the attitude she had chosen for the night.

The meal, as usual, was exquisite. On silver trays and gold-rimmed dishes the food was brought: petite crustless sandwiches of cucumber slices with butter, cheese with walnuts, smoked chicken with raspberry mayonnaise; and then fish, mutton, and an assortment of delicious vegetables.

Gervase surrendered to Sir Edward's plea to hear more of the Crimea. She spoke mostly of Florence Nightingale's heroic work and dedication, scarcely mentioning her own. Ives sat to her right, listening and saying little. His face was pale and she noticed he had lost weight. *I wonder if his confession has made any difference?* The thought touched Gervase's mind, and from time to time, while others were speaking, she managed to make a few remarks to him. He answered briefly, but finally during a lull in the conversation he said, "Father, I have something to tell you."

Sir Edward had a bit of mutton on his fork, halfway to his mouth. Putting it down, he asked, "What is it, Son?"

"Would it disturb you very much if I decided not to pursue the study of law?"

His question, Gervase saw, gave his father pause.

"Why, I thought you had settled on that."

"I think I decided to become a lawyer because I had no inclination for anything else. But I have another idea now."

"What's that, Ives?" Sir Edward asked sharply.

"I've been thinking I'd like to go into the business — that is, if you think I might be of some help."

Gervase saw a warm light glow in Sir Edward's eyes. "Why, my boy, that's always been my dream!" he exclaimed. "I thought you had no interest in such things."

"Actually, it's what I would like to do."

"That would make Davis very happy," Lady Sarah said. Then she dropped her head. Lifting it, she smiled bravely. "When he gets well, the two of you could work together."

"I'd like that very much, if he'd have me," Ives said quietly.

For some time the talk was about Ives' decision, but then his mother changed the subject. "If you're going to be living at home again instead of at your rooms in the university, I've been thinking that perhaps we could prepare the blue room for you."

"That was always my favorite," Ives said, "but there's really nothing much to repair, is there? It's all gone."

"What's the matter with the blue room?" Gervase asked.

"It's the room down the hall from ours on the second floor," Sir Edward said. "There was a fire in it. Pretty well wiped it out." He shook his head. "We were lucky that the whole house didn't go with it."

"How did it happen?" Gervase asked.

"Oh, there was a guest staying with us. He had a fire built and then went to bed, I think. A spark must have popped out on the carpet. It caught and the fire got pretty bad. He was nearly overcome by smoke, but he woke up just in time to crawl out of there. We were lucky the servants were able to keep it from spreading. Of course, the floor will have to be replaced. It would be quite a job to fix up the room but I've always wanted it done."

"I'd like it very much, but I don't want you to go to the extra expense," Ives said.

"Nonsense, my boy," Sir Edward said, beaming. "It will be something you and I can do together. You can do your own decorating."

The dessert came, vanilla tarts and fresh fruit, which must have been grown in a hothouse, since it was out of season. Sarah glanced across the table as she was sipping her coffee and said, "You look tired, Gervase. You're spending too many hours with Davis."

"That's right," Sir Edward said. "Only two of you, and someone there all the time."

"It's only eight hours on and then eight hours off," Gervase said with a smile. "Sailors do that all the time — except their watches are only four hours long."

"You're no sailor," Sir Edward said. "I think we ought to get a third person. Do you know someone you could recommend?"

"Oh, really, sir, that's not necessary."

"As you say, then, but the option is there."

Lady Sarah asked, "What about the trip we were going to make to the Continent?"

"I didn't know you were thinking of one," Roberta said suddenly.

"Oh yes, I've wanted to go for some time, but then Davis's accident came and of course it was off."

"You should go. We could take care of things here. You need the time off."

"Why, that's kind of you, Roberta," Sarah said.

"Do you miss your travels, Gervase?" Roberta asked.

"Oh, I've never traveled except to the Crimea, and that certainly wasn't a vacation." Gervase smiled and said, "You and I have one thing in common, Mrs. Wingate." She was making an effort to be pleasant. "We both would love to take a trip to Spain."

"Oh, that's your desire, is it? To travel to Spain?" Roberta said. A peculiar expression had crossed her face but she said no more. When finally the dinner was over, Roberta excused herself at once and went to her room.

⤛⤜

As soon as she stepped inside her door, Roberta began pacing the floor. "How could she possibly know that I said something about going to Spain?" She stopped and stared fixedly at the wall. "The only time I ever said that was on the day of our quarrel at the cliff." She remembered it clearly then. She had been pleading with Davis not to divorce her, and reaching for something to offer him, she had taken his arm and begged, *"Let's go somewhere. Let's go to Spain. I've always wanted to go there. Take me and we'll work this thing out."*

Now, standing absolutely still, Roberta was face-to-face with an inexorable truth.

"No one knew that but Davis. He *had* to have told her — so he must have regained consciousness!"

She started pacing again. She clasped her hands together, not noticing that they were trembling. "I've got to leave here," she said frantically. But when she reached the clothespress and opened the door, she stopped. "No, I can't run away. Where would I go?"

Roberta thought of her plight for a moment, fighting off panic. Ives had broken it off with her and she despised him for it. When he told her they were through, she'd been filled with a blind hatred for him. She'd railed at him like a fishwife, but later, after she calmed down, she'd decided that she didn't really care. There were other men, and Ives was weak.

But the problems Davis's recovery would bring into her life loomed as large as a mountain. She forced herself to sit. Leaning over, she pressed the heels of her hands against her forehead and tried to think clearly. *I've got to find out if he's come out*

311

*of that coma. If he has, I don't have any choice!* Suddenly a vague solution began forming itself in her mind. Her eyes narrowed and she whispered, "If he's come back, he'll have me sent to prison. I can't bear that! I'd rather die!" She became quite still and glanced at the clock. It was only ten. "She goes on at twelve. I'll find out then. The window — she always leaves it open for the fresh air." She nodded, as if coming to a decision, then got up and began pacing once more.

As soon as the clock struck midnight, Roberta slipped on a warm navy blue coat with a hood. She pulled the hood up and waited for another few moments. Then she went to the door and opened it cautiously. She looked both ways down the hall and saw no one. Quietly she stepped out, pulled the door shut, and made her way to the side entrance of the house. She went outside and the air was cool and crisp; overhead the stars were bright and a full moon shone. She moved around the house toward the north wing, and when she got there, she saw the light shining out of the double French doors and the two windows that flanked it. Stealthily she approached the near window and could hear a voice as she did. Placing her feet carefully, she found that she could barely see over the lower part of the window. As she glanced in, she saw that a fire had been kindled in the fireplace and was burning merrily. Gervase was sitting in a chair beside Davis's bed, her back to the window, reading.

Keeping perfectly still, Roberta listened as Gervase read from the Bible. Roberta was startled once when an owl made a cry very close to her. She flinched and almost uttered a sound but clamped her lips tightly together.

On and on Gervase read and Roberta grew stiff and cold. She could not see Davis clearly, for Gervase was blocking her view. Nearly thirty minutes passed, she guessed, for she heard the mantel clock strike the half hour. *Twelve thirty. How long is she going to read?*

Suddenly Gervase closed the book and put it down. "Well, that finishes the book of Isaiah." She got up and said, "It's quite a wonderful book, isn't it?"

Roberta knew, of course, that Gervase always talked to Davis as well as read to him. It had seemed a foolish thing to her, but now she heard the sound of Davis's voice answering, and she froze, unbelieving. Yet there it was. His voice. He was speaking. He was out of the coma!

"This means we'll be reading Jeremiah next." Davis's voice came to her clearly. "That's always a good one, isn't it?"

The enormity of his recovery caused Roberta to feel faint. She closed her eyes and pressed her forehead against the windowsill. *He's conscious, and that means prison for me!*

Finally she shook off her weakness and, lifting her head, looked in. Gervase said, "Davis, I think we should tell your family how well you're doing. It's not fair to keep this from them."

"You may be right, Gervase. I just wanted to wait until I was able to take care of myself."

"But you're healing so well. Why, I believe you could walk now."

"Let's see if I can."

Roberta watched as Gervase threw the sheet back and helped Davis swing his feet over the edge of the bed. He was holding her shoulders and she was encouraging him. Roberta saw him pull himself to an upright position and heard him say, "Just one step. That's all I ask."

But his legs were too weak. Roberta saw him make a wild grab. His arms fell around Gervase's neck and as he went down, he dragged her with him. Gervase was laughing, however, and that infuriated Roberta.

"Come along. Get back in bed. You're not quite ready for the Olympic Games yet."

Roberta watched Gervase help him up. When he was upright again, his arms were around her, holding on for support. She saw them suddenly stop, and she had a clear view of Davis's face, and she heard him very clearly when he said, "You're always my good angel, Gervase." The look on his face struck Roberta. *He's in love with her.* The thought stirred a hatred in her, and when he lay down and she saw the same look on Gervase's face, Roberta suddenly moved away from the house.

She crept back to her room without being seen and shut the door behind her. Pulling off her coat, she threw it down. Rage consumed her and she walked the floor. *The two of them. They're so . . . holy . . . reading the Bible! It's been going on for years. I knew it! That letter writing couldn't have been all that innocent.*

But with the anger, fear came also. She stopped dead still and whispered, "Both of them know the truth about me. Even if Davis died, she'd know!"

At that instant she knew that Davis and the woman must die. When she had pushed Davis off the cliff, it had been in a fit of rage. Later the plan to administer poison had been carefully crafted but it had still failed. This time she would be sure!

All thoughts of sleep were gone, and for over an hour Roberta roamed her room. At times she would force herself to be still, but soon the restlessness, brought on by fear, would come.

Finally she prepared for bed, but when she blew the candle out and drew the cover over herself, her eyes were wide open. She trembled at the thought of being shut up in a prison, she who had never suffered any inconvenience. She certainly would die first!

For hours she thought, tossing and turning, but one idea became paramount. *How can I get rid of them both?* She could not rest. She got up, put on a robe and slippers, and began to pace the floor. Growing cold, she poked the fire until the logs flared up again. As they did, suddenly fragments of the evening's dinner conversation came to her. Sir Edward had said, *"A spark caught the carpet, and the poor fellow nearly died."*

Holding the poker in her hand, Roberta stared at the yellow flames leaping upward. She did not move for a long time, and then she straightened and said, "A fire." She bit the words off, then looked at the blaze again, and a smile touched her lips. "A fire," she repeated and stood looking down into the flames.

# Chapter Twenty-Eight

Ten days had passed since Gervase's dinner with the Wingates, and since that night Roberta had been different. Gervase had become accustomed to her icy manner and obvious dislike and was taken aback at how amiable the woman had become. She mentioned this to Davis, who said instantly, "Be careful, Gervase. She's a good actress and she hates you."

Davis's progress was dramatic. He had even taken a couple of faltering steps two days after the dinner. He was very unsteady but obviously over the crisis, and both of them knew it was only a matter of time before he was completely well.

The days had passed swiftly and Gervase had worked hard. She slept soundly and woke with a feeling of joy. But at times the future would come to her, and she knew that as soon as Davis was well, she would be leaving Kimberly — and him. He was a married man and there was no answer to that.

She was thinking of this on Thursday evening during her shift. She stood and stretched, arching her back, for fatigue weighed heavily upon her. Glancing at the clock, she saw that it was still an hour and a half from midnight, when Margaret would relieve her. Going to the window, she considered closing it for a moment and then decided to leave it cracked. The fresh air, she thought, was good for Davis. But it was chilly in the room. She walked to the fireplace, removed the fire screen, poked the fire until the logs crackled and sent orange sparks swirling up into the chimney. Replacing the fire screen, she went to stand beside Davis. He was asleep and she smiled to see how peaceful his features were. She almost touched his hair but then drew back her hand. *Let him sleep. He worked hard and he needs it.*

Going back to the chair, she picked up the copy of *Oliver Twist* that she had been reading to Davis and tried to read, but her eyes burned. She blinked and then heard the door open. Thinking it might be Margaret coming early, she turned — and at once rose to her feet. "Good evening, Mrs. Wingate."

"Good evening, Gervase." Roberta was wearing a light-blue dress, and her petticoats held it out as she moved toward her. Over the dress she wore a thin linen jumper fastened at the neck with a single broach. "How is he tonight?"

"Why, very well." Gervase was puzzled, for Roberta had never come this late. She watched as the woman went to Davis and stood staring down into his face. Roberta stayed there for so long that Gervase wondered at it. "He ate well tonight."

"Did he?"

"Yes, and as you can see, his color is better."

"Yes, he's very much improved." Roberta turned to face Gervase with an enigmatic smile. "Do you really think he'll recover?"

"Why, yes. His muscle tone is much better."

"What about his other functions? Any sign of improvement there?"

Gervase hesitated. She knew what this woman was, yet still there was something about her that was pitiful. She considered for a moment and said, "I think he's going to get better as time goes on."

"I think I'll sit with you awhile. You were about to read to him, I see."

"Well . . . yes, I was, but —"

"Go right ahead. I'll take the chair by the fireplace. It's cold in here. Do you always leave the windows open?"

"I believe in fresh air."

"It is healthy. Go right on with your reading."

Gervase did not know how else to handle the situation, so she sat, opened the book, and began to read aloud. She heard the swish of Roberta's petticoats but could not see her, because of the angle of the chair.

Roberta moved to the fireplace but did not sit down. Her eyes were glittering and her breath came in short gasps. She had steeled herself for this moment and now stood poised, as if she had reached a fork in a road and knew that one path might be fatal. She had slept little for over a week as she went over and over her plan to get rid of Davis and Gervase, trying to think clearly but finding her thoughts clouded by rage.

As Gervase read, Roberta examined the supply of firewood in the U-shaped cast-iron rack. She had paid careful attention to this and saw that the logs, as usual, were divided up into large ones and smaller ones. For a moment she could not seem to move, and then she picked up one of the small logs. It was no more than three inches in diameter but it was solid oak and heavy in her hand. Holding it tightly, she stared across the room. Gervase's back was to her, and her voice droned on. She was wearing a tiny cap but that would do nothing to cushion the blow. Roberta moved forward, the carpet soft under her feet. It was an old carpet and thick; it would burn readily. When she was three feet behind Gervase, she raised the log over her head. For one brief moment she remained immobile, fixed and solid and as still as a statue. She felt an impulse to turn, replace the log, and leave the room, but she did not. She had slept so little and she felt a fierce determination to survive. She swung the log as a batter would swing at a ball, and it delivered Gervase a grazing blow on the side of the head.

Gervase's voice broke off and the book dropped from her hands; she slumped sideways, then tumbled to the floor and lay still.

Breathing hard, almost in a broken gasp, Roberta leaned forward and saw that Gervase was unconscious. The blow had broken the skin, and the crimson blood began to show in the wound. The white cap had fallen off and Gervase lay there awkwardly, half on her back and half on her side, one arm trapped beneath her. For an instant Roberta thought she had killed the woman, but she saw that she was breathing, her chest rising and falling quickly.

A shock ran along Roberta's nerves when Davis's voice rang out. "Gervase!"

Roberta looked up. "So," she sneered, "you've recovered. Come back to life, have you, Davis?" She advanced toward him.

Davis was struggling to pull himself into a sitting position. His eyes were filled with rage and he cried out, "What have you done, Roberta?"

"You forced me to do it, Davis! You should have died! You told her I tried to kill you, didn't you?"

"Roberta, you're not yourself. Go get help."

"You'll get no help, Davis. You brought this on yourself. You should have died. It would have been much easier."

Roberta raised the log and swung it again. Davis managed to lift an arm but only partly deflected the blow. It hit him on the neck and he cried out. Roberta raised the log again, and this time the end of it caught him on the temple and he fell sideways across the bed.

She stared at him for a moment and then murmured, "It's your fault! You brought yourself to this!" She whirled and replaced the log. Hurrying to the French doors, she opened them, went out, and returned with two gallon jugs filled with lamp oil. Immediately she began pouring the highly flammable liquid on the carpet and splashing it on the heavy drapes that hung over both windows. All around the room she spread the oil, but she did not notice that much of it was seeping into her petticoats as it sloshed out of the narrow mouths of the containers.

Roberta's eyes had a wild, mad look in them as she emptied both jugs, but then she heard a cry and saw that Davis was regaining consciousness. He turned his head and his eyes focused on her as she put the containers outside. She had planned it out — she would light the fire, take the jugs, and go back to her room. She would give the fire time to kill Davis and Gervase, then she would sound the alarm with the story that she had smelled smoke.

She went to the mantel, where the box of matches always sat.

There was no hesitation now. She had gone too far for that. She heard Davis call out her name and turned to him. "It's too late," she said.

"Let Gervase go. I'm the one you hate."

"I hate both of you!" She ignored Davis's cry and saw with some alarm that he had thrown himself off the bed. He had a cut on his temple, and though he could not walk, he began crawling across the floor toward Gervase.

Roberta struck a match and threw it down. The flame caught at once and ran over the carpet. She watched as it leaped to the curtains and spread rapidly throughout the room. She gave one look at Davis, who was almost at Gervase's side, then crossed the room, struck a second match, and threw it in another puddle of oil. It flared up instantly and she gave a laugh, her eyes crazed.

⟨≫⟩

"The meeting was vurry good, Margaret," Brodie said. The two had returned from an evangelistic meeting at the chapel they were attending. They had entered the house and she had brought him to the kitchen for a late supper, for the meeting had been long.

Margaret poured the tea for Brodie, set it before him, and said, "I'm going down to tell Gervase that I'll be in a little early."

"I'll just go with you. Perhaps we might have a prayer for the dear man."

The two left the kitchen, speaking softly, for the house was quiet. Everyone had gone to bed. It was nearly eleven.

As they approached the door to Davis's room, Margaret suddenly let out a cry. "Look, Brodie, there's smoke!"

"It's a fire!" Brodie shouted and threw himself forward. He touched the door and found that it was hot. He yelled, "Fire! Fire! Everybody up!" Then he opened the door and turned to shield himself as smoke boiled out.

"We've got to get them out!" Margaret cried.

Roberta heard Brodie's cry and knew she had waited too long. She whirled to leave through the French doors, but as her skirt swirled, its oil-soaked hem passed through the flames rising from the carpet. At once the flames ran up her dress, and before she had taken two steps, she screamed, for they had caught the material as though it were the wick of a lamp. She began beating the flames, and the pain in her hands brought a louder scream. She fell onto the burning carpet, then sprang up and ran, blind with panic, her body on fire. The pain was unendurable! She ran into one of the French doors, breaking the glass, and then the flames seemed to swallow her. She fell against the drapes, grasped at them, and they came down over her, ablaze. She gave one more brief cry and then was silent.

Davis had reached Gervase. He saw Roberta start for the door and then she seemed to ignite, the hem of her dress catching and the flames rising. He called her name and watched in horror as she collided with the French door and pulled the burning curtain down on herself. He heard the other door opening, but the smoke was so thick that he could only barely see two forms. He saw that Gervase was moving then, but the flames on the carpet were creeping closer.

Suddenly hands were on him. He looked up to see Brodie, who had tied a handkerchief over his face. "It's all right, Mr. Davis," he gasped. "I'll get you."

"Get Gervase!"

"I've got her," came Margaret's voice. Both she and Brodie were bending low to avoid the smoke. All around them the flames were going up, and there was a roaring sound.

Davis felt himself being lifted. Brodie had picked him up as if he were a child. He carried him out to the hall, and as Brodie set him down, Davis saw Margaret dragging out Gervase.

The smoke had gotten into Davis's lungs and, sitting against the wall, he began to cough. He was confused and could barely see, for his eyes had been blinded by the smoke, but suddenly he heard his father's voice. "Quick, get them out away from here!" There was a great to-do and then many voices came. He heard his father yelling, "Get the fire out! Brodie, take Davis and Gervase outside, where they can get some air."

And then Davis saw his father's face. He blinked and whispered, "Father."

Sir Edward's eyes widened. "Davis, you're awake!"

"Yes. How's Gervase?"

His father, overcome with emotion, could not speak, but Davis's eyes were clearing and he saw that Gervase was sitting up. She looked confused. He cried out her name, but just then his mother suddenly threw her arms around him. "Davis, you've come back!"

Davis suddenly remembered the blazing torch that had been his wife. "Roberta," he whispered. "She's still in there."

"Brodie, go to the outside door and see if you can help her!" Sir Edward cried.

⚬⚬⚬

For a time all was confusion. Gervase and Davis had been carried outdoors by some of the servants. The yells from the servants fighting the fire were muffled, and Lady Sarah was weeping and holding Davis's hand. Sir Edward was kneeling by Gervase, who still seemed groggy. She had a large lump and a cut on the side of her head. Mr. Bob, whom Margaret had retrieved from Gervase's room, was on her lap, nuzzling her. Margaret quickly finished attending to Gervase's wound and then ran to help Brodie.

"I don't know how it all could have started — the fire, I mean," Sir Edward said, shaking his head. He could not take his eyes off his son.

At that moment Davis realized what he had to do. Everything in him rebelled against speaking the words that would protect the woman who had tried to kill him and Gervase. Deep inside he knew that a black hatred lurked, ready to burst out. But at that moment he knew he could not speak the truth — not ever! *I must forgive her — or it will destroy me!*

Taking a deep breath, he said, "I think it must have been a spark from the fireplace that caught the carpet. Gervase, I think, had gone to sleep, and when I heard the flames and smelled the smoke, it was too late."

Gervase and Davis exchanged glances. Both knew that the truth would never be spoken by either of them.

"But what was Roberta doing in there?" Sir Edward asked.

No one answered. Brodie came over to them a few moments later. He was blackened with smoke, his eyebrows singed. He stood breathing hard and Sir Edward asked, "How is Mrs. Wingate, Brodie?"

Brodie licked his lips and looked at Davis. When he spoke, his voice was harsh, for his throat was raw. "She's gone, sir. Margaret tried to help her but it was too late."

"She must have gone in after the fire started," Sir Edward said heavily. "Somehow she got caught in it."

Davis stared at his parents, then looked at Gervase. "I expect that's the way it must have been, Father," he said quietly and closed the door on his tragic history with Roberta Wingate.

# Chapter Twenty-Nine

Sir Edward stood beside Brodie McLean and stared at the shell that remained of the north wing. All of the first floor had been destroyed and the second was gutted as well.

"It's a wonder the whole house didn't go up, Brodie," Sir Edward said. "You and the others did a magnificent job of saving it."

"Thank you, sir. I think the good Lord is responsible for that."

All the servants had turned out, and a bucket brigade had been formed to fight the fire. Brodie and the other men had soaked blankets and had gone in to beat out the flames wherever possible.

"How is Mr. Davis, Sir Edward?"

Edward Wingate turned and faced Brodie squarely. He could not speak for a moment, but finally he swallowed and said with some difficulty, "I thank God that he's all right."

"How did it come about, sir? I mean, one day he can't speak and can't move, and now he's talking and able to move his arms and legs."

"Dr. Thompson has a theory about that. He thinks that the shock of the fire itself woke Davis from that coma. He is not sure but suspects that what caused the recovery was the sudden panic Davis experienced when he awakened to find himself in a blazing room. In any case, he's certain Davis is going to be all right."

"That's fine news, sir, very fine indeed!"

Sir Edward suddenly turned away, took out his handkerchief, and dabbed at his eyes. Brodie looked off into the distance, feeling a warmth for his master. *He has a good heart in him, he has indeed. And who wouldn't have a warm heart to get a son back from the dead, as he has?*

Sir Edward gave his nose a blow and then turned to give a half-embarrassed laugh. "I'm not much of a one to weep, Brodie. I think the last time was when I was ten years old, but I can't seem to stop."

"I think better of you, sir, and it's what I wud do myself."

"Well, there'll be a bonus for you and the others for working so hard. How are your hands?"

"Oh, they're fine, sir. Just roasted a little bit." Brodie flexed his huge hands and grinned broadly. "God bless you, sir." Then his face darkened. "I'm sorry about Mrs. Wingate."

"We'll never know what happened, I suppose." Sir Edward shook his head. "Well, God is good. I must go in and check on my son."

Brodie watched him enter the house and then looked at what had been Davis's room. "The good Lord, indeed, has come to this house," he said.

⟞≈⟝

Margaret MacKay turned her head to one side and studied the swelling on Gervase's temple. It had gone down. "No need for a bandage, I think, but it was a bad bump."

"Thank you, Margaret." Gervase turned and smiled faintly. She had been silent since the fire, and now her color was pale and she seemed to be hiding behind some sort of wall.

"What's troubling you, Gervase? Mr. Davis is cured, thank God."

"Yes, Margaret, and I'm so grateful for it."

Margaret sat beside Gervase. The two women were in the sitting room. The fall sunlight threw itself on the floor, illuminating the rich colors of the Indian carpet. Margaret had said nothing to Gervase, but now she remarked, "I know that things are not what they seem with this fire."

Instantly Gervase looked up and met Margaret's eyes, and her voice was unsteady as she said, "Why, what do you mean?"

"Too many things don't match up. Brodie and I have talked about it."

"What sorts of things?"

"For one thing, Sir Edward's theory that you went to sleep and the fire caught. That's ridiculous! In the first place, you'd never go to sleep while tending a patient. In the second place, you would have heard the fire or felt it before it got out of hand." She held Gervase's eyes and waited for the younger woman to speak. "What do you say to that?"

Gervase looked down at her hands and remained silent. She had been filled with confusion ever since she had awakened from the blow she had taken, and now she whispered, "I don't know. I can't say, Margaret."

"And then that bump on the side of your head. The fire didn't do that." Once again Gervase only shook her head slightly. Margaret watched Gervase and said, "Me and Brodie found the two jugs outside the French doors. They were empty but had been filled with lamp oil."

Quickly Gervase looked up. Davis had told her about the containers. "What did he do with them?"

"He got rid of them. He didn't know what to do and we prayed about it. I think I know what happened, Gervase."

"Well, you must never say anything, Margaret. It wouldn't do any good. The poor woman is dead."

"That she is. May the Lord have mercy on her soul. Is there anything else you want to tell me?"

Gervase's eyes were troubled. "I've wanted to tell you for some time that Davis was getting better, but he didn't want it known until he was sure it was going to be permanent and he was able to be a whole man again. I felt guilty not telling you but that was what he wanted."

Margaret smiled suddenly. "Did you think I didn't know? You must think I'm blind, girl. Mr. Davis tried to hide it but he couldn't always keep still. I waited for you to tell me but you never did."

"I'm so sorry, Margaret."

"Well, I forgive you."

Gervase was anxious to change the subject. She forced a smile and put her hand on Margaret, saying, "When are you and Brodie getting married?"

"He's very impatient."

"And how do you feel about it?"

Margaret smiled. Happiness glowed in her eyes. "I'd marry him today if he said the word, but he wants to do it proper."

"Yes, I'll have to help you make a dress, and we'll plan the ceremony. Where will you be married?"

"In the chapel, he says. Won't I be a sight, big as I am, coming down the aisle. I'll look like a locomotive in white."

"You'll be a beautiful bride, I promise you."

The funeral had been hard on everyone. It was well attended, but the casket of course was not open. Davis endured the ordeal very well. It had been his decision to have the services as quickly as possible, and now as he sat in his new bedroom at Kimberly, looking out the window, he found himself unable to think clearly about what had happened. He turned his wheelchair at the sound of a faint knock. "Come in." When Gervase entered, he smiled. "Gervase, I've been hoping you'd come."

Gervase sat across from him. "I've just seen Ives. He said he's been talking with you."

"Yes, he has." Davis shook his head. "He confessed the whole thing to me, the whole story. He didn't know, of course, that I had heard him when he confessed it before. I thought it best to just let him speak."

"He looked terrible, Davis."

"He's going to be all right. He's going into the business, and that pleases Father very much. I forgave Ives, of course. It'll take a while for him to accept my forgiveness. He feels awful."

Gervase sat quietly as Davis began to speak about his physical progress. "I'm walking much better, Gervase."

"I'm so glad," Gervase said and her smile came then. "You're going to be as strong as you ever were."

The two of them carefully did not mention Roberta or the fire for some time, but finally Gervase grew agitated. "I've come to tell you something, Davis."

"Tell me what?"

"I've got to leave here." Gervase shook her head and her hands were unsteady, so much so that she had to hold them together. "Too much has happened. I'm so mixed up and confused."

Davis was watching her carefully. "To tell the truth, so am I. It's been like a kaleidoscope, and . . . well, we won't speak of it again, but I wanted to know how you feel about Roberta."

Gervase looked up quickly, surprise on her face. "Why, I pity her, of course. The poor woman!"

"I think she was not entirely sane. She was an unhappy woman and I feel that I wronged her somehow."

"Why, Davis, how can you say that?"

"For better or for worse — that's what I promised. With Roberta it was worse, but there it was. I promised and I didn't stay with her. I went off to war. When I came back, I wasn't much of a husband. If I had shown more love, things might have been different."

Gervase did not answer for a time, and then she said, "I don't think so. You mustn't live with guilt."

"But why must you go away?"

"I need time to think and my work here is done. You don't need a nurse anymore. Margaret is going to stay until the wedding at least, and I think she and Brodie will make their home here afterward." Gervase rose and said, "I don't want any long goodbyes. My things are packed."

Davis stared at her. "You're leaving right now? Today?"

"I've got to get away. I hope you'll understand."

Davis hesitated, then said gently, "Perhaps you're right, Gervase. We both need time to get over this terrible thing." He put his hand out and she took it. He squeezed her hand and said, "God be with you. Every day of my life I'll be thankful to the Lord for what you've done for me."

Gervase tried to answer but suddenly could not. She turned and left the room, saying, "Goodbye, Davis."

The door closed and Davis sat looking at it. He could not blame Gervase, for he knew that he himself was unable to think clearly. He shook his head, wheeled himself around, and then stared out the window again.

# Chapter Thirty

A light snow had fallen, coating the park with a gleaming luminescence that made it look like a fairyland. As Gervase walked along, she passed a group singing Christmas carols. She stopped for a time, listening, then moved along, thinking of the Christmases she had known as a child. They had been very lean indeed. There came memories of her mother, her eyes laughing as she watched Gervase open her small presents. From there her mind moved to the Christmases at Kimberly. They had been rich with the smells of roast turkey and pies and cakes.

Finally she retraced her steps toward the room she had rented while working at Miss Nightingale's hospital. Gervase had gone out that night because she was lonely. During the weeks since she left Kimberly, she had learned to isolate herself with work. She had heard regularly from Margaret, had gone back on the one day for her marriage. She had seen Davis only briefly, and the two had exchanged greetings, and then she had quickly returned to the city.

The snow began falling again, tiny flakes at first, but as the sky thickened, they became larger, until finally they were as big as shillings. Gervase, who always loved the snow, looked up and felt them touch her eyelids with tiny frozen fire.

When she returned to the apartment, she saw Margaret standing by the door, tall and bulky in a new coat. "Margaret!" she cried and rushed forward.

Margaret came to her at once. She enveloped Gervase in her arms, hugging her so fiercely that Gervase cried out, "Margaret, you take my breath!"

"Well, I'm so glad to see you."

"Will you come up to my room? It's not much, but I can make tea and I have some cakes."

"That I will."

Fifteen minutes later the two women were sitting at the small table. Margaret was eating cakes in single bites and talking a mile a minute.

". . . . and Brodie is now going to be the chief gardener for Sir Edward."

"And where will you live?"

"In the old gardener's house. It has two bedrooms, you know, and we'll need them."

"It's always nice to have a guest bedroom."

"Well, this bedroom will have a very small guest."

Gervase stared at Margaret and then burst into laughter. "You're going to have a baby!"

"Isn't that wonderful? Me, Maggie MacKay, a mother."

"I'm so happy for you."

"Oh, you should see Brodie. He's the proudest thing you ever saw."

For a time the two talked about the child to come, and finally Margaret said, "You've asked about everyone else, but what about Mr. Davis?"

"Is he back yet from his sea voyage?"

"No, but he writes as regularly as the mails permit. He even congratulated me when he heard that Brodie and I were going to have a baby."

Gervase kept her eyes fixed on Margaret as she spoke. Then she broke her gaze and said, "What about Mr. Ives?"

"Well, that's good news. He's doing so well. Sir Edward is so proud, he's about to burst, and Lady Sarah too. He's taken over at the office. All the things Mr. Davis used to do, he's learnin' 'em so quick that you wouldn't believe it. Sir Edward tells us that he has a natural gift for the business and likes it."

Gervase expressed her happiness over this, and then finally she sipped her tea, put the cup down abruptly, and asked, "Did Davis ever say why he left?"

"Not to me, but Phoebe heard him tell his parents. You know how she is. Always eavesdropping. Well, anyhow, he told them that he had to get away and straighten out some things within himself."

"I hope it helps him."

"Now then. When will you be coming to Kimberly for a visit? Everyone longs to see you."

"Well, I'll come when the baby's born. You can believe that," Gervase said, smiling. Then she said, "Now, how long can you stay? Miss Florence will be so glad to see you and to hear the good news."

❦

When the new year of 1858 arrived, Gervase put in a full day at the hospital. It being a holiday, many of the attendants went home, including the nurses, and she was glad to volunteer. It made no difference to her, for one day had become like another. It was growing late in the afternoon, however, when Miss Nightingale came to her and said, "Gervase, I want you to go home. You were here before dawn this morning and you've worked too hard."

"Oh, I feel fine, Miss Florence."

"You go home and get some rest. That's an order." Florence smiled and put her arm around her. "I don't want my best nurse to wear out on me. You go along now."

Gervase would have preferred to stay. She liked to work such long hours because she slept better at night, but one did not argue with Miss Florence Nightingale!

Slipping on her heavy coat and fur cap, she left the hospital. It was growing dark now, but there was still light enough so that the dying sun cast its gleams on the snow which capped the buildings. In the streets the snow had been turned to dirty, yellow slush by the passage of carriages and wagons, and she got her feet damp while crossing them. She had reached her apartment building and was ready to open the door when she heard a voice.

"Gervase!"

Quickly she turned and saw Davis. For a moment she could not speak, she was so surprised. He was wearing a long gray overcoat and a black fur cap, and he was smiling as he came to her, holding out his mittened hands. She thrust out her own and he grasped them, saying, "You look wonderful, Gervase."

"Davis, I didn't know you were back!"

"I just returned yesterday."

"Have you been to Kimberly?"

"No, I wanted to see you."

"You look absolutely reborn, Davis."

"I feel that way." He hesitated and then said, "Could I come up?"

"Of course, unless you'd rather go get something to eat."

"No, I just want to see you — and of course Mr. Bob. You still have him?"

"Why, certainly. What would I do without Mr. Bob?"

The two entered the building and went upstairs. Gervase asked, "Would you make the fire or should I?"

"Oh, I'll do that."

Gervase took off her coat and began pulling down the elements for a small meal. "I don't have much here. It would really be better if we went out to eat."

"No, let's not. It'll be cozy in here. This is a nice place."

"It's very small. Just the sitting room and the bedroom, but I've been comfortable here."

Gervase's mind was racing. She could not get over the shock of seeing Davis and how well he looked. She watched as he started the fire expertly, and saw that he was moving easily. When he had it going, he turned to her and said, "Now, let me look at you." He put his hands on her shoulders. "You look fine, Gervase, absolutely beautiful. But then, you always did."

Gervase could not answer, for her heart was suddenly full. "Where all did you go?"

"Let's fix dinner together. You do the cooking and afterward I'll do the cleaning up. While you're at it, I'll tell you about my trip."

She put together a simple dinner of chops, potatoes, a shepherd's pie, and for dessert a cake she had baked two days earlier. She set the food on the table, listening as he told her about his voyage.

They sat down to eat and she asked Davis to ask the blessing. He bowed his head and said, "Thank you, Lord, for this food and for this time that Gervase and I have together and for all your mercies. In the name of Jesus." He looked up and said, "It smells good. I missed your cooking. You were always the best cook in the world."

"Except for Aunt Martha."

"Well, of course, she is the champion."

As they ate, Gervase wondered at the ease in Davis's manner. His eyes were bright and there was in him an eagerness she had not seen before, except perhaps when she had first gone to Kimberly.

After the meal, he insisted on helping wash up, managing to break one dish. She laughed at him and he shook his head with chagrin. "I'm as clumsy a man as ever drew breath."

Finally they drew up two chairs facing each other before the fire, which crackled and snapped and popped, giving off a warm glow.

Their conversation slowed and a silence fell between them. Davis stared into the fire, the yellow flames creating shadows on the planes of his face. He seemed caught up in deep thought, and finally he turned to her and smiled and said, "When I left Kimberly, I was as confused as a man ever was. I was miserable and unhappy, and the tragedy that broke over us — I couldn't get away from it."

"I felt that way myself, but it was worse for you," Gervase said quietly.

"Well, day after day on that voyage I prayed, and I couldn't shake off the guilt. I had the idea that I might have done something to change everything, but after two weeks the peace of God came to me, Gervase. It came all at once. I was up on deck. It was night, almost midnight, I think, and I was beaten down and thought I would never know peace. And then all of sudden — I wasn't even praying, I think — something came into my heart, and it was as if a huge burden were lifted. And from that moment to this I've been able to live with the past."

"Oh, Davis, I'm so glad." Gervase smiled and added, "What did you do then?"

"Well, I worked on my novel. Not the old one. A brand-new one. And Gervase," he said, his eyes glowing as he leaned forward and spoke rapidly, "it's as if someone were dictating it to me. It's going to be a good one. I wrote day and night and I'm halfway through with it. Others went to see the sights; I worked on the book. I have it in my suitcase. I want you to read it."

"Of course."

"Gervase, I asked the Lord what to do with my life, and I'm not going back to the office. Ives has taken over in a wonderful way. I think you can guess what I want to do."

"What you've always wanted to do, Davis. You'll be a writer. I know you will, and you'll be good at it."

"I may be the world's biggest flop."

"No, you won't. And even if you don't become another Charles Dickens — and indeed who could; there's only one Dickens — even then you'll be doing what you want to do."

Davis suddenly rose and pulled Gervase to her feet. "There's one other thing I settled with God, besides that matter of guilt and what I want to do for a profession. Can you guess what it is?"

Gervase suddenly smiled. "Does it have anything to do with me?"

"I could never fool you. Yes, it has something to do with you. I want you to marry me, Gervase. I don't know when my love for you changed. At first it was just love for a child who needed love, but over the years you grew up, and now you're the finest, loveliest woman I know. Will you marry me?"

Gervase suddenly understood what Davis meant about the peace of God coming over him — for it came to her at that instant. She realized that this was her calling, to be a wife to this man whom she loved with all of her heart. She put her head up and as he kissed her, she clung to him.

When he lifted his lips, he said, "I may not be able to make a living."

"Then I can support you by working as a nurse."

Davis Wingate laughed and shook his head. "I've always wanted to be a parasite."

Gervase put her head on his chest and he put his arms around her. She felt as one might feel who has come home after a terrible storm at sea and sailed into a quiet harbor. She knew then that this man would be a haven for her for the rest of her life.

Mr. Bob had grown bored with the talk. He had been lying before the fire, blinking, watching the two as they spoke. Now it was time for more serious things — such as a snack. He reared up and caught his claws in Gervase's skirt and pulled until she looked down. Then he looked up and said piteously, "Yow?"

# The Spider Catcher

*Gilbert Morris*

He is a young Welshman who for-sook the family shipbuilding busi-ness to study medicine ... until, poised at the brink of a brilliant career, tragedy broke his heart and shattered his dreams.

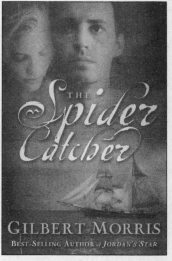

She is a daughter of London's inner city, a woman-child weaned on life's harsh realities who has learned much about fending for her living and her virtue but little of what it means to be loved.

Thrown together by circumstance, Rees Kenyon and Callie Summers head across the ocean toward a new life during the stormy begin-nings of the American Revolution. As a new nation struggles for independence, Rees employs his medical knowledge to save lives, and his shipbuilder's skills to build the potent fighting vessel known as the "spider catcher."

But it is Callie, whom Rees scooped from the mud of the London streets, on whom his own life will soon depend ... and who can help him find for himself the faith, hope, and love he has taught her.

Softcover: 0-310-24698-9

*Pick up a copy today at your favorite bookstore!*

GRAND RAPIDS, MICHIGAN 49530 USA

WWW.ZONDERVAN.COM

*The Ultimate Journey.*
*The Impossible Decision.*

# Jordan's Star

*Gilbert Morris*

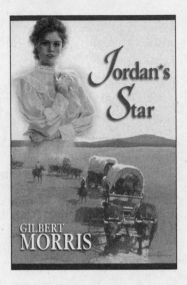

Bound for the Oregon frontier, Jordan Bryce and her new husband, Colin, a dashing ex-mariner, face danger from both man and nature: a deadly buffalo stampede . . . tragedy at a river crossing . . . hostile Indians . . . and hatred within their wagon train, escalating from bitter words to the point of bloodshed. All that separates the Bryce's party from disaster is seasoned leadership, the skillful guidance of Ty Sublette, and the hand of God.

For Jordan, the journey west is more than a trip into an untamed land. It is a passage from a teenage girl's romantic fantasies to the wisdom and character of womanhood. But nothing can prepare Jordan for the testing that awaits her beyond the journey's end. There, in the face of staggering circumstances, she will face an impossible decision . . . as two good men—one wounded by past grief, the other branded by his own impetuousness—struggle with the demands of faith and honor on behalf of the woman they love.

Softcover: 0-310-22754-2

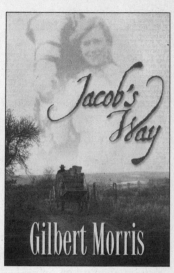

> *An Epic Story of War, Regret, Love, and Forgiveness Set in the Post-Civil War South*

# Edge of Honor

*Gilbert Morris*

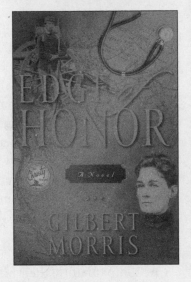

Quentin Larribee is a surgeon—one of the best. But in the confusion of one of the Civil War's last, desperate skirmishes, the hands devoted to healing bring death to William Breckenridge, an enemy soldier in the act of surrendering. Now the deed haunts Quentin.

A bright future lies before him, with marriage to the lovely Irene Chambers and eventual ownership of her father's prosperous medical practice. But it cannot ease Quentin's troubled conscience. Honor compels him to see to the welfare of the dead man's family. Quentin moves from New York City to the little town of Helena, Arkansas, where he attempts to save the wife of Breckenridge and her children from financial ruin.

*Edge of Honor* is an unforgettable novel of redemption and honor, where good is found in the unlikeliest places and God's unseen hand weaves a masterful tapestry of human hearts and lives.

Softcover: 0-310-24302-5

*Pick up a copy today at your favorite bookstore!*

**ZONDERVAN**™

GRAND RAPIDS, MICHIGAN 49530 USA

WWW.ZONDERVAN.COM

We want to hear from you. Please send your comments about this book to us in care of zreview@zondervan.com. Thank you.

GRAND RAPIDS, MICHIGAN 49530 USA

WWW.ZONDERVAN.COM